HIGH DIVE

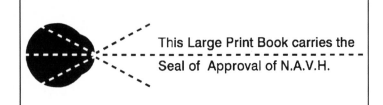

This Large Print Book carries the
Seal of Approval of N.A.V.H.

HIGH DIVE

JONATHAN LEE

THORNDIKE PRESS
A part of Gale, Cengage Learning

GALE
CENGAGE Learning

Farmington Hills, Mich • San Francisco • New York • Waterville, Maine
Meriden, Conn • Mason, Ohio • Chicago

GALE
CENGAGE Learning®

Portions of this book first appeared, in slightly different form, in the following publications: *A Public Space, Narrative, and Tin House.*
Thorndike Press, a part of Gale, Cengage Learning.

LIBRARY OF CONGRESS CATALOGING-IN-PUBLICATION DATA

Names: Lee, Jonathan, 1981– author.
Title: High dive / by Jonathan Lee.
Description: Large print edition. | Waterville, Maine : Thorndike Press, 2016. |
   © 2015 | Series: Thorndike Press large print reviewers' choice
Identifiers: LCCN 2016002190 | ISBN 9781410489128 (hardcover) | ISBN 1410489124
   (hardcover)
Subjects: LCSH: Large type books.
Classification: LCC PR6112.E413 H54 2016b | DDC 823/.92—dc23
LC record available at http://lccn.loc.gov/2016002190

Published in 2016 by arrangement with Alfred A. Knopf, a division of Penguin Random House LLC

< Large Print >
Fiction

Printed in Mexico
1 2 3 4 5 6 7 20 19 18 17 16

FOR ALFREDA MAY LEE
(1915–1996)

how difficult it is to remain just one
person,
for our house is open, there are no keys in
the doors,
and invisible guests come in and out at
will.

— CZESŁAW MIŁOSZ, *"Ars Poetica?"*

CONTENTS

■ ■ ■ ■

INITIATION

1978

■ ■ ■ ■

When Dan was eighteen a man he didn't know took him on a trip across the border. It was 1978, the last week of June, six days after the British Army shot dead three Catholics on the Ballysillan Road. The car smelt of vinegar from fish and chips and the man had a scarred bald head and two jokes, one about the Brits and the other to do with priests. He seemed to be steering Dan somewhere near Clones, big square-tipped fingers drumming at the wheel, little jolts of surprise in his eyes sometimes as the road invented itself. He had a lavishly ugly cauliflower ear. He touched it several times as he drove. The crowded grey houses of Protestant Ulster gave way to light, to colour. You could feel the wind here and smell the grass. There were Derry buses streaming with red-and-white scarves. Flags in green and white and gold were wrapped around the branches of trees.

The bald man unleashed a magnificent burp as he swung the car onto a dirt track. The dirt track led down to a square of land enclosed by elms. Dan saw daisies, hay bales. A gleam of Coke bottle in the weeds. Beyond the bottle in a margin of shade a dark Land Rover was parked.

"Don't you worry yourself about the vehicle," the bald man said. "No one stops it, see? He'll be thinking of a Saracen for Christmas."

Dan tried to smile. "So that's . . ."

"Yeah?"

"It's Mr. McCartland, is it?"

"Oh," the bald man said, "I'd reckon so." With his seat belt still fastened he began pawing around in his jeans pocket for something, the touchy bulk of his body contorting like he was trapped in a torture chair, but a flattened packet of chewing gum was all that his hand retrieved. He looked at Dan and laughed. "Should've thrown you a can for the journey, shouldn't I? A drink would've tightened the dung."

The weather this morning was storybook pure. Big yellow sun. Smooth blue sky. A single white cloud as drawn by a child. It seemed the kind of day when nothing serious could happen. A day to drink eight pints and get burned. There weren't many days

14

like this in an Irish year; they asked to be remembered. He walked with the bald man towards the Land Rover, sharp grass going flat under their boots. Cottages were scattered around this land, detached places fronted by tilted fence posts and low open gates, window shutters swagging on tired hinge pins, properties that promoted an idea of privacy without ever quite needing to commit, and he too felt exposed, open. Sorely underprepared. He'd had no notice that the car was coming for him. Sweat was already forming at the base of his back. His leather jacket was cool but heavy. He'd heard so many stories about these initiations, the things they put you through before you could properly join, but he knew too that tall tales were Belfast's stock-in-trade, the false often boosting the true.

A thin guy climbed out of the Land Rover. He wore specs and a smart shirt, sand-coloured trousers. Could this really be Dawson McCartland? He looked like an accountant. He pulled two large dogs out of the Rover on a long forked lead. One was gold and the other was brown. "Good morning," he said in a nasal monotone, nodding as if to prove that he meant it.

Dan went in for a handshake. Instead he received the dog lead. "I'm Dan."

"Well," Dawson said, removing his specs, "that's a relief." His blurry eyebrows were joined and from under their awning he stared. A twinkliness to his eyes. The corners of his mouth upturned. With a hanky he wiped at the lenses of his glasses. The dogs were barking and pulling on the lead. He looked like a man struggling to contain some huge and mysterious amusement with the world and glancing down at his dogs now he sighed. "Away in the head they are, Dan. I love them more than my wife, these animals. Is that wrong, to prefer them to her?"

"Dog lover," Dan said.

"Are there others?"

"Others?"

"In Ireland, who love their dogs. You seemed to be assuming a category."

Dan waited a moment. "Just a thing people say," he said.

"On the whole I think of us more as cat fellas, Dan. Independent. It's the Loyalists who are the dogs. Got any pets?"

"Me?"

"You."

"No."

"Not a rabbit, or anything?"

"No."

"Chinchilla, maybe? Budgerigar? It's going to be tough to let you volunteer without *something,* y'know. Freedom fighters need a mascot."

There was a long pause.

"I'm just pulling your chain, Dan. You're with friends. This interview's going to be very informal."

The bald man was yawning happily, eyes sliding towards the trees, and the squirm of nerves in Dan's stomach began to settle a little. "The lad's not much of a talker, Dawson."

"You don't say," Dawson said. "Might be a doer instead, eh?" He took a pack of Newports from his pocket. "Want one, Dan? I'm a great supporter of silence."

"I'm OK."

"You?"

The bald man chewed gum. "Given up, haven't I."

"On life?"

"Fags."

Dawson lit up and took a drag. "Same thing, I'd argue." He stood there smoking, crackling with his own peculiar charisma, the kind of self-assurance Dan had only recently learned how to fake. Every movement with the cigarette was well mannered, expert, measured and tight, as if designed to counter rumours that he could be a vi-

17

cious brute. With great delicacy, as Dan leaned back into the breeze, Dawson tapped some ash away and let smoke escape a smile. "So," he said to the bald man. "Business. Tell me about young Dan here. What's he got going for him apart from his looks, his height? Who recommended?"

"Mad Dog," the bald man said.

"Which Mad Dog, though?"

The bald man sniggered at this. Paddy was quiet, diminutive, aways keen to understand, with a careful moustache and small blue eyes he had a knack of keeping steady. He was ten years older than Dan and if he really was known as Mad Dog it would be a joke, Dan thought. Like calling a small man Big Tony. A ladies' man Gay Sam.

Dawson said, "You'll have to excuse us, Dan. The best nicknames get overused. Same in every army. We forget what the reason was and then there's this dearth of imagination, isn't there? A dearth that's affecting the world. How d'you get to know Paddy Magee?"

"Collecting bullets," Dan told them.

"Yeah?"

"Yeah."

He had cousins who lived around the Ballymurphy Estate. When the RUC took on Republicans there, news crews from all over the world came to watch. Italians staying at the Europa would pay five US dollars for a plastic bullet. They tried to give you lire but you laughed, told them you didn't have a big enough bag; they liked the pep in that chat. The Americans would pay upwards of ten. If the bullets were still warm you could scratch names onto them, which the Japanese enjoyed — souvenirs from a dangerous trip, a bystander's excitement at violence. A personalised bullet commissioned by an Asian and engraved to order could catch as much as fifteen. On the downside the commissioner might easily disappear and then you were left with something you couldn't sell on. Dan's friend Cal had spent half his adolescence looking for a second Haruto. From the Ballymurphy you could see the Black Mountain, a thousand shades of green made dark by all that rain.

"Not a bad little business, I imagine, Dan."

"It was all right. Don't do it much now."

"No?"

"I'm concentrating on odd jobs, electrics."

"So I hear. You and a sham, was it? For the bullet collecting?"

"Yeah."

"Anyone I'd know?"

"Cal."

Dawson tilted his head. "Has he a sur-name, this Cal character, or is it a Cher ball-tickler sorta situation?"

Dan laughed. "He's no Cher, Mr. Mc-Cartland."

"Dawson."

"His name's Cal Doherty."

Dawson considered the sky. "Nothing's ringing," he said. "I've succumbed to im-pure images of singing angels, is the thing."

"He suffers from a —"

"Oh, I know Cal. Nice lad, altogether. Face like a dose of haemorrhoids but he's nice despite it, isn't he? I'm very wary of pretty fellas, Dan, I've got to tell you. A pretty guy or girl has something they're worried'll get spoiled, y'know? My wife's dead on — you'd be lucky to have her company, Dan — but she's only got one eye, there's the thing." He crouched down to screw his cigarette into the ground. Care-fully he folded the stub into a tissue, pock-eted it and lit another Newport. "Wears a patch. Scottish by birth. As for me, I've actually got some English blood in me, y'know? Touch of Welsh too. Some say it disqualifies me from doing this job, but that's the type of wonky thinking that'll cause wars, isn't it? Lack of faith in empathy. Tell me: are you a fan?"

"Of empathy?"

"Yeah."

"I don't know. I suppose so."

Dawson's lips pressed thin, resisting a fresh grin, and his eyes seemed to glitter again. "It's worth pondering on. If you don't have it, a little of it, you can't think yourself into another person's shoes. You can't countenance, let's say, that I could wear yours with conviction." He bent down to pat his dogs, took a long look at Dan's boots and stood. "No," he said. "Lack of empathy's a tragic flaw. Ever read any Shakespeare, Danny?"

"Why? Did he invent flaws?"

"Ha. I like you already. You're warming up nicely. But no. Not even God, the old fucker, could make such a wondrous claim." He inhaled and blew a smoke ring. "Wonder where He's holidaying sometimes, don't you? Not giving Ireland much time, is He?"

"Probably He's got a lot on."

"Depressed or drunk, like everyone else. But no, I like a bit of Shakespeare, Danny. That's all. I don't read it anymore, but it's *in* me, you know? Like the Irish lingo. *Seirbhís. Slán.* Now. Mick. Will you go fetch the bags from the Rover, please? The ones with the gear in them. That'd be grand."

Mick. Gear.

21

Dan watched Mick receding and returning, settling the bags on the grass, shirtsleeve riding up around his grudging wrist and flashing part of a blue tattoo. Tongue of a hanging snake, maybe, or flick of a mermaid's tail.

Dawson said, "Do us a favour, will you, Dan? Play with the animals awhile. They don't get out much, they're like old Mick here. And Mick and I have deep stuff to discuss."

At Dawson's instruction Dan unzipped the green bag. It contained three tennis balls, a baseball bat, a warm six-pack of beer. He walked towards the trees with the tennis ball that looked least chewed.

Branches leaning and relaxing. The whispered resistance of leaves. Thinking: first stage of the interview must be over. Doing as he was told.

He threw the ball up high and retrieved it from their jaws. Amazing the amount these dogs drooled. The brown dog had patches of yellow on its tongue but it moved, on the whole, quicker than its golden friend. They competed to catch the ball on the bounce, weaving in front of each other — slipstream, overtake; slipstream, overtake — never clashing but always seeming like they would.

Should he be asking more questions? Showing more initiative? He'd been advised by Cal to stay silent unless spoken to. Probably that was right.

Every few minutes he looked back. Dawson and Mick were paying him no attention, which had to be a good thing. In his days of reading the pulps he never hankered after flight or the ability to cling to buildings. Invisibility was the most precious of the superpowers.

He tired of the damp tennis ball, exchanged it for a hunk of dried-out bark. The dogs chased it down and brought it back. Dan sprinted alongside them with the bark dangling from his hand, stopping and starting, lifting it up and lowering it down. After a while it burned to breathe. He knelt down to scratch their ears and watch the bob of their tongues. Some people said dogs were stupid, pure dim need and pure dim gratitude, but he saw in the spark of their eyes a special intelligence. Footballers calculating angles, movement without doubt.

"Here we go!" Dawson shouted. "Round 'em up."

Dan clipped the dogs to the lead and jogged. The two men were nodding and laughing, squinting in the sunlight.

Dawson said, "Was just sharing an anec-

dote a guy called Clinkie told me. He's
straight out of the blocks, is Clinkie. Want
to hear it?"

"Sure," Dan said.

"Clinkie says to me, he says Jesus is on
the cross and the guys either side of him
aren't thieves. So, what are they?"

Dan shook his head.

"Well, Dan, if you knew Clinkie you'd
want to say they're gays. But no. Clinkie
explains to me they're political activists,
working against the Roman authorities.
You've a pair of Republicans either side,
getting crucified. And Clinkie says —"

"I've heard this."

Dawson raised his big eyebrow. "What's
that, Dan?"

"I've heard it," Dan said, "from a couple
of people. I remember now. Romans are
Brits. Samaritans are Catholics. Jews are
Protestants. First person welcomed into
heaven today would be a paramilitary, Jesus
talking to Dismas the thief, You will be in
Heaven with me today, et cetera."

Silence.

"Well," Dawson said. "Talk about spoiling
a story."

There was the lazy sound of a bumblebee.
Mick spent some time scratching his face.
As Dan looked down at the grass Dawson

24

said, "I enjoyed watching you with them, Dan. My dogs. Beautiful beasts, eh?"

"Yeah."

"Myself, I'm not much of an athlete. A wee bit short on the breath, you know? I need a little can of special air." He took an asthma inhaler out of his pocket and revolved it in his hand. For a moment he looked utterly lost. "Anyway, I'd better head. Sadly I've an appointment with a fella who's lived too long." He waited a beat, shook the inhaler, took a puff and held the air in his mouth. "Birthday party. Fortieth. Bloke's mad as a bottle of chips, y'know, but we've got him a ping-pong table."

"That's it?"

Dawson laughed. "Well, we'll throw in a couple of bats and a ball, for sure."

"I meant —"

"Yeah?"

"I'll just — I'll wait to hear something, will I? Wait to hear whether I'm in? I'm keen, Mr. McCartland. I'll work hard. I — I want to help the cause." He could feel another future going grey.

Dawson raised his chin and blinked. "Listen, Dan. I've heard —" One dog barked and the other dog whined. "I've heard that you're useful. Is that right? Chaps at that Matt Talbot Youth Club. They say to me, as Patrick did, Now there's a useful guy."

"Pool," Dan said. "Snooker. That's probably all they meant."

"Come on now. No games. Ireland's been modest too long. What are you good at, besides spoiling a story? An example. Let me think. My wife, the one-eyed one, she's your bona fide whizz in the kitchen."

Had they really brought him here to talk about hobbies? He chewed his lip, lined up some thoughts.

He hadn't been a success at school but he was good at some things, small things. He had a talent for remembering. He was confident he'd be able to recite the right bits of the Green Book if all this went well and they swore him in. He could give them whole passages from the Bible too. Lines from the pulpit seemed to lodge in his head; he liked the slant and pop of bygone language. He could draw a map from memory, replace a tyre without a jack, run a decent hundred yards and lift some heavyish weights. He could masturbate three times a day and still tug out a fourth before sleep. He was good in the garden, good at sorting his mother's drugs, good at making bets with other kids and good half the time at winning them. He did some DIY for the

26

community: bits of plumbing, guttering, electrics like his father used to do after the job at Gallaher had gone. He was proud of his country and he thought it was OK to be proud.

"I'm not modest," he said. "I'm just shy with new people."

They chose to take this as a joke. One of the dogs bit playfully at the folds of skin around the other's neck.

"Do y'know how to use an auto, Dan?"

He found himself looking to Mick for an answer. "No," he said.

Guns. A lot of the boys he knew wanted to join the Provos so that they could play with guns. Whereas his own reasons for wanting to join were . . . What were his reasons? To make a difference, long-term. To end the occupation, change people's minds. To help fix up gutted businesses and protect the Catholic corner shops. To do service to the circumstances of his father's death and to the fact that two of his brother's friends, James Joseph Wray and Gerry McKinney, had been killed by the British Army on Bloody Sunday. Gerry unarmed with his hands in the air saying "don't shoot, don't shoot," after which he was shot in the chest. James Joseph unable to move.

"One at home," he said. "For protection.

But it's not an auto, and I never fired it."

"Interesting. Hear that, Mick? Prefers picking up bullets to popping them. I bet you Danny's the guy at a party who sticks to the hard H_2O."

With a snigger that seemed stolen from television Mick zipped up the bag that had contained the balls. He opened the other one, took out a shotgun and a handgun. The handgun he gave to Dan.

"Feel it," Dawson said. "Lovely weight, no? Tend to jam, the autos, is the only thing. And now, if you don't mind, you'll shoot the dogs."

Dan laughed. No one else joined in. Their faces were flushed and attentive but there was no hint of humour at all.

"Or," Dawson added, "you can shoot one of them. Fifty per cent. You seem to be a left-hander — is that right, Dan? I could probably look after one dog. The thing is, looking after two, I don't have the time, y'know? It's cruel to have them."

Still their expressions gave nothing away. Dawson blew his nose.

"I'd keep hold of the lead with the other hand," Dawson said. "When you fire, I mean. Otherwise we'll have a dog running around causing mischief, covered in bits of the other dog. Ugly, it'd be."

Mick snapped open the shotgun. He looked inside and closed it again. His eyes settled on the ground and his bald head shone.

"Is this a joke?" Dan said.

Dawson shrugged. "I'm asking you to stiff two dogs for me, my friend. I could do it myself, but they're my dogs, and I've had them exactly a year. So, do me a favour, save me from having to kill my own, will you?"

"Is it loaded?"

Dawson smiled again. "I was told you were useful, Dan. Have I been misinformed?"

"Like I said, I never used an auto."

"Same principle. Automatic. Manual. The thing they have in common is, you point them at something, squeeze the trigger, and the something stops being a problem."

"These dogs aren't a problem."

"They're a problem for *me*, Dan, you see." Hard and low in the voice now. Grave. "I'm starting to wonder at your team skills. I'm starting to think you lack a bit of the interpersonal."

Dan looked at the two dogs and they looked back at him. Wet eyes. Wet noses. Excited. "I could take one home. Or both. I've got time to look after them, Mr. Mc-

Cartland, and money for food."

"I like to get tight, Dan, but that doesn't mean I'm tight."

"No, of course."

"You've just joined an army. Time to wind your neck in, Dan."

"All I meant was —"

"You want to take on some new dependants now? Your ma not enough? The brother in the special home?" Dawson shook his head. "You think the British Army hesitate when they shoot dogs on our streets, corpses on the Falls to show us they're keeping an eye? Nothing was ever changed by squeamish men, Dan. History clears away the blood, records the results, but that doesn't mean the blood wasn't there. An Ireland occupied by the Brits will never be free. An Ireland unfree will never be at peace. Do you believe otherwise? Do you prefer to stand back and observe? Are you a watcher, Dan, is that it, you like to watch?"

Mick looked shifty now, embarrassed to be here. Again he touched his ruined ear. There was something newly benign in the calm sag of his mouth. A vulnerability, surely. It was Dawson who'd become the more brutish of the two. His thin neck had reddened, his thin lips had parted, his silver tongue was whipping up more words.

Maybe the brown one, with the patches on its tongue. Maybe that one is sick. He wants me to kill the sick dog. He'll tell me afterwards that it was sick, leukaemia or whatever, and I'll have passed the test.

With a steady left hand Dan lifted the gun and pointed it at the brown dog's head. Be a person who does instead of says. With his right hand he gripped tight at the dog lead. Go on.

He thought, This would be easier if the dog was ugly, if the dog was a rat, if the dog looked angry or unkind, and these thoughts made him sure he was being weak.

If he got it between the eyes — the complex eyes, keen, watery they were — he'd kill it quickly. But if he aimed for the body he'd reduce his chance of missing. A body shot and then a follow-up? That's what the RUC tended to do with guys they could label terrorists. But the other dog would be tugging, trying to get free, maybe covered in blood? Scared.

The brown dog looked at Dan, expectant, breathing through its mouth. The other had gone flat, nose nuzzled into the grass. Mick seemed — could this be right? — to be putting bits of toilet paper in his mouth. He was sticking the damp wads in his ears.

31

"I'll incentivise," Dawson said. "If you don't shoot one of my dogs, Mick here is going to kindly shoot you."

"Kindly?"

"He's not unkind. Watch him around the bars of Belfast. He's kissed all sorts of horrors."

"This is a wind-up."

"Is it?"

"Why would you shoot me? I'm asking to join!" It was a wind-up. It was. He lowered the gun. "I'm not shooting any dogs."

"It's your choice," Dawson said. "I've made the three options clear."

"Three?"

"Shoot a dog, one. Get yourself shot, two. Number three, you can shoot us. Although, for that option, you'd have to get cracking."

"This is stupid."

"We'll give you three seconds to finalise your thoughts, Dan."

"This is, what's the point of this?"

"Three."

"Come on."

"Two."

"Please."

"One."

Mick lifted the shotgun. He pointed it at Dan's chest and fired.

The slam of impact. Shock of his body

thrown back. A noise that put him deep inside himself.

As he hit the ground his senses ceased to function. There was darkness, silence. Only the slightest light swirling through the old dim world, sluggish as the cream his mother put in coffee.

He was groping for where the wound must be, the wound. Block the blood. Should have killed the dogs.

The leather of his jacket felt smooth. Nothing wet. Nothing ripped. Entry. Where was the entry? Slowly certain things came into focus: wind-swollen trees, a bird in blue sky.

He rolled onto an elbow. The Land Rover was pulling away, its tyres giving up dust. Mick was standing over him, holding out a massive hand. There was sand and white stuff on the ground. Grains? Rice? Some on his jeans too. Dry white rice.

Mick's cool shadow. It looked from his face like he was shouting, a muscle jumping in the jaw. "Doctor the partridge," he seemed to say. The ringing in Dan's ears changed in pitch. His chest hurt, his skull hurt.

"We fiddle with the cartridge. Pack it with a bit of basmati."

"What?"

"Ruining the local carb market, the rice, so we steal it from the Indian importers. Slows the flight of the thing right down. Sorry if you hit your head."

Dan spat. "I might've. But I might've shot the dog."

Mick laughed. "Yeah. But as initiations go, not so bad, eh? Next time a gun's pointed, you'll up your game."

He had no clue where the handgun was. It wasn't in his hand or anywhere near his hand. The dogs were moving wildly, happily, the lead snaking through the grass.

"Useful to confirm his initial impressions," Mick said. "There's that too. Thinks you're more of a distance man, doesn't he? Your DIY skills. Devicecraft. More and more he's looking to the mainland. First lad to call his bluff." He pulled Dan up into a warm embrace.

Dan blinked and tried to hide his shaking hands.

"It's over."

"What is?"

"Welcome to your new life."

■ ■ ■ ■

ONE:
UNACCOMMODATED
MEN

1984

■ ■ ■ ■

1

After her Wednesday-morning swim Freya bumped into Mr. Easemoth. He was her old History teacher at Blatchington Mill, the benevolent dictator of Classroom 2D, a man always striving for facts. You got the sense it was pretty important to him to feel he was misunderstood.

They exchanged a few words about the hotel. He grinned palely in the sunlight and said her future was bright. Mentioned also, awkwardly, that her father had given him a call. They'd discussed university options.

"Very proud of you," Mr. Easemoth said. "As well he should be."

"Thanks, Mr. Easemoth."

"Some of those marks were among the best in Brighton, I'd guess."

She smiled. "Thanks, I appreciate it."

"No," he said.

"What?"

"Thank *you*. A pleasure to teach."

Overhead a seagull screamed and wheeled. "Well, I guess I'd better . . ."

"Oh, of course."

"It's just."

"No no, don't let me hold you up."

The quality of his smile in this moment made her sad. "See you soon then, Mr. Easemoth."

"And give my best to your father."

Walking. The breeze on her legs. Brine in the air. She was wearing a brand-new electric blue miniskirt. And would she ever actually see Mr. Easemoth again? What had undermined him above all in the corridors at school was not his sinusitis, or the stains in the weave of his tie, or even his anticharisma. It was the unfortunate rumour that he possessed a micropenis, and probably that part wasn't true.

On rare September days like this, people in Brighton didn't hang about. They threw off their drizzled raincoats and raided drawers for gaudy shorts. They cooked themselves on towels and bobbed about on waves. Gulls tottered across rocks, heads dipping low and feet lifting high, the motion mirrored by a kid checking his shoe soles for chewing gum. Old men watched the water through wavy iron railings and old women sipped tea outside cafeterias.

The purple-and-pink signage of the hair salon was up ahead. Also the ice-cream guy. She could murder a 99 with double flake, but there was a long queue on the left side of the van.

Wendy Hoyt was the second-cheapest stylist at Curl Up & Dye, a curvy hypochondriac whose own bleached locks — an advert, a warning — took up a massive amount of airspace. With Wendy, headaches were often imaginary tumours. Back pain amounted to osteoporosis. She'd had suspected failures in all the main organs, suffered a non-productive cough caused by contact with livestock, and her neck bore a hairspray rash that she preferred to blame on sea breeze. Freya didn't pay much attention to Wendy's catalogue of invented catastrophes, but at the same time had an instinctive sympathy for people whose catastrophes didn't get much attention, so it was a sort of draw and she kept coming back.

"Thought any more about it?" Wendy said, tightening the gown around Freya's neck. There had already been a discussion about why her hair was "pre-wash-wet," a connected warning about the coarsening effects of chlorine, and a bonus tip about a girl who got pregnant when swimming because a boy had been masturbating in the shallow end. The hairdryers had been on. Wendy was breathing hard. The neon beads of her necklace shifted as her bosom rose and fell. From the top corners of the mirror hung two squiggles of silver ribbon that had survived the nine months since Christmas.

"I'm thinking maybe not," Freya said.

"We have more fun," Wendy said, winking. "Works like catnip in discos."

"Huh."

"I'm practically harassed. Blonde would flirt with your skin tone, too."

"Maybe."

"Different, I thought you were after. But if you want to stick with the flat brown look, we could always go side-ponytail, or fringe. Your friend Sarah — uni now, is she? — I gave her a lovely Cyndi Lauper."

Wendy took a sip of cranberry juice, a drink she claimed was effective in warding off infections. The wall behind the mirror was the colour of a fine lime. Another wall was pink, a third was purple. A girl sweeping up hair clippings was humming a chorus-only version of "Borderline" by Madonna, an undeniably awesome song, and her T-shirt said "All the Way to Wembley" under a picture of a gliding gull. Freya closed her eyes and imagined, for a moment, sitting here at Mr. Easemoth's age, having the same conversation, counting the same neon beads around Wendy's neck: three overlapping strings, twenty on the bottom, eighteen in the middle, sixteen on the top.

A lot of time passed. At least half a minute.

"OK," she said. There was new heat in her skin. Live dangerously, right? "Cut it all off, Wendy, and turn me blonde."

Wendy raised an intensively pencilled eyebrow. A customer from Hove walked in. Several things told you a person was from Hove. In this instance it was the explosion of silk scarves around the neck.

"You're sure?" Wendy said.

"Yep."

"*All?*"

"No! To here, basically, and then bleached. Or highlights. Yep, highlights. But nothing that will look ginger."

Wendy's features formed a grimace. She was an expert grimacer.

"On a skinny little girl like you," Wendy said. "A girl who's pretty in that waify sort of way . . ." She took a further slurp of juice. With great caution she placed the glass down on a ledge. "Here's what I'm thinking. This is the question on my mind. It's whether you have the neck for it, Freya.

Because, as your adviser, I've got to say a lot of light is going to be falling on that neck, is the thing, and — with your cute little features — going shorter might make you look a bit, how to say it . . ."

"Boyish?"

"Ethiopian orphan," Wendy said.

Freya lifted her chin and studied herself. What orphan-like qualities would a bob cut reveal? She was pale, brown-haired, brown-eyed, ordinary, but in the mirror now a starving Ethiopian stared back at her. She crossed and recrossed her legs. Barbed comments were Wendy's brand of friendship, but they could also be a kind of contagion. You walked out of there worrying about problems you probably didn't have.

She thought about the Grand, her impending shift behind the reception desk. Her father, the Deputy General Manager, generally managed to fix it so that on Wednesdays she only had to work the afternoons. He too was a customer of Wendy Hoyt. On a quarterly basis he got his head, eyebrows and ears done, a 3-for-1 deal the barber refused to do.

"Tell you what," Freya said. "Just the usual trim."

"Yeah?"

"Yeah."

The decision cast a spell: her heartbeat slowed. She felt herself relaxing back into the comfy disappointment of her life since leaving school.

"Better safe than sorry, eh?"

"Probably," Freya said.

"Let's get you washed, then, with that strawberry stuff you like, and you can tell me your plans for Maggie Thatcher."

2

Philip Finch, known to everyone but his aged mother as Moose, was driving to the hotel in his fail-safe Škoda 120, a car the colour of old chocolate gone chalky. His window was wound down so he could tap ash onto the street and blow smoke out of the side of his mouth. It was important that his daughter shouldn't have to inhale his mistakes. She was in the passenger seat wearing her classic early-morning look: black skirt, white blouse, an elegantly expressionless corpse. Her hair had been cut yesterday. He saw no discernible difference. He told her it looked very good.

They passed the Dyke Road Park and the Booth Museum. Freya started rummaging in the glove compartment, a minor landslide of cassettes. There was a system and she was spoiling it. "What are you looking for?"

"Music."

"We're five minutes away, Frey."

She yawned. Blinked. Considered the windscreen. "It's hot," she said.

"There's some Wayne Fontana and the Mindbenders in there. That one I played, where were we?"

She sighed.

"You're sighing."

"Nothing good has ever been produced by a Wayne, Dad."

"Untrue," he said, and fell into a long dark reverie from which he emerged with the name Wayne Sleep.

"Who?"

"Or . . ." Where were all the other famous Waynes? "John Wayne."

"Surname," she said.

"That makes him a deeper form of Wayne. His Wayneness is in the blood."

"Probably a stage name," she said. Which, now he thought of it . . .

He changed down another gear — these conversations were precious — and told her she shouldn't write things off until she'd tried them.

"Like travelling, you mean."

"Like university," he said. "Travelling, Frey. There's nothing special about travelling. This right here is travelling — going to put those back, at all? You can find yourself and lose yourself in this very car, this town."

"Thrill a minute," she said, but he thought he saw the flicker of a smile.

She was eighteen years and a dozen days old. Just yesterday, it seemed to him, she'd emerged out of an awkward bespectacled adolescence — a phase in which she'd temporarily lost the ability to be appreciative, the ability to be considerate, and the ability to be apologetic, all while causing a great proliferation of opportunities for these states to be warmly deployed. He'd noticed, of late, a big upsurge in the number of masculine glances clinging to her clothes, and also in the ways she didn't need him. Seldom asked his advice anymore. Knew how to deal with difficult customers. Would one way or another soon be leaving him behind. Her mood swings had settled into a dry indifference, a much narrower emotional range. At times he felt nostalgia for her earlier anger and found himself needlessly provoking her. University! Careers! When might you learn to lock the door?

With her pale skin and dark eyes and button nose, that fatal way of raising the left eyebrow in arguments, Freya was increasingly a Xerox copy of Viv, back when they'd first got together. There was an awful pregnant pathos to this: your perfect daughter becoming your then-perfect wife, slinking into a future where she'd fall prey to certain enterprising, highly sexed individuals who were suped-up versions of the once-young you. He sometimes overheard summer staff at the Grand talking in an advanced language of sexual adventure, discussing what he assumed to be new positions or techniques. The Cambodian Trombone. The Risky Painter. South-East England Double Snow-Cone. Did anyone still do missionary? The future bares its breasts and laughs, a gaudy county fair.

Truth was, Moose hadn't had sex in a while. The one great difficulty of his job was the fact of being surrounded, at all times, by people engaged in sexual communion. Guests were having sex against walls and on hushed carpets, in storage cupboards and on sea-view balconies, in gooseneck free-standing baths and walk-in showers and probably just occasionally on beds. Forty-five. Too young, definitely, to have taken retirement from romance. But it was more of a redundancy-type situation, wasn't it? A severance. Lust running on without opportunity, not unlike a headless chicken. People still occasionally made remarks about his appearance — remarks interpretable as compliments — but he was often too busy to follow up on such leads. He'd had only a handful of flings with women in the years since Viv had left him for a guy called Bob; Freya at that time was thirteen. Possibly he'd have to relax his no-guest rule. There was always someone lonelier than you were. He struggled sometimes to shake the idea that his early life had been all about an excess of sex and a sense of bottled potential, and that these things had, in the rich tradition of life's droll jokes, been replaced by an absence of sex and a sense of wasted potential.

"New skirt," he said.

"No."

"New haircut, though."

"We've covered this," she said.

He flicked the indicator. Reminded himself to waterproof the passenger window. Masking tape before autumn really kicked in. They passed a Labrador walking a lightweight woman.

Frey mumbled something.

"You've become a mumbler," he said.

"Wendy told me to tell you hello."

"Did she? That's nice. How was she then? Still dying?"

"Yeah. Bit more each time."

"Good hair though."

"Hmm."

"I bumped into her in Woolworths a few

weeks back. Forgot to say. Complained to me about an ingrowing toenail. I thought it might mark a new move into realism."

"No," Freya said. "There was no mention of toes. She was back to brain tumours and surgeries."

"Shame."

They rolled on through Brighton's breezy, straight and safe-looking streets, lamp posts spaced out and rooflines designed to rhyme. Girls in white denim walking, ponytails flicking. Women in smart dark jackets, narrow at the waist and wide at the shoulders. Crazy baggy T-shirts giving gangly kids space to hide. The summer not yet over. That special summer hum. The Prime Minister was coming to stay in a few weeks' time. He knew her visit was a route to promotion. To future GM opportunities in Oxford or Bristol or Durham, wherever Freya ended up studying. Money too. His current £14,000 a year didn't go that far. He needed to provide and provide. He'd earn more as a doorman or a bellman — those guys built houses out of one-pound coins — but if you were a doorman or a bellman you were a doorman or a bellman for life, addicted to tips and shorn of the chance to advance; he'd seen it happen many times. A salaried position had a future. That was the idea, anyway.

Left onto the King's Road, a modest milk float trundling past them. On his right, the vast glittering sweep of the sea. Late-season holidaymakers, towels slung over their shoulders, crossed the street to reach a warm swerve of shore. Grey stones and beige stones, some slick and some dry. The British approach to sunburn was simple: get out there and upgrade yesterday's patchy burns into something of more uniform severity. The recklessness of his own heat-seeking people made Moose oddly proud. Paint was peeling from the candy-floss huts, faded seaside glamour.

The Grand came into view, one of the loves of his life, a giant white wedding cake of a building facing out onto the English Channel. The wide eaves, the cornices, the elaborate brick enrichments. The Union Jack slapping high. He loved the twiddly little features and their special arcane names. One hundred and twenty years of stinging drizzle, of corrosive sunshine, of the salty gales and acidic bird shit it is every coastal town's cross to bear.

What he loved most was walking into the Grand with his daughter at his side. Yes, I created this person, look. A tiny moment of ego in an industry that was all about accommodating others. His favourite doorman, George, waved as they got out of the car. George who always had an umbrella in his hand, forever expecting rain, and touched every bit of luggage the moment a car boot opened, for once your hand was on the handle a tip was almost certainly yours. Then Dave the Concierge with his wide friendly face and breath that always smelt of aniseed, a strategy to conceal his fondness for Scotch. He bowed for Freya in mock-theatrical style, a move that made her laugh each time. Derek the Bellman simply nodded. It was said that he had a picture of Bernard Sadow on his dartboard at home, the guy who'd invented the suitcase with wheels.

Within these Victorian walls, Moose's style was excessive. The Grand was all about excess. He was living through excessive times. He didn't have the money or inclination to wear expensive suits, to buy designer gel to sophisticate his salt-and-pepper hair, and although he had a head for maths he lacked the inner shard of ice that was probably required to make it rich in merchant banking. So instead he wore his navy-blue Burton suit — a suit for a man who was neither tall nor short, neither fat nor slim

— and created little performances out of thin air, words and gestures that made his guests feel special, his name badge pinned close in on the lapel, his tie hanging over the nearest portion of his title, concealing the word DEPUTY, leaving only GENERAL MANAGER, a promotion without the salary or associated sense of pride. His stage was the lobby's Persian rug. He liked the thick cream scrollwork of the ceiling, the gleams in the bends of the luggage trolley, the decorative panels that made him think of Malted Milk biscuits, the soft wattage of elegant lamps. He liked the Merlot-coloured curtains keeping the parlour rooms calm. The heart of house was dingy corridors and piles of dirty laundry, but the front of house, the areas guests saw once they had passed through the glittering wings of the revolving door, was full of the warmth of opulence, the mellowing air of antiquity, the fragrance of fresh flowers. First thing you felt coming in — the door's revolutions slowing — was the hush of wise furniture inside. Duet stools and wing-arm chairs. The Gainsborough nestled under the first dramatic arc of staircase. It was upholstered in Colefax & Fowler Oban Plaid.

"Mr. Barley, how's that nephew the newscaster doing? Lovely profile in the *Argus.*"

"How was that champagne, Mrs. Harding? Did it live up to the no-hangover guarantee?"

"I'll get that console table replaced, Mrs. Mathis. A woman of your stature should not have to stoop."

"A sea-view suite?"

"Some aspirin?"

"A doctor?"

"A florist?"

Smell of fresh coffee in the morning. Tea and cakes come afternoon. Toothbrush sets behind the desk. Hundreds upon hundreds of condoms. Knot cufflinks by the dozen. People were very regular in what they overlooked, and also in what they left behind: pyjamas, handcuffs, once a prosthetic leg. Moose was a secular man. He would have liked to remove the Bibles from the rooms, or else to add copies of the Koran, but they were hugely popular among the summer staff — the thin pages were apparently handy for rolling joints — and if a thing made you feel better, and you practised it discreetly, who really had a right to object?

On days when ambition and regret got the better of him, when lost opportunities stuck to his shoes like bubble gum gone to ground and created ugly slouching strings that halted progress, he told himself that all human life was here. Yes, the affairs. The stuff everyone always asks you about. Definitely those things. But people also got engaged and married here. They received phone calls telling them their parents had died. They conceived children. They blew out candles.

He was happiest of all when talking to guests. If it wasn't for the editorial influence of deadlines and to-do lists, he could easily pass whole days discussing their get-richer ideas and much-mourned ailments, the Platonic ideal of a pillow, its consummate softness and girth. He liked to know every guest's name and to slowly fill out the lives underneath. When regulars were the kind of people who enjoyed saying hello he tended also to know the names of their children. When they went about their days closely guarding their privacy he nodded and smiled, held a mirror up to their reticence. Hospitality involved an aspect of surface flattery but also of deep familiarity. It was a peculiar combination of density and gauze. You were reading people all the time, reading and reading and reading, and only occasionally was his apparent fondness for people false. The odd smile delivered to a slick pinstriped guy who was really no more than a slippery fish in the sea of his own possessions. The occasional compliment to a woman whose post-operative breasts were even more determinedly inauthentic than her eyes — eyes that were blank screens upon which brief impressions of felt experience flickered. In the main, people were kind if you were kind. They wanted to have a good time. You gave them the best and worst of yourself. The huge lie that you would escalate their complaint to Head Office. Telling the truth, almost always, when you wished them a very good stay.

Mrs. Harrington from room 122 was doggedly crossing the lobby, swinging the walking stick she rarely seemed to need. Old Mrs. H was one of the Grand's most reliable regulars, and she only ever stayed in room numbers that added up to five. Many front-desk staff had learned her proclivities the hard way. "Room 240 is lovely, Mrs. Harrington." "I'd prefer not to, dear." "Room 301, perhaps?" "I'd prefer not to."

"Punctual as always, Mrs. Harrington."

"You," she said with a hospitable grimace. "Still poorly?"

"Poorly?"

"Pale."

"Me?"

"Roller coaster," she said, and traced a

wavy line in the air with the ferrule of her stick.

Moose tried to laugh but managed only the maintenance of his current smile.

"Arm pain," she said.

He felt his smile fail him. "How did you know?"

"You confided."

"Did I?"

For a moment her eyes slid sideways towards another regular, Miss Mullan. On every other week of the year she was *Mr.* Mullan, chairman of a FTSE 100 toiletries company.

"Perfectly fine now, thanks, Mrs. H. Little sprain. I'm not dead yet."

"Geoffrey said that. My Geoffrey, before he died."

"I'm sorry," Moose said. "That was thoughtless of me."

Mrs. H couldn't move her shoulders much, so to indicate a shrug she simply turned the palm of her right hand towards the ceiling. "His death," she said. "Second-best thing that ever happened to me."

"What was the first thing?"

"Motorcycle," she said, and continued her voyage towards the restaurant. The breakfast crowd parted as she waved her stick on a low axis from side to side, as if it were white and she were blind, the wood knocking at shins and kneecaps, opening a path to where the best table was.

With Freya safely installed behind the reception desk, her chin on the heels of her hands, still frustratingly bad at disguising her boredom, he did his usual check of the restaurant (tidy) and the lavatories (shiny). He walked up to the first-floor storage room, where the hotel held long-term luggage and other items like cribs and wheelchairs. There had been a spontaneous staff party in the hotel last night and sure enough he now located, in a dusty corner, a few dozen miniature bottles of booze. A condom wrapper too. Jesus. An untouched Marathon bar. Interesting. He ate the Marathon and found Mimi from Housekeeping. Asked her to put the unused items back in the minibar cupboard and ensure that it was double-locked. No 1-1-1-1 combinations on padlocks, please. Then, coming down the thickly carpeted staircase, careful not to touch the handrail and impart unnecessary smudges, he passed Chef Harry's temperamental tabby cat, Barbara. Usually she begged for food. Lately she'd been depressed. Gave him a withering droopy-whiskered look that seemed to say "What's the point?"

"This is as good as it gets, Barb."

She pinned her ears back and yawned.

He asked Marina, the Grand's Guest Relations Manager, whether there'd been any further press enquiries about the conference, or any changes to the block-booking numbers supplied by the Prime Minister's secretary's secretary. There hadn't been, so after he'd marvelled at the wondrous way she blew upward at her hair between sentences, the soft fringe fluttering darkly, he took his disappointment and arousal to the cupboard he called his office. A memo to finish. A briefing pack on important guests. Documents authorising the installation of extra security and CCTV — nine cameras, twelve, the requirements kept shifting. Paper sprouting from his IBM Wheelwriter. No natural light in here. Assuming the overall manager stepped down in a few months, as planned, and assuming also that the PM's visit was a major success; assuming all this and assuming that the Group Executive Committee was as good as its word, Moose would soon be moving upstairs into an office with a door plaque saying "General Manager." Overall control. Decent salary. Sun and sea view. He wished he were not so reliant on recognition, but it gave him the little lift he needed to get through each seventy-hour week.

Paragraphs taking shape. Letters sometimes interlocking. Clack clack clack and only four errors. The dyslexia always an itchy label on his thoughts, irritating his attempts at eloquence. The calendar on the wall showing sun touching fields and *September* festooned with breezy leaves. He was in the habit of crossing out each finished day, boxes of cancelled life, a pencil not a pen, as if he might at some point want to reinstate a long-lost Tuesday. The filing cabinet had his little gold statuettes on top, men with torsos that were upside-down triangles. They were standing on the edges of diving boards. Along with the hatstand, these were his favourite office items.

Did he own any hats? No, technically he did not. But built into his belief system these days were a number of convictions — never take taxis, never be afraid of combining carbohydrates — and one of them was that a hatstand was something every man ought to have. The thing about hats was, you never knew when you might want to start getting into them. Freya had said to him, "Why don't you use it for coats, in the meantime?" But his daughter was missing the point. He was saving the hatstand for a hat. He could picture it: the first delicious instant when, with casual carefulness, he'd toss onto one of its lovely curling limbs an Ascot cap, a Balmoral bonnet, a beret, a boater, a fez or a fedora. It was a small moment of magic he'd stored up for the future.

He reached for a folder entitled "Conservative Party Visit" and began to refine his strategies, taking breaks only to phone universities and ask them to send more prospectuses.

In the afternoon there was a meeting with the following agenda:

1. Alarm clock roll out. 201 + spares. Testing committee. Features. LED light? Serving the long-sighted, late-sleepers, etc. (PF)
2. Napkins for functions during conference. Scottish supplier. Problem? Conference blue? (PF)
3. Snagging request from Cameron House. (PF)
4. Training prog for additional temporary staff. (PF)
5. Canapé vote. (PF)
6. Fax machine installation. (PF)
7. Mitigating annoyance of CCTV for non-conference guests? (MV)
8. Towels not soft enough — what's the point of trying to be cheap on

fabric softener? (DN)
9. Riots. (PF)
10. Irish protesters. (PF)
11. Security threats. (PF)
12. Any other business.

In the "any other business" section of the meeting — so seldom used for anything except birthday announcements — there was a discussion about the fact that the hotel hadn't suffered an overflowing bath for the best part of nine months, which was thought to be a record. There was also a complaint from a maid about further strings of semen found on floral-pattern curtains. Who *were* these curtain fuckers? What was their plan?

Once item 12 was dealt with, the ever-sleazy Peter Samuels asked Fran a mischievous question. She was the p.m. Housekeeping Manager, a black lady with striking eyes. Turndown, purchasing, scheduling. Thirty-two staff under her command.

Fran said to Peter, "Nah, no no, not what happened. *Here*'s the story. OK. So. The wife came out of the bathroom, yeah? Wet and naked." Fran paused for effect. Silence fell around her. Only Marina smiled. Perhaps she'd heard the story already. "And this guest, she's wearing nothing except a skimpy little white towel tied up around her hair. This is when I'm covering for one of those useless summer girls, Veronica the Vomiter, you got it." A nervous laugh from the assembled staff, two of whom had personally recommended Veronica for the job. "And she says to me, this guest, her tits out, her arse out — everything out — she smiles and says all casual, 'Carry on, darling, but shut the curtains, will you? I don't want the neighbours seeing me naked.' "

Hush around the table. Men full of longing leaned in. "What did you do, Fran?"

"Well," Fran said, "I carried on making the bed, didn't I? And then I explained to her, real polite, that if the neighbours saw her naked they'd shut their own fucking curtains."

The room exploded. Fran had worked in hospitality for the best part of three decades. Her principal complaint about the Grand was that tights weren't supplied with the uniform.

As the sky over the Channel became a deep purple, only a few fragile coral swirls surviving up high, Moose took a seat in the bar area for his pre-dinner beer and cigarette combo. His Zippo was engraved with the words "To Viv, Love Phil." His ex-wife hadn't shown much commitment with her smoking. Marina came over, clutching a pack of menthols. Moose provided a flame. The best thing about smoking was that people like Marina sometimes asked you for a light.

He dropped a twenty-pence piece into the till, opened a packet of crisps, pulled up a chair for her. Pictures of famous guests adorned one wall: Napoleon the Third, John F. Kennedy, Harold Wilson.

"Take a holiday, Moose," Marina said. "A couple of days you could spare, no?" She lifted her arms. A little pink yawn as she stretched. He noted once again the miraculous mundanity of her elbows, tiny angry creatures that seemed too awkward to belong to her body.

Technically he was, via a dotted line, Marina's boss. But the clash of continents in her voice gave the Grand's Guest Relations Manager a worldliness he couldn't ignore. Also: he was still suffering a little from The Infatuation. He took to heart everything she said and respected also the fact she didn't explain too much about her past. Viv used to say there were two types of person in life, past tense and present tense. Viv had seen herself as a present-tense person, which gave her an excuse never to discuss what she felt about a thing that had already happened. She'd dwell on that thing silently instead. Marina, though, was genuinely present tense. She inhabited it. Owned it. Male staff members at the Grand waded through the myths that surrounded her, enjoying the feeling of being stuck. The story that she'd once been married to an adulterous game-show host in Argentina. That she'd previously been a model and a children's entertainer. That recently, on her thirty-eighth birthday, a woman with short blonde hair had proposed to her in a café in the Lanes. No one quite knew what was true.

"Want one?" he said.

Marina shook her head.

The first three crisps he ate individually, seeing how long he could keep them on his tongue before succumbing to the crunch. The rest he crammed in quickly.

Taking a fresh pen from a drawer, hunching over a 42-page hospitality brochure, Freya began to fill in, with black ink, every pocket of negative space in the letters "b," "g," "e" and "o." At the western end of the reception desk lay ten paper clips, placed there in readiness for a task not yet determined. At the eastern end, in a pool of shadow, the Guest Registration Book: a thick volume containing information on room rates and check-in dates, but also several ambitious doodles of penguins caught in rainstorms and a regularly updated note entitled "TOP FIVE LIES TODAY."

Actually, sir, the singles are all exactly the same size.

Madam, I'm so sorry. If there was <u>any</u> way to upgrade you, I would.

Really, it's been my pleasure.

The GM enjoyed meeting you too!

Of course I remember you, Mr. Norton. It's

really great to see you again.

A guest asked for his key. He had a thin officious moustache on his clammy top lip. It looked like it had crawled there in the search for a warm place to die. She closed her eyes sometimes and saw the whole hotel going up in flames, re-forming as a structure made of pink reservation paper, all the neatly pencilled words settling as ash on the floor, but pulsing a little as they lay there.

Her shift today would run until 7:30 p.m. Her principal role, during this time, was to sit behind the reception desk without falling asleep or killing anyone, in particular herself or a customer. She played with her hair, curling it around a forefinger as she had on multiple previous summers. There were a few guests talking in the lobby. One guest on the stairs doing some kind of back-stretching exercise. In the bar area opposite men played chess and sipped gin and ton-ics, surrounded by antiquated swank. Jorge the Barman was reading the splayed pages of a newspaper, a skyline of whisky bottles behind him. He was handsome in a damp kind of way.

One of the chess players in the bar area she recognised from yesterday. While her father was in a meeting this guest had called her "extraordinarily useless" for not knowing the name of a shop on East Street. The guest next in line, overhearing this, had been extra nice to her to compensate. A queue for the reception desk often broke itself down this way: nasty — nice — nasty — nice. When a customer had been audibly rude to you, your options opened up. It was possible to give the next guy in line the coffin room and hear no murmur of complaint.

The lobby's clocks ticked, hands angling for different hours. The air filled with the delicious smell of cakes and scones, the scent mingling with the sweetness of fresh-cut flowers. People padded softly across oriental rugs, pausing to look at art in ancient frames. Still lifes and landscapes. Oil paintings of sea scenes. Glossy ladies with lapdogs. Horses drawn out of proportion. There were an awful lot of kings in capes.

"Split ends": the phrase didn't even begin to cover it. The ends of her hair had been put through a mini blender this week. £8 that trim had cost her. Considering she was paid £1.60 an hour to sit behind this desk, watching people come and go, life actually genuinely passing her by, the price tag was nothing short of criminal. Usually if someone assaulted you it was free.

Lost in the curves and slopes of her

penguin pictures, rubbing her dry eyes, she heard the familiar whirr of the revolving door and began to sit up straight. The man entering the hotel now was unusually young: mid-twenties, she guessed. For a September guest he was also unusually good-looking and tall. You wouldn't hesitate to call him a "guy," and in the wake of peak season most of the men who stayed at the Grand could be better described as "chaps," or "fellows," or some other form of upper-middle-class address you might, if you were a silver-haired person from a similarly creamy kind of background, be tempted to preface with "Jolly good" or "Hello, old." He didn't have the drowsy smile. He didn't have the soft, outdated face. He didn't have a thin tense wife on his arm and he wasn't even swinging an umbrella.

He made his way from the door to the desk. He was carrying two sports bags, one on each shoulder. He was wearing a good leather jacket. It seemed a little heavy for the weather. Barbara — her foot in the air, her tongue on her bumhole — reluctantly raised her head. She'd been adopted by Chef Harry in the winter of '79 and had subsequently developed a generous figure, plus certain unresolvable issues with authority. She was not in the habit of making needless moves. Freya had time to wonder if Barbara sensed what she sensed: the guy's air of competence; the fact he'd probably be a dab hand with a can-opener. She had time to think that he must be here to ask for directions. Time to convince herself that he didn't plan to stay here at the Grand, with its massive oak reception desk, a shelter for hillocks of fuzzy dust, swamps of chewing gum, several miraculous cobwebs, Snogger Dave's bogey collection, battered stickers saying "Rad!" and "Pow!" and, until Freya purchased a deadly spray from Woolworths last week, a complacent oversized spider whose death she'd immediately mourned. No one cared about the areas the guests couldn't see.

He was right in front of her now. She arranged a curl of hair over her collarbone, pointing it towards a space that she might, on a more confident day, have called cleavage. She watched him touch his own hair. It was dark and sharply parted. He was wearing a smart white shirt under his jacket, tucked in at the waist. His stubble was thickest in the cleft of his chin.

"Welcome to the Grand!" she said.

And he said, "It's nice to be here."

His face was one of those that looked even better when it was moving. His eyes were greenish-brown.

"You'll be checking in?"

"Yes please."

"And do you have a reservation?"

"Yeah," he said. "Roy Walsh."

She flicked through the Guest Registration Book and got the pink notepad ready. "And did you already put a deposit down, or —"

"No, no deposit. But I'm happy to pay cash up front." He opened a leather wallet and a new-car smell escaped.

There was talk of the weather. His tone was neutral, empty, like the drained voice of a teacher. But unlike Mr. Pickford or Mr. Easemoth, his expression wasn't weary, his bearing wasn't broken. He didn't come from a world of corduroy and borrowed novels. His back was straight. He looked bracingly awake.

"Just the one night, right? That's what it says here."

A smile began to break on his face. "Actually, if it's not too late, I was hoping to extend to three."

"Three nights?"

"That's what I was hoping."

"Let me see. I think you're probably in luck."

Luck, though. He didn't seem like a

person who needed it. Probably he made his own. That was what everyone was supposed to do in life, she'd been told. This despite the fact that the people who told you so never went on to explain *how* you might make your own luck and were often wearing, at the time when the advice on luck was dispensed, very unfashionable shoes.

She seemed to be on her feet. Sitting down again straight away would make her look like some ditzy freak in an exercise video. "Half-board?"

"Why not."

"OK. That's sixty pounds a night. So, a hundred and eighty overall."

"Great."

"Would you like to pay for the first night now?"

"I'll pay it all."

"Up front? You don't have to."

"Might as well. Do you know which number you'll put me in?"

"Sorry?"

"Which number room."

She took a quick glance at the registration book. "629 is vacant. A nice room facing the sea."

"629. That's great, thank you."

"Maybe you'd like to see the room first? I

71

can do that for you."

"No no, that'll be grand. That'll be fine."

Did he mean it, though? Was he being overly polite? Sixty a night was a lot of money. She had a good feeling about this man Roy Walsh. You could tell straight away whether someone was kind, and he was kind. Kind customers were sometimes too nice to ask for what they really wanted. With this in mind she waved at her father.

"Have you come far?" she asked. "Was your journey OK?"

"Oh," Roy said. "The train was like it always is."

"It's a work trip?"

"With a bit of pleasure, I hope. Colleague of mine might stop by a couple of times. I assume the room has a desk?"

Before she could say "yes" her father arrived. He shook Roy Walsh's hand. "Welcome, welcome," he said.

"Dad, maybe someone could show Mr. Walsh room 629?"

She said this and a little pantomime of deferrals ensued. He didn't want to see the room. He said he was in a bit of a rush. Everyone apologised and their words overlapped and she could feel herself beginning to blush.

Her father walked away. She marked Roy

Walsh's name down on the grid. Acronyms were printed next to room numbers. NB (no bath). WF (wooden floors). SB (small bathroom). NL (near lift). The only letters next to 629 were SVB, for sea-view balcony. She'd done what she could for him.

"This your summer job?" he said.

"This? Sort of, yeah."

"And sort of no?"

"Well, this is the never-ending summer."

"Ah. I know the feeling."

"You do?"

He blinked. "My dad used to get me doing DIY every summer, then in the evening playing snooker with him. Those weeks could drag, not being outdoors, though it's better looking back."

She opened a fresh pack of registration cards. "My dad's got me helping out here. I haven't applied to university yet, basically, and Moose — that was my dad and he's called Moose, unfortunately — it's a busy time for him. Some important guests are coming in a few weeks. Not that every guest isn't important, obviously."

He smiled. "Obviously."

"Some of the summer staff are staying on."

"Do many of them stay the night?"

"Sorry?"

"You know, live in. The staff."

"A few do, yeah."

"You should travel."

"Pardon?"

"See the world," he said, smiling again.

She'd been thinking about that. She told him so. Marbella or somewhere, if she got some money saved.

"Marbella." He seemed about to laugh. "Good plan. I hear it's nice there."

"Have you been anywhere in Spain?"

"Me? Never. Every now and then, though. Every now and then it occurs to me to go."

"Better weather," she said.

"I suppose that's a part of it, yeah."

She thought of telling him about her better-than-expected A-level results. She thought of telling him about not being sure university was for her. She thought about admitting that up until last month she'd thought Oxbridge was an actual place, rather than two places made to mate as if by way of a posh schoolboy prank — the kind of prank she wasn't sure she had much time for at all. She thought about saying she had friends who would be enjoying Freshers' Week soon and that university was actually an extended drinking game — probably he'd been, could confirm it — but wasn't real-world experience actually more important? She blinked twice before explaining all of this and then decided not to explain at all.

Was his accent shifting from sentence to sentence? She couldn't quite pin it down. In Scotland she'd only been to Edinburgh, and in Wales only to Cardiff. She'd never been to Ireland and had never explored the North. It was grim up there, her mother used to say, but then again Vivienne Finch considered a lot of things to be grim. Life. England. America. Love. People who ate meat or called the wrong things "ironic."

He said, "So the VIPs are coming soon, you said? Other than me, I think we established."

"Yeah. We've had JFK here, in the past. And Napoleon number three also stayed. But nowadays, basically, although I shouldn't say it, we actually don't get so many VIPs. It's a big deal when one comes. I guess more people are going to exotic islands and stuff."

"Or Marbella."

She laughed. "Exactly."

"No film stars, then?"

"No. Just Mrs. Thatcher. The whole thingy. It's the Conservative Party Conference thing. Last time she was in Brighton she stayed at the Metropole, so, you know . . . Then last year they did it in Blackpool." It was all public knowledge, but she lowered her voice nonetheless. She wanted him to feel like he was receiving a secret. "So, Mr. Walsh, if you wouldn't mind just signing this . . ."

He looked down at the Guest Registration Card, the pen in his left hand. He signed it slowly. "What room will you stick her in, do you think? I hope it's no better than mine." He smiled again.

"Ha, well. I'm not really meant to say."

He nodded. His eyes politely died. She tried for an apologetic smile. He picked up his two sports bags from the floor.

As he put the key in his pocket he said, "OK. Thank you." It was a cold thank-you. An empty OK.

She said, "My friend Derek here can —"

No no, he said. No need to bother the bellboy with my luggage. See you later on.

He walked towards the lift but didn't press the button. Turned left through the double doors, maybe looking for the downstairs loo. Unusual, actually, because people almost always waited to use the en suite in their room. People put privacy first.

What exactly had she done wrong? She'd begun to think they had a rapport going, and in no time at all that rapport had collapsed. She wrote it down on a page of the

Guest Registration Book — *rapport* — and it didn't look quite right.

Derek came over, shaking his head. He was amazing at making guests feel warm and fuzzy, at playing with their kids and complimenting their grandmothers, and at then turning that warmth right down to zero and fixing them with an icy stare. The stare said: "Yeah, motherfuckers, time to tip me, you thought this was free?" It was a strategy that had resulted in him owning two types of car.

"Wow," Derek said. "Just, wow."

"Lay off," she said. "I tried."

"Too tentative, man. If you're going to say it tentatively, like, 'Oh *maybe* please *maybe* can my friend take your bag?' you might as well just do the usual 'Can I get the bell-man to help you, sir?' No. No no no. You've got to *tell* them, Freya Finch. You've got to say 'My *good* friend Derek here *will* take your —' "

"Bags, yeah, I know."

"Got to help me get my kill rate up," he said. "This girl is just wow, you know? Like insane expensive." He paused. "You could hang with us sometime if you wanted."

"Derek," she said, "you're not normal."

He shrugged. "I thought he was going to be one of those guys that comes up with the balance line. You know, bag balanced on each shoulder. No need to help me! I'm balanced!"

"I'll get the next guy," Freya said, and Derek traipsed away.

She opened the corporate brochure and continued adding ink to the letters "b," "g," "e" and "o," but the project had lost much of its lustre.

She was happy. Overall she was. But — she played with the yellow master key for Roy Walsh's room — she'd also been thinking recently that she was maybe suffering from a lack of something, a smallness or thinness, a stuntedness even, like there was a higher plane of being she wasn't reaching for. Her blatant failure to impress Roy Walsh seemed in some way to confirm this. Wimping out of a progressive haircut was similarly damning. She visualised the higher plane of being as a hard-to-reach shelf in the herbal shop on East Street, but the point about higher planes was that they were, presumably, unimaginable. Like God's face. Like Tessa Sanderson's training regime. Like a boy who wouldn't try and shove your head down on a first date, and who didn't try and twiddle your nipples like a radio dial. What tune did they expect her breasts to play?

She thought she might pay a visit to the top-floor storage cupboard, where someone usually hid some wine. Then she thought: what if I just let myself into Roy Walsh's room, walked up to him, took control? She'd noticed lately that lust and boredom shared a bed.

When her final break of the day arrived she took a short walk along the King's Road, turning back when her fifteen minutes was almost up. A man was collecting for charity. She gave him twenty pence. Didn't look, actually, at what he was collecting for. Up ahead the hotel looked like a gesture, a huge white symbol for something, but it was surely rare for symbols to come so comprehensively covered in bird shit. Three gulls were perched above the entrance, not looking at each other. Freya watched them fly up as she approached. As the birds settled back down they altered their configuration, one from the edge now taking centre stage, their wings not touching and no squawks exchanged, but a definite team nonetheless.

At 5:15 p.m. a fresh weirdo approached the desk.

"I'd like to book the restaurant, if I could," the woman said. "Intimate table with a view, please, for six this evening."

She leaned forward, elbows on desk, and touched her mouth with her fingers. "Intimate," she said.

"Sure," Freya said. "Actually, you can always do that just through there, in the restaurant, but I can definitely help you here too."

The woman blinked.

"I can do it for you. It's no problem."

"That's what I was hoping," the woman said. "Good. Good." There was a dead fox around her neck. It looked somewhat surprised to be there. She had a way of touching it as her body swayed from side to side during sentences. There was lipstick on her teeth. Her eyes searched various sections of Freya's face with a grim and happy hopelessness.

"So you'd like to book a table for 6 p.m. this evening?"

"Six? No no. Six *people*!" The woman laughed like a drain or a minor sewage works. "An intimate dinner," she said. She played with her purse, emergency yellow, a cyclist on a bike in the dark.

"That should be fine. What time would suit you, Ms. — ?"

"Cooke," the woman said. "You can call me Mrs. Cooke."

"What time shall I book you in for, Mrs.

Cooke? Your party of six?"

"Oh. Eight o'clock?"

"Great."

"We may be a little late, though, I should warn you. No more than about an hour, though, I would say."

"An hour later than eight o'clock?"

"Possibly."

"So more like nine, you might say?"

Mrs. Cooke's smile tightened. "Perhaps safer to bring our menus at nine, as it were, yes. Unless you work in increments. No one does, though, do they? Will you be the one serving?"

"Me? No."

"So many people, aren't there?" The tongue moved across the two front teeth and further blurred the lipstick stain. Freya tried to meet Derek's eye, but he was doing his napping-while-standing thing. He only really woke to the rustle and clink of cash.

Mrs. Cooke said, "What's the cuisine, would you say?" and made a rolling motion with her hand.

"Modern British, with a twist."

"A *twist*?" At length Mrs. Cooke weathered this blow. "It isn't French, then?"

"No, sorry. It's not French."

She clutched her fox and frowned. A man in a maroon bow tie and matching cummerbund crossed the lobby's complex rug. The chandelier dripped light onto his wife. He waved at Mrs. Cooke and warmly she waved back.

"They have no politics at all," Mrs. Cooke whispered when the couple had entered the bar area. "Can you believe it? Not even at the local level. Almost as bad as the windscreen wipers. Left right, left right, left right."

Barbara meanwhile was having her third nap of the day, occurring within a whisker of her first and her second. She had picked, for her rest area, the middle of the lobby floor. When Mrs. Cooke's husband arrived downstairs, wearing the shiny bewildered wince of a baby, he leaned down to tickle Barbara's tummy, saying "Good kitty" as his spectacles slid down his nose, and she bit him hard on the hand.

4

Chef Harry was a ruddy, sarcastic, manic-depressive former professional player of darts who, after one of his strenuous lock-ins at a favourite pub, often arrived at work, Moose had noticed, wearing a shirt with the words HIGH-TON HARRY on the back, several sequins missing. He'd recently added to his repertoire of light lunches on the Grand's summer menu a Strawberry Risotto with Fine Champagne Jus. It was a dish he generally topped off with what he referred to, in his squeaky children's-entertainer voice, as Parmigiano Stardust. Tonight, at home, Freya had adapted this into a less fussy and flashy and far more delicious dish, replacing the strawberries with bacon bits, the champagne with extra chicken stock, and the Stardust with tiny planets of proper mozzarella. Moose was spooning additional portions onto a plate garlanded with small blue flowers.

Freya cleared her throat.

"What?" he said.

"I was just thinking."

"About what, though?"

"Nothing."

Unlikely, he thought, swallowing. One of the great understated tragedies of human-kind was that people were always thinking about something.

He eventually cornered her into telling him this: he needed to be careful he didn't become fat. In response he pointed out that his stomach was mostly muscle.

"Is there science behind that?"

"I'm eating," he said.

A little speech ensued. She said you should get healthy again, you smoke way too much and you've been coughing a lot. He said I'm more than in shape but thanks for the concern. She said I don't think you *are* in shape, at least not the shape you should be. He said you're mistaken. She said I don't think I am. He said yes, you are, and you're mistaken about not being mistaken.

Alas, this was when an ill-timed coughing fit caused risotto to shoot out of his mouth. It made a grainy landing on what she went on to describe as her "all-time favourite sweatshirt, ever." An argument ensued as to how that could really be so. He'd seen her, just the other week, cutting its sleeves off, and using a ruler to mark a line along which the collar was also cut. That didn't sound like a way to treat your favourite sweatshirt, did it? In fact, it no longer looked like a sweatshirt at all. She wore it slack, the shining ball of one shoulder exposed.

"OK," he said. He lit up a cigarette and pushed his plate towards her. Every fibre of his humanity was focused at this time on the business of not coughing again. "Let's go for a morning swim tomorrow."

Her face relaxed. "Not too early, though."

"It'll have to be."

She sighed and rubbed miserably at the little beige stain.

They sat in silence. Something Moose had learned over the years was that, in silence, the past could be relied on to resurface. His memory seemed to flourish in quiet conditions, like a monk or a bucket of popcorn, and he began remembering now how, on a crucial day four months ago, he'd ruined a nice white shirt with a similar stain to the one just inflicted on Freya. A slippery gherkin was to blame. It had exited a recklessly overpacked pastrami sandwich. He'd been sitting on a bench, looking at the sea.

He remembered reading a piece in *The*

Times. An announcement that the conference would be held in Brighton this year, a thin article next to an advert for cricket-bat oil. The Conservatives were to continue their pattern of alternating between Brighton and Blackpool, the article had said, and when he phoned Group headquarters that afternoon they had additional intelligence: the booking was up for grabs. Apparently the Metropole had fluffed its chance at perfection in '82 by failing to stock a sufficient amount of Denis's "special water." The Prime Minister's husband was an easygoing man, but gin shortages greatly tested his patience.

Moose had punched the air three weeks later. A call from the Prime Minister's office: in response to his "impressive letter," they wanted to take a look around. He prepared fully, faultlessly, and on the day — the mustard stain notwithstanding — everything at first went to plan.

Four blokes in grey suits arrived. Also a woman wearing shiny heels. There were dark swipes of something interpretable as loneliness riding the lower curves of her eye sockets. Already he liked her a lot. His excitement began to toss and turn in his stomach. They walked around the hotel, nodding and making notes. He took them to room 122, the suite where the Key VIP (for they insisted on speaking in code) might wish to stay. He took them to the restaurant and the bar. He took them to the Empress Suite, a function room with five-star refinements and stunning sea views, top-spec audio-visual routing, and complimentary high-concept seafood for Christmas parties booked before 5 November. He took them to the car park and two of the men measured the precise inclines of the ramps. Then, instead of climbing back into their Jaguars, they said they would take a stroll along the seafront. He escorted them out of the front entrance and told them in brief the story of the West Pier. The grey-suited guys shook his hand one by one and the high-heeled lady gave him a two-second smile. Sandwich, he thought. They'll be wanting a late lunch. He nearly warned them about the amount of mustard in the Pastrami Slammer from Tony's Café. But then he thought no no no don't do that don't do that and sure enough as he looked on and lit up a cigarette they hooked right and entered the Metropole.

A small war ensued. He wrote a twenty-page proposal. He laminated it and velo-bound it at his own expense. The proposal set out in extensive detail the Grand's facilities and security procedures and Head Office's willingness to bolster staff headcount as required. CCTV no problem at all. Events management included in the price. £2.50 corkage if they preferred their own wine. He didn't slag off the Metropole. He went for a stately tone shorn of all exclamation marks, jazzed with the occasional winking semicolon, as if there were no real contest at all. He read and edited. Took Marina's comments on board. Vivienne's ghost was also there, lurking somewhere behind the head of the anglepoise, suggesting small punctuation changes and tiny shifts in syntax.

He waited.

A letter came.

We would like to provisionally reserve 150 rooms.

He'd won!

(The Grand had won.)

There was sparkling wine in the bar that night. The pleasantly strange guy everyone called the Captain turned up, downed two glasses in ten minutes, and disappeared into a night full of excessively bright stars of the kind Moose had once painstakingly glued to a large piece of black card — an early art project of Freya's for which he'd been awarded a Highly Commended. Jeremy

Garner from Group headquarters draped an arm over Moose's shoulder and said, "If this goes well, Moose, I think I can see you right at the top of this tree."

"Tree?"

"Good work. *Very* good work. Overall GM, I'm saying. You know Nipster's stepping down, yes?"

He didn't know, but now he knew with his whole soul.

He began imagining a two- or three-year tenure as overall manager at the Grand, followed by a hotel in a red-brick university city, followed by an appointment to one of the great hotels of the world. He imagined the Grand obtaining a reputation as the Lady's favourite hotel — her mentioning it in interviews — and people beginning to call it, colloquially, the Lady Hotel. Then he started to think this perhaps wasn't a good idea, that the Lady Hotel sounded like a cheap King's Cross brothel. You had to be extremely careful, in the hospitality industry, with both names and numbers. He'd once talked to the Front Office Manager at the Ritz at a conference in Sevenoaks. The guy told him they used to have a "George IV Suite," but that one of their best customers, an overseas gas billionaire, had one day refused to stay there because he thought it was only the fourth-best suite in the overall category of "George." If it hadn't been good enough for him, you could bet it wasn't good enough for the next big gas billionaire who arrived. Empty rooms cost you money. Gas gas gas. The Ritz renamed the "George IV Suite" the "King George Suite" and profits returned to normal levels.

The woman with the tired eyes and beautiful business cards had asked him to call her if, in the weeks leading up to the visit from the Key VIP, any guests at the hotel acted "in any way abnormally." But was she half joking when she said this? Playing up to an over-glamorised idea of the riskiness inherent in having the Prime Minister stay? There were a few recent guests who fitted the profile she'd described — male, not regulars, young among the Grand's demographic. Mr. O'Connor. Mr. Smith. Mr. Walsh. Mr. Danson. But each of them was polite, and each seemed relaxed, and each had only checked into a room for a few days. The risk was surely from people staying right up until the Prime Minister's arrival. These people, the woman had said, would be vetted.

The only suspicious thing about Smith was his shifty-eyed wife, the only suspicious thing about Walsh was the amount of room service he was getting through (never one Coke, always two), and the only suspicious thing about Danson was his voluminous toupee. As for O'Connor, he was clearly here to take advantage of the nightlife. There was very little room, in the tight leather trousers he wore to dinner each evening, for sinister plans to be hidden.

Abnormal. The concept was relative. Was he supposed to tell the authorities about the man six weeks ago who'd offered to pay extra for yellow bed sheets? The American steel magnate's wife who'd wondered if Moose could "reduce the ocean noise"? If you looked at people closely, you realised most of them were acting abnormally most of the time. It was what made life in the hotel interesting. That and the careful choreography of guest experiences, the perfect neatness of the rooms and the attractive symmetry of the meals, the world reduced to a manageable scale and the decor refusing to change.

Seven a.m. at the public pool, making good on his promise. Exercise, exercise! Well, he was exercising. Doing as his daughter advised. Around him were splashes, shouts. The clunky suck of wet feet walking. Shoulder-deep in water a thought came unrequested: Why not try a dive?

It had been a long time since his diving days. Confidence gets thin. He couldn't picture himself doing the somersaults of old, but neither did he feel he belonged in the shallow end over there with the loose-skinned oldies, discussing Terry Connor and cancer. These men were the work of a half-hearted taxidermist; age had emptied them out. Five breathless lengths he'd spent trying to keep up with his daughter. It dampened a guy's esteem to be panting after just five lengths. He hauled himself out of the pool and joined the queue for the tower, a line of lean boys waiting for a dive.

Wearing swimming trunks rescued from his thirties he was a magnet for their smirks. Fair enough. It was nice to be a magnet for something. There was a time when his stomach was a thing of alien precision. Crunches, kettlebell windmills, prone plank. Would any of these kids believe it? Why were they even awake at this hour? He thought the lady over there might be a teacher of some sort. Overhead a body fell through the air.

The high-dive platform was a long grey tongue stretching out from the top of the tower. Ten metres. Three storeys high. A near-vertical metal ladder was the only way up. He stood in line and tried to look bored. Freya swam to the edge of the pool and watched him, head bobbing, a beautiful person he'd made. In response he extended his spine, puffed out his chest, becoming father-shaped. She continued swimming. Touching the wall, turning, breaking away. All of her freedom unthinking. Last night's ale was thudding in his head, squashing fine memories of mozzarella.

When it was his turn to climb, each rung felt cold and hard under his feet. He took two rest stops to let out his smoker's cough. Above him the grubby glass ceiling, September clouds breaking up beyond it, sunlight restless on tiles. There used to be a second pool next door where the women had to go. A few years ago they floored it over for badminton. Up high you could hear the dull *pop-pop* of the shuttlecock, the scribble-squeak of fast-moving shoes. Blinking, he clambered to stand.

That first look around: such a shot of eerie beauty. It took him straight into his past. Chlorine gave the air up here a hazy un-crackable quality, everything a chemical blue. The only higher creature was a seagull relaxing in the rafters. Trapped *and* relaxed: it made no sense to Moose.

The kid in front of him had loosely knitted limbs, that slouchy bellboy way of making youth seem like a secret, and when he reached the end of the platform he pulled a pair of red goggles over his mop of dark hair and turned and said, "Do you think my watch will make it? This says, like, ten metres resistant."

"Should be OK."

"Yeah?"

"Yeah."

As Red Goggles retied the cords of his shorts Moose inevitably gave in to the impulse to look down. He was surprised to find himself beginning to reel — arms out for balance, take a breath. With slow caution he glanced again. A number of coloured floats and armbands down there now. The landlord of the Cricketers flirting with a hefty lady. Freya standing on the tiled lip of the pool, arms crossed. This was a place of echoes and the achievement of private targets. If someone's foot touched your foot, they apologised profusely.

It was supposed to be only two at a time up here but with Red Goggles hesitating, trembling, a new person arrived on the platform. He was a squat Coke can of a man on whom a desperately stretched swimming cap sat. The first thing he did was explain he didn't have all day. Then he looked around, his knees seemed to go soft, and with a shudder and a muttered "fuck" he took the ladder back down. When Moose stopped smiling it occurred to him to do the same. Pride before a fall.

Red Goggles was finally primed to jump. "Fear does not exist in this dojo!" he cried, and with that announcement he cannon-balled out of sight. He wailed all the way down and the impact, when it came, was closer to a crash than a splash. Sparks of water flew up. The surface healed.

The way the warm platform eats up the evidence of your presence. The way it shrinks your footprints to the size of a child's, then an animal's, then a nothing. The water was a tiny cool blue sheet that seemed, in these moments, to want to break your smallest bones. His heart was beating light and fast and a shift of cloud threw half the pool into shadow.

On the tip of the platform were two dusky oval shapes formed by all the feet that had gone before. He settled his soles on these ovals, blinked to stop the walls turning. He did his first high dive at the age of twelve, looking at his own awkward knees and rubbing his sweaty palms against his stomach, his father cheering him on from below. His father who seemed to come alive when watching his son succeed, a man usually so carefully contained within himself, shy and jokey and perhaps a little bitter, sharp features that made his moods look worse than they were.

Hurl yourself into the soundless blue or take the ladder back down. No-no-no and yes-yes-yes.

Oh, fuck it. Always was an over-thinker.

He was only forty-five and there was nothing much wrong with his muscles and Moose now found the arrogance to bounce, to ask the air for eloquence, just like he used to do over and over when competing at a meet. As his feet began to leave the platform he knew he was getting only half the push he used to get but he was up now, up, blood hurtling through his body — the friction of travel in his teeth.

Yes, he thought. This is what it's like.

Loosely bound to the room around him now, held by no ties at all, everything hushed and hesitant as it is before an accident. He tucked into a somersault, drew his knees into his chest, fingertips touching shins. Sky. Tiles. The whole gleaming ceiling of this old public pool. Colours bled into one another as a second somersault came. Through his knees a flash of water as he tumbled towards the tank. Fast now. The windrush. Steady.

Spotting the ceiling for the final time he moved from tuck to open pike. His body thinned as he arced down into the pool with the beauty — the overdetermination — of a dream. Forty miles an hour. Back straight and toes together. Hands angled to make a hole he could climb inside. For a moment he was Louganis, gunning for gold, an odd hovering perspective on himself. The water opened without protest. The warm green world took his weight.

Advice from his old coach Wally came to mind. Bending your back underwater gets your shins to vertical. Spreading your arms stops air bubbles breaking upward. Heart beating quick in the deep, feeling himself starting to smile, water creeping in through his lips as he awarded himself a 7 out of 10.

Moose lingered beneath the surface a little longer than necessary, enjoying the leggy shadows and livid pools of light. He broke into the sharper air, drew breath. Blurred shapes became precise. The lifeguard seemed to be clapping and the boy next to Red Goggles cried "Skill!"

Poolside he stood tall, water streaming from his body, the bones in his chest on fire.

"Show-off," Freya said.

"Sportsman," he replied, panting.

"Big splash."

"Untrue."

"No water left in the pool."

He risked a glance at the tank and saw that it was full. He told her she wasn't a very supportive daughter. In response she touched a throbbing vein in his shoulder. "Huh," she said, very thoughtfully. There were moments when love burned up in his throat and he didn't quite know how to move.

That morning at work he felt immense. His elation was up there with the time Viv had said through trembling lips that she'd marry him. The time he first held his newborn daughter in his arms. The time a couple of years ago when he'd seen Louganis attempt a 307C, the so-called Dive of Death, and pull it off with style.

It wasn't until sixish, trying to get the end-of-day admin started, that a thick tiredness began to cling to Moose's thoughts, rendering everything slow. If he had gone to university. If he hadn't assumed, stupidly, that a life in sport might open up. If he'd been the sort of person to stick at teaching — the sort not to see a deathly circularity in that noble profession. Might be a guy at

the head of something now. Head of department. Headmaster. Able to give his daughter
more than she needed. Instead, at university,
if he eventually convinced her to go, she'd
have to stack shelves on lectureless days to
help pay the rent on a room. He decided to
have a ten-minute power nap, his frequent
solution to the ifs of introspection. If you're
going to get stuck in your own head for
hours, might as well make it a dream.

There were a lot of rooms free, the hotel
only 30 per cent full this week, but he chose
a single on the top floor. He lay on the
carpet so he wouldn't crease the sheets. His
reveries had no right to unmake such a
beautiful bed. He took it all in from a low
angle. The mahogany wall shelves. A little
oak corner cupboard. An antique gilt over-
mantel mirror. A cedar chest of drawers that
smelt like a fresh pack of pencils. Like
fatherhood the hotel made him bigger. Like
fatherhood it kept him tired. The carpet was
soft, the curves of the lamp were soft, he
was asleep.

"Moose?"

He was surfing a cheeseboard on a wave
of ice cream.

"Moose? I tried to knock. Are you OK?"

Through waterlogged lashes he saw a
hand reaching down towards his arm,

fingernails on his forearm that were perfect pastel moons — moons that belonged to Marina.

The double *o* she emphasised in Moose. The way she brought out in his name a friendly farmyard innocence no one else seemed to know was there. When he opened his eyes fully she was smiling and sitting on the edge of the bed. One leg was swung over the other, the shine of the tights and the curve of the calf, a glittery little shoe hanging off the tips of her toes. She moved a stray hair from her forehead, a sleepy gesture that killed him.

"Hell—" he said. His chest hurt. His back hurt. He abandoned his attempts to get up and he cleared his throat of static, the recent teenage swings in mode and tone. "Hello, Mari. How's life?" The ceiling light gave her an absurd little halo.

"Good," she said brightly. Skin and hair. Health. She was looking down at him with curiosity but sidestepping the obvious question (why the hell are you lying on the floor?) because she was better than that, or knew him well enough to see his plan, or accepted that he was a man who got himself into tricky positions.

"I looked everywhere," she said. "And then I remembered this is your nap room."

"It's been a while."

She nodded and smiled, looked at the ceiling. He stared again at her hands. They held some of the few available hints that the better part of her thirties had passed. The nails were perfectly attended to, but the flesh around the knuckles was weathered. Slight bumps, pretty gullies, prominent estuaries of faint blue veins around which wrinkles formed. Also the tiny lines squinting out from the corners of her eyes and the way her skin seemed to have thinned around the cheekbones. Such flaws gave him hope. He planned to find more over time.

"Is there a problem, Mari?"

"Problem? No. I would not say problem." She patted her knee. "A small issue with humane resources, maybe."

"Oh?"

She nodded. "But if this is a bad time . . ."

"Do I look ridiculous down here, Mari?"

She shrugged. "Yes," she said, her eyes flashing the way they always flashed when she said "yes," like it gave her great pleasure to be positive. "You look a little ridiculous."

Those flashing eyes. When she was angry her rages were legendary. Last December a lazy male member of staff, caught in a web of lies after an incident involving a smashed chandelier, had backed into a Christmas tree to get away from her. The lobby had been bright with broken baubles, shards of light reminiscent of the incident that had first caused her fury. James Newman swept up the mess with tears in his eyes, mouth closed, straightening the tree as she issued instructions.

More common, though, were the moments when she would stretch and sit back in a chair in the midst of a crisis. On these days she'd explain to an employee, using no more than ten or twelve words, exactly what he or she should do to address the concerns of the guest in question. Confronted with particularly rude customers, she'd shyly glance away from their abuse. They'd begin in the silence that followed to feel a little awkward, their blood starting to cool, and that was the moment when she'd turn her gaze back upon them, eyes fuller than ever, and their awkwardness would harden into fear or confusion or simply melt down to nothing. "Excellent" was a word she used to good effect. They trundled away, dazed. Excellent? What was excellent?

He and Marina had first got acquainted when he was in the midst of a long losing streak. He'd come back from New York, out of work, Viv left behind in the care of that guy called Bob. Being cuckolded by a Bob had felt like a new nadir in the already low-lying terrain of Moose's middle age. Was she only interested in people with stupid names, or what? He was searching for a new place to live, seeking refuge in the familiarity of Brighton, forced to spend weekends receiving advice from his outspoken mother, abandoned careers in teaching and private tutoring and diving and diving coaching behind him. (Also the aeronautical engineering plans that his mother liked to tell her friends had never quite got off the ground.) Separated from his wife. A newly motherless daughter at his side. Three thousand six hundred pounds in debt. If he'd met Marina at a better time in his life, he might have given off an aura of achievement. Sometimes an aura could be enough. Sometimes an aura was everything. The paradoxical thing was that he so respected her reluctance to lower her standards. He viewed her lack of attraction towards him as a sign he'd been right to try. Meanwhile her unreachability made her more and more alluring.

She was saying something about him working too hard.

"No no," he said.

"Yes yes," she said.

"Just making sure everything goes well for

the conference. Putting the hours in."

"The promotion."

"Oh." He waved a hand around to better dismiss the idea.

"It's Karen."

"What is?"

"The humane resources issue."

It would be a terrible thing if anyone ever corrected Marina on this humane versus human stuff. It would be a gleam of uniqueness gone. "Tell me," he said, and closed his eyes to picture the problem.

"It seems she has been getting herself involved with a man with marital entanglements."

"As in?"

"He's married," Marina said.

"Right. I see."

It was quite fun lying here like this. A hint of what therapy might be like?

"There was punch," Marina said.

"What, like fruit punch?"

"Like fist punch."

"Oh."

Marina coughed. "Yes. She punched the married man just outside the hotel. Well, outside the Conference Centre."

"Not ideal, but it's probably not our problem, if it wasn't on our property."

"The married man is a guest, though,

actually. The one who Karen punched."

Moose opened his eyes. "Fuck."

"Yes. Was a guest. He left now."

"That Stephens guy?"

"How did you know?"

You could always tell. There was something primal in the eyes of certain guests.

"Anyway," Marina said, "I am dealing with it, but I know you like to know." She uncrossed and recrossed her legs; he looked away.

"A complaint isn't what we need right now, Mari."

"How would they find out?"

"I don't know."

"I think they are busy running the country. You look tired these days, Moose."

"What?"

"Tired."

"Thanks, Mari."

"No problem," she said, smiling. "Don't make a habit of staying late, yes? A man needs balance in his life."

"You're right, I suppose."

"It is not healthy to get as stressed as you do."

"I don't get stressed."

"Obsessed, I meant."

"That's a worse word. You're going the wrong way."

"Yes?"

"Yes." He closed his eyes again. "You're a good therapist, Mari."

"I learned from my therapist. She is good."

"You have one? What could you possibly need one for?"

Marina shrugged. "Back home everyone has a person. The men cheat, and the women are beautiful. Anyway, she said — my therapist said — that happiness goes *outward,* not inward."

"Wow," Moose said. He sensed there was something profound nestled in this idea, something worth rummaging around for. "What do you think she meant?"

"I think she meant what she said."

"Right. Of course." There was dust balled up underneath the radiator, fleecy dust that had no business being there. "I did a dive today, Mari."

"Boys," she said, shaking her head.

5

Mornings at the beach were often beautiful. No choice but to admit it as true. There was none of the haste of the afternoon. Less of the intrusive arguments between adults. Less gross rubbing of groins. Less mating rituals. Less slapping of bad kids' bums or spreading grease onto hairy backs. The expanse of pebbles sloping down to the water's edge was uncluttered. You could pick your spot and make it your own, the way you made your bedroom your own. Not so much with posters and branded duvet covers as with pure familiarity: knowing the shades and textures that filled every bit of your domain; knowing which stain was the beer stain and which was blood and which loose floorboard concealed the cigarettes you'd stolen from your dad. The air glowed. The sea was full of colour. Everything was rich with light and warmth. Even the seagulls seemed relaxed, content to ride the wind with rigid wings or glide down with care for bits of weed, saving their techniques of total intimidation for the lunchtime crowd and their cones of delicious chips.

She was sitting on the beach beside Susie, both of them sipping pulpy orange juice through straws, shivering slightly in the sunlight. Sarah and Tracy had both gone on holiday this week, a break before starting uni. There would be new friends waiting for them at uni, probably. *Boy*friends, definitely. Colourful anecdotes forming in her absence. But there was still the beach, and she was here, and Susie had been left here too.

"Four o'clock," Susie said, and casting her eyes at that angle Freya re-engaged with a game they often played: imagining themselves into the lives of strangers.

"A police detective," she said. "You can tell from the choice of snack."

"American," Susie said.

"No, Canadian. If he was American it would be a *ring* doughnut."

Susie nodded in acknowledgement of this self-evident truth. Her neck was long and pasty, a length of white icing, and her hair was a mass of fiery orange spirals moving in the wind. A pensive expression bunched the freckles on her face. She was too thin and tall for ordinary clothes, and too gingerskinned for ordinary make-up. Her limbs had the look of objects recklessly arranged, liable to come apart in the event that they were ever required to coordinate for sport. She liked to wear black T-shirt dresses in natural fabrics with dark green tights underneath.

"Background?" Freya said.

"He used to live and work in Canada, where his mother is from. But he got frustrated with the way the local government aids and abets drug addicts there, by supplying them with needles. But he's actually totally wrong. Because you're better off giving them clean ones than letting them spread disease." Susie slurped at the last of her juice, the sleeves of her thick cardigan pulled down to her fingertips. An agitated expression came over her. "Also," she said, staring at the guy in question, "he hated the way, in Canada, surveillance of criminals was curtailed by the lawmakers? He *loves* surveillance. Makes him massively horny."

Massively horny was one of Susie's favourite phrases. In Freya's mind it always conjured a lumbering caveman. They looked out at the West Pier. Surfer John, made so small by distance, was paddling on his board, waiting for a wave. He was another of the hotel employees, a year or two older than both of them. A number of the female staff members took their breaks at times that allowed for a glimpse of him here.

"Still looks good in a wetsuit," Susie said.

Freya agreed this was no mean feat.

Susie clapped her hands. "He loves to follow people around. He spends a lot of time finding out who people are linked with, how they manage to afford their cars with apparently no job."

"Surfer John?"

"No! The maybe-detective."

"Oh."

"He thinks about surveillance while he's doing the deed."

"Yuck."

"Don't judge me, Frey-Hey. It's him who's the sicko. He sleeps most days 'til around two in the afternoon. Then he wakes up for another wankathon."

Freya wiggled her toes between pebbles at this unpleasant thought, then resolved to put her shoes back on. "And he's up early today because . . ."

"Because," Susie said, "he's become so proficient at surveillance that he can't shake the sense that he himself is being watched."

"Good detail," Freya said. She was impressed.

They agreed the maybe-detective was in

Brighton on holiday. They agreed he couldn't shake off the idea that he was being watched. They agreed he couldn't get any privacy and it was stressing him out. The world was intruding on him at night — noises, nightmares. John fell off his board and they started laughing.

"In the mornings detective man is all over the place."

"In the mornings he can barely walk! Look at him. He blatantly forgot to put his belt on."

Into the pinpoint world of Freya's imagination came a detailed image of the absent belt: thick brown leather with a complicated buckle. It was lying on the floor of the man's hotel room, a place further back from the beachfront. Mini white plastic kettle. Iron that stains your shirts. Brown-and-green carpet in a diamond pattern. Type of place she and her dad stayed for a while when he split from her mum and the year in America ended. Then she started picturing Surfer John in the hotel room instead. This proved to be distracting.

"What do you think of John's trainers?" Susie said. He'd left them, together with a small rucksack, a stone's throw from their chosen position.

Gulls had arrived. They were studying the

111

sea. Freya shrugged. "They look fine. Pretty average trainers, if you ask me."

"Huh," Susie said.

Freya turned to confirm that this "huh" was a "huh" of disapproval, which it was. She looked at Susie's hands. They were in her lap, unmoving. Ordinarily Susie's hands were in motion, gesticulating desperately while she explained the extent of some little-known injustice in El Salvador or Israel, or worrying at the wooden beads on her neck-lace as she panicked about whether a boy liked her or not. Today her beads caught the sun and sent milky spots of light up into the shadowy area under her jaw. She man-aged always to look misplaced.

"OK," Freya said. "Forget about his train-ers."

"An African kid," Susie said, her voice suddenly raw. "That's who makes that brand. A sweatshop."

"Is that definitely a fact, Sooz?"

Susie raised a wispy orange eyebrow. The limits of knowledge in its strictest sense rarely marked the confines of their conversa-tions. When they were in people-watching mode it was all about how much detail you could apply to a life before it crumbled; how plausibly you could deform people's histo-ries. "We can make a guess," Susie said. "We

112

can guess that, like most branded trainers, they are made by children overseas."

Here it was again: her habit of rushing her attention to stories of exploitation, as if the words themselves were a form of emergency aid.

"I didn't buy John's trainers," Freya said.

"But you buy other ones."

"So do you."

"Plimsolls."

"Sweatshops."

"Made in Northamptonshire! In nice places!"

"The manufacturing isn't down to me, Sooz. It's not my problem."

"Whose problem is it, then, Frey-Hey? Your tennis shoes. Those nice heels you wear to work?"

"I don't know."

"Exactly," Susie said, and shook her head as if she'd won.

"So you basically asked me about his trainers as — what? — a kind of trap?"

"That's ridiculous," Susie said.

"A trap so that you could say that I represent some kind of Western ignorance?"

"Maybe you do," Susie said.

"Because I buy shoes?"

"It's an idea."

"Because I don't ask the girl in Coast

113

Sports a hundred questions before I get myself some trainers for running, or a swimsuit for swimming?"

"It's an idea."

It was an idea. An annoying one. Freya let it drift out to sea. She focused on the sight of Surfer John catching the crest of a wave. It was a small wave, and his balance didn't last that long, but for an instant he was serene.

She loved the moment when waves broke, the moment when the walls of turquoise grew toppings of white foam that spread along their length and hung, bubbling in the air, as the wave curled itself into a forward roll. She loved seeing water crashing against the West Pier, its delicate legs. She thought John must love these moments too. It seemed wasteful, somehow, that they hadn't spoken about it.

"Do you ever think about your mum?" Susie said.

"What?"

"Your mum."

She hesitated. Motivations. "No."

"Whatever. Just asking."

Freya shut her eyes. "If I'm ever a parent, Sooz, I'm going to remember that the only rule, basically, is that you shouldn't take sides. You shouldn't say stuff about the other parent. Our cleaner says —"

"You have a cleaner?"

"Yeah."

"How much do you pay her?"

"I don't know. That's not . . . It's Sandra from the hotel, she only comes once a fortnight."

"Interesting."

"Sooz, cleaning's what she does."

"Through choice?"

Freya sighed a deliberately heavy sigh. "I'm not a receptionist through choice. We're not forcing her. And what I was going to say about my mum is that —"

"*You* are not forcing her."

She tried to unpack this, find the trick in it. "That what I said."

"Huh."

Freya picked up a large stone. A big seagull waddled towards the maybe-detective and flew off with his doughnut wrapper. Suddenly the only thing all the other seagulls wanted was that exact doughnut wrapper. She turned the stone over in her hand.

"Look," Susie said, "I've got something to ask you."

"What?"

"You know I said about that protest?"

"What protest?"

"Outside the hotel, when Thatcher arrives."

"You didn't tell me about any protest."

"I did. I fully did. But anyway, they won't let us in the hotel, obviously. We're protesters. It's them against us. So there's a limit to what we can do. But I was thinking you'd be perfectly placed to, like, get involved . . ."

"What are you after, Sooz?"

A pause. "Stink bomb."

"What?"

"Something like that, anyway. Shake things up a bit. Show her how we all feel about her. That her policies, that her attitude —"

"Stinks."

"Yes!" Susie said. She looked astonished that her message had got through.

"But I'm not even sure I think that," Freya said.

Susie shook her head and lay back on the stones. The joy seemed to fly right out of her. "Pathetic," she said to the sky. "I knew you wouldn't do it."

One of the reasons why Susie wasn't in Freya's Top Five Friends anymore — why a couple of people Freya never really saw at all had managed to edge Susie out — was that she never fucking listened. Her inattentiveness turned your worries into insignificant trifles, things which floated free of reality. Susie prided herself on being honest and open about everything, confronting issues other people would prefer to keep below the surface, on doing lots of stuff for charitable and political causes, on nothing she did being for herself, but when she grew silent it was a tactical silence, it served her needs. Every little gesture was intended to have an effect on other people. Silent like she'd been over the trainer comment. Silent like she'd been when Freya had gone to Sally Lander's party even though they were supposed to hate Sally Lander. Silent like she'd been when Freya had asked Sarah to be the one friend who joined her and Moose on a camping holiday in the Lake District two summers ago.

Suspicious of beaches, Susie was. Unimpressed by oceans. It was an attitude which seemed at odds with her membership of Greenpeace, but, there you go, that was Susie. She thought anything picturesque was frivolous. She was always asking Freya why she wore lipstick on nights out. Like many people who felt that their talents were under-acknowledged, Susie spent a lot of time looking at her watch.

"You're annoyed with me," Susie said.

"No."

"You're always annoyed with me these days. I've left, like, *six* messages at the hotel these last few weeks. I even saw you, last Monday, disappearing into the kitchen, and I asked Karen whatserface, the one with the dead sister —"

"Brother."

"It doesn't matter."

"It probably does to her."

"To see if you had two minutes for a talk or anything, and she came back from going to find you and said — one hundred per cent lying — that you weren't working today. And why would she even say that?"

Freya didn't respond to this. There were things in her life, small fractions of the whole, that she chose never to look at. It was easy. She did it all the time. She heard herself saying, "I've got to go."

"But we were going to hang out." A stitch of grief had sewn itself between Susie's eyes.

"Yeah, well. I've got this date tonight, and another shift before then."

"Someone's taking you for a big dinner?"

"Yep," Freya said, though the date was just another invention. "While the African kids starve."

"You're mocking me," Susie said. "I never said you shouldn't eat."

"But it's what you don't say, isn't it?"

"That's the same with anyone! You could accuse anyone of that!"

"Sooz, did it ever occur to you that it's not a very nice thing to do to my dad, to try and disrupt them all when they're staying at the hotel? I mean, why not focus on the Conference Centre?"

"If you're a real friend you'll do it. You'll think of the bigger picture."

"But this whole thing, it's important to him. It's his chance to get promoted, feel good about himself."

"And what isn't? What *isn't* important, Freya? The government? The Prime Minister? The way this country is going? The unemployment and the money *wasted* on *sham* wars and the massive divide between rich and poor and all the fancy people in London and then people without any food up north and striking miners and the *total* lack of interest in trying to soothe the *racial* tensions in our community, or solve unemployment?" She was getting shouty. Her hands were flapping and her freckles were blurring. "If those are cool enough reasons."

"OK, whatever. If you want my dad to lose his job, go ahead."

"The protests are going to be massive," Susie said. The words came with the engineered airiness that told you they were a

119

threat. But then, in a more natural voice: "So you should probably let him know, or something. You know, security. It'll be peaceful. They're only talking about some chanting and a prank to get publicity."

With each word Susie's confidence seemed to wane. Freya said nothing. Surfer John was coming out of the water. He was carrying his surfboard under one arm. He didn't seem to feel the weight of it at all. His hair was dripping. His wetsuit was shining. He flicked the hair out of his eyes.

"Hey," he said, smiling. "How's it going?"

"Not bad," Susie said.

"Yeah," Freya said.

The sunlight made John's cheekbones look nicer than usual. His hair seemed blonder, his eyelashes darker. He was breathing slowly. "Cool," he said. "See you guys later, then." He retrieved his bag and shoes.

"Look," Susie said, "we'll mainly be outside the Conference Centre, anyway. You know, on the day Thatcher speaks. The singer from the Angelic Upstarts might be coming. And they're letting us use songs from the *Two Million Voices* album? And the guitarist from that Belfast band, Stiff Little Fingers, he might be there too."

"Nice," Freya said.

"Our group. The Collective of the Discontented. It's basically an alliance between a lot of smaller liberal and socialist groups who are depressed by what they're seeing. I mean, it affects all of us. Bad things will happen, my dad says, if we don't shift this country away from the right."

Freya shifted slightly to the left. The palm of her right hand hurt from the stones.

"And you need to take the public with you," Susie continued. "It has to be a change from within. Which is why we're collaborating with these musicians, and this new Paul Weller thing called Red Wedge. The idea is that rock people, bands, who want to get Labour into power, are collaborating with grass-roots organisations to do that. A cultural — they call it a cultural revolution. Though the problem with Weller, my dad says, is that he seems too much like a working-class boy made good, like pursuing individual success and achievement, which is, you know, what's portrayed as a Thatcherite success story . . ."

"Yeah," Freya said.

"You could join us?"

"Hmm."

"You could come along now, to this planning meeting for the protest."

"Yeah, maybe."

"Thatcher wants to privatise everything, Frey-Hey. She wants to privatise *people.* Brigid says she's so obsessed with this, like, this *dependency culture* —"

"Who's Brigid?"

"— that she can't see what she's doing. Nobody's saying she's evil. OK, some people. But the results of what she's doing are most definitely bad. She thinks everyone is responsible only for themselves, and that's that, the only kind of rule there is. No community. No society! Everyone separate! That's a sucky way to live. Don't you see?"

"Maybe we *are* separate," Freya said. She wasn't arguing. She was trying to think it through. "Maybe it's fine sometimes to back down on a point, or not care, or be separate from others?" She hated this feeling, the sensation of trying and failing to get her arms around something big. The way political opinions seemed always to be expressed with a total sureness of tone. The way that sureness was at odds with every true thought she'd ever had.

"You're so wrong," Susie said. "You're just wrong."

"About what?" Freya said, but no answer came. She watched her friend standing up, her long legs unfolding awkwardly, the motion bringing to mind the setting up of an ironing board, Sandra the Cleaner, Sundays, steam rising from her father's shirts. She listened to the sound of Susie's plimsolls crunching loud and then soft across the rocks.

She looked out at the water and thought of Surfer John. Imagined him still there, paddling. She thought about whether Susie might sometimes have a point.

For a while, it had seemed something would happen with John. He liked to tease her about the fact her surname was Finch and also about the fact that, on account of her having worked in the hotel during various summers, she was senior to him and other part-time student staff.

"Freya Finch, you're at the top of the pecking order," he'd say.

And then: "To be in your position must be quite a birden?"

And also: "You are aviary talented receptionist."

And often: "Honestly, I'm not trying to ruffle your feathers."

He knew his lines were lame and that knowledge, together with his toned arms and the idea he might be kind, was what had first drawn her towards him.

Their timing was off, though. The rhythm, the sequencing, that elusive whatever.

Nights where they'd bump into each other in the pub and stand drinking and laughing, him touching her shoulder during an anecdote and never anything more, letting the crucial moment slide away into a semi-awkward goodbye, which was among the better ways a thing could end.

She and Karen were in the lobby talking about a low-on-laughs sitcom called *Bottle Boys* when two people came down the staircase, carrying bags. It took a moment for Freya to see that this was Roy Walsh and another, shorter man. Freya said hi to both of them. Roy said hi back. Karen smiled. The shorter man, older, touched his moustache and glanced away.

"How's your stay been?" Freya said.

"Oh," Roy said. "Been great."

"Yeah?"

"Yeah. It's a beautiful place you have there. Really beautiful."

You could see in his eyes that he wasn't lying. An appreciation of the picturesque. Those eyes were more complex than the eyes of boys her age. A greater amount of noticing. She looked again at the other man — maybe he was a mute? — and thought about what Roy had said when he checked in: "Work with a bit of pleasure, I hope."

Brighton . . . Pleasure . . . A single guy checking in alone and appearing now on the staircase with another man, blushing . . . The way she'd thought there was a spark of attraction that first time at the front desk, but had seen it die away so quickly.

God, it was obvious. Roy Walsh was blatantly gay.

"So you're checking out?" Freya said.

"No no," said Roy. "We're just running a couple of errands."

She looked at the bag he was carrying and at the bag the older man was carrying.

"Maybe we'll catch you later on," Roy said, and something in his eyes introduced a crackle of doubt again. Bisexuality was a thing she'd heard about. Maybe he was bisexual. It must be nice, good, maybe even much better, to pick a person rather than a gender.

When the men had gone she tried to continue the conversation with Karen, but it had lost most of its energy.

6

His daughter found him in the drying room, trying to establish the veracity of a reported rodent sighting. He was also trying, more half-heartedly, to locate among the laundry Mrs. Anton's lost pearl earring. Being down here made you long for open air, but in the open air it had been drizzling all morning. The coastline had fizzed up like a badly tuned TV. He hated how quickly guests blamed the cleaners for missing items. Did they think there was a nightclub in town where all the cleaner-robbers gathered, wearing just one earring each? Wearing just one stolen sock, and waving around that important piece of mislaid paper that the guest just happened to have left crumpled up right next to the waste-paper basket?

Freya said, "I mean, seriously. I just went home, forgot my sandwich, totally soaked, and there's like a — like a *landslide* in the hall." She looked at him. Wet hair was hanging over her face in threads. The drying room was dark and soupy, full of ambushing damp. Her perfume cut through it cleanly. "Like, *twenty* of them!"

Several thoughts occurred. The first was: good that she's making her own sandwiches, because those baguettes from Amadeo's add up. The second was: annoyed or simply pretending to be annoyed? Third: get an umbrella. Fourth and finally, he didn't know what she was talking about — not at all. "Twenty," he said, buying himself a little time. He tried to picture things in multiples of twenty but managed to think only of canapés — canapés on a platter presented to Margaret Thatcher, who in this particular vision was for some reason wearing a peach-coloured spacesuit.

"Those huge prospectuses."

"Ah, those."

"Twenty!"

"Right."

She was wearing a skirt much shorter than was ideal, or even acceptable, but probably it wasn't a good time to mention it. It was hot down here. Water fell from her clothes. He sneezed and said, "There were three yesterday too. I put them in the kitchen for you. The process for next year starts soon, Mr. Easemouth —"

"Ease*moth* —"

"— said. You're still thinking History, right? Or is it English now? If you don't apply in time, Frey, it gets tricky."

"Mental," she said, shaking her head. He waited for more, but nothing came; the word was a free-standing judgement.

"Lots of exciting choices. That's all I'm doing. I'm giving you choices that I —"

"Wasn't given, yeah." She shook her head again. "God."

"Don't bring Him into it," Moose said. "You think He'd be running this shit show so badly if He'd got a proper education? Look," he said, "you've seen the pictures on TV. It's crazy. If you want to have a comfortable life these days, you've got to get an education."

"You're that guy. That mental dad. You actually are." He thought he saw an earring on the floor. "You've been in disguise for a while, but it's you. It was like a sorting office or something had exploded. I told you —" was she going to cry? Really? To cry at this? — "I told you I don't even know if I want to go."

"Then you should apply," he said softly, "and keep your options open." It wasn't an earring after all. It was a small pebble or a little piece of cheese. He nudged it with his foot. "No wonder there are rodents."

"What?"

"If you don't know yet, then keep your —"

"University," she said. "University university university university. University. University. *Obsessed!*"

He tried to calm things down, began to succeed, began to think less intensely about the question of how cheese had found its way onto the floor, but then he slipped on a well-meant phrase about the future and that one slip sent him free-falling into an argument. He never let her make her own decisions, he was always trying to interfere, he thought university was amazing because he hadn't been, so what did he actually know, he always thought stuff he hadn't done was amazing, he was always nagging, nagging nagging nagging, and couldn't he see that she wanted a bit of time to think, that she'd just stopped doing exams and exams and exams, all that structure and no time to live, to *live,* and why was a degree so important, and couldn't he just be pleased with her results, and had it done him any harm not having a degree, had it really?

"Well, actually —"

"No," she said.

He tried to stick to questions, because —

a useful customer service principle — there was a limit to how aggressive a statement could seem with a question mark at its end. Did she really want to work behind the desk in this hotel for another summer and the summer after that? Did her good exam results at a mediocre state school like Blatchington Mill not show that she had great potential at degree level? Was her pessimistic view of higher education something to do with her mother being a lecturer? Because that's the last thing Vivienne — yes, why not, let's bring Viv into it — because that's the last thing Vivienne, wherever she was now, would have wanted. Defining yourself in opposition to other people was really no way to live.

This last line was the most provocative of all his statements, liable on another day to cause him serious injury, but her eyes relaxed and he watched as her thin arms crossed underneath the V of her sweater. "You just want to make me — this is it — into the person you want me to be."

Which was unfair. Utterly unfair. Because what he really wanted was for *her* to want to make herself into the person he wanted her to be. Such was the great hope of fatherhood.

The wine-cellar hatch went up and Jorge

climbed out, closely followed by Sasha, the latter pink of cheek and laughing, a rare occurrence indeed. "Was there a problem down there?" Moose said. "A problem requiring both of you?"

"Que?" Jorge said. He was fond of feigning incompetence with English when caught fucking summer staff.

"Jorge," Sasha said, tugging at his sleeve, "we've fixed the problem now, so let's go."

Freya said, "If you're so keen to get rid of me, I'll be buying a ticket somewhere soon, like I said to Roy — to Marbella — so whatever."

She left. Jorge left. Sasha stood for a moment staring at Moose as if she had a question in mind. She was a changeable girl, Sasha. She could be warm and she could be cold and it could all be within one sentence or glance. She would smile at him but be unable to keep the smile going. She sometimes squeezed his arm. She knew too well the effect she had on most men. He had concluded she had no soul. In the moments when her worked-up warmth faded and her other self was exposed, Sasha was like a house slowly losing electricity, emptying, the TV flickering, the lights fading, the radio's song dimming, the fridge humming thinly into silence, and this again made him think of his ex-wife.

Sasha said she'd found out that Jorge's hourly wages were a little bit higher than hers.

"Not now please, Sasha," he said.

She sighed and disappeared up the stairs. The tumble dryers rumbled on and on. The earring was nowhere to be found and neither was the reported rodent.

His daughter so frequently misunderstood his intentions. His allotment of life was pleasant but undeniably narrow. She was better than he was, a more talented person, and he wanted her to have a whole blazing field of sunflowers. He wanted to tell her that unfulfilled ambitions pile up like unopened post and can clutter a person's life. He also wanted, at a more bitter and seldom acknowledged level, to explain to her how fatherhood had destroyed his solitude. Explain to her that he used to think — really *believe* — that he would win an Olympic medal on the diving board. That Viv had in fact been the one pushing for a child. That if one of them was ever going to end up as a single parent he never expected it to be him. That motherhood had finally seemed to kill Viv's already-slender sexual appetite and that, if it wasn't for the feeling of aloneness this abandonment had left him with, he might never have poured quite so much love into his daughter, into their early-morning routines with Lego and milk, into the intimacy that left him feeling needed again and brought an almost-pleasure to the hot Sunday task of ironing all her school clothes.

When Freya moved away, who exactly was going to take her place? Was it selfish to think of the gap she'd leave in his life? Needy? Hospitality, fatherhood: service industries. Eighteen years in which every-thing he did was worked around her. More than four of those with just the two of them, no Viv. At least if she was at university they'd be in the same country. He could visit for lunch on his days off. Maybe on *all* his days off. He'd take her and some grinning boyfriend out for drinks, torture the guy in inventive ways. And was it inevitable that he'd become his mother, moaning at the lack of phone calls from one's child, and that Freya would become him, moaning about the moaning? When she went away for weekends he always felt at first a rich sense of possibility. He told himself he would succumb to the advances of one of the lonelier women in the hotel and that he would roll around with this woman on the sofa, cook her eggs for breakfast, drink lunchtime wine. But slowly and surely that sense of possibility would always flatten and sink — there was no rolling around and he drank the wine alone and often the wine was beer — and he'd get up for a bleary, wheaty midnight wee and see that his daughter's bedroom door was open, no one inside. He'd think, Soon it'll be empty forever.

He rubbed his arm and caught a glimpse of Barbara. She was scowling but nonetheless permitted him to stroke her. After a while she rolled onto her back, legs akimbo, so he brought her a fresh bowl of Whiskas.

A little after four Moose was coming down the hotel's sweeping spiral staircase, down and down, 123 steps over which a rich dark carpet flowed, when he started to feel very tired. He noticed also that his jacket was listing to the left. He paused on the first-floor landing and began redistributing coins between flap pockets, aiming for equilibrium, picking out from palmfuls of ten- and twenty-pence pieces those thin squiggles of cigarette-packet cellophane. He caught sight of his reflection in the banisters. Even allowing for distortions, he looked pretty bad. The lobby below seemed gloomy, sleepy. His mouth felt full of putty. Sticky. Odd.

He sat down without deciding to sit down.

There was a vase on a console table and it wasn't centrally placed. Little things like the central placing of vases created a sense of symmetry, perfection. Overall design. He would recentre it. Another centimetre to the left. You can make an imperfect dive seem perfect if you focus on position and posture. Posture at the edge of the tower. Hips forward. A straight lower back. Posture as you're about to leave the board, as all the energy in your dive is applied. Posture as you tuck: show the judges just one leg, knee close to shoulder and heel close to body. From overhead it would be clear that the tuck was split. A judge up high would see that your knees were apart. There was no judge up high. The judges always sat side-on. Fuck. He was not feeling well.

He needed to stand up. The Grand's staircase appeared curiously soggy. He tried to make sense of the grandfather clock on the landing, but grandfather clock sounded like the wrong name for what the grandfather clock was. This was stupid. He got up.

A bolt of pain in his chest. His first thought was the Wo of Wow. His tongue in the roof of his mouth. The carpet. He fell.

He was on his back staring up at the ceiling.

Sandra the Maid nearby. He wanted to signal to her. There was no power left in his body. What was this? Pain insisted on its preeminence. Everything else was play. Footsteps. Her upside-down mouth. Hideously it opened. The new bitter clove of pain in his chest started to expand and to involve his shoulders and his soul. All in all, this was far from ideal. Sandra was running down the stairs shouting, "Someone!"

Others. People flocking. The next ten minutes seemed to happen underwater. A busy green blur coming through the crowd. A paramedic ripping open his shirt, sending a button spinning.

"How old are you?"

"Forty-five."

His shirt open. They tilted his head. The carpet rough and warm under his ear. On days when he might be required to help out behind the bar he kept the belt buckled slightly to the side, so the metal wouldn't scratch the joinery while he was serving. Save the wood. Avoid that grating sound. They undid his belt buckle and loosened his trousers; a friendly comment about his boxers. They *were* comedy boxers, strawberries in sunglasses designed to be amusing, but he had given no one permission to see them or speak of them. The pain was cooling, was it? Thinning. He was just so tired. Something very cold or very hot against his hip. A metal canister. A tube. At the end of it a mask. They strapped it to his face. It seemed like a toy, the elastic so thin, and that brought fresh hope that this was all a strange game.

"Breathe," they said.

He thought he heard Freya's voice, someone trying to fob her off, and he wanted to explain that she was smarter than all of them put together, that if anyone could help him it was her.

"How old are you?" the paramedic said. Kindness. Hair. A big blurry nose into which all her other features fell. He adored her for speaking so softly.

"Forty-five," he tried to say, but the number was muffled by the mask. He said it again and the pain in his veins was amazing. Everyone standing around looked huge. He was scared of all the ways they might hurt him.

Lying here undressed in the hotel with five or six people managing his movements, every illusion of power and privacy vanished. He was a dust mote among them. A zero, a speck. They made comments he couldn't respond to. They moved the canister and it knocked his knee.

Tongue-tied. He never knew what the phrase meant until now. All bets were off. All hands to the pump. Took the clichés right out of my mouth.

"How old are you?"

Four, five.

"We need to know that you know."

His eyes started to close. Shut out the world. Thin dreams through which his father's voice rippled along with his Uncle John's. A little to-and-fro joke the two of them liked to do in their unexplained mock-American accents.

What's the difference between ignorance and apathy, Tom?

I don't know, John, and I sure as hell don't care.

Someone slapped his face. He heard a voice much like his own mumbling the word "Promotion."

"What did he say?" they said.

The pretty paramedic asked what he'd had for breakfast. Did she mean his first breakfast or his second? She asked him who the Prime Minister was. Margaret Thatcher! She's coming to stay! She asked him what year it was. '84! '84! She asked if he had any pets. No. She said she owned a small brown dog. Her dog was called Potato.

As the light withdrew from the room he thought: I wish I'd had another child, a son, what would the son I never had be doing now? And then he thought: I could love a woman with a dog called Potato. A woman with a dog called Potato could be exactly what I need.

■ ■ ■ ■

Two:
The Flight of
a Dive

1979–1984

■ ■ ■ ■

1

Dan's first op for the Provos was in darkness, an alley off the Falls Road, half a decade before Dawson McCartland would ask him to become Roy Walsh. He was crouched with his back against a rough brick wall and a man called Colum Allen was beside him. Colum was sometimes called Hallion or Hallinan or the Welsh Saint, the last of these nicknames persisting despite his energetic claims to have no Welsh in him at all. He was tall and thin with a great vein forking up the left side of his neck. Even in the dim you could see it flickering. It moved whenever he spoke, which was always. His leg jerked up and down. Punching his palm was a frequent hobby too. Nodding his head. Biting his fingernails. Humming. Singing. Some of the many daily ways Colum relieved the pressure of being Colum.

"Predetermined is what it is." Colum's

voice was a quick whisper. "Last time was unlucky, isn't it? Whole season unlucky. Fuckers this season are on the ropes. Inevitable. Fuckers home in an ambulance. Been lucky. Got a destiny that's not what they think, to be sure."

Chance and fate, Dan had started to see, were a great pre-occupation of guys engaged in reckless deeds. He didn't trust Colum to do a good job. Didn't trust him to keep his mouth shut after. It was exhausting to think of all the ways he didn't trust him and why had they been paired together? Dawson kept telling Dan he'd be able to work soon with Patrick. Kept telling him Patrick was too well known to the authorities now — couldn't be the face of operations, only the brains, needed help. Dawson kept saying Dan and Patrick would make a great team one day, but here he was, teamed with Colum Allen, talking football.

"Agree with sacking Steiny? How could a man. How could. But a man gets no silverwear for the Celtic, his history is history, isn't it? Fuckers got short memories is what they've got. Anyway —" he coughed — "this your debut, is it?"

Dan stood for a moment to grant some relief to his legs, then went back to crouching and squinting. Occasional shapes animated the gloom at the end of the alley. Occasional voices too. There was advance word of RUC raids happening here tonight. The idea was for Dan and Colum to disrupt the raids as much as possible. They had gear on the ground in two zipped bags.

Nerves. When Dan was nervous he didn't gibber or fiddle with his hands like Colum. Instead, basic questions surfaced. Such as: What am I doing here? Or: Will I end up with a bullet in my brain? Another cool wind was picking up grit. They waited.

"Paddy's your man, is he?"

Dan was silent. Disconcerting to think a guy as simple as Colum could have a read on your thoughts.

"Internment, was he?"

"Yeah," Dan said. "I think so."

"Whole year?"

"No idea."

"Two?"

"Dunno."

"Fuckers keep their secrets."

He knew exactly how long Patrick had been interned by the Brits without trial. But he'd also learned that it was unwise to give your facts away for free. Sharing less — sometimes less than was decent — made the other person uncomfortable. In an uncomfortable silence, people gave you more of themselves. The RUC had apparently come at dawn to pick Patrick up. The whine of the Saracens, bulky six-wheeled monsters, being slipped into a low gear. A dimmed stage, dark vehicles, blackened faces, not unlike the expected scene tonight; the occasional white blotch from a Catholic paint bomb. The whole of your life in Belfast was organised around light and dark, visibility and invisibility, silence and sound, information and secrecy, the private rubbing up against the public and making you feel tired. None of this Dan said to Colum.

"Heard about your initiation," Colum said. "Aye. The dogs. That one's getting nice and famous. Though I expect he was only preparing Your Majesty for obstacles others might raise."

Don't give in, Dan thought. But he gave in. "What did you hear?"

Colum grinned and scratched his neck, staring at the ground as if it were the future. "Other option, course, is he just wanted to give you nightmares. Dawson McCartland's nice like that. Fuckers love a good nightmare." He clicked his fingers. "My first time? They gave me a gun and an address and that was that."

"I won't be doing any of that stuff."

"What?"

"House calls."

"Ha," Colum said, and allowed himself an unusual pause. "Demoralises the police, stiffing them at home. Shows all the other police there's no place that's their own to relax, they said. Hadn't even occurred. I was even younger than you, probably. I was seventeen. So I'm realising quick I'm going to have to get a ride into an Orangies' area. And I'm realising a certain amount of planning needs to be done for the runback, though I've got only a day to do it. So the day comes and I'm wearing a Rangers badge, right? Though it kills me, so it does. And I'm wearing a pair of Beatle boots I got hold of from a fat lad. And all the while they're not telling me much about this guy I'm going to stiff or any real advice, tips if you will, but I'm used to that, aren't I? Grandfather used to be an Ulster fiddler, a virtuoso in Donegal — really. Took an awful reddener when he forgot his music one day. None of those fiddler men would let you in on their performance practices, no way; that's what I'm sayin'. It's a similar thing. So anyway, I go and stiff the guy and his wife comes screaming into the hall, looking at the pool of blood. Cool as anything I was. Just did the thing and left."

Dan nodded. "Sure." People were always

heroes in their own telling.

"Yeah," Colum said. "It was only once I got back to my district and had my first pint that the whole thing went right up on me. Shaking all over I was. Been shaking mostly ever since."

He had Dan's attention now. Night clouds moved across the moon. In a brief breeze an empty can rolled towards them and Colum's shoulders did a jump. They laughed.

A whining sound. A few thin flickers of light. Colum got up. "Here we go," he said, newly hard in the face, oddly impressive-looking. He picked up the bags. They ran to the end of the alley.

"Wait."

Dan did as he was told. The black Saracens were creeping along the Falls, slow and certain. The walls flanking this section of the road were painted black, a mass redaction of the murals of Bobby Sands and other heroes. The sound of heavy boots. Foot patrols moving behind and alongside the Saracens. Even if Colum had brought his gun with him, there was no way you could see the men well enough to snipe them. All of the officers were wearing black. Anything else would have spoiled the decor.

They watched as two RUC men broke down the first door to a Catholic home. The groan of the wood giving in. Dan's heart going hard. In the first open bag a dozen plastic bottles. Each of them was three-quarters full with white paint and water. "Quick now," Colum said. They scrambled to unscrew five or six lids. In another bag they had waterproof sheeting tied around chunks of dry ice. They started squeaking fragments of dry ice into the open bottles of paint, screwing the lids back on. Colum slapped Dan's face. "*Quick,* I said." Running.

Out into the open road. They got alongside the Saracens, a taste of smoke in the air, a soulful adrenalin building. A woman dragged out onto the street was saying "Don't you touch the inside of my house!" Men from the foot patrol were running into her home and another man, lank and stooped in the dim of the moon, had his hand around the woman's mouth. Colum hurled the first bottle. The lazy grace of it in the air and the little crackle and pop as it hit bodywork and exploded. Better than when they'd rehearsed. Perfect. White paint sprawling out on the Saracen, white paint dripping and pooling. Dan hurled two bottles. His blood was swaying. Hurt to breathe. Neither exploded. He needed to throw them harder, higher. Colum was shouting "Pots and pans! Pots and pans!" without a single tremor in his voice.

Dan went to ground, grit in his elbows, and pressed more fragments of dry ice into bottles. He sprinted, the bags banging on his shoulders, and threw a bottle at an RUC man — missed — but then one of Colum's bottles looped and the man's uniform was half white and the man yelled, fell. Another Saracen backing up to the front door of the next Catholic home to be searched and torn apart. Another throw. Dan was screaming "Pots! Pots! Pots!" and like magic windows were opening all down the street. Colum must have lobbed another bottle high — Dan could see it coming down almost at a vertical — and paint exploded over the roof of a Saracen. A precision hit. He'd got Colum all wrong. Loved the man in this moment. Loved him. Catholic women were leaning out of windows banging pots and pans. The whole street waking up and making noise, ensuring others rose and joined. Don't let these men rip our floorboards up. Don't let them call our freedom fighters terrorists. Some of the women were throwing glass bottles stuffed with burning hankies towards the blotches of white, tiny bursts of fire near the targets, three and then six and then more. Other women were in the street in nighties. They were standing in the way of the Saracens and banging their pots and pans above their heads, shouting "Put the fires out if you like! Go on then!" Shouting "What's a taste of water then? Give us a shower!" All this as Dan ran into another dark alley, the last of his bottles used up, changing into clean clothes and beginning the long jog home.

In training he tried to show that he was hungry for knowledge. There seemed to be an infinite supply. There was more artistry to violence than he'd ever expected, more technique and philosophy. Months rolled by with only paint-bomb operations. Less a war than an apprenticeship — someone finally taking him under their wing. They told him they thought his future was bright.

In a warehouse space that smelt of raw meat they taught him how to open and split a shotgun cartridge. They taught him that candle wax in the tip made it hold together on impact. Mercury in the cartridge made it more deadly. Garlic purée in the cartridge put poison in the blood. They taught him to smear axle grease on a bullet to make it fly through reinforced doors. They taught him to pack cartridges with rice to slow them down. They showed him all the things you could do with the looped brake cable of a pushbike. A knife in a body needs to be twisted upward. Bulletproof glass has a blue-green glint. If a friend's car is stolen, call Sinn Fein on this number. If a friend's family is persecuted, call Sinn Fein on that number. Golf courses are for golf and the storage of weapons. Some people relax by emptying magazine after magazine into oil drums, tree stumps, the tyres of abandoned cars; others prefer the cold sophistication of invention, electrics, tricks with cassette-recorder parts. You can hammer away at Semtex with a rolling pin, shifting its shape to fit a suitable space. You can do anything you like, just don't get any on your hands. On his nineteenth and twentieth and twenty-first birthdays Dawson sent packets of cash.

2

A book called *Everyday Baking* lay open on the kitchen table. Dan nibbled at his lower lip, pretending to pay it close attention. Every now and then his mother would ask him to call out an amount or instruction and whatever reply he gave would cause her to come up behind him, freckled forearms resting on his shoulders, floury hands made rigid in concern for his clean shirt, as she leaned down and kissed his ear. This whole gesture of affection was, he knew, a way of perusing the recipe page and checking he hadn't fucked things up. It was expected that her sons, left unsupervised, would fuck things up. All three of his older brothers had moved away. Bobby, deaf, to a special home called St. Joseph's in Stillorgan. Tom to Scotland where he worked on a farm. Connor to America, happy to spill his secrets, each letter alive with new girls' names. Lisa. Mary. Kimberly. Dawn.

Six oz softened butter, the recipe said. Six oz granulated sugar / caster sugar. Two large eggs, quarter-pint strong coffee, three tablespoons whisky. She was making a coffee cake. Halving the relevant amounts, presumably; the two of them would never get through it otherwise. It occurred to him to check this with her but he opted instead for a swig of vodka and water. There was an unspoken agreement that he would not challenge her while the oven was on, and a supplementary understanding that he'd challenge her rarely when it was off.

"Do you want some of those potato wedges?" she said. "As a starter, tide you over?" She was moving towards the fridge, the dull thud-thud of his father's old five iron measuring out her steps. His mother had a hip issue, needed a stick to walk, but in the kitchen there was an unexplained preference for the golf club. "Are you hearing, Dan? A potato wedge I said."

He shook his head. An image came loose. Last night's dinner was an old sock, a blood clot and some pieces of warped plastic. Main courses were her undoing. She was better off sticking to desserts. His mother's cupboard of accompanying condiments was a treasure trove of precious clues. If it arrived with mint sauce you knew you were looking at lamb.

"You'll get yourself drunk," she said.

"Hopefully."

"You'll want a biscuit the Gallaghers brought round."

"What biscuits?"

"After you got Cal to reinforce their door."

"On the house."

"What's that, Dan?"

"Cal put it on their house on the house. He didn't charge."

"Well, that's grand. If you hold this a second I'll get your biscuits down."

He smiled. "Really, Ma, I'll save myself for dinner."

A short, thin woman who lived to fatten others up. Fuzzed-peach cheeks. Skin potato-sallow. Her arms of late looking empty, sausage casing squeezed of cheap meat. He knew it shamed her how little he ate. The slow-motion movements of his fork. The non-committal way he moved the food around his plate, picking, toying, never taking a second helping, never mopping up excess sauce with the bread. Hating the idea, in truth, that you'd want to take a clean hunk of bread and make it soggy. Toast was the thing he loved. Slice after slice in the morning, crispy at the edges and butter-supple in the middle. Bread was sufficient to keep him broad and strong if he added tinned fish during the day. Also those protein-dense snacks Mick's brother procured for free from . . . He didn't know where they were from.

A pip from the lemon in the bottom of his glass. Touch of citrus made vodka and tap water into a proper drink. The window bleary with steam and last night's grease.

Many things about his mother remained a mystery to him, but he felt sure she was at her happiest when preparing food. There were still times when she went out to gather ingredients, but increasingly he tried to limit these excursions. The problem wasn't so much her lack of mobility as her recklessness in the open air. If she saw an RUC man on the street she wasn't beyond spitting at him or striking him, a frail woman swinging her stick and slinging abuse and bringing herself to ground in the process. In a fighting mood she was a nightmare to protect. Immune to reason. Deaf to it. Twice the RUC had retaliated, one officer with his truncheon and the other with the back of his hand. The second blow, administered a few months ago, had drawn one of the only real teeth from her mouth. Dan had come around the corner from the post office. He saw his mother on the pavement, legs spread, thick brown wrinkled tights. The RUC man was standing over her. The tooth was in his mother's hand, extraordinarily long at the root, the slightest speck of blood on enamel that was the colour of mustard diluted and stirred. She looked down at it like a child with a new toy. The RUC man grimaced, tried to help her up, said she'd gone crazy and fallen. Possibly this was true. She said she'd been hit. The RUC guy seemed lost in a loop of wondering what he'd done or wondering how she got so good at lying. Dan found himself memorising the pattern of moles on the man's face: one upper right on the hairline, three on the left line of the jaw. "That's my mother," Dan told him. "Be careful, that's my mother." And whether surprised by the evenness of Dan's response or slow-plotting his next move, the RUC man simply stood there, arms at his sides, until Dan had got his mother halfway home.

An incident like that happened and you called Mick Cunningham. You imagined him at the other end of the line, pressing the receiver to his ruined ear, light pooling on the lunar landscape of his head. Cunningham called Dawson McCartland. Dawson McCartland called Mad Dog Magee, Chief Explosives Officer, your main reporting line. Magee circled back with you and the chain of command was a figure of eight, overcomplicated, tiring. There was a rule that you didn't deal with personal matters personally, and another rule — linked — that authorisation for operations had to go through central command. It was a way of sanifying a plan, sweeping away elements of emotion. Useful in more than one respect.

His mother hobbling towards the stove, golf club clutched in her little blue fist. She positioned herself in the tight right angle where the cupboards met the drawers, freeing up all her fingers for chopping and peeling, the breaking of eggs.

It had been on TV, the RUC man's death. The guy's face in a box in the top right corner of the screen. A mole there, three here, telltale acne scars. A car bomb, the newscaster said, and later Mick would say to Dan that it had comprised three RDG5 grenades with five-second fuses, four ounces of TNT a piece. Someone had filled a ginger-beer bottle with sugar and oil and taped it onto the grenades. Someone else had added a juice carton of petrol. Someone. Someone. The contraption was attached to the steering column of the RUC man's personal car and it sent him sky-high. The *Belfast Telegraph* ran the headline

"PROVOS TAKE CREDIT FOR NEW FIRE-BALL." At the weekend the *Guardian* picked up on the story. Someone sent Dan a clipping. Underneath the main piece was a box headed "WHO ARE THE RUC?"

Since 1922 the Royal Ulster Constabulary has had a dual role, unique among British police forces, of providing a normal law enforcement police service while, at the same time, having a remit to protect Northern Ireland from the activities of proscribed groups.

Did *Guardian* readers need to be told what the RUC was? It was shocking, if they did. His mother had yawned and put the newspaper to one side.

He'd spent a long dreamless night thinking about the RUC man with the moles, wondering if there hadn't been a better solution, wondering if he was wrong to have taken his mother at her word. A beating — that's all he'd been after when he made the call. But to get a beating arranged he'd had to share her account of what had happened, and what sort of man hits an old woman? A pathetic man, a dead man. Move on.

Pans hanging down from hooks above the stove. These were a biding presence. His mother's concentration, while cooking, was quite something to behold. The way her face coloured and her small blue eyes became unblinking. Her whole body seemed to coil as she creamed the butter and sugar. Her shoulders remained rolled, her back bent, until the bowl contained a cloud. She cracked eggs with one hand as the other hand continued beating and then there was the expert sieving of flour and salt, the three quick taps on the rim of the sieve, the slow circles made by her wrist when it was time, the precise time, to fold the dry ingredients into the moister part of the mix. When she said the word "syrup" to herself, a reminder of some future stage in the process, her tongue seemed to lick real love into the word, the language a sugary treat.

"One to two chopped hazelnuts," he said. "For decoration, apparently."

She moved behind him and leaned her forearms on his shoulders. "Later," she said. "They'll be for later."

Stirring darkness in. The process of adding the coffee to the batter brought a new alertness to her features. With all her weight on the five iron she stretched up to retrieve something from the cupboard — a cake rack — and he was on his feet but she had it now, refusing help, whispering, "Pan, whisky, springform, syrup." He could sense within her movements an excitement and anticipation that other parts of her life could not provide.

The phone rang. He moved into the hall. At the other end of the line a man exhaled in an even rhythm. Dan put the phone down and then took it off the hook. He returned to the kitchen table and drank.

"Who was that?" his mother asked. She had a way of flaring her nostrils when suspicious.

"Electrical job for the club. Lighting."

She smiled. Grateful for the lie? From the garage came the barking of dogs.

"Almost forgot myself," she said. "Jan Henry? From the Donegall? She told me my fortune this morning."

Jan was a Protestant, one of maybe two or three his mother was happy to talk to. She got all over town, didn't mind crossing the line to read a palm.

"She said, first of all, that I'm soft and spongy these days. That I'll be picking up vibrations from the universe. Positive vibrations, she confirmed. She said I'd be continuing to receive the benefits of wisdom."

"That was first of all."

"Yes. You think she's loony?"

"I think she's loaded."

"Loaded?"

"Her life's a dander in the park."

"But do you believe it, Dan? That there's good news ahead?"

"I do," he said. "But I wonder how much of that news it's in her gift to predict."

"She's gifted."

"I don't deny it."

"Well then."

"I've seen her car."

"She said we were our own worst enemies, Dan."

"That's a stretch," he said.

"It's what she claimed."

"She exaggerates."

"No no."

"She's a storyteller. Accept her for what she is."

"No, Dan, no. A cleverer woman there isn't around."

It was frightening and frustrating how easily she was deceived — by fortune-tellers, by door-to-door hacks, by her own son. The first big lies he'd told her came when he was an adolescent. Hidden magazines and skipped classes, little untruths that left him guilty and weary. But at some point the effort of remembering and repeating each fiction had taken on the shape of a game. Fatigue gave way to a determination to succeed. He began to realise he was good at lying and with each operation now he became more and more set on protecting her from the truth. That's how he thought of it: protecting her from the truth. It was as if within the walls of his own life there was another person being born, an alternate Dan growing strong in secret. You had to work for what you believed in. It was the only thing a decent person could do. His father had said it was one of life's few lessons. That and don't mix your drinks.

"You'll be on the right side of history." These words had seemed absurd when Dawson had first said them. But these days Dan felt, with increasing confidence, the rightness of what he was doing. Volunteering offered him a purpose. He nurtured it. He was reluctant to see the bulk and heft of his own opinions whittled down into something more subtle. He'd seen, among many other volunteers, that subtlety tended to sit side by side with doubt.

"We need types like you," Dawson had said. "Idealists with a brain." But being an idealist, if that's what he was, didn't obligate him to tell the truth, did it? It meant *adhering* to the truth, probably. A bigger truth, a conviction and a faith, which was something different. And why would he tell his mother that they had received another threatening call? Why would he let her lie awake at night thinking Prods wanted them dead? Why would he make clear to her that specific people, actual individuals who had this actual phone number, wanted to see the end of him and the end of her because — despite believing in a similar God — their ancestors disagreed over the sufficiency of Scripture, the completeness of certain words in a book, the authority and office of the Pope? He was determined to keep her in the dark. She knew there were risks in living around here. (There were risks living anywhere, she said; there are risks in every town around the world, and why should I be forced out of my home?) A man breathing hard down the line would add nothing to her armory.

The tinkle and squeak of cutlery now. "Shall I wet the tea?" she said.

"No thanks, Ma."

"Go on."

"I'm fine with the drink I have."

Another sip of vodka. She shook her head.

These days his doubts tended to surface in very specific situations: after a glance from a neighbour; sometimes after sex. A girl on the mattress in the garage. Sad Samantha from the Falls. Samantha who was always calling him cold even though, in the private spaces of his head and heart, nothing would stay still. After making love, questions filled the space vacated by desire. Were the other three Catholic families on this road receiving the same anonymous calls? What did it mean if they weren't? He'd watch Samantha fall asleep, her face alive with light from his father's hurricane lamp, the glass chipped in two places and going slowly grey. He slept in the garage when violence was high. Lately that meant almost always. Best place to protect their home if anyone broke in. His mother thought he liked to sleep there to stay cool.

Lately he'd had to introduce, much to his mother's consternation, a household rule that only he could answer the phone. He told her it was important that their telephone number be perceived as his business line. She'd frowned at that and then offered, with no diagnosable irony, to be his secretary. Keep a diary, she said. I could keep a diary of your plumbing jobs, electric jobs, your wire-work and the like. To hear her offer this made him want to cry.

People said they couldn't find work in Belfast, but as far as he was concerned there was plenty to go around. You couldn't rely on an employer because most of them were

Prods who — fair enough — wanted Prods. So then: work for yourself. Between 6 a.m. and 11 a.m. each day he did lighting for businesses and homes. Between 3 p.m. and 9 p.m. he mainly focused on plumbing. In the interim hours there was the army, and that took up more and more energy. The peelers seemed to think he was gainfully employed (which he was) and honest (which he mainly was). In a neighbourhood where half the people were on the dole, he wasn't a priority problem. One or two liked to rough him up a bit, call him a Fenian cunt, but they had never once handed him over to Special Branch. No one had connected him to the Provos.

His mother cleared her throat. "So that Dawson man came round."

He looked up from pictures of cherries reclining on icing. "And you were going to tell me when?"

"Would it be important?"

"What did he say?"

"That man."

"What did he want?"

"Well, I asked him if it was an electrics query, didn't I, and he said yes. He said it very probably was."

"Very probably was."

"You know how he'll talk."

"You answered the phone."

"You'll listen. He came round in *person.* A mouth for mystery that man. Said, 'That's right, it's an illumination issue.' Illumination issue! To describe the lights!"

She returned to her work. The kitchen's one light — a long fluorescent tube, 60 watts, drywall patching involved — made a ghost of her. He felt sure the loose skin falling from her throat was a new thing, like the thinning of her hair this last year and the swelling of her ankles before that. The ageing process, with its small adjustments, seemed to pick on one or two small items at a time.

When he was growing up in this house there had been a picture of a long-haired Jesus in here, above the fridge. The dull buzz from the fridge had seemed to creep so coolly from Our Saviour's eyes and his half-smile seemed to speak of a love for acid rock. In the background of the picture was a woman in a blue veil standing in a burning bush. As a child he'd always looked at it and thought, If the bush is burning she should go stand on the grass. The parables he liked best as a kid were the ones based in common sense. It took him years to start despising their simplicity.

His father had loved that picture of Jesus.

Stared at it in the early days, when they still said grace before meals. Why did they stop? It was hard to recall. Buried the picture with him. A new suit, a new tie. He had looked much smarter in death than he had in life. Hair combed and skin smelling of cologne.

His father's necktie had been secured with what the undertaker called a half-Windsor. To Dan's eyes the knot looked lopsided. He was fourteen. He wanted to improve it. To improve it he had to remove it, put the tie around his own neck, remind himself of the rules. He felt he was dressing for school but after the funeral he didn't go to school for weeks. He walked the streets instead, met people who told him they'd look out for him, pay him for little jobs. Once the knot was nice he slipped the tie back over his father's head, unsettling only a little of the make-up on the ears.

He finished his vodka and excused himself for a few minutes. "Got to feed the dogs," he said. He let them chase each other around the small garden in tighter and tighter circles, until one rolled over and they fought. When you scratched behind the brown one's ears his eyes went dreamy and slow.

3

Dan found out about the Grand Hotel operation in March of '84, the week of his twenty-fourth birthday, a quiet celebration at the Harp. Many of the volunteers in the pub that night were people he didn't know. At times, talking to them, he couldn't shake the sense that they were soft. There was a langour about them. A blurriness to their beliefs. It seemed rare these days for recruits to be put through the kind of initiation he'd experienced six years ago in the field with the dogs, or to be put through any initiation at all. There were worries about retention. Bobby Sands's body had been cold too long. An army needs its poster boys.

For the fourth or fifth time in his life, drink in hand, the lights in the bar he was in went off and he heard the whine of the Saracens. The door broken down. The Brits charging in over splintered wood. Paras puffed up by flak jackets worn under their tunics. Ireland at night was a repeating dream.

"Could have knocked," said a drinker, staring down at the ruined door. There was laughter. The Paras said sit on the floor. Everyone groaned and sat on the floor. They wanted information about someone called Micky McGee. No one knew a Micky McGee, or else knew so many Micky McGees that it was impossible to pick among them, and the added complication was that there were people in that bar who would rather have died or lost a hand than told the truth to a Para. Dan sat with his elbows resting on his knees.

One of the Paras started pouring pints of ale. He asked what was on the table next to Dan. Bottle-shaped. Wrapped in silver paper. No one said a thing. It didn't take a genius to work out what it was. The Para wasn't a genius. He took a sip of beer and asked again. After a certain amount of asking his face had the coarse blush of a good bolognese and he allowed the beer to run on from the tap. It began to flood the floor.

This was above all a waste of beer so Dan stood up to explain. "It's my twenty-fourth," he said. "Five of us at our table. One of them brought me a present. The others are certified cheapskates."

More laughter. Mick Cunningham shouting "I'm no fucken cheapskate!" The beer tap was still running. The landlord looked broken. Beer pooled on the ground and broke out in thin streams that carried sawdust and dirt to the walls.

One of the Paras asked for the bottle. People for some reason were looking to Dan. He nodded. No point battling these guys on every single thing. Hand to hand the bottle was passed to the Para. The Para unwrapped it and made a show of being impressed. "Good Scotch," he said, and helped himself to a slug of Scotch. "Not bad at all. Really."

A second Para took an interest in Dan. Said: "On your birthday it's customary to do a dance."

"What?"

"Do us a jig, if you please."

"Fuck off."

A third Para fiddled with the radio behind the bar, found an Irish tune. *Da di di, da da, da da.* Sweaty brow. Greasy eyes. All the sticky charm of a congealed school meal.

"Do a little Taig dance. A little Irish jig."

"Get lost," he told them.

The Para who'd been pulling pints now pulled the bolt of a Sterling down. "Have a go," he said. "It would be lovely." Two of the younger Paras looked to the floor in shame, guys whose sense of fairness perhaps hadn't yet been pressed away, and one tried and failed to intervene.

Dan standing. The room silent. He told the Para he wasn't in the mood to entertain.

"I think you should."

"No."

"How sure are you?"

"Fuck you."

"Doing a little jig for a minute, that's all I'm asking. Save your friends some trouble."

He didn't even know a jig.

The Para with the Sterling pointed it at Martina's bare legs. This act of unsubtlety extracted a groan from the crowd.

Martina looked up at the Para. "I dare you," she said. Her defiance made Dan twitchy and proud. The anger she'd managed to salvage from a short cruel youth, all the shit she'd sucked up her nose while her father watched, all the poison pinned into her veins.

"Dare *him,*" the Para said, and pointed at Dan. Seemed to be under the misapprehension that he'd said something terribly clever. "Go on, boy, just a little dance for this girl here. Do that and maybe I won't take her out back for a prize."

There was the exchange of swear words.

There was Martina's hair being pulled. There was another of the Paras saying, "This has got to stop, Rob." There was Jim Callaghan getting a baton in the ribs for intervening. And finally there was Dan standing there, in the middle of the floor, shifting his weight from foot to foot, the Paras clapping, cheering. One or two of the drinkers were clapping too. Most were staring down into their drinks.

Afterwards Martina drew her legs into her chest and sat by the window, saying nothing.

At the end of the week, waiting for the shame of the dance to cool, telling himself his life would contain no more moments like that, thinking of things he should have said and done, he came home early from an electrical job and decided to work on the garden. Quiet was what he wanted, the quiet only your own private land can provide. His mother was over at the club playing cards. She was a fierce cheat. Twice he'd had to beg them to restore her membership, and last week he'd promised a council of intimidating old women, frowning behind slow blooms of cigarette smoke — Mafia lords in a fucking film — that he'd be happy to provide transportation to other members of the club *should they see fit to exercise the*

Christian principle of forgiveness. He'd nailed it with that form of words. The Christian bit was of limited interest to these old girls, but the offer of free transportation was a tangible earthly perk. Heads turned. Words were whispered. If he could promise a touch of assistance to those who struggled for lifts, who were less mobile or lived alone, well then, yes, they might see fit to overlook the unfortunate incident, which they were sure had involved no malice. It would be a nice gesture, altogether.

The sun today was low in a cold sky. Made his teeth hurt to look at it. He closed the kitchen window and went searching for some gardening gear.

On his knees in the cupboard under the stairs he tried on his father's gloves. Too large. His father had been sausage-fingered. Big angry hands on a quiet determined man. A miracle, really, that he could do the fiddly work he did. After leaving the tobacco factory he'd retrained as an electrician and odd-job man. Said that the freedom inherent in self-employment more than compensated for the lack of security. By working nights and weekends — a peculiar kind of freedom, it seemed to Dan then — he'd earned just enough money to buy the family this narrow terraced house on what was then a safe, mostly Catholic street, and to pay down the mortgage each month. The back garden was a source of pride and worry. Every week weeds would sprout between paving stones. Every Tuesday morning, for fifteen minutes, his father would pull them up.

Growing up in this house Dan had seen riots break out in '69. He'd seen the British Army mobilised to restore order. He'd looked on, with mounting excitement, as the barricades went up between Catholic and Protestant communities. By climbing trees you could swing yourself over to the other side, hide-and-seek, play You're the Brits and We're the IRA, chanting warnings, your voices charged with drama, bright with it, giving off imagined glory. He'd stood side by side with Jackson, a crayon-eating kid from the Ballymurphy, as authorities pulled the trees down in August '69. In July of 1970, during a gun battle around the Falls, he was forced to stay indoors with his mother. The safety was as smothering as this cupboard. Gunshots cracking through the dark. To be a ten-year-old boy prevented from fighting — it had struck him as bitterly unfair.

Rust had made a hole in his father's shovel. There were blisters of rust on the spade. Rust and dried mulch had ruined the garden shears and you could barely open the blades.

In a plastic bag in the cupboard he found rinsed-out soup cans that his mother was keeping for what? Made him think of coffee-jar bombs hurled at Land Rovers. He'd seen his older cousins spring-load and throw them in fits of youthful excitement, an excitement he'd been desperate to take as his own. At some point the civil rights marches became minor riots. He went on a march with his dad, Connor, Tom, a family. The rainy weather had no effect on their mood. Adrenalin, sense of purpose. People broke rank and punches were thrown. Sound crowding in on you, people grabbing at your clothes. A brick struck his father on the head, side of the head, temple. Didn't see the moment of impact. Saw the deepening bruise. It was more than sad. His father on the ground, one eye half closed, rain falling on his pale face, washing it. He might have survived if the police had listened. They said he was faking. They said it was a trap. One, in desperation, kicked his father in the stomach — a way to prove he was alive. His father didn't move. The policeman shuddered. What do you do when the people making the rules aren't interested in fairness? When they choose who to protect based on religion, race, history? The police are scum. People who join the police are scum. Dan hurried through this thought and went out to buy new tools.

Brand-new serrated grass whip in his hand, eleven-inch blade and a hardwood handle. The patio was a thin little runway of paving stones, modest but clean. Flower beds bordered it on three sides: tangled briars, creeping thistle, the hollow stems of other plant life he couldn't fairly name. He'd let domestic duties slide. It felt good to tick off some jobs. His great discovery, coming out of adolescence, was that being busy gave you energy.

Three hours he worked at trying to clear the weeds. The grass whip, while effective for ripping into stubborn stuff, was curiously unsatisfying to wield. To get any rhythm going you needed to angle your body in an unnatural way. As time passed pain collected along the right flank of his back. Twice he managed to embed the tip of the blade in a fence post. The effort to extricate himself from these errors was tremendous. After a third comic wrestle, jerking and pulling and cursing as the blade refused to budge, he decided to leave it there. He began using a severed stem from the most mysterious weed group in the garden, the stuff that looked a little like bamboo, to thwack and flatten nearby brambles. The simplicity of this new method pleased him: Nature against Nature. Before long, though, the stem broke and he admitted to himself, with a reluctance that tugged hard at his biceps and thighs, that it was time for the shears and the rake.

He clenched his jaw against the sound of metal combing stone and then there was another noise: small metallic rattling. The back gate began to grumble, the hinges started to rasp. He took the trowel in his hand as if that would help and watched as a shoe came into view.

Dawson McCartland. The perennial interrupter of progress. "Danny," he said. "Nice day for it, eh?"

"Average."

"Average is nice," Dawson said. "Don't underestimate the pleasures of average."

"Try knocking next time, please."

Dawson's eyes did a second sweep of the garden. "You always were very polite."

He wished he'd never given Dawson a key, but what were the options? All of the excuses had seemed to write their own solutions. "My mother is always looking out the window." Tell her to draw the curtains. "The neighbourhood kids kick footballs over the fence." Tell the kids to kick their footballs elsewhere. In the end he'd given Dawson what he prized above all else: access. If you lived in a Catholic area, as Dawson did, you were always looking for places to hide gear. You were safe from burnouts but vulnerable to searches. The advantage of being here, an odd one out on a Protestant street, was that everyone assumed you'd never be so stupid as to risk keeping weapons in your home.

With great delicacy Dawson picked a piece of lint from his shirtsleeve. He seemed to be waiting for a conversation to occur to him. These days he was less of an accountant in appearance. More a flamboyant lawyer. He wore suits with silk linings. Starched white shirts with double cuffs. Every day seemed to bring a new set of cufflinks. Some thought he was aping his daddy, a partner in Madden & Finuncane, and the other thing in development was his impatience with direct questions. Statements he'd answer. Mumbled asides he'd deal with straight away. But in the years they'd known each other Dan had noticed, more and more, that if you decorated your thought with a question mark you rarely got him interested. He'd wait in silence for

179

another sentence, working towards a topic in his own time, on his own terms, sideways, a guy working a piece of furniture through a door.

"You should get yourself some gloves," Dawson said. "Those hands'll blister up."

"Nice of you to worry."

"Protecting my investment."

"You need to feel the stuff."

"Come again, sweetheart?"

"With your hands, to feel them, the weeds."

Dawson began excavating something from the corner of one eye: a loose eyelash or a thin moon of sleep. He put his glasses back on and raised his heavy eyebrow. "What's that stuff, then?" His nod was directed at the bamboo-like weeds marshalled skinny against the fence, impossible to uproot.

"I don't know."

"Spring-cleaning. Nice idea. Out with the old and in with the new, get your cassie looking nice."

Dan watched Dawson's gaze fall on a particular paving stone. The slabs around it were chalky with scratches. If you lifted the unmarked stone, as Dan did most mornings in a fit of something that could look to the untrained eye like paranoia, you saw a wooden hatch. The hatch opened onto a disused well shaft. You darted your hand down, keen to get the daily check over with, searching out a piece of thin rope wound around a nail. To tug on that rope and feel the necessary weight was a relief that bordered on bliss.

Dawson said, "Not having a *general* clear-out, are we?"

"Fuck off."

"Ah."

"Ah what?"

"Ah you're pretty when you're angry."

"It's risky, Dawson. It's bad enough that the garage is a lab."

Detonators, chemicals. A hundred empty bottles under ancient cotton sheets. Dan could picture it all as he spoke. Overhead the sun was getting lost behind a film of cloud but there was still a spring warmth in the air, apricot scent of cowslip.

"You'll be rewarded, Daniel."

"What for?"

"Aye. You're on an upward curve."

A number of expressions chased one another across Dawson's face: vulnerability, viciousness, an extraordinary half-comatose brand of introspection.

"What is it I can help you with, Dawson? You still haven't said."

"Bad mood you're in for sure."

"No."

"I have a nice plan."

"Yeah?"

"Yeah. Very nice, very special."

Always a game. Liked his nice plans to be revealed with theatrical slowness. "Tell me the plan, then, before it's autumn."

Dawson readjusted his shirt cuffs. He liked no more than an inch of white to show where the suit sleeves ended. His eyes alighted on the grass whip stuck in the fence post. "A scythe," he said.

"Grass whip."

"It's not a very subtle sculpture."

"It's stuck. Give me a hand with it."

"My oxters'll get sweaty. It's always the lefty that goes first." They grabbed the handle and pulled. "Reaper came, did he, Dan? You pulled a quick judo throw on him?" The blade squeaked out. "More and more you're my hero, Daniel. I think of you as a supernatural."

Dan made tea. They drank it in the garden. The saucers were side by side on the step and Dawson's biscuit remained untouched. No one ever saw Dawson eat — not ever. Dan had heard various theories. An intestinal complaint. A protein-only diet. A belief that being seen with your face in a sandwich ruined the myths a man created for himself. The other thing he never did was linger in the house. He worked on the assumption every building was bugged. He thought if a man was going to be caught he might as well be caught outdoors.

Dawson lit up a Newport. "Want one?"

"Why not." It was useful, when talking to a guy like this, to have something in your hand.

Eventually Dawson said, in a much quieter voice than before, "We've work that needs a man of your skills, yes? You'd have seen the two house calls we made to those UVF members last week. Arosa Parade, near the Grove? Doing a job on the Loyalists in the heart of their territory, Danny. Important work, for sure, but —"

"Small."

A nod.

"And?" Dan said. Then he rephrased, careful to avoid a rising intonation: "And you have me in mind, I assume, for a follow-up. To which I'd remind you, I don't do guns."

"Or knives. Or paper clips. I know, I know."

"I'd be working with Patrick."

"No. This one's lonely. We're having a try for keeping Patrick uninteresting. Mad

183

Dog's got a big job coming up."

It was bait, this comment. Jobs so big that you couldn't work in advance of them? They didn't exist. Couldn't work *after,* for a while — that made sense. "What's his big job, Dawson?"

"Curiosity's another of the tragic flaws, Danny."

"Fine."

"Still not read your Shakespeare, have you?"

"Enough, Dawson."

"Unaccommodated men," he said, and blew a smoke ring. Dan watched it widen and die. "Every society's got them at the edges of the public space, haven't they? But no, we need to put Patrick on the subs bench a little while. The op he's on — it's not for you. Though tell me, what do you think of the name Roy Walsh?"

Familiar somehow, but Dan couldn't place it. "I picture a glittering jacket," he said. "Grinning game-show host."

"I've just come from a little Army Council meeting, is all. We're toying with a couple new aliases."

The piece fell into place. Roy Walsh was the name of another volunteer. In which case, hardly a good alias.

Dawson listened to Dan's concerns, blowing smoke again. "Opposite," he said. "Confuses the old authorities, so it does. The real Walsh is a Red Light right now, see? In the Special Branchy books. Which is to say, given he can't visit the mainland, he's got an alibi tighter than Gerry Adams's arsehole."

"Heard it was pretty loose."

"No," Dawson said thoughtfully. "*Verbal* incontinence, that's Gerry's main issue. My own idea of a CEO? Leave a bit more to the imagination. Be a bit more like God." He took his asthma inhaler from his trouser pocket and twirled it in his left hand. Then he pocketed it again and took a nimble drag on his Newport. He said, "Forget Patrick's job. This other one I'm putting you on is plenty big. Large impact, high value. But simple, for a man of your skills."

"They're all simple in the strategy rooms. It's when you're there, sweating into the Semtex, peelers approaching you east, south and west — that's when it gets tricky."

"You go north, in that situation, no? Simple. Easy. I tell you, for me it'd be a fucking relief to go north. Instead I'm stuck at home, strategising, with a one-eyed woman who's always nagging me to go south."

Dawson waited for the laugh, accepted it

with a wave of his hand, smoke creeping out of his mouth. "I disgust myself daily," he said, crouching to press his cigarette into a paving stone. "Also, you're the expert, but it's not advisable to sweat into the Semtex."

"You're thinking of a car charge, I suppose."

"There's been enough charges under cars," Dawson said. "There's been enough Nissan Sunnys and Land Rovers. This one's an *arty* kind of operation. Right up your street."

"Local."

"Everything's local. The wonders of transport. This one's across the Irish Sea. Larne–Stranraer ferry. You must be familiar? It's being used — you'll like this — to move fifteen Brit Army trucks a fortnight. *Fifteen*. Two- or three-ton trucks, it seems. Ones bringing blankets and uniforms from Scotland. Supplies for the Province troops. Comforts, so they can be well rested when they kill us."

"You'll never get the kind of volume of fertiliser, or whatever you're wanting, onto one of those."

"*We* are on there. That's the point. Not fertiliser — a human presence. I know that's tough to grasp for a robot like you. For a guy who fiddles with wires for a living. I'm a people person. Our army is full of them. It's only your area that's chilly. So I'm talking about a flesh-and-blood volunteer, Danny, a civilised human person, someone who doesn't operate at a remove from reality. Sixteen-year-old lad, very mature, cousin of McCluskey C. He's a ship's hand and — screw Mick's mother — he's noticed a pattern. He's noticed that the fifteen trucks get loaded at Stranraer every other Saturday morning, arriving at Larne in the afternoon. The last three of the trucks are, he says, packed with soldiers."

"You're just giving me facts," Dan said, refusing a second cigarette.

"You asked for facts."

"I asked for nothing."

"None of us does. *Óglaigh na hÉireann*. The Army of People Who Ask for Nothing."

"Objectives," Dan said, but at that moment Dawson's eyes widened. Voices were coming through the fencing: the home of Ancient Jones.

A second, two seconds, and Dan recognised these voices as the talk of people on TV. Muffled but neat. Scripted. Ancient Jones was ninety-four and the best kind of Protestant around, but he liked to have the volume as high as his heating. Twice Dan had helped replace blasted component parts, fried audio elements. When he was hot, Jones opened his windows wide. He sat there flooding half of Belfast with sound waves from obscure wildlife programmes, repetitive weather reports, golf. An alternative to taking off one of the jumpers his bulky niece kept knitting.

"Elderly," Dan explained.

Dawson frowned. "Objectives. The objectives will become clear when you hear the plan. The plan is to plant one of your speciality packages at the side of the road and take out the last three trucks on a Saturday afternoon in two weeks' time. Ones that will be packed full of soldiers returning from Scotland. Sitting ducks. Quack quack quack. No need to get our gear on the actual ferry."

"Single-lane traffic."

"Yes."

"Parked cars."

"No."

"Lay-bys."

"One."

"Civilians."

"Not a touch."

It sounded doable, possible. Certainly not off-the-scale absurd, which he realised now he'd been hoping for. Because how could he refuse a clean, high-impact job like this?

He was enjoying his lighting work at the moment. That and the plastering and driving, and trying to learn his Spanish for a half-hour each night. *Puedo, puedes, puede, podemos.* Secret operations gave a buzz and as a result they wore you away. With languages he'd keep his options open. Widen out the places he could live and work if things got worse. Spain. France. He'd have enough money in a few years to get out of here. By then he would have done his bit to save the place, he'd be able to pay someone to look after his mother, maybe take Bobby with him, clumsy deaf Bobby, get him out of St. Shitpit. And at the same time the idea of the ferry job was swelling in his mind now, taking on detail and colour, and there was an ugly excitement to it all — a challenge to be met.

"What would you need, Danny? What doings to make it happen?"

Dawson had moved closer, the pearly buttons of his shirt giving off a gleam. Ancient Jones's TV was blaring facts about sharks.

"I'd want a caravan."

"Caravan?"

"As though a family is having a weekend away."

"Good," Dawson said. His features had settled into a look of grudging respect. "And what would you need, in that caravan? Three trucks to take out, remember."

"One thousand five hundred of mix. Home-made. Get one of your more competent Red Light lot to make it."

"Good. Clear. Now the detonators."

"If I do the job, which I'm not saying I will —"

"You're briefed. It's agreed."

"If it's something I can do justice to —"

"Listen to yourself! You sound like a bloody pub singer down the Shankill! Five years ago —"

"Six."

"— you were an innocent babe. I like innocence. I pay a premium for it."

"I'll bring my own detonators. I've had it with the quality of detonators being produced. You risk everything and then the operation whimpers into nothing. It's stupid there isn't a standard agreed testing procedure, in advance. It's not rocket science."

"And I'm not the Pope," Dawson whispered, crouching to stub out his cigarette. "When you're appointed Chief Explosives Officer, you can issue these decrees, can't you?"

A hot pause. "Patrick'll be in place for years."

"Unless he goes out with a bang."

"I want in on it," Dan said.

"You what?"

"The job that Patrick's doing. The bigger one."

Why? Why had he said it? Why had he offered himself up? He didn't know himself well enough to say. Career progression? Pursuit of a thrill? Misguided loyalty to Patrick? Wanting to be at Patrick's side if risks were to be taken? Patrick who'd also lost friends on Bloody Sunday. Patrick who'd trained in Libya and knew all there was to know. Patrick who said one night as they sculpted Semtex in the warehouse that he and Dan were joint captains of a submarine. You put a periscope up, you see an enemy warship, you know your job is to sink that ship. Focus on the target. Remember it's a target. Planting a bomb or pressing a button below deck. Same thing. Identical. In wars people die every day.

Dawson looked at him with dire eyes and said, "Pushy. Where did your modesty go, my little choirboy?" Then he sighed, chewed his thin bottom lip, glanced at the gate. "It's a seaside jobbie. You know Patrick's been involved with some mainland thinking, yes?" He was barely audible now; Dan leaned in. "Beach towns, cities. Stoking a few fires."

"You were right. I'm not interested. After La Mon you're mad to go that route. Tourists, restaurants, hotels. What about the Council directive? That stuff's a PR disaster."

"I knew a woman in PR once. She was nice despite it."

"You're away in the head to be thinking along these lines."

"This particular plan, it changes everything. It's the end of everything, Dan. After this job, give it ten years, there'll be peace."

Dan laughed.

"You have things to learn," Dawson said. Dan was surprised to see he'd hurt him. "A stiffing is all about timing. Get it wrong and you're out on your ear."

"Who's getting stiffed, then?"

"An assassination of a political figure. It works, but only when they're already at a low, you know? That's why the Kennedy thing made him into a dead god. He'd never been at a low enough ebb. When a leader's shown their cruel side, and there's a significant pool of haters within the moderates, and said leader has already made herself into a monster, even within half of her own country . . . Watching soldiers starve. Being brutal to the poor. Ignoring the north and the west . . ."

"You can't seriously be talking about this."

"I'm always seriously talking. Haven't I told you before? Greatest tragedy of my life is people think I'm joking." He bent down to remove a bit of soil from his shoe. "The conference. The hotel the Cabinet will be staying in."

"The whole?" Dan said. "Come on, the whole Cabinet?"

Dawson smiled. "If you want more, you'll have to come in for a meeting. The warehouse tomorrow."

"The losses."

"Legitimate targets. One or two staff, perhaps, but if they're hosting our targets they're legitimate too."

"Staff are collateral damage, at best. Don't kid yourself."

"You'll be surprised how contagious kidding yourself is. Every one of them is part of the political elite."

"Maids, cleaners?"

"Serving the elite, then. The point is, Dan, you change, with one blast —"

"Timed in the night, to limit losses?"

"You change everything." Dawson sighed and looked around him, lowered his voice even further. "Whitelaw's Deputy PM. He, in the first instance, assumes power. We'll need to talk about this in the warehouse."

He glanced again at the fence.

He couldn't really be suggesting this. He couldn't really be serious. "If he lives, you mean. And she . . . because we're talking about *her*, aren't we? She might not, you know."

"No, she might be a vegetable instead."

"And Whitelaw."

"Whitelaw's weak. Voices on the line suggest he won't be in the hotel on the night, anyway. So he takes power. And it doesn't take him long to see, with his experience of us to date, that he needs to put in process a free Ireland."

"Alternatively —"

"Alternatively? Alternatively this conversation is coming to an end. But alternatively he hands over to Tebbit. That would be trouble. But, much more likely, Heseltine. Heseltine's always hated Thatcher. Urged more moderation upon her, behind the scenes. He *knows* she made a bad play with Bobby Sands. Most of the Cabinet are looking for a way out. You don't let a man martyr himself in front of the camera. With Heseltine as PM it's the same end result."

"Which is?"

"We get our country back."

Bobby Sands on hunger strike, waist all

withered, the awful embroidery of his ribcage.

"It's not my place, Dawson, but it's huge. I mean, as a statement. Think about it before you —"

"You're right," Dawson said. "It's not your place."

"But come on, what if —"

"If we don't eliminate them all? We say that was never the intention. We wanted to show the mainland's not secure. It's almost more effective. A symbol's a symbol. A lot of thought by bigger brains than yours has gone into all this, and I have somewhere I need to be. This isn't going to fail, Dan."

Vigilante attacks. The contagious spread of surveillance. Dan could see ways for it to fail. "To take out the Prime Minister, though. Come on."

"With her in place there'll be no peace, Dan. You're acting like this hasn't been talked about before."

"There's a difference between talk and action."

"Not when one follows the other, same sentence, same breath. With her in place . . . She thinks she's the queen of us, Dan. Queen of our land, governing from a distance, quoting fucking Victoria. Even my mammy wouldn't quote from a queen, Dan, and she named me from a book called *Mosquitoes*. Thatcher might govern in her own tight circle but she's no right to power here, none at all. She's queen of nothing, and we'll treat her with the same respect she's granted us. Let her taste a little bit of equality. Let us take our freedom back. If you were in on this operation, Dan, you'd be the luckiest man alive. Go down in history. The guy who made sure no more civil rights men got finished — with a bullet, with a stone. It'd be the last job you'd ever do."

"Because I'd be locked up in the fucking Maze, that's why."

"Possibly. Though you seem to be one of those buoyant little jobbies who resists the flush. If anyone's getting scooped it's probably Patrick. He knows he's owed the prestige. Men get tired. He'll take his dog to the far side of the fair, same as you want to do."

He took his asthma inhaler out again and inhaled. Held the air in his mouth for a good few seconds and then opened his lips, relaxed.

"Explore it."

"What was that, Danny? Did the individualist speak? I was sucking at my can."

196

"Explore whether he needs a second man."

Dawson smiled. Ancient Jones's TV blared. *"Certain toothed whales,"* Attenborough's voice said, *"can generate 20,000 watts of melodic song. It's a song that can be heard for many miles."*

"Been reading a book about Leonardo," Dawson said. "Your scythe got me thinking on it. You know how he sold some of his more obscure sculptures?"

"I'm sure you'll tell me."

"He sold them by telling people they couldn't have them. By saying they were already sold." He shook the asthma inhaler and took another puff. "We've all a lot to learn from artists."

4

You choose the parts of the story to tell. It's the only way you can make it yours. Eight days before Brighton there was news. Loyalists had bombed a meat-packing warehouse on the Springfield Road, a building that had stood in the shade of Greater Shankill. Dawson said they should go and inspect the damage. "See what we can do."

Dust and a scorched plastic bag. Flies buzzing and alighting on the ribs of pigs. There was a thick smell of iron in the air and people were rummaging through debris, side glances from gaunt faces; some meat already packaged was able to be saved. After a point you had to look away, turn inward, but inwardness had its problems too. His thoughts went to the call he'd received from his brother Connor last night. One of those conversations that consists of a single question approached from different angles: What have you got yourself mixed up in, Dan? It was dark how far information could spread, its liquid capacity to escape you. There was a night as a boy when Connor had pissed himself. Dan remembered laughing.

They were sitting on large metal storage cylinders. Dawson today wore jeans and a T-shirt, his arms and neck thin, the neckline too baggy, a portion of his hairless chest revealed. The change of costume made him a child. He played with a bottle cap as he talked. He pulled three Polaroids from an envelope.

Dawson said a young girl had been walking home with her older brother when the device went off. It was well known, he said, that Catholic schoolkids used that side alley over there because it snaked down to the Ballymurphy. The first Polaroid of the girl was a profile shot. Nine or ten, Dan guessed. She was a strawberry blonde, smooth-skinned, with faint auburn freckles. Perhaps there was a slight twist of grief in her eye. The second picture was another profile shot, the other side of the girl's face. The eyelid here was huge, swollen. Her skin was wet and red, pitted, and the cheek seemed to want to slide into the nostril.

"Blast injuries," Dawson said. "For the sake of killing off some Catholic jobs, they spoil a little girl."

A man used his walking stick to prod a piece of meat. The meat leaked thin liquid as it moved. There was corrugated roofing leaning against a ruined wall. A priest arrived with a weeping old woman. They began to mutter Hail Marys.

The third picture was of a man in his twenties laid out on the ground with his eyes completely closed.

"Your bomb ends the other bombs, Danny."

What was England, back in the day, before they started killing for land? A tiny offshore island, Dawson said. An island sad and cold.

"Why show me these?"

"This girl's father said to me . . . he said . . . he said, is this what we get for . . ."

Could Dawson really be fighting back tears? Something unconvincing about the swift onset of grief, the glistening eyes, the bony hand that moved from his chin to his knee like an actor's sure gesture on a stage. It was left to Dan to guess at what the girl's father had said.

Is this what we get for being good parents?

Is this what we get for not rocking the boat?

Is this what we get for teaching our daughter to turn the other cheek?

Who'd bombed the meat-packing warehouse? Not him. Not Dawson. Not anyone they knew. Blame lay elsewhere, with designated enemies, so why did he feel so guilty? Anger was the emotion Dawson must have hoped to stir, but he felt no anger at all. Nothing dissolves, nothing affrights. There was the rising sense, during this moment and a dozen others like it, that Belfast's carnage stole not only the victims' lives but large parts of the witnesses too. You disintegrated into the recriminations, the headlines, the pictures. You scattered yourself into proofs, warnings, suspicions, arrests. You rode out into the dark outrage of others, saw human loss shaped towards political ends, and though you hoped for the occasional gleam of uncontaminated compassion it seemed that the world was dimming. He remembered laughing at his brother and his piss-wet bed sheets. He was struck by his father for laughing.

Second thoughts? Yes. He'd had second thoughts, third thoughts, fourth thoughts. But doubt was a disease, a sentimental curse, and in the long run his actions would save lives. A new prime minister. Politicians seeing they were vulnerable on their own doorstep. Seeing that this war could cut both ways. The beginning of the end of apathy, maybe. The start of an understanding. And if one or two innocents died, if that occurred and couldn't be helped, it would be no worse than what happened on the Falls every other day.

The truth was that on an operation you felt clean of guilt and will. It was day-to-day Belfast life that made you dirty. The nowness of being undercover, the sprint of adrenalin in your blood. It seemed to have a purifying quality. Everything you did was so silently precise, every step had to link so carefully to the next, that when you finally lay down at the end of the day your mind was a vast empty space. No doubt, no regret. All miseries for a moment receded. They made space for the satisfaction of a job well done. The gloom stayed away provided that, the next day, you got up at five to do the same again. There was something nimble about deceit. He tried and failed to remember a time when he'd felt appalled at the thought of it all. He pictured his mother going to church every Sunday, the glare of stained glass coming alive in summer, loneliness of winter dusk gone. A recent revival of her interest in religion. He wondered if she was ever praying for him. It made him sad to see how much faith she put in Jesus Christ when Christ, for his part, never seemed to have heard of her.

The Grand Hotel. You could hear in the name that a collapse was overdue. Nothing noble stays whole forever. Shakespearean, Dawson would say, though Dan preferred to see it as a simple daily process of decay: metal turns to rust; plant life turns to mulch; fixtures peel from walls and people have to die.

The official plan — documented and shared with those who needed to know — was that it would be Patrick, not Dan, checking in at reception. Patrick was insistent that, if things went wrong, he would take the prison time alone. The Brits would look at the long-delay timer. They'd know someone with experience had built it. They'd look to Paddy. Paddy would say he'd checked in alone, built it alone, planted it alone. Leaked Council papers could back him up. It's not just the Brits who can leak information. Only one head would fall.

"Then why doesn't he check in himself?" Dan said. "Why not do it in reality, instead of just on the record?"

Dawson, hearing this, had laughed. "What I described is what happens if it all goes tits up, Dan. If he gets caught. But we don't want it tits up, do we? We want it all tits down."

Patrick was a man who'd done time, a man on police files, a man masterminding a dozen other jobs right now. They couldn't risk losing their Chief Explosives Officer to the H-Blocks — not by having him walk up to the desk and ask for a room, a simple matter of admin. What if the hotel was under surveillance? Dan's face was unknown to the authorities. He could check the hotel was safe, report back overnight. Patrick could wander into the Grand the next day, straight up the stairs, mute, confident, a colleague coming to discuss a job, and join Dan in the room. If things ever went wrong Patrick would simply say, "It was me. I'm Roy Walsh. Done." The lie would sprawl out from there. People remember nothing of consequence. Hotels are a world within a world, a million strangers' names.

If this seemed to Dan like a solid explanation, it still wasn't the one he'd wanted. He wanted to hear that he'd earned the trust of the Council. The Larne–Stranraer ferry job had come off well, no civilian casualties. Three vehicles rolling in flames. Nine army men dead. A pure act of war to the extent any act of war can be that. One charge failed to do its trick, the only thing marring the op, but he was always telling them about

the fucking detonators, never did understand why they didn't seem to prize precision each time, and it was noted on the
relevant files that the defect was not his
fault. So: he was doing well. He wanted to
hear that they'd selected him purely on
merit for the important job of walking in
and asking for a room, then assisting Patrick
with the engineering upstairs.

"Tell me," Dan said during a cold moment four weeks before, "are you sacrificing
me? Is that it? No bullshit."

"Patrick has other plans," Dawson said.
"Other seaside ops in the pipeline. Think
we can use his face every time at every desk?
No. Think I came up the Lagan in a bubble?
No. He'll be there when the important
stuff's done, and on the official version
you're clean."

Ferry and then rail. Fewer security checks
than air travel. He and Dawson drank vodka
and Coke on the train down from Scotland.
They sat on Brighton Beach watching
seagulls walk and fly. And why was Dawson
accompanying him here? Scared he didn't
have the commitment needed? Other people's worries found a way towards your own.
There was a team spirit in panic. Do I have
the commitment needed? Do I really?

Schoolkids sprinting along the beach in

plimsolls. Thoughts of Physical Education, the old concrete playground at his school, wearing his gutties, running around in circles in the cold, the warming smell of vulcanised rubber — a shadow of the scent you caught in class when you erased an answer from a page. When a breeze rolled in from the Channel the gulls paused to re-arrange their wings. A better future. A fairer one. "Stand up and be counted," Mick liked to say. "Then sit down and get cunted."

You had to remember you were at war. Catholics burned out of their homes like heretics. Occupied territory. Legislative power held back. Impose a dictatorship and call it democracy. If the average Englishman knew all that was happening in Belfast they'd cheer him on, they would, they would . . .

"Before I watch you go in," Dawson said. "Before I do my disappearing act. Before all that, I want to make clear that we're clear."

"We're clear."

"Are we, though?"

"We're clear."

"One more."

Dan sighed. These team talks were de-pressing. "We're clear."

A shabby man in a red jacket walked along

the shore, crazy hair, chattering to himself, happy.

"I ask for three nights. I pay cash up front. The hotel has space for me to extend my stay. They tell me my room number. I place it in the mental floor plan. I ask for another if necessary."

"Chess."

"Snooker. I've got no time for chess."

"One move and the move after that, Danny. Something unbeatable about the sound of two balls crashing together. The last good thing, don't you think, that British Army officers invented?"

Worlds disappearing into pockets. The excitement of travel. Clean geometry, safe ballistics, each ball suspended and directed. Touch and withdraw with a thin polished cue. Resettle and aim. Dan blinked.

"I tell the receptionist —"

"In your nice rehearsed English accent."

"I tell her I'll pay cash up front."

"You run an electrical business. You've a job at the Metropole. You didn't want to stay there because you don't like to mix business and pleasure. You've added on a weekend to breathe some fine sea air, and your father always said this hotel was the-oh-most-wonderful-place."

"Don't bring him into it."

"You need stories in reserve, Daniel. Don't volunteer them. Sure. But you need them there."

"And if for some reason I've been watched. If Special Branch come down the stairs."

"Or out of the back office. Or up from the basement. Or out of the sweet eyes of a nearby old lady."

"I ask what's going on."

"You show them your surprise."

"I give them the story, and if after a certain number of hours they seem to have something on me, then I say —"

"What do you say?"

I refuse to cooperate but this does not mean I'm guilty. I would like this noted on the record. I wish to be represented by Madden and Finuncane.

"Even if they've dragged you back to Castlereagh," Dawson said. "Even if the walls are white and the door is white and the floor tiles are white and the blanket is white. You'll sit there, naked, refusing to wear their wee white pocketless clothes, won't you? And what will be in your private world?"

"My what?"

"Come on, get it on."

"I'll start to write in my head a book about glass."

"Glass!"

It was a thing. He'd read a chapter in a library book, made some notes. The way its mass production came to change the world, showing up muck and clarifying perspectives. Mirrors, monocles, windows. Light entering rooms, touching floors, illuminating enclosed spaces and framing a view. Think about that and conjugate his verbs. *Yo escapo, tu escapas.* Something about the Spanish language made him want to laugh. The laughs were few these days.

"Glass," Dawson said again, seeming to find something disturbing in the word. He tossed a stone towards a seagull. "Your gift for self-deceit, Dan. What a beauty of a gift it is. Pushing through panels to get at the plumbing behind, braiding wires between your fingers, wrapping secret little things in cellophane . . . I knew from the start that you were a distance man."

"I go to the downstairs lavatories."

Dawson leaned forward and scratched at his ankle. "Woof. Dead on. You watch out for the cat that seems to like to bite the shite out of everybody."

"Four cubicles there'll be and I'll check. If they're all vacant I go into one and flush."

"You make yourself a nice soft blanket of sound."

"Stop interrupting."

"The old sounds of the hotel's plumbing overhead."

"I unzip the bag that holds the bedlinen and towels. I smooth Vaseline through my eyelashes, my eyebrows. I use bog paper to dab away the excess gloop. I get my tub of hair gel —"

"Jimmy's Wet Look, I hope. Supporting Bobby."

"And I run some through my hair. Keep the hairs from falling out. If I need to take a crap I take a crap there, downstairs."

"Everything's evidence," Dawson said. "Remember that, eh?" He put on a David Attenborough voice. He liked to do that these days, a reference to Ancient Jones and his screaming TV. " 'Unlike the grey wolf, the spotted hyena relies more on sight than smell —' "

"Very good, Dawson. You should have your own show."

"Already have, more or less. You don't think this is *reality*, do you? Now. When you're back we burn it, Danny. The bedlinen, the clothes, even those nice new shoes. Burn it and forget and do your gardening. They'll call you an animal, but forget it all. This is more serious than other jobs you've done. This is a big wee deal for you. I want everything back, to burn. I want you back, Pinkie, for the hero's welcome."

"Pinkie?"

Dawson hurled a stone. Toddler wandering nearby. Mother shot a disapproving glance. Dawson dipped his head and said, in a low voice, ashamed for maybe the first time in his life, "Carry on then, carry on."

"I put the gloves back on and I go upstairs."

"The lift, I suppose?"

"Stairs. Put my sheets over their sheets, on the bed. Change the pillowcases."

"And you stay the night, wait for Patrick. And when Patrick's there . . ."

"Finalise plans. Fire exits. Intelligence."

"And the last day of your stay."

"We do the job."

The 555 timer.

The 470K ohm resistor.

The 5m ohm resistor.

The PNP transistor.

A poetry even to the grimmest of things. Everything given its beautiful due.

He would unwrap the slab of Semtex from its wax paper. He would pop the bath panel. He would set the timer, bury the bomb, and they'd get themselves back home.

"No."

"No?"

"When Patrick arrives your thoughts stop. You do whatever he tells you to do."

Stones protesting under Dawson's arse. Looking at Dan with new energy now. Speaking in a rich warm voice, a kind of incantation. "The Lord Chancellor," he said. "The Chancellor of the Duchy of Lancaster. The Lord Privy Seal, the Chancellor of the Exchequer, the Chief Secretary to the Treasury. The Chief Whip, the git, the slimy perv. The Minister without Portfolio. The Minister of Agriculture, Fisheries and Fuckery. The Secretaries of State for the Home Department, for Foreign and Commonwealth Affairs, for Defence, for Education and Science, for Employment, for Energy." He coughed. "For Environment." He coughed again. "For *Health.* Trade and Industry. Transport. The Prime Minister, the Deputy Prime Minister. The Secretaries of State for Scotland and for Wales and for good old Northern *Ireland.*"

They listened to the sea.

"I know. I'm ready."

"Are you, though? There might be extra days, Dan. When it's planted, we might send Paddy home, and ask you to stay extra days."

"No. Pointless."

"Info. We'll keep in touch. You've got the

pager, haven't you? If a guy's got an electrical business, he needs one of those these days."

"I'm not sleeping in that room while the thing's maturing under the bath."

"It'll be meditative."

"Dawson."

"Like a fine little cheese. But look, there might be no need. Depends on whether we need to keep an eye, find out more about the Iron Vagina's movements, make adjustments to our Plan B before you get back to Belfast, doesn't it?"

"And the Plan B would be . . ."

Dawson grinned. "You've got to picture it, Dan. The result. Focus on that. Build a little moat around yourself. Imagine this little city burning."

"It's not a city, it's a town."

"Really?"

"Yeah."

"Well then," Dawson said. "Let's call the whole thing off." He looked up at a girl in a short skirt walking by. "It's like Belfast could be, this place is. But with a better class of quim. You're rehearsed?"

"I'm prepared."

"It's a long old timer, Danny. Four weeks a-ticking. I'm trusting you and Paddy."

Dan said again that he was prepared. It

was true. He really was. He felt that if a bullet was going to hit him now it was coming from a gun that had already been fired.

But then: there's always the unexpected. That's the real juice of life. He wasn't prepared for the embarrassment and self-reproach he'd feel when, departing from the script, he'd hear himself asking the receptionist which room they would put Thatcher in. She might remember that. And he wasn't prepared, either, for the way that, looking at her skin unspoiled by make-up or injury, he'd sense within that receptionist girl not arrogance, not ignorance, not the hoped-for signs that she liked to serve the ruling elite. The way he would see only an openness to life, and a need to be liked. She would blink a lot. She would touch her hair. He liked the weary belligerence that darkened her face each time she put pen to paper. She was an uncertain and determined person, and in that uncertainty and determination he was surprised to find something he recognised. He saw it for an instant and then forgetfulness came, affording him its useful distance.

How many staff members would be there in the early hours of 12 October when the bomb, on its long delay timer, would explode under the bath? Couple of night porters, probably. That's all.

Twenty-four days,
Six hours,
Six minutes.

A poem by Daniel in the lions' den.

With Patrick in the bathroom of 629. You know the moment will stay. The blood shining in your veins, the room alive. Ready to begin your work.

The lino felt oddly liquid under his hands. The press of it through rubber gloves. Objects arranged around them looked like floating debris. Things that were shipwrecked, lost.

Patrick's gloves were old, a superstitious thing. One forefinger had split a little at the tip. Patrick had black tape wound around it. In that black tape there was truth. They had planned this, rehearsed. They were not here on impulse.

The 555 timer. The 470K ohm resistor. The 5m ohm resistor. The PNP transistor. You could convince yourself you were making any number of contraptions. The mere fact you were making anything at all helped grant you part of the distance you needed for the job. In the midst of creation you couldn't envisage the myriad ways in which your work might destroy or be destroyed. The electrolytic. The capacitor breadboard. The jumper wires, the battery.

What sometimes came to mind when he was working on a device was a day in his childhood when he'd built a bookcase. Laying out pieces of paper with his father, screws and spanners and nails, screwdrivers and hammers and cold beers with beads of coolness on the cans. It didn't matter that the bookcase, once built, held only four or five books and a load of worthless tat: candlesticks, crystal dogs, paperweights; items from his mother's collection of clutter. The point was to build the thing, to have it there in the room. The bookcase cast a shadow across the mantelpiece most mornings. It pitched photographs and wilted plants into blackness.

The 555 timer. You had to put it in its own bit of space. It had to be free to breathe, the output connection pointing to your right. You had to move it to the dead centre of your breadboard, framed by the rows of tiny holes. The advantage of building your timer device at the operation site was that you were less at risk during travel if a stop and search happened. You were carrying ordinary old wires and video-recorder parts, an electrician on a job. You could show peelers an electrician's calling card with a phone number on one side. The number would go through to an answerphone and on that answerphone you'd have Martina's voice, its staggering gravel, saying the lines are all busy, please leave a message, someone from Sunnyside Electrics will return your call. You built a history for yourself and made people a part of it. They felt involved; they started to exist within its architecture. Dawson in his more lyrical moods liked to say the world was full of people who in their daily lives looked without seeing, felt without feeling; people who wanted to be carried away by a wave of false logic more soothing than what they knew.

They're halfway through their work when Patrick whispers words about the tourists outside the hotel, men and women clutching their shiny travel guides, seeking out the Royal Pavilion, the Regency architecture, the Victorian aquariums, the Pier, the pebbled nudist area beyond Duke's Mound (had he been reading a guide himself?). Good for them, Patrick said. He envied them and wished them well. The men and women on Britain's streets were on the winning side of a war, and on the winning side you barely knew there was a war at all. You didn't spot the cracks in the pavements, the weeds in the joints, the empty ice-cream shops with damp external walls, the blistered paint, the rusted bars on basement windows, the bird shit, the rain stains, the homeless people, loss. Ten minutes passed. Fifteen.

Patrick. Patrick who, during internment, served two years in detention without trial. Patrick who'd spent some of his childhood in Norwich. Patrick who believed British cities and towns were where the war could be won. Patrick who said you don't get an enemy to listen by shouting loudly from afar; you do it by whispering in their ear. It amazed Dan how simply you could summarise a life. Never felt at home in Norwich. Came back to Belfast to help with civil rights. Got locked up. Became the Provos' best bomber. An army feeds off injustice. The stories of its soldiers are only strange when stripped of context. Build a moat around yourself.

Wasn't full-on IRA when the authorities got hold of him. Patrick had existed only at the fringes. But the aim of the arrests wasn't so much to catch IRA guys as to catch innocent people you couldn't get a proper

219

court order against. People who, being Catholics, might have information about suspected terrorists. "Take these people," Patrick said to Dan. "Shake them up. Burst an eardrum. Blacken an eye. Terrify them into staying well clear of Republicans. That's their powerful, simple idea." You killed the cause by isolation. Picked a guy up again and again until other innocent people said, "Oh, he must be involved with trouble," at which point the isolated guy was at the RUC's mercy. If he got a bullet in his head people would have a narrative to hand that explained why he deserved it.

Patrick asks what happened with your father. What happened, what are the facts? The fact your father worked eighteen hours a day in the tobacco factory. The fact he made the move into odd-jobbing around town in pursuit of greater freedom. Plumbing, wiring, checking timber for defects. Shakes, knots, resins. The hole in a brick is called a frog. Preparing the installation of lighting systems; testing equipment; balancing on scaffolding; pushing wheelbarrows along planks; swearing like he was supposed to swear, a manufactured vulgarity that cost him a little of who he was. He was doing whatever he could to get by and to purchase that shabby family home. Someone decided to toss a brick at his head. His eyes became mere things, marbles. A son sees that and what does he do? Tidies his talents into a different channel. There's more to say but what's the point in saying it, in going on and on when life itself can be so brutally abbreviated? A random act. Can't even pick a culprit. System itself is bad. Take apart the system. Dan imagined the tourists outside the hotel coming into this bathroom and gathering around, cameras suspended from treated strings around their necks, special shapeless walking shoes in creative shades of beige, watching him make the timer for this bomb. He imagined them saying, Ah, he wouldn't have done it if his daddy hadn't died like he did. Might as well say he wouldn't have done it if he hadn't been born. All of us love a single motivation. Saves us from thinking too hard.

Moving pieces around. Keeping the gloves pulled high around the wrists. Fingertips feeling no slackness.

You had to attach your input leads to the left flank of the board. The intention wasn't to connect them, just to keep the lead wires in place. You had to thread the lead wires into a chosen hole near the input. You needed to connect the wire lead from the RST of your 555 to the board, nice and slow, and then you had to use your jumper leads to connect up the two holes that you'd used to attach the RST and input. You were creating a circuit path with these basic tools, something that connected the pieces, the world shrinking around you to the size of a smoke ring, forgetting that this floor was a bathroom floor, a bathroom floor in an expensive hotel on the south coast of England, a hotel where the Tories would stay for their party conference in three and a half weeks' time. Form a bridge. Form a link. Get the body of the resistor aiming upward, a needle on a compass pointing north.

■ ■ ■ ■

THREE:
DEPARTMENT OF
HEARTS

1984

■ ■ ■ ■

1

People say drugs cause dreams, but during his first twenty-four hours in hospital it was mostly memories that came. People and scenes washed in and washed out, a structure stolen from the sea, and a doctor playing with a twenty-pence piece began offering high-speed advice. Monitoring, lifestyle, myocardial. Nurse, perhaps a cappuccino please? A myocardial infarction, the doctor said, using his two fists to demonstrate the difference between myocardial and some other cardial, saying "pop," saying a heart really looks like a fist covered in blood, saying smoking and fatty foods, saying any recent uncommon exertion, saying physical or mental stresses or family problems, saying in forty-five minutes we're going to clear that artery of yours, don't try and say too much in the meantime.

There would be a little screen.

Like a TV screen?

Yes, Mr. Finch, black-and-white screen in the theatre.

Call me Moose.

Mousse? As in the dessert?

As in the animal. Animal.

Are you amenable to students being present to observe? Three, four. Picture of a little bonsai tree, really. One little twig shape lengthening, that's all. But they'll learn so much from you, they will. Young. Doing their degrees. Going to be fine. Futures ahead of them. Simple procedure. Done it a hundred times. Futures. That and a few days in bed and you'll be out of here. The rest is really up to you.

His mother telling him at the wedding, and before the wedding, that he was making a mistake. Didn't listen. Didn't worry. There was something reassuring about marrying a woman your mother wasn't convinced by. It underlined to you the fact that you weren't marrying your mother.

Mr. Waldman's father-of-the-bride speech had contained only one joke — good to get Viv off my hands! — but Moose in his groom speech had the audience roaring, joke after joke about things Viv did and didn't do, and when he sat down Viv put her hand on his wrist. He thought, She's proud of me, that was a good speech, I worked so hard on that speech to make her proud. In the corridor five minutes later she slapped his face. "Performance!" she said.

"What?"

"Performance!"

He didn't understand the accusation. She refused to elaborate. If he was performing he was performing for her, for her friends, for a family from whom he'd always wanted more love than he got. It was the first of many times he'd see her pretty neck go blotchy with rage. Not the best of starts. She cried when they drunkenly fucked that night, a bed covered with itchy red petals. He lay awake thinking of words that rhymed with wedding. He thought of shredding. Maybe dreading. Spreading. At times he lamented the fact he'd been born with a somewhat unsubtle mind.

Where was the paramedic with the big blurry nose? Where was Potato the Dog? People so easily swam in and out of your life.

The theatre. Mr. Marshall pulling his mask to one side. Mr. Marshall saying, "You're about to feel much better."

His tongue feeling clean. A huge weight lifted from his chest. But weak, still weak, the white lights of the theatre. Bluish smocks and masks. The dreamy creamy space emptying out. Performance. Two students who'd observed the whole thing standing in the corner, solemn, waiting to be told what to do. A distant nurse saying, "The boy said he fell on it in the bathroom!" Distant people laughing. Water. A plastic cup. Performance. Most delicious water he'd ever tasted. Light dimming and his daughter, sleep.

Growing up in Brighton, not yet known as Moose, he'd been told on many hundreds of occasions that he was destined for great things. This seemed like good news. He chose to believe it. He was good-looking, bright, popular, sporty. The idea that his heart would one day falter? That he would keel over before achieving what he wanted to achieve? Ridiculous. Absurd. As crazy as thinking life itself would one day stop shaping itself, however crudely, around his needs and wants. As unimaginable as the idea that he'd one day have such a precocious ear for failure that he'd mishear almost everything else. His heart was healthy, its welfare was secure, its beat was steady and vital and it was — like him — carefully contained, unbothered by the world, a private preciously effective thing that functioned without thought or doubt. Picturing his knowledge-less boyhood self now, he couldn't help but laugh. The laughing hurt him even more than sighing did. The pain brought him briefly out of a thick half-sleep and made him ask, "Is my daughter still here?" A nurse wheeling him along a corridor told him to try closing his eyes.

His supposed destiny as one of life's trailblazers took strength from all the occasions when kids his own age, and a healthy few dozen from the years above, chanted his name from the sidelines at football games. It took strength from the huddle of parents who often invited him around for tea after he'd hit a hundred runs or taken five quick wickets. It took strength from the local newspapermen — doughy, tired, deprived of light — who vied to steal from him some quick remark or meaningful reflection on the nature of Talent every time he won (aged 14, 15, 16 and 17) the 200 metres and 400 and 800 metres in the South-East of England Regional Schools' Junior Athletics Championships. And it took strength (how could it not?) from seeing his own face in the *Argus* under the unforgettable headline "BEST YOUNG SPORTSMAN BRIGHTON'S EVER SEEN."

There was a song certain girls sang while watching him take his shabby grammar school to the National Championships Finals in three different sports. It was a simple song, not much imagination to it, and it followed the tune of Fats Domino's "Ain't That a Shame." "Ain't That The Finch" they'd cry after the ball had left his boot and crashed past the keeper; "Ain't That The Finch." Sometimes he'd hear a depthless, muzak version of the same anthem in the playground, walking between buildings, crossing the concrete, pausing to pull up his socks. He'd look up and see girls from the school opposite, fingers clawed into the fence. They were singing to him, *serenading* him, fighting off impending fits of giggles. Once they recovered from these giggles one of them would generally ask if he was going to be at the Electric House come Friday. Demonstrating the unflustered ease that only the most adored of boys could afford, untouched by the super-abundance of love which met his every move, he looked at them and unleashed one of his trademark Shrugging Smiles. A good-natured smile. An excellent shrug. "Maybe," he'd say.

They nodded slowly, like he'd told them the future.

The Electric House was a local landmark around which the teen population of Brighton carried out the deadly serious business of hanging around. They hung around chatting. They hung around drinking. They hung around practising their kissing. They spent a lot of time pretending to inhale, or coughing. If you had a blind date with a girl they'd arrange to meet you at the Electric and it was a tradition of the time that they'd tell you the exact section of pavement on which you should stand at the designated hour, often referencing chalk marks set down specifically for that purpose: an "X" or an intimidating tadpole squiggle. Seldom did they keep him waiting long. It was a beautiful thing: his luck, his ability; the way the world moved to his tune.

On Christmas Eve, behind the changing rooms of the big drained Black Rock swimming pool, Angela Hebbethwaite opens her coat, a coat with shoulders covered in snow, and lifts up her several jumpers, permitting him to touch her breast. The left one, the soft floury texture of it. With wordless joy he fondles. The best Christmas present he's ever had.

"I'm going to be the next Don Revie," he tells Angela.

"I believe in you," she says. "You're quite tall."

She tucks her boob back into her bra. A

drunk Santa staggers past. They listen to Santa having a wee against the wall.

At this time there were definitely one or two friends and family members who predicted his downfall. It was said that by pursuing so many different sports to County level, then England Under 16 level, he would sacrifice his studies. It was also said by his soon-to-die Auntie Janet (appendix, Wandsworth) that it was "an inevitability" that once The Finch hit sixteen the extraordinary upward curve of athletic achievement that had marked his life to date would begin to level off. Even his mother appeared ready to accept elements of this hypothesis. With her constant curbing of expectations and reminders that "life follows complex patterns," she seemed to agree that a boy as bafflingly popular and successful as her son would, at some point on the perilous path to adulthood, blink and lose his way. If his father pushed her to give reasons for this lack of faith, she sometimes cited, with the stiff air of someone called to give evidence, Philip's occasional tendency to speak of himself in the third person.

The Finch was just a persona, a character other people had made up. It saddened him that his mother didn't seem to understand.

In response to what he couldn't help but

see as doom-mongering by the senior fe-
males in his family, he did reasonably well
in most of his exams. It was essays that were
his undoing, but he got extra help from
Miss House and Mr. Phillips in English and
History. He worked hard — hard-*ish* — and
was in the unusual position of being considered a role model by both pupils and teach-
ers, so it was perhaps no surprise when he
was appointed, following an internal school
process which he liked to think of as demo-
cratic, as Head Prefect. People told him he
fulfilled the role with composure, style and
a stringent sense of fairness, and he
shrugged off their praise, neither embold-
ened nor embarrassed, his only concession
to immodesty being his readiness to make a
detailed mental note of their words, remembering certain shapely turns of phrase or
terms of praise in case they came in handy
at a later date. A job application. A self-
awareness test. Stuff like that.

His dad was a local postman of nine years'
experience, a man with a tendency to sweat
in all seasons, and having his son appointed
to the role of Head Prefect seemed to give
him more vicarious pleasure than any of the
pursuits on track and field ever had. This
was confusing, given how much emphasis
the family had previously placed on sport.

Soon after the prefect appointment letter from the headmaster arrived he glimpsed, one night, through a crack in the kitchen door, his father sitting at the scuffed pine table on which they always ate their family meals. The memory of this moment is clear even through the veil of drugs. Everything quiet and well lit. His father alone and holding the document in both hands. His lips were moving minutely as he studied it.

Several days later, The Finch's father was chatting to the Carrs. The Carrs were neighbours with whom the Finch family shared a small front garden, a love of films, and absolutely nothing else. On this particular day, as The Finch and his father stood in the driveway and Mrs. Carr clutched her garden shears, Mr. Carr asked Mr. Finch what being Head Prefect at a school like Varndean actually involved. It was astonishing to witness the manner in which his father — known throughout the village as being punctual and taciturn — responded to this question. He stood tall. He draped one warm arm across his boy's shoulders. He relayed, with faultless fluency, the entire inventory of responsibilities which came with the role. He had memorised the letter verbatim.

Did they have money? Not much, not

really, but always a penny for an iced bun. You could get it delivered with the milk each morning. He was never one of the unwashed kids at school who wore plimsolls even in winter or was always being sent to the nit nurse under suspicion of infestation. Sunday mornings at the Sunday school, drawing miracles and parables on unevenly sized pieces of paper, wondering what the point of prayer was, and then there would be home-made lemonade in the church hall, bitter zest that clung to your gums, and wonderfully involved periods of paper-aeroplane construction, games that made all the worship stuff worthwhile, and after that everyone would stop at the old air-raid shelters on the way home, jumping off them in increasingly complex ways, touching ankles twice or thrice, cutting their hands and grazing their knees, all to summon some brief blaze of adrenalin to resurrect their lives from the stupor Father Simon's words had induced. On one such air-raid-shelter stunt he landed awkwardly, feeling the shock that normally crept up his shins advancing further than before, all the way up to his right knee. Pain grinding there. Pain sending him home in stages, limping and pausing, limping and blinking, limping and hoping he'd done himself no permanent harm.

Twinges of pain would resurface when, in his final summer at the school, he donned the Varndean athletics vest for the very last time — but only on the home straight, and it was nothing a post-race bag of ice could not correct. He still won the 200 by a clear two seconds.

His cousin Elizabeth was into gymnastics. Seeing her do a cartwheel during the family performance segment of Christmas Day celebrations, he asked his parents if he could join one of her classes. His father and mother discussed this over subsequent weeks and then informed him that they loved him unconditionally, regardless of whatever his preferences might be. What exactly did they mean? He could go to gymnastics, yes.

Gymnastics made him feel whole in a way that all the other sports he was pursuing didn't. It tightened his arms and back, gripped his stomach muscles. In mid-air every part of him felt hard. He was something cleverly put together, complete. His coach told him to start swimming twice a week as a way to improve core strength.

One winter's morning when he was nineteen and still living at home, deciding what to do with the rest of his life, or deciding at what point he had better decide it, he took a bus to a pool a few miles away with the intention of swimming his usual lengths. When he got there, he was told he'd have to wait until eleven. The pool was being used by the Brighton & Hove High Dive Club. From a café on the second floor of the leisure centre building he watched the training down below. A man in suffocating swimming trunks teetered on the edge of an absurdly high platform. He flipped himself into the air and twisted and flipped again. The certainty of the process. The fearlessness. Gymnastics with higher stakes. Masculinity and daring. The adoring glances of girls.

Only one swimsuited witness seemed immune to the exhilaration. She was sitting on a fold-out chair by the pool's edge. The tiled floor around her was splodged with coloured towels. She had her arms crossed, her legs crossed, and her skin from this distance looked cold but lively, shimmering, a source of cool light, all but a few dark hairs tucked under a rubber cap. She had a graceful nose, long shins. A few years older than him? The training session seemed to be wrapping up. Time to hurry downstairs.

Her toenails were painted green. She took

a pair of glasses from on top of a towel. Wearing these massive black frames, and still also wearing her swimming cap, she looked like some kind of exotic insect, or a librarian from the future. This was Viv, his eventual wife. She had no head for heights, she'd later say. She was only there to support a boyfriend. Didn't seem at all fussed that the cap and glasses made her look uncool. Therefore, clearly, she was cool. She was the coolest person he'd seen. Lack of self-awareness has its own perfect appeal.

Those downturned lips, though. The unmoving mouth. He didn't consider back then that a sullen look might be the sign of a sullen person, or that she might be a person whose defining characteristic was sullenness, or that this alluring young woman's inner tonnage of glum might be sufficient to send her sinking, throughout her twenties and thirties, into hot black holes of depression. Or — here was an idea — he *did* consider all this. It was exactly what drew him to her.

He stopped staring. Located a man in a tracksuit who was issuing directions. Said to him: teach me how to do this. Thought to himself: forget the gymnastics, forget the football, forget the possible trial for Surrey CC. Probably he was realising, at this time, that he wasn't getting significantly better at these sports. He'd improved at a faster rate than his peers but had then begun to plateau. He was living in a town where he was once revered, and was now well liked, and where he feared he would soon be simply recognised. He needed a new challenge.

The decision not to go to university. It took a while to begin to regret it, and to feel bitter about his parents discouraging him. Having not been to university themselves — having known no one except Fancy Harry who had — they were suspicious of what three years of no income might achieve. They pushed him to accept an offer of a teaching job at Varndean. Headmaster Perkins had included within this offer — Maths for the younger pupils, Physical Education for the seniors — a harrowingly sensible-sounding line: "It's always prudent to have a fall-back plan." No mention was made of the risk factor inherent in this philosophy. A person with a fall-back plan is actually pretty likely to fall back on it.

Years later, a scrapbook in one of his mother's cupboards. It was with a smile that he located the article he remembered so well from his youth, the one with the headline "BEST YOUNG SPORTSMAN BRIGHTON'S EVER SEEN." But looking at it now, wrinkled and yellowed, he saw that there was a question mark after the "SEEN." And how had he missed it, this question mark? What sort of mind failed to spot the rising intonation, the air of qualification, the tentativeness of the whole headline? A punctuation mark, you told yourself. Just a way to end a sentence.

When he looked at the journalist's name it was Daniel Rhoden, a family friend. The only quoted expert was his cousin Billy, a Varndean alumnus who came back to coach hockey each Easter term. Billy whose desire to make a pleasing impression was such that he shaved twice a day until he died at thirty-nine, knocked off his bicycle in some little-visited part of Kent. The experience of seeing this article, of pitting remembered reality against its frozen proof, was a slow electric shock for Moose. The jitters kept going for months.

There are times when your own childhood has the gimcrack feel of a tale told to friends over ale. When it feels like a bar in an old hotel, no television playing, no radio playing, a space that exists outside of events. Crouching before that dusty cupboard, looking at that scrapbook, he wanted desperately to know which page of the *Argus* the article had been printed on, and what the other pieces in the newspaper that day might have had to say, but the information he needed had been trimmed away. Context had gone in the kitchen bin.

2

Inside the Royal Sussex the floor was fiercely mopped. A smell of disinfectant rose up around her. She was back in Ward 3 but couldn't see him. Possibly he'd been moved into a private room? The nurse over there would know, but she was busy being screamed at by a guy in a pinstriped jacket. As the man's face became a plum that ripened and promised to rot the nurse stood there nodding, smiling, head inclined to the side, as if researching an essay on rage.

When the man was out of energy Freya approached the nurse. She was taken to a room that was white and lacking in clutter, a massive improvement on the ward. Everything had a clean, tense neatness — the symmetry of the stacked-up magazines, the flowers sprouting stiffly from their vase, the untouched tissues in their perfect yellow box. By far the worst-looking thing was her father. His skin was as bloodless as his last cigarette and one apparent side effect of the heart attack, unmentioned in the Coldean Library's medical books, was how it worsened a person's snoring. She listened in appalled amazement as a ten-second impression of a hay-fever-suffering pug segued into the slow sound of two wounded warthogs making love. She popped a fresh piece of Hubba in her mouth, wished she'd brought her Walkman and a few of her tapes, and at that moment, a bit shaky, needing sugar, feeling warm, thinking there must at least be a Coke machine somewhere — the NHS should surely invest in machines — she swivelled on her heel and saw, too late, a guy skidding around a corner wall with white coat-tails flapping in his wake. His brown eyes came to a halt an inch or two from her face. She thought of maple syrup.

"Right," he said. "I was just checking on the patient. Thought I might have heard a cry for help."

"That's just his snoring, I think."

"Really?"

"Yeah."

The doctor — was he old enough to be a proper doctor? — tilted his head to listen. "And you would be . . ."

"Daughter."

He took a step back. His face was stubbly

and sun-kissed, shaped by flattering shadows. "Pleased to meet you then," he said. "I'm Dr. Haswell."

"Seriously?"

"Seriously."

Haswell. She was impressed. It rang so rhythmically on the ear, was agreeable and grateful in equal measure, sounded wholesome and hopeful. Finch, by contrast, suffered from its extreme brevity and associations with seed-eating. For a long while she'd had a feeling that, in some distant language, her surname meant vomit or saucepan.

The nurse who'd suffered the shouting bout was coming back down the corridor. As she passed Dr. Haswell she said, "Too young."

"What?"

"Coffee, right?"

"Hot water and lemon," he said.

"Black coffee," she sang.

"Hot water and lemon."

"With milk, then."

"Can you stand it," Dr. Haswell said, "if I just have water and lemon?"

"Tea," the nurse said with a skimpy smile and promptly disappeared.

"Sorry," he said. "It's just — Monica, the ward nurse. She's nuts, that's all."

"Pretty."

"Do you think?"

"Yeah," she said, and coughed to let him know that the subject was now closed. "So, is he OK?"

"Oh, she's fine. When I said nuts —"

"*He.* My dad."

"Ah, yes." Standing tall Dr. Haswell offered a friendly frown and proceeded to pinch the bridge of his nose. "Mr. Marshall got that artery unblocked, as you know. I'm not expecting any major problems."

"How come he's a mister rather than a doctor?"

"Marshall?" Dr. Haswell checked over his shoulder, then fell into a whisper. "Power. No longer needs it. But your dad's comfortable, currently."

"Why did he get moved off the ward?"

"He's lucky. It's not a reflection of medical needs, as such. Hotelier, right?"

She nodded. The lighting in this corridor was weirdly unrelenting.

She'd been in the ward late last night. Her father had been sitting up after the operation, the operation that everyone here seemed to prefer calling a "procedure," but conversation had come only in woozy bursts. Waking this morning she'd felt a shadow of that post-exams feeling — empty,

achey, somehow caught in an anticlimax —
and also a small sense of wonder. It seemed
amazing to her that a whole week behind
the reception desk at the Grand could
contain so few achievements when, here in
the hospital, in two hours flat, a clogged
heart could be unclogged.

"Complications," Dr. Haswell was saying
now. "That's the main thing to watch out
for. That and instilling a healthier lifestyle.
The heart's a tricky muscle." He paused for
a moment and his brows became depressed.
"We need to keep an eye on things, but a
couple of days will be fine, I should think,
and your father really is in the best possible
hands."

Freya watched as Dr. Haswell, clipboard
tucked under one arm, glanced down at his
own palms. She allowed herself a moment
of quiet outrage at his arrogance. Someone
needed to tell him, without unnecessary offence, that Brighton was unlikely to play
home to the medical profession's best possible hands. That it was, in fact, unlikely to
play home to the best possible anything.
That *his* hands, moreover, were not scuffed
enough, not torn at by sufficient experience,
to be classifiable as Best Possible or even
Best-in-Breed. How old was he? Mid-
twenties? Straight out of medical school,

even. But it was true too, that despite his youthful looks Dr. Haswell gave off an aura of expertise. There was something about the set of his forehead, about the sophisticated mahogany furniture of his face, that suggested cloistered learning. Medical knowledge, definitely, but also other areas Freya had little experience of. Skiing. Multiple gym memberships. Birthrights, etc.

"Your dad said you've recently been celebrating some great exam results? Sounds like congratulations are in order." He glanced down at her bare legs, as if these were owed the better part of the commendation. "With A levels like that you could pursue medicine, I suppose."

"Not really," Freya said.

"No?"

"Didn't do sciences."

"Ah," the doctor said. "Yes, you need to be able to do the maths . . . Your father's already been mentioning some VIPs the hotel is hosting in a couple of weeks. Something to aim for is always good. Hollywood types, I expect?"

"Politicians."

"Ah, right . . . The conference?"

"Yeah."

"Well, he's got age on his side."

"Has he?"

247

"He's not even middle-aged yet, not really."

She thought about this. "He's forty-five."

Dr. Haswell tapped his clipboard. "Yes, exactly."

She popped another piece of Hubba into her mouth. Her father's snores stopped and started again. "How long does the average man live to?"

"The average? I forget. In the UK, seventy-seven or seventy-six, maybe."

"He's over halfway then," she said.

"In a sense."

"He's very much in the middle of his ultimate age, in all senses. Fast approaching the final third, in fact."

"Well —"

"Listen, Anthony," she said, and watched his brown eyes go wide. It was a good trick. People always forgot they were wearing name badges. It was the same at corporate functions at the Grand. "I'm just doing the maths."

Anthony Haswell grinned and looked away, his eyes tracking back to her with cautious warmth, and there came from inside the room a groan combined with a creak. "Welcome," her father said, "to the not-so-grand hotel." You could tell he'd been waiting for a chance to use the line.

■ ■ ■ ■

Wandering around the Grand in a dark suit and clean white shirt, making mediocre jokes and taking control of minor crises, her father could still look handsome. In here, under bright lights, wearing a tight short-sleeved tunic thing that appeared to be made of paper, he looked old. For how long had his eyes looked this grey? When had his ears become fluffy? Pale, pale. She could smell fag smoke on his skin as he beckoned her forward for a kiss. His lips were cold on her cheek.

She thought it best to hold his hand. A big hand, full of rough knuckles and veins, klutzy as a crab. She held it. Holding her dad's hand felt weird. She slipped from his grip and poured him some water. Her leg was jigging up and down, no reason.

"So how come you look like a dead person?" she said.

He sighed and closed his eyes. "Frey, you get it from your mother."

"What?"

"Blunt when nervous. A reluctance to beat around the bush."

"The only thing."

"What is?"

"It's the only thing I get from her."

He coughed and winced. The wince was sizeable but the cough was small, way short of a proper hack, a kind of diet cough that seemed to admit he wasn't as good at getting stuff out of his throat as he was at throwing stuff in. Last night she'd put a toothbrush in her mouth and cried. She'd felt angry with him, and sorry for him, and then scared and confused, and now she was a bit defiant again, or an aimless combination of everything.

"Your mother said once, after half a lifetime of accusing me of beating around the bush, and urging me to cut to the chase, that she'd discovered from a fellow Linguistics lecturer, an Australian guy, that it was actually, etymologically speaking, essential to do one before the other."

She looked at him.

"In bird hunts. It was important for participants to first beat around the bushes. Because only then could other participants cut to the chase, which meant to catch the quarry in nets. Something like that, anyway."

"Right."

"Beating *about* the bush is of course the more popular variant now."

"If I admit that this is gripping, can we talk about your health?"

A seagull squawked outside and they both looked up, with curious choreography, at the room's tiny window. The sun, not knowing what was appropriate, had risen this morning as usual. The weather couldn't last. The stinging drizzle and leaping foam would return, people hunkering down into the collars of their coats, that special British wince reserved for walking in the rain. A gold test tube of light extended from the sill to a far corner of the floor. Freya felt a little hot, a little woozy. She crossed and recrossed her legs, blew upward at her hair. A kid rode past the window on a bike, no hands. A blur of wheels, the *click-click-click* of Spokey Dokeys.

"So," she said. "I mean, what's the situation?" Information, please. Information.

He shifted a little in the bed. "Everyone has off days, Frey. I'm already feeling better. Aspirin, it turns out, is a lifesaver. Aspirin! It can't be bad if the thing they're giving me now is aspirin. The procedure —"

"The operation."

"Was a success."

There was silence for a while. The word "success" seemed to take his thoughts off on a tangent.

She waited and then said, "Dad?"

"Yeah?"

"You know Grandad? Your dad?"

"Used to," he said, smiling weakly again.

"Am I right in thinking . . . ?"

He hesitated. "Heart attacks are very common things, Frey. You've got to die of something." He scratched his head. "Poor choice of words."

"Right."

"But he was — it was a different situation."

They sat in silence.

Ordinarily her father could talk at length about any number of subjects. His main complaint over the last few years was *her* silence, the more refined allegation being that when he asked her about herself — on the way home from school, over breakfast, on the drive to work — she became what he called an elective mute. What he didn't realise was that after school she was all talked out, and in the mornings she was deliriously tired. They were completely the worst times of day to catch her.

He was particularly obsessed, recently, with the idea that she should go to university. This despite him being a living example of the fact university wasn't everything. He'd never got a degree, but alongside his diving and all those random jobs he used to do, teaching and tutoring and dive-coaching and the extra money from moonlighting as a concierge in that New York hotel, he'd managed to listen to radio programmes about almost everything. He was, for her, a bearer of information: the next exhibition at the Booth Museum, upcoming rates at rival hotels like the Metropole. When he was healthy his blue eyes shone. Those eyes *knew* things, knew and knew and knew. He could fix a car and unblock a pipe, he could say "You're welcome" in Swahili and "Train station" in Mandarin, he could recite passages from that *Tristram Shandy* book her mother had given him in a special edition. He could reel off the first 200 digits of pi. He didn't seem to see any value in these abilities, but Freya did. She was, though she'd never dream of saying it out loud, impressed by him. And if in life he'd failed to live up to the expectations he'd had of himself, which was what her mother always described as Your Father's Big Problem, then it seemed to her that those failures related to the real world, not to his education, and therefore fell short of proving that university was worth doing. He'd never actually been to China, or places where they spoke Swahili. He never made it past class six of a language course. You couldn't always say that he was good at finishing things.

Around two-thirds of the way through executing a long-cherished plan he appeared to get massively bored. He'd begin unblocking a pipe on floor four of the Grand — save the hotel some money on a plumber — and then, when an extra hour of work would have completed the job, he'd tire of the task and call a plumber. He'd buy himself some discount jogging gear for Christmas, spend New Year's morning doing pre-run stretches, and then make himself a coffee and act like the run was done. He never seemed apathetic about a thing until the exact point at which he was apathetic, and then the thing was dead to him forever.

"They're running some further checks on my heart," he said. A quick spurt of words like he was overcoming a stutter.

"I know."

"OK."

"OK."

"OK."

It was going to be OK, wasn't it? She looked at him.

There'd been a girl in History who'd overcome a stutter. They'd made a thing of it at school assembly last December, and when she got up to give her speech about overcoming a stutter, guess what? Yep. Awful awful. It was so awful Freya had given her a bar of chocolate afterwards, a bar of the size you usually only find in airports. Giant Toblerone. "Snow-Capped" limited edition. The sharp peaks were probably not that good for the roof of her mouth (the roof of the mouth and the tongue's relationship to it were apparently key to the overcoming), but it was a gift and, like all gifts, it was the thought that counted, and failing that the resale value. The playground at Blatchington Mill was a vast black market: caffeine pills, candy sticks.

She asked him if it was still serious. He said probably not. She asked him whether he'd have to have another operation after the remaining tests. He said they'd know more in a couple of days.

"Even if they do their tricks with another artery," he said. "Even then, it's no major thing. It's like clearing leaves from a gutter, a different gutter."

"So your veins are gutters, in this analogy."

He pursed his lips. "It's like fixing a bit of wiring, Frey."

"Wiring, though — it's complex."

"You're thinking of the Napoleon Suite. That was down to a bad electrician."

"What if *these* electricians are bad?"

"Who?"

"The doctors."

He seemed to consider this closely. "They're expensively educated."

"How can you tell?"

"Their vowels. Their assumptions."

"This is bad. This is, I mean, heart attack, I mean — fucking hell."

"Appears I may have eaten a few too many fatty foods," he said.

"Yeah, no shit."

"No," he said, "the digestive system is working well."

"You're not funny, Dad."

"You're not funny either, daughter."

They went on like this for a while, touching on the dangers of Mrs. Peachsmith's driving (she'd given Freya a lift here last night) and whether it was possible to blame his current health on the stress induced by Lady Di's abuses of refuse-collection etiquette. Di lived opposite. She'd been putting her bin bags on the Finch household's section of pavement each Tuesday. Once or twice under cover of night Moose had moved them back to their proper place with notes attached. Last week a response had arrived taped to the windscreen of his Škoda: *This car belongs to a very silly man.*

She asked him if the nurses were treating him well. He said yes, of course, NHS, brilliant brilliant. They'd given him this amazing little room to recuperate in. Loads of privacy. It was a word he kept using: privacy. She thought of Susie and her lectures on private life vs public life, apathy vs activism, on terrorist attacks and the distinction between victim and witness and culprit, and her dad said with fake cheeriness that there was a TV lounge somewhere down the corridor. Strictly, this wing was probably for patients with unaffordable private health plans. Lucky.

"How did you get that Marshall guy to move you here?"

"There are various ways to get an upgrade, Frey. As a front-desker you should know that."

"Shouting?"

"Come on. Shouting sometimes works, fine, but then the front-desker resents you, don't they? Items like your fox drape may go missing . . . Anyway, saying nothing — that never works. And being quietly rude is the worst of both worlds. Best method?" He shifted in the bed and winced. "You tell the person in charge that you appreciate how busy they are, but you'd be hugely grateful for anything they could do for you, and then you give them a tip."

"You gave the doctor a *tip*?" She was a

little bit appalled and a little bit impressed.

"Voucher," he said, yawning. "Twenty-five per cent off doubles. Keep some in my wallet at all times. Only applicable during low season, of course."

"No one's ever given me a tip."

"No?"

"Well, a couple of times. And you feel . . . I mean . . ."

"I feel right as rain," he said, and a mean desperation rose up in Freya. Please, she thought. Please do not go on to explain my mother's investigations into that phrase. She was with another man now, her mother. Back in London it seemed. Postcards sometimes came stamped from "Mount Pleasant," which was almost funny given how mean she could be.

"Well" — might as well lie — "you're looking much better than yesterday, anyway."

"Yeah?" He nodded. "That's good. Really good. Marina said I looked washed out. That I looked blank."

"Blanco," Freya said.

"Ahhh," he replied, winding up into his mock-Mediterranean accent, "so you speaka da Spanish?"

"If you're going to travel around somewhere you've to make an effort, haven't you?"

He looked defeated by this, shoulders sagging around his breastbone like a tent around a pole. Duke of Edinburgh expedition. Hills, winds . . .

"Had a few new guests arrive," she said.

His features lifted a little. "Who?"

"A couple of people."

"Good. That's very good."

"Someone on crutches. I put him in the old RAF guy's room. He finally checked out."

"As in?"

"As in he checked out. Paid his bill. Went to Worthing."

" 'Went to Worthing' would make a pretty good metaphor, actually."

"For a lawn bowls competition, he said. Televised. Does that happen?"

"Only on earth."

"Also a couple of honeymooners."

"Rose petals?"

"Already arranged."

"The non-itchy ones. The fake whatsit ones."

"Yep."

"What about the little strawberries in chocolate tuxedos?"

She stared at him.

"Thatcher won't even turn up," she said. "That's my bet. She'll have booked the Metropole too, kept her options open."

Moose gave her a stony look and she felt a prickle of guilt. Why the need to jab at him, even now? Why did she feel, at some level, *annoyed* that he was ill?

"All I meant was, her plans must change all the time. So you shouldn't get your hopes up, right? She could still end up in the Metropole again, so I'm just saying don't rush your . . ." What was the word? "Your recovery."

Her dad's stony look had become his Special Stare. It was the stare he used to give her when, hearing her returning from one of her nights out with Sarah or Susie, he'd wake in his armchair and ask her into the living room for "a chat." She'd walk through the door and sit down next to him, narrowing all her remaining energy, all her concentration, into making short sober sentences that corrected the boozy drag in her voice.

She got up and moved to the end of the bed, smoothing out a blanket. She remembered the grapes. "Here you go," she said. "This is, you know, supposed to be the sort of thing that helps."

"Thank you. That's very . . . thank you, Frey."

He plucked some grapes and held them cupped in his right hand. Reached for his water glass with his left. After a sip of water he began to wrinkle his nose. She leaned forward and scratched it for him.

"They're not bad, are they? Did you buy them with your own money?"

She shrugged. "They're grapes." A woman walked by in excellent boots.

"Any nuts?"

"No way. Is there healthy stuff you need?"

"I'd be interested in receiving some HP Sauce, Frey. Really interested. The food here could do, between you and me, with . . . something."

"Brown sauce is quite vinegary. You'd be better off eating the hospital food on its own, and then snacking on fruit or whatever."

"Vinegar is not the reason I'm in here," he said. "Vinegar is innocent." He plucked another grape and inspected it sadly, as if somewhere, engraved on its thin shiny skin, were the secrets to a healthy life. "Make sure you don't take on any extra shifts. Really, you don't even need to do your own shifts. Everyone would understand."

"Act normal, you said."

"I've been telling Marina to run the show. And maybe our esteemed General Manager will also show his face. Is he still on the jam-tasting trip to Yorkshire? He really is winding down. Happens when people are on their way out."

"I think he's doing that training series at the other hotels. Then New York to make links with the high-end travel agents there, is what John said."

"Oh."

"Yeah."

"New York."

"Yeah."

"Maybe we should move back there, Frey."

"Maybe you should stop smoking," she said.

He chewed. "I'll be out of here in a few days. This Thatcher visit's going to —"

"The promotion, yeah."

"Soon enough you'll be in Spain, eating tapas and swigging sangria, busily not-talking to boys. I might join you. I might have my pick of hotel offers in a year or two. Manage a famous one, maybe, in . . . I think I fancy Madrid. Marina can suggest places. I think one of her sisters lives in Madrid. If you do Spanish at uni, they probably offer a year abroad. Food for thought." After this speech his body slipped downward in stages and his eyelids began to droop.

Beyond a wall someone retched. Down the corridor a woman wailed. This place was a department store for sadness.

"I'll come back tonight."

"Tonight? Maybe spare pyjamas."

"OK."

"OK then."

"Cool, bye."

She kissed his cheek. Cool was a word she never, ever used.

Outside, a clarifying knowledge came over Freya: I am well, I am young, I am fine. Her relief for a moment overpowered her concern. The air was fresh; she was free. A cat walking along a wall. Pausing and diving down. You could hear in the distance tiny wavelets rushing in.

Only when she reached the corner shop and bought a drink did tears come again. Stupid. He was fine. She twisted the ring-pull off the can.

She passed the White IIart pub, the arm of the capital "H" crushed by last year's snows. She remembered her first ever kiss, the fake ID she'd had in her hand, Tom Williams's tongue in her mouth, the convivial saltiness of it, the unwelcome touching of her bum, and the unexpected moment a month ago, at a posh dinner to which all hotel staff had been invited, when she'd tried an oyster for the very first time and found that she fleetingly missed him.

On the pavement outside Amadeo's Susie was standing with two girls and a guy. Freya slowed and tried to find a way to — No, too late to cross the road.

"Well," Susie said. "Look who it isn't." As a greeting it didn't even make sense.

"Hi, Sooz."

"This is her," Susie said, turning to her friends. "I was just telling them. Saying that I knew someone who could give us access, but she didn't have any convictions, so."

"That's nice of you, Sooz. Thanks a lot."

"Nice shoes," Susie said, and the sneeriness in her voice was truly world class. One girl sniggered and the other shook her head. The boy was chubby and had a flop of blond hair, green braces over his shirt, and he held out his right hand and said, in the poshest voice she'd ever heard from a person under thirty: "Very pleased to meet your acquaintance."

"She won't be pleased to meet you," Susie said. "She doesn't care one bit about the cause."

"Shh," the blond boy said. "Now, Freya,

264

what's this I hear? You won't help us with a little stink bomb? It's just, you know, it gets us in the news. Stupid pranks, not much upset caused — inconvenience, right? — but when it gets into the news we get a few column inches to elaborate on, well —"

"The cause," Freya said.

"You catch on quickly. They could use you in the SWP."

"That's not what he's from," Susie said, too eager. "He's the LPYS. He edits *Social-ist Youth.*"

He smiled. "All true," he said. "And what do you do, Freya?"

There was a pause — she didn't know how to answer this — and all at once the girls and the boy looked at each other and laughed. It was a strange moment, more like a half-scene in a dumb nightmare than a real exchange. It left her feeling sick.

"Sorry," the blond boy said. "Didn't mean to embarrass you. But are you sure you couldn't help us out a little?"

Why did she want to cry again? Susie was staring at the entrance to Amadeo's.

"I —"

"Yes?" The blond boy was touching her wrist. Gentle. The girls whispered to each other.

"I'm not going to throw any stink bombs

around the hotel."

"Of course."

She had their attention now. It was the same as before. They were going to laugh again. "But there's a back entrance, where the kitchen staff smoke. I — I could *maybe* let someone in, I guess, if it's just for a joke."

"You legend," he said. "That would be excellent, really excellent." Her offer had stiffened their expressions.

"One person. On the Friday. But only if I know exactly what —"

"Chanting outside. A stink bomb inside. No damage done — you have my word, Freya. You're doing your bit for free expression."

Susie stepped forward and flung her arms around Freya — "I knew it, Frey-Hey. I knew" — and in this moment Freya thought of the time she'd asked Susie's little sister to name her ten favourite people. Six of them had been animals, two of them were her mum, and first place went to a plastic doll called Amanda Jane whose eyes were alarmingly large.

3

How the hell to get out of here? His contract only gave him six days sick pay a year. After that the cheques would stop coming. The unions had been bruised by Thatcher's assaults. In hospitality a few broken ribs. He hoped she knew what she was doing. Hoped he'd have a chance politely to ask her. To say, "Hey, Maggie, how about helping our industry?" But it was true too, that a couple of years ago it was impossible to sack bone-idle staff. They used to wave their union cards and grin, speak without respect. He wanted his employees to think of him as a nice guy, but the moment they took advantage it stung him. Now he felt gravely betrayed by his own body. The head of bloodflow. The department of hearts. I fed you, didn't I? I watered you? I did my bit to relieve your urges? There was that time I rubbed moisturiser stuff on your skin. Still you decided to go on strike.

Mr. Marshall was leaning into the room, his head crowned by irrepressible grey curls, his face expressing the exact combination of compassion and apathy that made doctors good at their jobs. His features were lengthy. His shoes had a frightening shine. A heart that would probably never fail him. A body that had probably been run for many years on death-repelling breakfast juices, improbable quantities of exotic fruit, the fine sea spray of expensive sailing boats gliding cleanly between private islands.

"Is the sun in your eyes?" Mr. Marshall said. "I'll get a nurse to get that sun out of your eyes." He stepped back into the corridor. "Monica!" he said. "Sun out of his eyes!" But Monica, whoever she was, didn't come.

"Actually," Moose said, "I like to see the trees."

"Trees," Mr. Marshall repeated, frowning. He seemed to be wondering how a man of his abilities had failed to factor them in. "You still living up on the old what's-the-name?"

"Brighton Heights."

Marshall frowned again.

"That's just what we call it. Because . . . well, there's the hill, if you remember. And it's an ironic thing, because it's not that high really, it's not like you're up there with the gods looking down, though you do feel a bit separate to your surroundings. Also, when we were out in New York, Freya and I ended up visiting these sort of relatives who live in Brighton Heights in Staten Island, which has these grand old houses, and a lake that's really a reservoir. It's a long story."

"It sounds it," Mr. Marshall said. "You've got to do what the young chap says, Moose."

"Dr. Haswell?"

"Haswell. Right . . ." Haswell whose eyes had a hard athletic intent, cold as the mints Moose used to eat before a diving meet: sugar-packed and powerful, the tingle-fresh sense you'd burnt your tongue. "This is our show," Marshall was saying. "Chance to return a favour. No use getting down. Couple of days. Hope to keep you in this nice little room. I'll never forget that party for my fourth."

"Fourth?"

"Marriage," Mr. Marshall said.

"Oh. That was your fourth, was it? Our pleasure to host you, anyway. Maybe bear us in mind for future . . . celebrations."

"Thanks also for the voucher. Look after the pennies and the pounds look after themselves. A heart requires care. No fags yes. No spirits yes. Cut down on those crisps and sweets you keep squirrelled about your person."

"Energy," Moose said. "I work long hours, like you." He objected to the word squirrelled.

"Look after it, or one day it'll be total blackout. Ticking time bomb is what people say. Tick tick. Tick." Mr. Marshall sneezed. "It's all nonsense, more or less, but however it helps to think of it." With an unpleasant lusty look he inspected the contents of his handkerchief. "Like I said, the only thing a heart really resembles, if you've actually held one, is a blood-soaked fist. Break too many knuckles and you can't go on fighting, yes? And you want to keep fighting, don't you? Fighting against the body's immemorial attempts to make us all look and feel like shit." Briefly he barked with laughter. "Is that wife of yours still carrying on with an American chap?"

"Ex."

Marshall's hand shot up to his ear. "She is then, is she?"

"Carrying on with him in London now, I think. Or with someone else."

"God," Marshall said, running fingers through his hair. "Jesus." For about five seconds he looked fiercely upset. "You're in pain?" he said.

"No. It's actually fine."

"You're sure? I can get them to up your intake."

"My heart."

"Yes?"

"Ever since Viv went, I've tried to keep it away from attractive, feisty women. I've done it many favours. I've tried to preserve it." He allowed himself a gentle smile.

"Well," Marshall said, "I wouldn't say you've done it *many* favours. But best advice I ever heard? Marry someone mediocre. Medically what's on your mind? I'm here to help." A quick glance at his watch.

"I suppose . . . Well, I guess the only thing is that I'm still slightly nervous that this might happen again, or what this means for me, and so on . . . I haven't had a chance to really discuss my — well, my condition fully with anyone, because obviously you're all so busy and everything . . . So that's part of the nerves, I suppose, though I'm definitely not complaining."

The admission of nerves. The request for more attention. Moose could see straight away that he had made a double mistake. The truth was there in the shine of Mr. Marshall's eyes, little hoops of light that were interpretable as distaste. Wanting on a great scale — that's what made people

271

shameful. Nervous patients were the medical equivalent of needy hotel guests, probably? The light sleeper, the hot-water junkie, the badly asthmatic anti-allergen guy, the vegan woman who dislikes meat almost as much as people made of it.

Mr. Marshall held one foot behind him, your basic quadriceps stretch. "Nerves are natural, Moose." He shifted to the other leg too quickly to reap a reward.

"You want to hold for thirty seconds at least," Moose said.

"Heart attacks make doctors nervous too. People are always surprised to hear there are still, in this day and age, uncertainties around the most appropriate treatments, yes? Bed rest, for example, has been for most of my career the most simple and established of ministrations for the kind of infarction we've been looking at here. But just the other day I read a journal piece — well, was told about one — suggesting that, in a forty to fifty male like you, the prevalence of deadly blood clots in the legs should force a reappraisal even of the bedrest strategem."

"It's a comfort to hear all that," Moose said.

"Stay off the smokes, yes? The cigars."

"I don't smoke cigars."

"Quit smoking. All of it. Assume, every time I stare at you, that what I'm saying is give up smoking. Do that and you'll be fine. Best thing? Get some bed rest."

Narcoleptics, Moose thought. Of all hotel guests, narcoleptics are the most highly prized. Shut the door. Leave them be. Rarely hear a peep. When they get hungry they order to the room. You charge them extra even though it costs you less, frees up the restaurant to squeeze in more covers.

In hospitality the thing that killed you was headcount, the sheer size of the payroll in a luxury place. That and the two hundred towels washed each day, the sourcing of vintage lampshades, the touching up of rooms every Monday and Friday: suitcase scuffs, shoe marks, loose plaster, broken mirrors. The maintenance required was amazing but you did it without thinking, just got on with the jobs, and maybe that was the secret? Today he'd spent a lot of time speculating that his life would be better if only he spent a lot less time speculating. He'd been thinking of Viv too. Her puzzling combination of confidence and insecurity. She was the kind of woman who'd turn up at a fancy-dress party holding a photo of the person she was meant to be.

Mr. Marshall had gone. From the corridor came the clinking of water glasses, an affable social sound, restorative and daily. It was the afternoon.

Monica the nurse, laughing.

"No no," he told her. Her happiness was lifting the pain in his chest. "I'm serious. Never need to pay for that stuff."

"What, *ever*? Come on, you're teasing me." Not pretty, no, but something invitingly inquisitive about her dark mouth, the way it was never wholly closed.

"Look," he said, "think it through." A moment of hesitation, of industry guilt, but it gave way soon enough to his desire to entertain. "Try this at my hotel and there'll be trouble, but here's the thing. At the desk, at check-in, say you'd like a no-smoking room. Then go up to your room and open the minibar. Mix yourself a couple of gin and tonics, eat a nice chocolate bar, throw the mini whiskies in your suitcase. Then light up a fag, smoke it, flush the stub down the toilet, and go downstairs. Complain that your room smells of smoke."

"No," she said.

"Yes. People do this. A small group in the know. Seasoned travellers. Downstairs, the person at the front desk apologises and assigns you a different room — probably a better one, because no one wants you complaining twice. Then they get house-keeping to check out the reported smoke-smell. Housekeeping confirm they can smell it too. Front desk send a bottle of wine up to your new improved room, though by then you're already drunk."

"I can't believe it."

"When you move rooms on the same day you check in, it leaves virtually no trace."

"What if I emptied out the whole mini-bar, though? *Everything.*"

"That's what I'm saying. In a way it's even less suspicious. We get loads of faded rockers staying. It's not unusual to be asked to empty out the minibar completely, before they arrive, and therefore not unusual for the minibar attendant to discover that he needs to completely refill a given minibar. Applying charges — it's not his job."

The nurse sat down on the end of the bed and then got up again, shaking her head, ringlets swaying. "You win. My mind is blown."

"The other thing is, at the end of your stay, when they apply the minibar charges to your bill, you could just say, 'No, I didn't have anything from the minibar.'"

"That simple?"

"Yeah." Why was he saying all this? Why was he spreading the word? "The truth is no good front-desk agent will accuse a customer of lying, whatever the situation. You think we want to go through your bins looking for little bottles? They know the minibar attendants make mistakes. Peer in. Mess of bottles. Ticking little items on a chart. They know papers and room numbers get mixed up. Human error. They know other fallible people copy those details onto the guest's bill. They know some temp-staff maids drink a couple of gins while they clean and then blame it on the customers. They know summer staff sneak into vacant rooms and smoke, have a party. The only thing that shows you're lying is if you give an over-complex excuse. If you just say, 'Didn't have anything,' we take it off your bill in a heartbeat, and then you eat and drink for free."

She gave him such an excellent smile.

Performance.

He experienced a moment of thinking this hospital wasn't so bad, of thinking the enforced removal of all motion from his life might even be a blessing. The feeling did not last. He was napping three or four times a day. In the afternoons he was nicely heavy with doziness. Quickly it began to amaze and depress him that, during these colour-ful breaks in consciousness, time still seemed to pass. He woke to find a trolley had moved. A clipboard had disappeared. Situations changing and him playing no ac-tive role at all. And he was tired too, by the effort of recalibrating all the reference points in his life. Having one heart attack increased the likelihood of others. Dying at fifty of an exploded heart was a distinct pos-sibility now. That would mean his twenty-fifth birthday — twenty-fifth! — had been a halfway point in his life. He resented all the months spent having showers, the weeks spent brushing teeth, the days driving lost along thin grey roads with a map spread out on his knees.

4

One of the final times she saw Roy Walsh was in the bar at the Grand. The morning had been lit by worries for her father. The afternoon had been overcast. She spent most of it behind the desk.

George the Doorman came inside. He took his top hat off. He glanced at the list of returning VIPs taped to the inner rim. With a brisk hand he combed his hair. She watched him go back to his preferred position on the pavement, a safe distance from any awning-based birds, until eventually a customer arrived. She checked him in and it was painless right up until the moment when she smiled and handed him the key. He looked at it with something like disgust and announced that he'd like a free upgrade. Why did so many people wait until after the admin had been done? If they asked politely, pre-allocation, you were so much more likely to meet their needs.

"I'm with Britvic," the new guest said, as if this should mean something to her.

She lied and told him there were no suites available. She said the King of Nairobi was staying. That statement almost always put people in their place.

She went back to her Jumbo Jotter pad. Worrying about her dad had loosened other thoughts about her mother. It was like a buy-one-get-one-free kind of deal, except you didn't want the paid-for thing and you didn't want the free thing either. She'd been trying to set some of her ideas down.

Mum was often <u>bored</u> with life. Basically need to avoid that — e.g. remain only bored with <u>JOB</u>.

She stared at these lines, the forward tilt of her own handwriting. Why was it that, when in a bad mood, her mother had always tried to find ways of making everyone's character feel foreseeable? Everything people did or said was anticipated and discounted in advance. "Oh, you would say that." "Well, that's typical." She was a lecturer in Linguistics. Some days she saw cliché in everything. There was nothing malicious about it, probably. Her dad always said it was a symptom of The Depression. You could tell he capitalised it. But she seemed fully convinced that everyone's personality was locked on a single predictable track — except hers, because you could tell she thought of herself as unusual. It seemed to Freya that her mother, trying to reinforce this sense of herself as unusual, would sometimes make herself happy when she wanted to be sad, and sad when she ought to have been happy, and angry for the sake of being angry. She was committed above all to contrariness, was she? She wanted to keep people on their toes.

Some mothers threw parties. Mine threw crises.

She was quite pleased with these last two sentences. She thought they might one day be the seed of an extremely profitable screenplay. She opened *The Colour of Magic* under the desk and read a few more pages. Twoflower and the upside-down mountain and the dragons that only exist in the imagination. The characters' journeys were being controlled by gods playing a board game. She snorted at a line from Rincewind.

"My name is immaterial," she said.
"That's a pretty name," said Rincewind.

Light teased the lobby walls with slowly shifting mysteries. More clouds arrived outside. The patterns vanished. She checked the Band-Aid supply in the second drawer down in case Barbara decided to maul more guests. Barbara was on her back on the rug with her legs in the air, yellow eyes shining, a trap. Her purrs were alive with staticky crackles.

Fran came up. "How's your dad doing, Frey-doe?"

"On the mend, thanks, Fran."

"That's what I heard. Awesome. Give him my love, OK?"

People wanted the bare minimum of information. Something that wouldn't eat into their day but would nonetheless leave them feeling kind. Fran *was* kind, but she was also bored and busy, and in that respect she was like everyone else who wasn't famous, and maybe even some who were.

Freya looked down into the grainy swirls of the desk and thought about hearts. Felt the inside of her head loosening to sherbet, becoming a purring whiteness, a long bright corridor reaching out into the distance that was music-video pretty, pure. She wanted to tiptoe through it lighting candles as she went. Madonna. *Borderline.* What would it be like, to be that awesome?

She blinked. One of her thumbs, today, looked slightly bigger than the other.

The notepad was decorated with dandelions and bits of seed that were forever blowing sideways, trying to escape the page. She flicked past the message about Susie trying to get hold of her and also the message underneath about requested rearrangements to Margaret Thatcher's room. The key thing, apparently, was to have a number of low-wattage lamps close to the desk, so that her husband, Denis, mysteriously missing a second "n," could get some sleep while she did last-minute amendments to her speech. Dad thought this was a perfect detail: that someone would *plan* to do last-minute amendments.

She'd need to get out of here in the next few weeks. More than enough temporary staff to take her place. Even if it wasn't Spain. Even if it was just, like, *Bognor.* Her father said that meeting Margaret Thatcher would amount to a once-in-a-lifetime opportunity, but what actually was the point in doing something you'd never do again? It sounded very much like what her mother called Novelty Value.

Surfer John sidled up to the desk, looking unusually shifty. Could Freya, um, by any chance, um, cover his shift this afternoon?

4 p.m. behind the bar. You know I'm good for it. Didn't I repay your shift the other day?

"I'm visiting my dad again."

"Oh. Right." Surfer John rearranged his handsome hair and allowed a moment to pass. "And that would be a long visit, would it?"

She sighed. "You would owe me, John."

"I love you!"

"Four until eight, right? You'd owe me."

"You're the best. I'm going to . . ."

"Yeah?"

"Something nice. I'm going to buy you —"

"A car? A castle?"

"A fancy dinner," John said.

She laughed.

"No, I am. I've got to grab a lift to Camber Sands, and then I'll book you up."

With this mysterious promise, John left. A summer-staff kid came to the desk. He leaned on the oak all casual and said, "Hi, Freya, how's your dad?"

"He's dead."

"Shit! Really?"

"No," she said, and saw the excitement drain from his face.

On her break she took a walk and got annoyed. She was annoyed with herself for accepting the bar shift instead of visiting her father. She was annoyed that she had preferred the idea of the bar to the reality of the hospital. She was annoyed with the Royal Pavilion for looking too much like pictures of the Taj Mahal. She was annoyed with the predictably bright fabrics in the bohemian shops on North Laine. She was annoyed with the dismal iron canopy of the station, the fiddly white arches over side streets, the small sleepy bandstands, the half-melted look of the wavy seafront railings. She was annoyed by Surfer John and she was annoyed, most of all, by the Grand. The whole thing looked absurdly self-indulgent. The painstaking brickwork. The well-spaced windows. The cast-iron twirly bits on balconies. The flouncy sections of supporting white stone. Squint and they revealed their silly floral patterns, silly leaf patterns, silly seashell patterns. The whole facade seemed just that: a facade. It was the over-engineered, dramatic film-set frontage for 201 absurdly overpriced rooms in which the only concession to imagination was, what, the *slightly* varying configuration of the furniture? The building had the quaint lacy look of her grandma's flat in Hove. Did her grandma even know that Moose was ill? She charged through the revolving door and said hello to no one.

From a shelf under the bar she took a segment of lime and dropped it in her drink. Acid mood. Swirling citrus thoughts. The smell of nicotine competed in the air around her with the sharp vinegary scent of brown sauce squeezed into ramekins. Narrowing her eyes into a kind of safari squint, thinking that she'd much rather be at home watching David Attenborough tapes, she studied the half-dozen drinkers arranged around her. A few of the beige-jacket crowd sitting at a low table, playing bridge and making jokes about their wives. Also a local writer who liked to drink real ale while making notes in his bloodred notebook. ("Waves are amazing" was the only sentence Freya had seen.) And closer, sitting at the bar, a crossword laid out between his arms, was an eccentric guy everyone called the Captain. "The Captain of what?" Freya occasionally asked, but no one seemed to know. Her attempts to get some sense out of the Captain himself on this simple but apparently intimate issue had, as yet, yielded no success. He looked like the love child of badgers. White whiskery sideburns. Liver spots on his skinny cheeks. She stared now into the high frizz of his hair, bluish and electric, separate threads of it startled by light. His age was somewhere north of seventy. The high numbers merged into one another, top floors of a skyscraper, distant.

The one undisputed thing about the Captain was his natural habitat: Brighton's charity shops and second-hand stores, places where he could indulge his remarkable need to rummage. The Captain had an insatiable appetite for memorabilia. The very best of his discoveries found their way into a small enterprise three streets back from the beach: a "cultural institution" he called the Museum of Lost Content. To most, the museum — of which the Captain was Founder, Acquisitions Manager, Curator and the sole member of staff — was an attic flat filled with junk. But to Freya sometimes it seemed a place of liberating disarray. When the weather was bad she went there on her lunch breaks. The Captain never charged her an entry fee. He never seemed to charge anyone an entry fee. His ability to stay financially afloat was one of several mysteries that orbited his person.

"The eighth wonder of the world," he was saying now. The tatty leather elbow patches on his red jacket squeaked against the bar as he shuffled on his stool. Freya assumed he was talking about his museum, or reciting a crossword clue, but she was wrong.

He was referring to Marina. She entered the bar area pink-cheeked, pneumatic, holding a dusty lidless plastic box topped with crayons and Lego. The card players at the table to the left became tremulous of eyebrow and low of voice. The Captain cracked his fingers. A silver pendant bobbed helplessly on the swell of her breasts. An unusually low-cut little number. Lately Freya had felt herself slipping into a rivalry of delicate dimensions.

"Freya, darling, do you mind if I leave this box behind the bar?"

She shrugged. "We've got kids staying?"

"No, it's my little nephew. My sister is ill. I've got him with me later today."

"I didn't realise you had a sister."

"Seven," Marina admitted.

"You've got seven sisters?"

"Yes. And one brother. But he adds nothing."

"Zone Three," the Captain said, tapping his knuckles three times on the bar.

"I'm sorry?" Marina said.

"Seven Sisters. Between Finsbury Park and Tottenham Hale, in Zone Three, if I'm not mistaken. London Underground. Also a term to describe a loosely linked collective of Stalinist skyscrapers in Moscow. Yes, an unusual combination of Russian baroque

287

and Gothic. Saw a couple of them after the war."

Marina, rarely flustered, looked flustered. It was interesting to observe. She blinked and gave the Captain a quick strategic smile. "See you soon!" she sang.

"When you say 'during the war,' " Freya said, "which war was that, Captain?"

The Captain coughed.

She looked at the Walkers Crisps order form in front of her. A little job left by John. How was she supposed to know what flavour crisps Conservatives preferred? In his Memos With The Bad Puns In The First Paragraph, the GM kept telling everyone to "bolster supplies" and be "ready for any-thing." He made it sound like they were go-ing to war. It was the most boring war she'd ever been involved with.

She was hungry. The Captain reached into a jacket pocket. He pulled out a yo-yo and a curled Post-it note. The Captain's pockets were renowned throughout Brighton as sinkholes of buried treasure and sedimented knowledge. In pub quizzes at the Cricketers he was on occasion asked to leave his jacket behind the bar. There was a fear that the weight of encyclopedic wisdom lurking in its various compartments might tempt him to cheat (or, as the Captain himself put it, fleece, hose, bilk, diddle, rook, gyp, finagle, cozen, swindle, hornswoggle, flimflam). He pressed the Post-it note onto a London Pride beer mat, wrote something on it with a biro borrowed from Freya, and then put the note and the biro in his pocket.

"Um, I kind of need that pen?"

He pushed the yo-yo in her direction. "Swapsie?"

Why not. This was the new Freya. Yo-yoing. Impulsive. Soon-to-get-a-cool-boyfriend-whose-skin-wasn't-scorched-by-Clearasil. She took the yellow yo-yo and tucked her middle finger into the loop of string. With a backwards flick of her hand she sent it down towards the ground. Instead of whirring back up the thing left its string, hit the floor with a *clack,* and rolled away.

"The Games section of my museum is getting unwieldy," the Captain explained.

She'd liked Blatchington Mill. She had been OK at all the sports. The school had a reputation for being rough, but that reputation was spread by people who unfairly compared it to St. Catherine's. St. Catherine's was, as everyone knew, the kind of top-notch penitentiary where students took home the BBC *Songs of Praise* Choir of the Year trophy three years running. She made herself another lime and soda and gave the Captain another bowl of nuts. When the nuts were finished the Captain looked up.

"Are you going to come by tomorrow, Freya? To the museum?" He appeared to have retrieved the yo-yo from the floor. With surprisingly nimble fingers he was reattaching it to the string.

Maybe, she told him. It was a genuine maybe. There had been a time when she'd wondered if he might be a bit creepy, but that had given way to a sense that he was one of the more interesting people she knew. She suggested two thirty.

"Too bad," the Captain said. "Two fifteen tomorrow I plan to be at St. Paul's. A man without a schedule may as well be dead."

"I didn't know you were religious."

"I am interested in fictions of all sorts," he said. "Novels. Poems. Stories. Tales politicians tell. I've never found much that's fruitful in straight-faced facts. I don't *enjoy* them, you know? Can't make myself believe in them. Second-hand is what they are, they lack the raw stuff of absurdity, and people make the mistake of trying to be all-serious, as if life isn't funny, or all-funny as if life isn't serious. You can only get at the world if you do both. Life's a tune that accommodates a great many tones. Of course" —

he yawned — "most people are desperate bores. Lucian Freud once said to me — I know him a little, not to name-drop, and he once said to me this — he said, 'Captain, sometimes painting is like one of those recipes where you do all manner of elaborate things to a duck, and then end up putting the duck to one side and only using the skin.' " The Captain slapped the bar and laughed. "Good old Lucy! Terrible hunger for flesh, but . . . Life's the things people keep, the things they throw away. Here, good as new. I've lost my train of thought."

She took the yo-yo. "Who's Lucian Freud?"

"Prolific is what he is. You're probably one of his love children."

"If he's got money, that could be useful."

"I'll put in a good word," the Captain said. "If you're not going to galleries, keep up with your reading. I've been ploughing through some paraphernalia by this chap Joseph Mitchell. Know him? Bernard Mac-Laverty also. Not a better writer alive. If you read things, you have views on things. You never want to become one of those people who believe in nothing. It leads to the itsy-bitsy misery. A time to dance. I'm the second-greatest authority in the world today on the language of the seagull."

She asked him if he wanted another drink. She thought it might bring some colour to the unwhiskered portions of his cheeks. Her idea of old people was that they should look a bit autumnal. Did the Captain ever eat a home-cooked meal? Did he ever sleep in a proper bed? Did he really know Lucian whatsit? She didn't know; she had no idea. More mysteries, more hidden habits. More things pocketed within his private self.

He said no to another drink. "I'll lose my senses," he explained. As he did so, a shape emerged in the lobby. The shape resolved itself into Roy Walsh.

She swallowed and tried to write a quick script in her head. Witty things to say. Interesting things. Where were they? He saw her and waved. Came towards the bar. "Nice to see you again," he said.

"I thought you were . . ."

"Yeah. Had to extend my stay."

She asked him if he was staying because of work.

He shrugged and said, "What isn't?"

"Is your friend still with you?"

"Friend?"

"The guy on the stairs. He seemed —"

A smile. "Colleague. He had to leave, unfortunately."

"That's a shame," she said. "I mean . . ."

she said, and gave up.

The Captain studied the wall. The card players stared at their cards.

"Sorry," she said. "Captain, this is . . . well, he's —"

"Hi," Roy said, shaking the Captain's hand.

Time got fat on silence. The Captain leapt to his feet with unlikely speed. He offered Freya a pound coin. He always offered a pound coin. It was his best and only offer. According to the Captain, if you presented a pound coin in exchange for food and beverages and any other services rendered, it was a civil matter. Theft and a whole gambit of other criminal offences only came into play if you walked off without paying anything at all.

As the Captain's red jacket receded, Freya's eyes moved to a chunk of blue plastic in Roy Walsh's hands. "What's that?" she said.

"This?"

"Yeah."

"Satellite pager. A beeper thing. If someone wants to contact me about a job, they call a computer, then the computer notifies a satellite, then it bounces back or something like that and — who knows — this thing, it beeps." He smiled again.

"Intelligence," she said.

"What?"

"Artificial intelligence. All that stuff. I read an article about it."

He rubbed his eyes. There were new dark arcs underneath. "I guess it's not quite that," he said, "but yeah. Clever things."

Freya looked at him and looked at the pager. He knew stuff, owned stuff, had a proper life. Dr. Haswell and Mr. Marshall could fix hearts — that was how their adulthood was defined — and it seemed to her that Roy was also, probably, in the business of improving others.

"What is it you do again?"

"Me? Electrician."

Well, that made sense. Technical but practical. Everyone needed lights and . . . toasters. People needed toasters. She tried to hide her disappointment.

"What's your boss like?" she said.

"My boss? I guess you'd say I'm the boss, probably."

"Oh, right. So would you say you sort of *own* a . . . ?"

"Yeah, a small business, exactly. This thing's useful. The office lets me know about jobs when I'm on the move."

"You're a businessman, then."

"In a way."

"And your friend . . ."

"Colleague."

"He left because —"

"He had to go back to his other half."

"His other half?"

"Yeah. She wears the trousers. He's very under the thumb."

She shook her head.

"You don't know that phrase?"

There were these weird embarrassing holes in the things she knew, areas to patch over or fill in, and you never could guess when you'd fall into one.

"Siamise cat girl," he said.

She shook her head again.

"Rolling Stones."

"Ah."

"Under the thumb just means . . . well, what does it mean? Someone else controls you. I can't imagine that happening with you."

The compliment was only small, if in fact that's what it was, and she tried to control the heat in her cheeks. If Roy's friend was in a relationship with a woman who wore the trousers, then maybe both Roy and the male friend really were bisexual instead of homosexual, or maybe — this was a simpler, sturdier theory, and yet it required more erasure of assumptions — she'd misread every moment to date, and both men were only interested in women, in which case —

"I don't suppose you know a gym round here?"

"We don't have an arrangement. But there are a couple of places you could try for a one- or two-day pass. I could write them down?"

"That's kind. That'd be great."

"I suppose you exercise quite a bit, do you?"

"I do when I can," he said. "Used to do more. I like to run. Walk my dogs. You're a swimmer, right?"

"How did you know?"

"Thought I overheard something."

"Well, I used to be a swimmer. But now, not so much."

She wished she hadn't asked the question about him exercising. It was a little-girl question, for sure.

"You're very young to have *used to be*s," he said.

"Why? Don't you have any?"

"I'm a few years older than you."

"Only a few, though."

He held her gaze. "I suppose that's true. Old enough to know who the Rolling Stones are, though."

"I know them," she said. "I still go to the

pool. But I don't take it so seriously now."

"Maybe you should write down the name for me. Where do you go? I swam when I was younger too. I don't really know why I stopped."

"Probably the chlorine was drying out your tan," she said.

He was laughing. "This is a natural tan."

"Naturally."

"It's a natural tan and I'm deeply hurt by suggestions it's not, Freya. Where I'm from, people work hard for a bit of colour."

"OK," she said, stirring her lime and soda with a straw and smiling. She wasn't wearing her name badge. It was pinned to her jacket, and her jacket was on the stool. She rolled up the bright white cuffs of her shirt and took another sip. He'd called her Freya. It was the simplest of all pleasures, the cleanest and neatest, when a near-stranger remembered your name.

"I used to go with someone to the pool," he said. "And then, when she stopped going, I did too."

"Your girlfriend?"

"My dad, when I was younger. But then a girlfriend, yeah."

"And not anymore."

"No."

"What happened? Did she sleep with your

best friend?"

"You're funny," Roy said. "But no, my best friend is . . . You know, Freya, I'm not sure I'd say I really have one."

"No?"

He laughed and seemed about to say something important. Instead his face clouded with confusion, or regret. "With this girlfriend, it was all going great at first. This was at the start of the relationship, years ago. We were really young, that's for sure. But I was convinced I could hear old Cupid calling me, y'know?"

"And then?"

He shrugged. "Turned out to be a wrong number."

She gave a half-laugh, half-snort — exactly the kind of idiotic thing she was trying to eradicate from her range of responses.

"What happened after that?" she said.

"We used to talk on the CB radio. You won't know about that. Events took over."

"Events?"

"Yeah."

"Where are you from again? I can't re-member."

"I don't think we discussed it," Roy said.

"Hey," she said, reaching over the awk-wardness. "Have you heard of Lucian Freud?"

"Freud? Yeah."

"Do you like his stuff?"

"I guess I . . ." He shifted on his stool. "The name's familiar," he said. He laughed again. "Do I get a drink, then?"

"Shit! Sorry. I'm terrible at this."

"Swearing at customers," he said. "Sackable. Do you have a single malt?"

"We've got these, over here."

"Whichever."

"Yeah?"

"I'm not a big enough buff to be fussy."

She poured him a Glenmorangie, the one her father liked. She made a note to charge a cheaper spirit to his room.

"I thought you were more into vodka," she said.

His eyes went wide.

"Sorry. One of the things I've got to do, when it's quiet behind the desk, is copy down the room-service records."

He looked at the window. He had his left hand over the left side of his face. He nodded as if agreeing with something unsaid. "Where's your dad these days, then? Haven't seen him around."

"He's — well, he's been a bit unwell."

"I'm sorry to hear that."

"Yeah. Ice?"

"Definitely not."

He took two short sips and downed the rest.

"Long day?"

"Yeah."

"Another?"

He smiled. "I've always wanted to do that."

"What?"

"Drink a whisky in a top hotel like my life depends on it. I feel more heroic already."

She tried to figure out if she was being teased. "Depends if you call this a top hotel."

"Are you kidding? Look around you."

"That sewage smell yesterday. Would you call that five star?"

"Listen," he said. "First off, I didn't smell anything. And second, the hotel can't be held responsible for everything. An old place like this probably has a lot of two-and-a-half-inch pipes. And my guess is that a lot of these guests" — he nodded towards the card players — "have three-and-a-half-inch arseholes."

She laughed too long at this.

"Simple physics," he said.

They talked about the electrical business he owned. She asked if he wanted the same again. He said, "Unfortunately I can't stay." Despite never expecting him here, never expecting really to talk to him again, this felt very much like a fresh blow.

"How's all the planning for the PM's arrival going, anyway?"

"OK, yeah." A reprieve. "She's asked — there's all sorts of requests."

"Yeah?"

"Special foods. Special drinks. Cameras."

"Cameras," he said.

"They'll be installing a load of them."

"Of course. But already?"

"No, a week or so."

He was silent for a moment. "I wonder if you'll get to hang out with her, with Maggie. Probably her schedule's pretty packed. You'll need to locate a free window or two while she's here. Catch up with her views on apartheid."

"Apartheid?"

"Yeah."

"It looks pretty complicated."

"Once you know the score, it's pretty simple."

"No! The schedule."

"Oh." He smiled. "Fair play."

"It's changing all the time. There's a lot of *ifs* and *buts.* Look." She picked up her jacket. She took the document out of her pocket and put it on the bar. Roy Walsh looked at it for a long while. She was grateful to have steered things back onto a subject she knew something about, territory where she could hold her own.

"I see what you mean," he said.

"You're interested? I mean — you're into politics?"

"Me? No more than the next man. We're all into it, aren't we? It's just a case of whether we know that we're into it or not."

This seemed to her like an intelligent thing to say. It reinforced an idea she had of him as someone whose intelligence came from experience rather than books. Again she felt very young in his company, and when she thought of Surfer John and, worse, the boys she knew from school, it was like they belonged to a completely different gender to Roy Walsh.

In the bottom of her pint glass, all lime and soda sucked away, her face looked like a big pale moon of things never done. Skiing, waterskiing, sailing, sex in water, sex where the guy takes you from behind. The baking of seasonal biscuits, jalapeño peppers, Michael Jackson live, sushi, body piercings, bungee jumps, sky-dives, waterbeds, yoga, a Coke float made with more than two flavours of ice cream. Argentina, Botswana, Cambodia, a whole alphabet of adventure. But it was a face with potential, she thought.

"Shall I write down the name of the gym and the pool for you?"

"Please," he said, standing.

When he'd gone she leaned against the bar alone, rolling the word *please* through her mind. She put the schedule back in her pocket. Possibly she was an over-thinker. It was something she'd been thinking she should address. A dark spot at the edge of her field of vision was swelling and shrinking.

When Surfer John returned from Camber Sands he presented her with a stick of Brighton rock. He thanked her and hugged her. He looked at her strangely. It was as if he was seeing something new.

"What?" she said.

"Nothing," he said.

He asked her when she was free for the fancy thank-you dinner.

It had begun to rain outside, water rushing down the windowpanes in long wobbling lines, a heavy downpour that left her quite content.

5

Two hours before Marina was due to arrive, Moose awoke open-mouthed. He began to try to climb out of bed. An orderly came and helped him stand.

Shaky legs. When he'd checked into this place, his legs had been strong. The hospital was bad for his health. There was no other conclusion. Blisters on the heels of his feet, nappy rash on his arse. No man should ever have to utter to his daughter the words "buy me buttock cream, please." Making his way to the bathrooms, stooped and slow, he passed people whose eyes made him think of clouds and whose bodies made him think of bed sheets. Faces shining, suffering. An old lady on crutches. Child in a wheelchair. The damaged life in these corridors made God a senseless brute. What a team he'd become a part of! A group bound together by mistakes of the mind and body, errors and accidents and sharp turns for the worse.

A four-cheese pizza would be wonderful. The sad tiled floor was unyielding.

The bathroom mirror told him he belonged. His eyes were bloodshot and a mask of pallor still clung to his skin. There was no mistaking it: he was in the kind of condition where it's advisable either to thoroughly pull yourself together or to thoroughly let yourself go. The latter held all the allure. No more play-acting! Become a one hundred per cent mess! And meanwhile the rest of the world's men could carry on pretending, grinning, lifting their chins — putting space between themselves.

Great palmfuls of water were required to dampen his hair's enthusiasm for adventure. A few licks sprung up the moment he put down the comb. He shaved with an inch of luke-warm water lurking sunless and shallow in the basin. Listened to a man behind a pockmarked door straining to squeeze out a turd. Splashed his face, zipped up his washbag, went back to his hospital bed.

This morning Freya had visited again. She'd brought him a plant. He was grateful for the plant. A plant was a perfect gift. Earlier in the week an old diving friend had turned up with a whistle that made different types of birdsong when you blew it. One of the drawbacks of having a surname like

Finch was that a surprising number of people, at Christmas or on birthdays, thought it appropriate or amusing to give you bird-related gifts. Singing bird clock (green). Singing bird clock (brown). You Can Toucan can-opener.

Sometimes he felt that close friends liked to turn him into a bit of a caricature, the hapless hotel guy who used to be good at everything he set his mind to and was now thrillingly — perhaps even transcendentally — mediocre. When he played along to the idea they had of the arc of his life, everything was fine. They loved him to act flat and be one of humanity's genial, self-deprecating disappointments. But when he said something unexpected, something that was too harsh or too true or which he hadn't thought through — maybe reminding them that they owned their own fair share of badly blown dreams — they treated him like he was a bit of a spoilsport. So these days he kept quiet. Kept quiet just as he had when Antonia and Brian from the hotel had visited this morning. He could see it in their eyes. They'd come with the specific purpose of ensuring that the heart attack hadn't happened to them.

The plant from Freya was positioned on the faux-oak bedside table, sharing surface space with a water jug and a copy of the *Guardian.* The front-page headline read "PM'S POPULARITY SINKING," but the poll referenced in the body of the article showed Thatcher holding on to a narrow lead over Labour. There was also a ten-page pull-out about the birth of Prince Henry of Wales. The baby prince looked tricksy, sardonic, chubby, blotchy, and would hopefully cheer up his sad-eyed mum. Freya had claimed the plant was scentless, but the cheerful lily-pad-like foliage had a distinctive peppery perfume. Every hour or two he'd sneeze, and sneezes hurt his heart, his back, his arms and his eyeballs. The pain often dwindled down into a small knot above his Adam's apple, where with the aid of water it could sometimes be swallowed down.

Where was Marina? She was late, late.

On his third day ever at the Grand, after their shifts had ended at exactly the same time, he'd asked Marina if she fancied a drink.

"Maybe some other time," she'd said. And then, when he pressed her a little: "You know, I'm not going to sleep with you."

He thought he must have misheard. "Sorry?"

"I'm not going to sleep with you," she repeated.

"Sure," he said. "Right."

It had been a very exciting development. Here was a woman, a beautiful woman, a new woman who didn't know the ins and outs of his every mistake, and she was thinking about not sleeping with him.

Unfortunately Marina had, since then, been true to her word. The Grand's Guest Relations Manager wouldn't give him love. He knew he'd never be able to lie on tangled bed sheets with her, his ear against her belly, listening to the secret squelches of her stomach. He'd come to terms with all this long ago. There was the time he'd asked her to the cinema "as a friend" — universal code for Please Sleep With Me. There was the time he'd asked her, when they'd been spending an increasing amount of their spare time together, to join him on a weekend away in a luxury hotel in the Lake District to "check out how our competitors do it" — i.e. I Adore You. On both occasions she had politely declined and had leaned forward to give him, as if by way of consolation prize, a squeeze on his upper arm. Oh, those arm squeezes. They left him longing for her more deeply than before. Less sharply, perhaps, but more deeply — an old injury that creaks on cold days.

An orderly had smuggled him a packet of

cashew nuts. He'd hoped to obtain them for no more than 50p, but in the end had handed over an outrageous £1.20. The market here drove hard bargains: a captive audience, more buyers than sellers.

The strip lighting was unagreeable. The spongy walls exhaled an inertia. A nurse came and apologised again on behalf of Mr. Marshall that they'd had to give his private room to a "patient in need." What this ward needed was a skylight. Or: a sculpture here and there. Or: a jaunty purple chair. Redecorate! He did not dare to think of the hotel except in flashes, its soft-lit elegance and luxury. He longed for spring, could not face another winter of freezing winds, cold fronts skidding in from the sea, wet gloves dropped on pavements, the counterfeit solidity of snowmen, iced dog shit in the gutters, snow scraped from the King's Road kerbs . . .

Come on, old man, stay positive.

"Am I disturbing?"

He opened two eyes and closed a mouth. Marina.

"I."

"Yes?"

"It's good to see you, Mari."

"Good," Marina replied. "Are you enjoying your stay?"

He hauled himself into a sitting position. "The service isn't bad, now you mention it."

"No?"

He rubbed his face. "Francesca came in yesterday and said it gave her an idea. She's going to get all the Grand's carpets ripped up. Replace the vacuums with a couple of mops."

Marina smiled.

"Is everything OK?" he said.

"With staff?"

"With the building. With the preparations for the PM."

"Of course. And I've brought a friend to see you."

"A friend?"

"Yes."

"I must be losing it," he said. "I can't see any friend."

Marina leaned forward in her chair and spoke into a space south of the mattress. Briefly Moose sensed movement. "Are we ready?" she said. "Yes? One, two, three, surprise!"

The surprise came in stereo and very nearly killed him. Held aloft above Marina's head was a tiny boy with a wicked grin, no more than two or three years old. He had long eyelashes and an extraordinary mop of thick dark hair, shiny as a freshly tarred road.

"This is Engelbert," Marina said. "Remember me talking? My nephew. I'm taking care of him again today."

Engelbert took a lolly from his pocket, spun the wrapper off and started sucking. He looked quite happy suspended up there, his tiny jeans hanging low, his red T-shirt looking snug.

"He's a good workout actually!" Marina's face reddened. "The little man is quite heavy!"

Moose watched as Engelbert was lowered onto Marina's knee. It struck him as another of the universe's myriad unfairnesses that this kid had so much life ahead of him and would spend at least some of it in Marina's lap. "Well," he said. "Nice to meet you, Engelbert."

Engelbert responded with a blink.

"Is that . . . ?" Marina said. "The pool . . . under the curtain?"

"Yep. The guy's not well. I didn't want to make a fuss. I'm sure they'll deal with it soon."

He was remembering — what was he remembering? Freya as a four- or five-year-old, perfectly viciously cute, capable of breaking the heart of a passer-by with a smile or poked-out tongue. Daddy, why doesn't sick look the same as what you've eaten? He'd made a note of that somewhere. An early inkling of genius.

Marina had spotted the file on the floor by the bed. "You are working?"

"No, just catching up on correspondence."

"Don't make it a habit," she said.

"Give me a quick debrief," he begged.

"You are addicted."

"Debrief, please."

"There are no new guest problems. Nothing to worry about."

"What about the punching incident?"

"Nothing to worry."

"Is there going to be litigation? Do we need to tell the GM?"

Marina wrinkled her nose. Engelbert sucked on his lolly. A nurse stared at the vomit and looked at her watch. "Do you want to?" she said.

"Pardon?"

"Tell the GM."

"Well, I suppose it's dealt with now, is it? And the guy probably had it coming."

Marina nodded. "These men."

"Yeah." He tried to arrange his face into the expression of a man who was not one of these men but who was, nonetheless, a man. "By the way, for the napkins, I'm definitely leaning towards conference blue now. A supplier in Scotland."

"You are better at this than me. I don't care much about colours." She paused. "Are you staying optimistic, Moose?"

"That depends. Is it possible to be optimistic about life without being optimistic about your own specific life?"

"If you're still thinking in riddles you are all right. Did you cut yourself shaving?"

"Possibly."

Moose felt rather than heard Engelbert's feathery sigh. Time to make some effort. You saw a little boy and you wanted his approval, the future to give the past its blessing.

"So," Moose said. "Engelbert. What's your favourite flavour lolly?"

Engelbert narrowed one eye. "Big," he said.

"Good choice, good choice. Size is important. And — next question — how old are you?"

To this Engelbert also said "big," so Moose politely enquired again.

"Three," Engelbert said.

"Nearly three. Still a month to go, haven't you?"

"Three," Engelbert said, frowning, and Marina conceded the point.

"Is this perhaps your auntie, then?"

There was a pearl of saliva in the corner of Engelbert's mouth, on the side swollen by the lolly, and Marina dabbed at it with a tissue. "Auntie," he said. His stare announced that they'd already covered this ground.

"And can I assume your mother, Mari's sister, is a fan of the other Engelbert? The singer?"

The child looked alarmed.

"Mr. Humperdinck," Moose said.

"Urgh," Engelbert replied.

"Humperdinck."

"Urgh."

They had encountered another misunderstanding. Moose decided to croon out a lyric from Engelbert Humperdinck's classic "Release Me" by way of example.

Engelbert let a decent interval pass, then burst into a shoulder-shaking chuckle. "Silly!" he said, pointing a mini finger at Moose. "Big! Silly." The joy in his voice was pure — oh, it was pure. Instinctive, unimpeachable. It took hostage that childlike part of Moose that was still receptive to balloons and pink wafer biscuits, that sketched small turds in the margins of notebooks, that felt almost three years old.

"You're right," Marina told Engelbert, her

mouth hovering close to his ear, her long fingers smoothing his hair. "People can be silly, can't they?"

"*Him* silly," Engelbert said definitively. He looked a little put out.

"He's right. I'm silly. A note was actually left on my car recently, making a similar point."

Being singled out for comment by a fresh, miniature human: it was a very special feeling. Moose felt 20 or 30 per cent drunk. The pain massing in his chest as he laughed was not altogether unpleasant.

The three of them watched Nurse Monica Jones folding things, straightening things, stacking things, arranging things, packing things and lifting clipboards from the ends of beds. You could hear a high wind outside and imagine old leaves coming loose from great trees. There was something acceptable about death, something soft and almost amiable, until you considered the very specific inconveniences it would bring about. The fact you'd miss your daughter's wedding, for example. Miss the chance to remarry yourself. To be a grandfather. He'd never meant to stop at one child.

Marina was speaking. "Actually, Adolfa isn't any big fan of the Humperdinck you were talking about. She named him because she loves the music of Engelbert Humperdinck the composer. The German who did the *Hansel and Gretel* opera. Our papa was a musician. The Humperdinck you are thinking about actually took his stage name from the German composer, you know."

"You have a sister called Adolfa?"

"Yes."

"And she likes German classical music?"

"Yes. Why?"

"Just wanted to get my facts straight," Moose said. "Unusual names, in your family."

"This is coming from a Moose," she said.

He twisted a little in the bed, enjoying the spark in her expression, and propped himself up at a better angle. "They tell me I'll be out of here in forty-eight hours, Mari."

"Wow. That is great."

"Yeah."

"What will you do first, when you are free?"

"First? First, I guess I'll take a walk."

She nodded. "That sounds like a good idea."

A walk. Yes. He missed the greens and blues of the sea, the feeling of the water tickling between his toes on weekly beach strolls, triple-scoop ice cream in one hand — coffee vanilla chocolate, vanilla choc-mint choc-chip — and an enlivening can of Coke in the other.

"Being ill, Mari. It's really no fun at all."

"Yes. My sister has diabetes."

"Adolfa?"

"Yes."

"That's not good."

"She qualified for a clinic trial, in London. She will go there two days a week, for three months. So I will get to spend a lot of time with this special small person."

Engelbert smiled. Milk teeth white and aligned. And had the kid been tanning?

He asked Marina some more questions about preparations for the PM's visit. They talked for a while about the allocation of staff to different tasks. In the past she'd proven herself to be valuable counsel on subjects as diverse as boiler repairs and British dining-room etiquette. He'd recently found a book confirming her opinion that salt cellars and pepper mills should always be removed from the dining table after the main course. She understood hotel work was about putting on a show. He loved watching her backstage. Often she was drinking a Bloody Mary, the tip of her tongue removing pulp from her gums.

Perhaps the greatest mystery about Marina was her continued status as a single person. Her aloneness was an inalienable right but also a source of mass confusion among the Grand's male population. Jorge had once told Moose (over a plate of leftovers in Chef Harry's kitchen) that the game show Marina's ex-husband used to present on Argentinian television had involved, among other challenges, a segment where audience members had to fart on demand.

Engelbert leaned his head back into Marina's chest and studied Moose with an intensified, possibly rivalrous curiosity.

"So," Marina said, "how do you plan to prepare for the next heart attack?" It was as if she were asking about a long weekend coming up.

"Jesus, Mari."

"A man must be prepared for the worst thing. When I visited last, you looked worse. I didn't want to ask. But today, cheered up. Colour." She smiled.

"I'm forty-five. I'm young."

"My second husband? Forty-six when he finished."

This interested Moose. "*Second* husband?"

"Yes. I was twenty-five, skinny, full of love. Older men get older, this is the issue."

"Right."

"He fell out of a window."

"Oh."

"People bought me these cards, these flowers. Two hundred at the funeral. But it did not matter. He had begun to drink. Drink drink drink. All the time drinking. The pavement was the best place for him, in a way. This is what I came to see."

"Well, I'm sure he had his qualities."

"He had nothing in his favour. He lacked ambition."

"Well, you don't want a Macbeth in your bed."

Marina shook her head. "He was not Scottish, but the whiskies he drank, the cigars he smoked. They burned at his throat. He sounded like Kermit the Frog."

"Do you think . . . with the window . . . Do you think it was . . . ?"

"It is possible. I feel he was trying to cut himself loose from a deep misery."

"Oh, so he'd had a trauma?" For some reason Moose felt deeply relieved.

"The trauma was his whole life. Once he turned forty-five he couldn't even get a hard-up."

"On."

"What?"

"Nothing."

"He was *limp*, yes? You kiss him, you

319

touch his ear with your tongue, your hands stroking him, and nothing."

"___"

"Moose?"

"I'm fine."

"And he didn't care about my desire."

Moose swallowed.

"My desire to make films. Movies. I always wanted to be the woman version of Kurt Land."

"Oh."

El Asalto. Films about people in poverty, trying to make an honest life. People working out who they are in relation to the world, you know? And I was going to do a disaster movie too. An earthquake in Buenos Aires. But instead of an earthquake happening at the start of the movie, like in every other disaster movie, and people fleeing and some dying and others recovering, you know — instead of that it would happen at the *end.*"

"Why?"

She was silent for a moment. "Because sometimes the before is more interesting than the after, no? Heading towards the impact. What is beautiful about a dive? It isn't the splash, is it?"

He thought about telling her a good dive didn't involve a splash.

"I wanted to sing about what the lives were like before the quake, the day-to-day, what gets lost — that's the song I wanted to sing."

"Like a musical," Moose said.

She blinked. "No, Moose."

"Have we talked about this? You wanted to direct, to produce?"

"I went to film school for two years, but then the government changed again. There were the kidnappings. Then Cámpora. The return of Perón. Scholarships for film school was not the priority."

"I only ever really read about the Falklands," Moose said.

"Same with everyone. Now I am more keen on photography. I have three photographs in my first show next June, a thing in the gallery on Royal Pavilion Gardens. One is a pair of photos of the islands, in fact. Before the destruction and after. The other is of a pig. It's almost impossible to get pigs to look up, yes? So, it is an unusual photo. He looked up for me."

"Of course he did."

"This is why I don't want to progress higher. I told you this, no? Guest Relations suits me fine. I have time to pursue my interests."

"Right. No. I'll come to your show, Mari,

I will. It's great news. I didn't know about all this. I had no idea you wanted to do films and stuff. I'm going to definitely come. I'll probably buy something. One of the photos."

"You couldn't afford."

"No, right. So how much are we talking?"

"Expensive," she said slowly, extending the word beyond its means. "It would be nice to have you there, I will give you the invite, but if you don't come I won't pee on your grave."

"Much appreciated. Although, you'd be welcome to!"

You'd be welcome to. You'd be *welcome* to? What kind of unspeakable pervert was he? It was the latest in a series of missteps that edged him further away from her loveliness, her deep soft voice, her beautiful blunt talk and slow careful smiles.

"You should see a lawyer about your will, Moose. And an accountant. About the investments and trusts, things like this. Freya's future, in case. A backup, yes?"

Backup: somehow the phrase took the red right out of his blood. "I'm not going to die, Mari, and there isn't money to put in trusts and stuff. Forty hours and I'm out of here. Thirty-nine, almost."

"My papa used to say this: 'Only by

providing for family does the man achieve immortality.' "

"To be honest, Mari, I was hoping to achieve it by not dying."

"The world is bigger than us," she said, nodding. "Both my husbands were blind to this. My third fiancé also."

"Third?"

"You will probably be fine, but you must assume you will not. You cannot shut yourself off from the reality. No man is an Ireland."

He wanted to pick her up on the pronunciation, correct the error, but to do so would be petty and — after all — Ireland was an island, so it sort of worked, and the idea of islands was probably linked to the non-musical she wanted to make. He had to resist the lure of small things, irrelevance.

There was a long silence. Because what else was there? Apart from detail. Apart from the weird beauty of irrelevant things. His thoughts were drawn all the time towards silliness and insignificance. The bigger stuff could swallow you whole.

He wondered if the current silence was an awkward silence or a non-awkward silence. He thought probably it was an awkward one, but comforted himself with the idea that silences, like events, like good films, like good news, could maybe be perceived differently by different people.

"Engelbert," Moose said. "Look! Look at this!" He pointed at the strip of blue paper tacked around his wrist, inviting the child to play with it. Engel wasn't interested. He was nuzzling his nose into Marina's left nipple, eyes closed, his fingers clutching at her sleeve, his leg hooked over her thigh, never letting go.

"Oh, *Moo*se," Marina said, looking sad. "Do you remember when we met? It feels like years ago."

"It was," Moose said.

"Yes, exactly. Years. You were so muscly!"

It was a past-tense compliment, but he'd take it and cherish it. "Thank you," he said.

When the time came for Marina and Engelbert to leave, he felt a quiver of sad foreclosure. Marina leaned down, inviting him to kiss one of her bold, butterscotch cheekbones. Her hair smelt of fudge and for a lovely moment a strand of it was caught between his lips. Engel consented to a high five.

Was all this his fault, this heart thing? It was and yet it wasn't. He knew in some locked-up part of himself that he was responsible for his body's decline, and yet he also could not part with the gorgeously irresistible idea that everything was accidental.

He had been living in London when the news of his dad's death came through. Still young: twenty-two. At that time he spent his mornings tutoring maths students in a ramshackle east London building that smelt of mould, supplementing his income on Tuesday and Wednesday afternoons by lifeguarding at the London Fields Lido. He was also doing occasional bits of concierge work at a hotel owned by a friend of a friend. The lido job he did mainly to avail himself of free physiotherapy on his right leg in the little clinic out back. His knee was struggling under the weight of all the training Wally Clark was encouraging him to do on the ten-metre platform. Always tried to conceal the pain from Wally, but Wally always knew. He knew Moose was a very good diver, but knew too that he was never going to be a great one. That he'd started too late to be great and that while he might get a few statuettes from the smaller national meets, might even squeeze through the qualifiers for something as big as the Commonwealth Games, he was never going to bring home medals. The first time Wally had seen him dive he'd said, "What's with your arms, Phil? In mid-air you look like a moose." There was something inherently sticky about nicknames, particularly in the world of sport. False world, really. Made-up rules, achievements out of proportion. All part of the pleasure.

Undeterred by Wally's constant curbing of expectations, still more or less in the mind-set of the winner he'd been at school, Moose used to travel most evenings to the Merton School of Diving and Trampolining. The journey was slow on the way there and quick on the way back. After a session with Wally his shoulder blades felt like huge leaden wings and his brain, which for the previous two and a half hours had been tensely alive to every mischievously blunt instruction issuing from his mentor's lips, was rocked into a state of exquisite fatigue. At home he'd have a late dinner with Viv, and then she'd go back to her papers.

The call from his mother came on a Tuesday morning, around eleven thirty. He borrowed a friend's Ford, was in Brighton within an hour and a half, one wing mirror lost to a line of parked cars. His father was still on the carpet in the living room and the doctor from number 18 was there. A fatal heart attack while smoking in his favourite threadbare chair. No drama. Just fell over. Finished. His mother had dry eyes, was matter-of-fact, but her hands were shaking and shaking. The body didn't look like a dead body should look. His father had the faintly disgruntled expression of a man interrupted mid-task. His hands were on his stomach, peaceful, as if they realised they no longer had the right to reach for things. Pack of cigarettes next to him. Two Luckys left. Moose got a spare bed sheet and put it over the body.

Someone dies and a lot of questions are born, some of them overblown and others worth examining. What really was the point? What was the point in all that training, all that rigour and precision, the denying yourself ice cream, the desperate nausea after the two-hundredth sit-up? All his life he'd focused on exercising himself. After his father's death the me-ness of it all — the fanatical self-discipline — felt, for the first time, like selfishness. Would something bigger always intrude on your plans? When was the last time he'd done anything for anyone else? Shouldn't he and Viv be taking weekends away, having three-course meals somewhere? They'd only been married a year. Why hadn't he made it to his father's birthday dinner? Had his father's constant encouragements when it came to sports actually been a form of coercion? Was his mother, by showing no apparent interest in his athletic feats, the parent who in fact had granted greater freedom all these years — the freedom from expectations?

A few weeks went by without exercise. Thoughts were a sufficiently tiring self-obsession. His father didn't call to ask for updates on the dives he was trying. He didn't call because he was dead. For a while Moose had really felt that his father would call, would call him soon, and that they'd have a chance to discuss what the afterlife was like. It was the absence of all future communications that was so shocking.

The coffin was made from the wood of Aberdeenshire larches. Very durable. No chemicals. No polish and no stain. No screws, either; only old oak dowels. Cost him all the savings he had.

The idea a life could be boxed up into neat, discrete phrases. Probably it was bollocks. There were times before his father's death when he ate doughnuts for breakfast and curry for dinner and caught colds and didn't exercise for two days or three. There were times after his father's death when he went on long runs and went to the gym and ate expensive muesli in the mornings. The diving didn't stop straight away. He kept going. Years passed. He switched into and out of coaching. But something changed that day he saw his father dead on the floor. A turning point occurred.

Looking back, Moose's twenties and thirties felt fast and thin, somehow sketched in, important moments resisting depth. Whole years had the quick-scrawl quality of the notes Viv left on the fridge.

He and Viv tried for a child. There were miscarriages. Grieving for these lost children briefly brought them together, did it? Made them feel well suited, almost, to the marriage they'd rushed into. Then they got lucky, and he immediately thought, Fuck, what have I done? With the arrival of Baby Freya, his life widened out into the blur of family life. He began to eat a lot of chocolate. Got back in touch with Wally. Started helping him with coaching on Saturday mornings.

Fatherhood: the expense of it horrified him. More and more concierge work, saving up tips; he could do it in the evenings when Viv was at home looking after Freya. Less and less tutoring of little Cuthberts and Anthonys. Sunday afternoons travelling to his mother in Brighton.

At some point he and Viv stopped sleeping in the same bed (his snoring was the first excuse to surface) and at another point he became unsure whether women of his acquaintance expected a single-cheek kiss or a double-cheek kiss. He compromised by providing a friendly pre-emptive hug.

Vivienne began to go to a lot of academic conferences abroad. He became, for a while, the main carer at home. He felt like a single parent long before he was a single parent. He suspected her of infidelities. There were silent phone calls. There were receipts for dinners for two. There were coloured envelopes addressed to her in a small even script. But he didn't want to be the kind of guy who suspects his wife of infidelity, who shouts down phones and opens another's correspondence, so instead of confronting her about the potential affairs he tried to sleep with the babysitter.

"What are you doing?"

"What?"

"Why are you touching my face?"

"You're beautiful."

"Mr. Finch, I'm repulsed by what you're trying to do right now."

Repulsed. He felt sure Chloë, twenty-one and tanned, hadn't meant to use such an unforgiving word, or indeed to tell Vivienne what had happened.

What else from these years? TV became a

close friend. News of the Colour Strike, the postal workers' strike, the miners' strike, the Ulster Workers' Council Strike. Freya was quiet when images flickered on-screen. "UK needs a stronger leader, Phil." This from his Uncle Mick.

Then one day, in the newspaper, a gift. Next to an article claiming that Britain's economy had slipped remorselessly down the international league table, he saw an advert. Diving instructor — head coach — at an American university. A chance to do what he enjoyed in a place where no one knew him. An opportunity to experience the life of higher education that should have been his first time around.

His purpose would be to nurture young talent. It would be like maths tutoring, except there would be no more sedentary processing of textbooks, no more passed notes, no more rooms that smelt of farts, creativity exercised only in the labyrinthine daily excuses for unfinished homework. It would be like concierge work, except he'd get in shape again, and there wouldn't be such a need to be servile. There would be no more London, with its gloomy summers and endless protests and its winter of discontent — a winter that seemed to have expanded to accommodate many more months than a season reasonably should.

He cut the advert out. Put it on the kitchen pinboard. The idea of flight made him feverish.

Morningside Heights, Manhattan.
32 acres of land.
State-of-the-art facilities.

Probably he should always have worked on becoming a great coach rather than a great sportsman. His attempts to break out on his own as an athlete were supposed to have allowed him to get closer to living an authentic life, closer to that thing everyone agrees is to be desired above all else, which is freedom. Instead, the endless striving for independence had worn him out and made him hanker after everyone else's homogenous middle-class dreams: more security, more money, a better kind of car.

He got the job at Columbia on Wally's recommendation. Wally was a guy who always knew a guy who knew a guy. Being offered it convinced him that this was Fate. He had been selected, rewarded. The world had approved his plan. He told Vivienne it was a great opportunity for them both. Told her it would be good for Freya too.

But oh, the things Viv hated out there. The

summer humidity, the graffiti on the subways, the way it turned out that subsidised campus apartments were only for the academic staff on tenure-track. The Dean's secretary was very sorry if Moose had received the wrong information. Story of my life.

Eleven months into their time overseas, his marriage crumbled under the accumulated weight of her daily complaints and his technique (masterfully executed, he'd thought) of pretending everything was fine. She said that every time she rang the number you needed to ring to get a Social Security card, they asked her to state her Social Security number. She said that when she went into the bakery for a blueberry muffin, they pretended not to understand her. Tiny shifts of emphasis. Language — the thing she cared about most — conspiring to make her misunderstood. She couldn't get an academic position anywhere. Hadn't published papers here. Said he'd stripped her of her self-respect by moving the family out of England.

But she also kissed him sometimes and said "I love you" sometimes and sometimes — once — they went on an amazing trip upstate, and he felt again that she was the love of his life, so it still hurt badly, very badly, when she said she was sleeping with a guy called Bob.

This was how he remembered it. She was on the sofa in their small Manhattan apartment. She seemed to find her own admission of infidelity amusing. He saw that on the carpet beside the sofa, under her limp right hand, there was a half-empty bottle of gin. Half-full, he thought, but he couldn't change his mind. It was a half-empty bottle of gin.

He thought of the time he'd spent six weeks on the sofa after his father died, eating food from foil takeaway trays. The time he'd screamed at Vivienne that life was not right not right not right. The time he'd somersaulted off the board too close, way too close, daring it to clip his head, to make him bleed, to change his situation in some small or major way.

"I'm so sorry," she said. She'd felt ignored for years, she said. She was married to a man who preferred to spend all his time trying to make a living out of falling into water. A man who was content to fall and fall. Falling from three storeys high! Teaching others to fall! They'd never make enough money for Freya from that. "You're a dreamer!"

"No," he said.

"You are, Moose. Somewhere along the

line . . . somewhere, you mislaid the ambitions you had for yourself. Now you want to claim they were stolen. Yes, you are, you're a dreamer."

He blinked and his marriage was gone. She said she was going to make a life out here with Bob. Bob who loved her. Bob who knew her. Bob who understood her. Moose could stay here or move back to England alone. She was sorry. She was. "I'm sorry. So much of your life is repetition, Moose. So much of your life . . ."

"Is repetition," he said, and waited. If she was alive to this one cheap joke, maybe their relationship could be saved after all. But no, her eyes were cold, and he saw that the chilly sophistication of her sense of humour was one of nine or ten things that had doomed him from day one.

Bob had a place in Midtown Manhattan. Bob had three daughters. One was at Oxford. He'd beaten cancer, had Bob. Bob was a fighter. Bob owned an early Joan Miró sketch. Money if he sold it. Bully for Bob!

"You don't even like New York!" he said.

"Bob does. He likes New York."

"Bob sounds like a cunt."

"It's too late," she said, "for you to develop some spine." Comebacks were always something she was good at.

He thought, I love you, don't leave me, I love you. Who was she to take his daughter away?

"You can visit, Moose."

"With what money?"

"With all the money you keep saying you'll soon be earning."

"Fuck you."

"You haven't, not for a long time."

"Bob has," he said.

She looked at the carpet. "Yes."

"Ask her who she wants to live with," he said, and felt detached from the new chill in his voice. "Just ask her."

Viv looked at him with a flicker of something fresh in her eyes. He saw with disgust that he'd impressed her.

This conversation would come back to him over the years, slightly different each time. It was like one of those crazy tonsillitis dreams he'd had as a child, clutching a cool damp flannel to his face, his mother's diamond-shaped ice cubes shrinking in a bowl by the bed.

Vivienne asked Freya who she wanted to live with, and asked in the wrong way, just as he'd known and hoped she would. Vivienne *told* Freya what would happen. She said, "We're splitting up, darling, I'm so sorry. You'll live here with me." Viv was cleverer than him, undoubtedly. But despite or because of her intelligence, she had no feel for others' freedom, their need to believe they were in control, and he understood something of this — it was the biggest thing that life had taught him. As a toddler Freya had always complained when her mother carried her upstairs for a bath. On the nights when Moose was in charge, he took a different approach. He posed a question for his daughter: "Bath before or after dinner?" She made a choice and didn't protest when asked to stick to it.

In later years he'd waste a lot of time thinking about why Viv had so easily given up on their daughter. How Viv had seemed willing month by month to let a distance open up between them. Friends treated the situation with suspicion. It's a truth universally acknowledged that middle-class mothers don't abandon their kids. They looked at him like he must have threatened her, or beaten her, or slept with the babysitter. To one mutual friend all he could say, over and over, was: "I'm surprised too." All he could add was: "Maybe some women are different to others?" And also, magnanimously: "It wasn't that she was a bad mother." Which she wasn't. That was the sad thing about it. Wasn't even a bad wife — they were simply a stupid match. The sight of her sewing labels onto skirts and shirts and jackets, all her daughter needed for a new school term, looking over the bridge of those huge glasses. The constant vegetable casseroles. He came to think she was so very depressed at that time that she didn't want to go on living. Rather than killing herself, she wiped her life clean, started again, daughterless. But then again, this was only his version. They didn't talk much those last few years, not about anything meaningful. In the gloom of their marriage it was possible he had blind spots.

He closed his eyes and dozed, observing in his dreams a dozen dark mysterious trees. The way some branches stayed heavy in the breeze. The way others were subtle and reactive. He was hang-gliding over a forest, naked, the proud owner of a friendly erection. His balls were unrealistically big. Down below, Margaret Thatcher and her Cabinet waved and went about their business. He passed through several commas of cloud and swooped into a red lipless tear in the sky. In haste and natural expectancy of compliance he nodded at God and God nodded back. Then someone vomited once, twice, and God sipped a beer and burped.

6

She'd thought French. She'd thought Italian. She'd thought coq au vin with scalloped potato gratin, or tortellini with spicy sausage in a bouncy-sounding sauce. *Bon appétit, mademoiselle! Buono appetito, bella!* But no: her fancy dinner with Surfer John turned out to be a takeaway curry, two bottles of cava, a polystyrene cup sticky with watered-down mango chutney, and a bag of fractured poppadoms. She made sure to claim the least broken one as her own.

He said, "Can I come in and use your loo, before we go?"

"Sure."

"Can you hold these?"

"You brought booze?"

"It's BYO."

"What is?"

"The restaurant."

"Which one?"

"Not sure yet," Surfer John admitted.

"I thought you were supposed to be recommending somewhere? Booking some-where? I thought you were picking me up in your car and we were —"

"It's at the garage," John said. "Suspen-sion. Think I put too much stuff on the roof."

She waited.

"Maybe we'll have a drink here first, Freya Finch? My mum gave me these two bottles from her party."

This was how it went. This was how, tipsy on cava, she found herself having to retrieve, at 9 p.m., the Coastal Raj menu from the back of the cutlery drawer in her own cold kitchen at home.

They sat on the sofa and ate their food. Newspaper-covered cushions were on their knees and the plates were balanced on these. Her dad had bought the sofa last year second-hand from a woman in Littlehamp-ton. As the woman had pointed out other items for sale in her house, and explained her decision to let her husband run off with an acquaintance — "My mother said be kind to less fortunate girls" — a gold bangle had crashed up and down her arm.

"Are you happy, Freya Finch?"

She held her fork in mid-air. "Are you get-ting deep, John?"

"Just wondering," he said.

"Maybe. It depends. You?"

He shrugged like it was a stupid question. "Cool," he said. She saw that a scattering of dead hairs sat on the shoulders of John's T-shirt. This provoked in her a jolt of empathy: he too had had a recent haircut, maybe even at the mercy of Wendy Hoyt, though probably somewhere better. His ears looked pink and vulnerable tonight, borrowed from a less confident boy. She liked those ears and liked the feeling of liking them.

The cava bottle stood on the coffee table. A ripped bag of lettuce relaxed beside it. She was wearing her best knee-length dress, a little yellow number with polka dots and ruching at the shoulders. She should change into jeans, probably, but she was concerned about what that would say to him. She didn't want to get too casual, because that would mean giving up on the idea of leaving the house. A cocktail bar after food — that was the revised itinerary.

On the carpet was a leaflet that had fallen out of the *Argus:* a plea for support from the Society of Redundant Electrical Oven Salesmen.

"It's their own fault," Surfer John said

between mouthfuls. "They need to adapt to gas."

He retrieved the second bottle of cava from the kitchen. The window took the force of the cork. Fifty per cent of the booze frothed out on the carpet.

"Sorry," he said. It was his word for "I am failing badly at feats of manly endeavour."

"Don't worry about it," she said. It was her phrase for "Yes, you are."

They laid tea towels down on the dark part of the carpet. They drank beers they found in the garage. It occurred to her that if mice had peed on the cans then she and John might both die of a mouse-pee disease. They stared at each other, waiting for the next move. They talked about John's art. He'd done a foundation course. She thought it was an interesting combination within him, art and sport, but the mention of painting seemed to send him into a low-level trance. He rubbed his eyes. The skin around them took on the pinkish blush of a faded ketchup stain. He said he was really bored with working at the hotel, that his parents were asking him when he was going to move out, what he was going to do with his life, when he was going to start getting serious. He glanced up and glanced away. She realised he was nervous tonight, that he'd been nervous since he arrived. This gave her an unexpected feeling of power. It put her at the centre of things.

"Have you got a girlfriend, John?"

A smile crimped the corners of his mouth. "I don't know what you're suggesting, Freya Finch, but you're making me very uncomfortable."

She laughed at this and he laughed too.

She swallowed a very small forkful of chicken and rice. Took another gulp of beer. He pointed out that she was an extremely slow eater. Much quicker on the drinks, he said. She felt warm now, alert. Playful, attractive. The cork had popped; something had changed. But what was she doing here? The thing with John had been stillborn. Everyone knew this to be true. If they were supposed to be together, they'd be together by now, wouldn't they? Did she only want him in order to want somebody who would maybe want her back? She enjoyed being a small, thin, successful drinker. People assumed she'd be wasted after just a glass or two, but she could handle . . . How much could she handle? She hiccuped and the room seemed to dim.

When John reached for his beer the logo on his white T-shirt stretched and the muscles in his forearm flickered. "How's your dad?" he said.

"OK. He's hoping to be out of there in a day or two."

"Yeah? That's good. He needs to get himself a healthier lifestyle, that's all. Get down to the beach."

"He's on his feet a lot in the hotel."

"Yeah," John said. "But ideally the feet would be moving."

"Don't be mean about my dad."

"You're smiling," John said.

"I was thinking about him at this wedding, a party we went to for my cousin."

"Dancing, was he?"

"Yep, that's what he called it."

"Bad?"

"It definitely wasn't any dance I know. He was just causing his head, his shoulders, his two arms and his two legs to sort of tremble, pretty violently, at roughly the same time."

John laughed. "Diving's supposed to require grace, right?"

"Yeah. I'm not sure what happened. There are two halves of him, and in the middle there's this gap."

It was weird the way some words could enact the exact thing they described. "Gap" opened a gap. The silence threatened to last. But John, maybe sensing this, began telling an unexpected story. It was about a time, just before starting his art foundation, when he'd spent a long weekend house-sitting for family friends in London.

"They were a German couple."

"The owners?"

"Yeah," he said.

He'd been tasked with looking after their elderly red setter. Alas, the red setter had died on his watch, just lay down and died by the sofa on the Saturday. Died. He didn't know what to do. It was dead. Shit, what should he do?

"It definitely didn't seem appropriate to disturb their holiday," John said. "At least, not until I'd figured out what to say. You know, to soften their . . . their grief, or whatever."

On the Sunday, Wilhelm the red setter was rigid. Surfer John reasoned it wouldn't be long before he began attracting the attention of flies. He found the Yellow Pages and phoned a vet, and the vet referred him to a pet cemetery, and a taxi was too expensive so he decided to get the Tube.

"You got the Tube," she said. "The London Underground, with a dead dog?"

He was going to put the dog in its custom-made wicker dog basket. But what if kids wanted to say hi, what if kids on the Tube tried to pet the dead dog through the bars?

That would badly suck. "That was my reasoning, Freya Finch."

"So what did you do?"

"I ended up putting Wilhelm in a suitcase."

"John!"

"What? It seemed the right thing to do. What are the rules?"

He took the suitcase on the London Underground. At Hammersmith the lift wasn't working, so he began to lug the dog-filled suitcase up the stairs. An absolutely massive bald guy said, Let me give you a hand with that, son. No no, I'm fine, John said. But the bald guy insisted: I'll take it ten steps and then you can take it ten; it'll be a workout, mate. And then the bald guy took the suitcase and ran off with it.

Doing voices for the dog owner, the dog owner's husband, and at one stage for Wilhelm himself, John explained with new vitality how the post-holiday conversation with Mr. and Mrs. Mencken had gone. Yes, your dog is dead. Yes, your suitcase is gone. Unfortunately the suitcase and the dead dog were stolen at much the same time. He described all of this, and shared some of the swear words that were thrown his way in both German and English, and speculated as to what the thief must have thought when he opened the luggage with glee. From John's description of the event there seemed to emerge, regardless of the truth or falsehood of the story, regardless of her giggles, regardless of the attentive timing with which he delivered his lines, a portrait Freya was surprised to recognise: Surfer John was lonely. It had never really occurred to her before that handsome, popular people could be lonely. John could work a room at a party, for sure, but maybe all this time he'd had dreams of different rooms.

"Did you ever see the Germans again?"

He blinked. "Yeah. They still come round for dinner with my parents sometimes. They like to have weekends by the sea. What's weird is that Mrs. Mencken sometimes gets a little . . . despite the dog thing, she can get a little flirty."

"Well, you're a good-looking guy, John."

He rearranged his legs. He put his hand on her knee. "You're not too bad yourself, Freya Finch."

She looked at his hand. It had come out of nowhere, that hand.

"You have nice legs," he said.

"Have you considered poetry, John? I really think that's your true calling."

"I just think you're very cool."

"Why?"

"Did I already mention you're pretty?"

"What about my amazing wit? My brain? My drinking skills?"

"It's all connected," he said. He sighed. "Sorry. Think I might be drunk."

She moved her foot so that it touched his foot. They sat looking at each other. She looked at his arms. She pictured him balanced on his board. To be balanced like that was what everyone wanted.

She felt deep in the moment now, aware of every little gesture and breath, the seconds that flit by and the ones that fatten. There was a new energy within her, hustling for release. It wasn't about him, exactly. It was about a sense of risk, was it? Everything felt improvised, their pauses and word choices, their voices stupid but clear.

"I hope your dad gets, you know, completely better," he said. "I like him, he's like you, he's funny."

"I don't want to be funny."

"You make people smile."

There were times these last few nights when the house had seemed to grow around her. When it had seemed unbearable to be alone for another hour.

He leaned forward and she closed her eyes, but not the whole way; she could still see a version of John brushed by lashes. She waited. She sensed him assessing her. What if he didn't like what he saw? People saw different things at different moments in different ways. There were all sorts of ways of seeing. A stray fragment of poppadom crunched under his legs, or her legs; she wasn't sure. It would be seriously massively mortifying if he didn't, after this, make a move. There were heartbeats. Lots of them. Fuck's sake. I mean honestly. She moved against him. Pressed her lips to his. Warm taste of the almost-champagne. Wheatier hint of beer. Spice of sauce. He didn't use his tongue straight away, which was the sign of a good kisser. When the proper kiss came it was warm and deep, hungry. They were intertwined. He was on top of her. They kissed like that, her body taking his weight. It felt good, liberating, not to be able to move.

His left hand was under her skirt. He placed it between her legs and kissed her neck. His hand was warm between her legs. She kept thinking someone might see through the living-room window. They moved upstairs to her bedroom.

On the bed she was trying to decide if it was worse at this stage to risk being called a slut or risk being called a tease. She wished there was some safe position in between those two bald judgements where a person could simply *be.* The carpet was covered with her clothes, bags. There were water glasses everywhere, each in a different stage of fullness. She had tidied the room this afternoon. This counted to her mind as tidy.

His chest was broad and smooth. The elastic waistband of his boxer shorts left a pink line of pressure on his hips. His tan-line ran just below. He kissed her breasts. He pressed himself against her thigh. He was more handsome with his clothes off than he'd ever been with them on. This probably couldn't be said of most people. It stood in his favour. So did the volume of other girls who fancied him. She needed someone to need her. She didn't want to dwell on the vast unoriginality of that. It was nice to feel swept up into someone else's concentration. She had a sense that she'd been trying to stay away from mistakes, and that it might be better to let them occur.

The best part of the evening was lying in bed with him, watching her little black-and-white TV, their bodies almost touching. He seemed fine with the fact she didn't want to go the whole way. He had produced a condom in case it was needed, and the only passive-aggressive thing he'd done after that was to unwrap it and keep it nearby. He didn't try and twiddle her nipples. She was grateful for that. The unused condom lay there now on her yellow bed sheets, in the thin light of the TV screen, like a dead jellyfish, or a scrap of litter, or a length of sun-bleached seaweed — something the sea had coughed up in the night for beach walkers and dogs to behold.

■ ■ ■ ■

FOUR:
THE GRAND

1984

■ ■ ■ ■

1

From the back garden came the sound of splintering wood. Ancient Jones had hired someone to rip down his fence. He wanted it replaced with a tall stone wall and had ignored Dan's offer of help, and also his advice about planning permission. So many of Belfast's elderly saw no profit in the concept of compliance. A wall was a wall and if they needed one they'd have one.

"We got another threat," he said.

His mother was reading a book entitled *The Complete Encyclopedia of Practical Palmistry.* On a side table a plate of toast crumbs was positioned on a copy of *IRIS* magazine. "No no," she said.

"We did, Ma. In the night. You know we did."

"I know nothing. I'm a washerwoman."

"Letter box went. A note."

Her empty gaze floated up over the spine of the book. "You'll give yourself a headache, Dan."

"A headache's the least of our worries."

She sighed. "It's a mystery, is what it is. Mystery's *all* there is. People like making their threats. It's the same as the ideas about emigrating. They enjoy — Kathy's your example — talking up these ideas of emigrating to Australia, to all sorts, a load of made-up places."

"Australia's as real as Ireland, Ma."

"Like hell it is. Didgeri-bloody-doo."

"Some really do emigrate."

"And others don't."

"You'll play the percentages, is that it?"

With her slippered foot she nudged at a mug on the floor. "Will we go again?"

"Not for me."

"Go on now, wet the tea if we'll talk."

"I've no thirst," he said.

She yawned and put the book down. Spit sparkled on her dentures. Her chair had been in a different position yesterday, a yard or two closer to the lamp. She was always moving tables and chairs around the living room, repositioning the footstool and the porcelain, half killing herself with the effort. The optimum layout eluded her. He was not sure if she had a notion of perfection in mind, or if she simply liked the feeling of not-quite.

He was correct to tell her about the letters and phone calls. He judged that something could happen soon. There'd been dog shit through the letter box on Tuesday and again on Wednesday and if things were about to get worse she needed to know. There was the bomb too, due to go off in about forty hours — assuming this, assuming that. The bomb: an implausible afterthought. But it was the afterthoughts that tired you out, arriving as they did on top of your ordinary worries. No one would suspect him of being involved, but that didn't mean there wouldn't be recriminations for the community.

He'd held his mother's bony shoulders yesterday and tried to emphasise that the risk of burnout now was high. And what had she said, lifting his dad's golf club half an inch off the ground? "I've got the five iron to protect me."

It was almost funny. Acceptance, acquiescence: for a woman like his mother these were hitches in the swing.

He pulled the letter out of his pocket and read from it. "*Burn you Fenian cunts.* More or less plain, Ma? More or less blunt?"

"I saw it on the kitchen table."

"Good."

"I've read and understood the thing."

"And?"

"I thought it could've done with a comma."

"This house, gone. The value, gone. I'm not sure you get it. The memories."

With the word "memories" he saw her expression harden. She pitched herself forward, shaky, refusing his help, the golf club taking her weight. "Jesus," she said. "Is that . . . ?" She was eyeing the patio doors, her shoulders rolled, a twitching in her hands.

"What?" he said.

"No," she said.

"Yes," he said.

She was contemplating, probably, her own reflection in the glass. Reality sinking in.

"Jesus," she repeated. "No, no. I really think it is. Can it be? You've stirred it up, Dan. We're in all kinds of hell now. King of over-kings."

"What?"

"God save us."

"Ma?"

"Jesus Mary Joseph. We've no control, none."

She instructed him to open the patio doors. Seeing the mad voltage in her eyes he obeyed. He followed her outside. Chimneys were ranged against a pewter sky. A magpie was marching mutely along a length of rain-bright guttering.

"What are you on about?"

She shook her head and leaned on the five iron. "Knotweed."

"Not what?"

"Weed! That's what this is, Dan! The stuff you've been saying is bamboo! It's Japanese knotweed is what it is. I'm only now seeing this clearly."

What was she telling him? How should he read her? He tried to shut out the sounds of the fence coming down next door.

"This is the worst thing that could be happening to us, Dan. The McCluskeys have had a terrible time with the stuff. Terrible. They couldn't remortgage! And forget selling. *Forget* it. With this, forget it *all.*" She looked one way and then the next. Raised a weathered hand and let it fall.

"We're talking about the threats, or what?"

"Knotweed! Against the fence! You stirred it up with your whipping."

"But —"

"This is the worst thing, Dan. The worst. This'll cost us what we've got."

There was actual foam in the corners of her mouth. The worst thing. A weed. Did she really believe it to be true? He felt he was witnessing the culmination of some strange process. She'd been drifting day by day away from the woman she used to be, and now she was deep in some other realm, bobbing on illogical waters, utterly beyond the reach of reason. Her mouth was trembling. She was whispering "knotweed" over and over, different shifts of emphasis, forming it into questions, exclamations, prayers, protestations. Last night's rainwater sang in the downpipe. He heard it in gaps between the destruction next door. What the fuck did weeds have to do with mortgages, with moving her somewhere safe? He asked her. She didn't answer. What did Japan have to do with Ireland? Knots? Weeds? The Mc-Cluskeys? She was mumbling, pacing, conversing only with herself. He laid out each constituent piece of the puzzle but could not make a picture emerge.

The low murmur she used for Hail Marys. The chainsaw starting up again next door.

She turned to face the house, eyes down. She poked at the patio glass with the end of her stick. Another insect squashed, work lost.

"I ran the shammy over that. What's the point in me cleaning if —"

"You're going to have to sort it out, Dan. You'll have to be sure to sort this out."

"Me?"

"*You.* Who else? My only son."

Only one left here, she meant.

"Ma, I'm not sure you're with me. The letters. The phone calls. They're telling us we're on notice. This knotweed thing is not imp—"

"*Notice,*" she said, vicious. He watched as the power returned to her eyes. Impossible not to be impressed, ever since he was a little boy, by the gravity of this woman's dissatisfaction.

"Mother," he said.

"You're telling me you can't protect an old woman from some little shites?"

"Calm down now."

"You're saying, Daniel, you can't get some of your *friends* to help protect ourselves?"

He looked at her.

"The fact I'm old doesn't make me the fool. If you think me a fool you're not paying attention, Daniel. I've got the Bridge Club quarterfinals. An important match. A cake to bake. Cake. You'll deal with it alone, this one thing for me, one, sometimes, at last."

"We've an abundance of cake. We've got cake coming out of our fucking ears."

"It's one I'm doing for Annie, isn't it? Broken into again. Bakewells."

"Broken into?"

"Again."

She looked like she might cry.

"Who by?" he said.

"What a question."

"You mean?"

A further burst: "*Will* you sort the knot-weed?" She wiped her mouth with the sleeve of her cardigan.

Holding last night's letter between forefinger and thumb he said, "But I have jobs to do. I've to find us a place to move to. Be safe."

"If we sold the house today with those damn roots, those roots wrecking our foundations, your father's Beatles records and Rolling Stones records and all his furniture too? We'd be laughed at. Laughed. Same thing we should do to the teenagers."

"Who?"

"Letter writers. Scare-mongers. Children them all."

"They're not children."

"Oh, they are. Every man in this city's a child."

"Let me make you a cup."

"You'll have time enough to sort the garden *and* your jobs. You're lying low, are you not, now this mystery trip to the mainland's over? You're keeping yourself free? Dawson McCartland no longer lives in my

362

garden."

Silence.

She showed him her cheek. He kissed it.

While she was upstairs he sat on the floor in the hallway. He called Dawson. No answer. There had been no contact since the debrief, no news at all for days. He had done what he'd been told. He had stayed the extra nights. He had passed on information about the Prime Minister's schedule in case Plan B, whatever that was, was needed. They had asked him to get into conversation with the receptionist girl again, and he'd done that, found a few useful things out, so why had they then seemed so annoyed? Visibility, yes, but for the greater good — the bar was where he found her, it wasn't a matter of choice — and if there was a Plan B then the scheduling could be useful for the Plan B, and if the Plan A worked then what exactly was lost? It was him that stood to suffer if his face was remembered. It was him that stood to suffer if he remembered the girl's face. The cause would not be harmed.

Putting the phone down, picking it up again, trying to call Colum Allen to no avail. He dialled some of Colum's people in finance, planning, intelligence, ordnance.

He saw the receptionist girl swimming in a lake. He saw her smiling. He saw her thrown across the room by the blast. Finally he tried John C, one of Dawson's more lowly job-doers, the last man whose number he could remember by heart.

"Danny! Good to hear from you. I'm trying to unblock the old toilet. Same trouble as before. Did I tell you?"

John was one of those people who reported so many details about his life, minor and major — his allergy to shellfish, the moles he'd had removed, the latest fornications of his sex-addict sister — that you could easily be conned into considering him a friend. He was admired for his command of Gaelic and known for his collection of weapons.

"John, my messages don't seem to be getting through."

"They're being passed."

"Where to?"

"The paves."

"What?"

"The pavements."

"What?"

"Yeah."

He had the feeling John had started smoking the green stuff again. "If my messages to him *are* getting through, and he's not calling back —"

"Don't fret yourself, Danny. Y'know Dawson. He drops out of the old equation now and again. It's the wee who-ha."

"Are you stoned, John?"

"Not yet, but it's a fine plan."

"I need protection, John. I need to speak to Dawson. I need a couple of D-squad guys in my house. I've probably got a few days, only, before petrol comes through my letter box. Do you understand?"

John sighed down the line. "Plenty safe places we got, Dan. I think Seán made it clear, no? Even showed you some places. Get you and your mammy in there in a flash."

"Seán's an arsehole."

"Not a big one, though."

"How big an arsehole do you need to be?"

"It's an inverse proportion type-a thing," John said. "Bigger the arsehole, higher the rank. Squeeze a banana up that hole of yours? Middle-ranking. A melon? Top of the tree! But we've probably said enough, if you're on the home phone. My point being, Seán'll sort you. Seán's nice enough."

"He's not. He's not nearly."

"Relativity," John said, and hummed a tune. "Relativity, relatives, relative."

"My mother won't leave and she won't let

me sell."

"She's got a number of nimble moves, eh? Mothers. I know your pain. One of those problems a lot of people have got. But strictly —"

"John, you owe me this."

Five pounds of Semtex, three detonators wrapped in toilet paper, five battery packs fitted with tilt switchers and timers: this was what John owed him.

"Dan. Listen, Dan. Not to offend a rising star such as yourself, but dealing with family problems, it's not really my area of the manual, y'know?"

Dan let silence soak down the line. He hung up. There was a world of bottled energy in his arm. Thirst dragged at his throat. In the kitchen he poured himself a pint of water. Outside in the street he dropped the glass; it smashed. Dawson. Knotweed. Silence. Armies. Her name was Freya but it didn't do to remember names. Names were as bad as faces. Why was nobody answering him? A hero's welcome was what he'd been promised. Instead a door seemed to have slammed.

With the outsole of his shoe he ushered broken glass into the gutter. Gravel sitting in stony reserve groaned as it went the same way. He saw that all four tyres on his van were still slashed. He'd half believed they would mend themselves overnight. He placed enormous faith in the miracle of materials, in what materials could make and do each day, but rubber wasn't skin, it would never heal itself, and wishful thinking was the worst kind of thought.

2

Summer was bedding down into autumn. Days had begun to pass with surprising speed. She wondered if she was the only person in the world who preferred trees with no leaves. The branches looked dark and dramatic. Knots and crags were revealed. John's dad was a botanist so John knew some species' names. He introduced her to a few on a walk through Stanmer Park. Crab apple, common ash. She liked being able to name them.

Her father was back home now. He was spending two or three hours in the hotel each day and going to bed by eight o'clock each night. Eight was a child's bedtime but he was better, less pale. Standing up straight and walking without wincing. Fine. He was fine. He was counting down the days to Mrs. Thatcher's arrival. Less than five days! Less than three days. Staring out of windows seemed to be a new and involved hobby of his.

She yawned and wondered if John was her boyfriend. There seemed to be movement on the matter. She had bought him a new white T-shirt which bore eight words in raised grey lettering: I AM THE WRETCH THE SONG REFERS TO. She was pouring a lot of imagination into the minor nightly lies she told Moose to account for her whereabouts. He had no great problem with staff romances, but she was pretty sure he'd disapprove of one involving her. Exhaustion, though. Complacency. Her string of alibis was losing the taut quality of truth. Maybe she'd just tell him, get it over with. Maybe she'd just say, "Get over it, Dad." A girl like Sarah made no effort to conceal this stuff: I am a woman; I am a sexual being; I suck cock. The thought of your dad knowing this, though. On balance she'd rather die in a pit of irate snakes. Plus she'd not yet sucked John's cock, or any other cocks. Putting a penis in her mouth was on her to-do list, definitely, but it was positioned somewhere between Visit Newcastle and Try the Steak Tartare.

She was doing a few double shifts, saving money and getting the Grand ready, searching for a succinct explanation for why she felt a happiness now. This thing with John was not love, it could not be love, but it was something, and that was the beauty of it. She still held a desire to travel, but she held that desire more casually now. Why not stay based in Brighton awhile? Going to new cafés and bars. Producing notes on the proper set-up of rooms. The work wasn't interesting but there were small satisfactions in getting it done. Possibly anything could become an art form if you took the time to do it right.

At home, in the early evenings, before slipping out to meet John, she cooked risottos or soups for her dad, pouring leftovers into old Hellmann's jars. The jars had half-peeled labels ("Hell"; "man"; "llma") and she didn't respond to Susie's notes. Seeing Susie again would remind her how weak she'd been. Why had she agreed to let that blond boy into the hotel? The occasional first-thing-in-the-morning thought: got to find a way out of that problem. Too much to do, though. The last of Susie's messages had said: "Sebastian will be by the cook's entrance 10 p.m. Friday SHARP." She imagined Sebastian looking over Susie's shoulder as this was written, twanging his green braces with a concentrated calm, insisting on the capital letters without pausing to think that they would make the word look blunt.

Swimming again. She and John went to the pool together in the early mornings. He had a Volkswagen of which he was disproportionately proud. "74 Scirocco" apparently. The roof rack was decked out with a complicated array of belts and ropes. The car was destined to become a modern classic. She asked him if the definition of a modern classic was a vehicle that started three times out of ten. He told her this issue was unrelated. He owned the car and his surfboard and seemingly nothing else. He still lived with his parents. They had money. They resented having paid for his fine-art foundation course. She had seen some of his work now and could understand, in part, their resentment. None of it was fine and a lot of it didn't seem like art. An apple that resembled a pear was the best of his paintings. The apple-pear ("papple" he'd said) appeared at breast height on an Asian body. It half concealed a nipple. The other boob was obscured by a doughnut. But *he* called it art, and that was probably what mattered, and despite what his parents seemed to think, John wasn't lazy at all. He did more shifts at the hotel than anyone else. He threw himself into cold water. His readiness to exercise and to sit in easy silence afterwards were two of the things she liked about him.

It felt good to be swimming so regularly. She was reclaiming some lost part of herself. It was like finding money in an old pair of jeans. It was like discovering the jeans were actually pretty excellent. It was surprising how much fun swimming could be when there was no one shouting at you to go faster, no one telling you to tighten your technique, just the warm smooth joy of moving from wall to wall.

Long-axis drills, girls!

Streamline, Finch, S-T-R-E-A-M-L-I-N-E.

Focus on the blast-off! Dolphin kicks! Doll, phin, kicks!

A one-metre breakout? I've seen ping-pong balls stay under longer.

Which never made any sense, actually, because why would you bring a ping-pong ball into a pool?

John treated Freya like she was a swimming genius. This she also liked. He asked for advice despite his own proficiency in the pool. She could see why people retreated so deep into relationships, forgetting to bother much with friends. There was a kind of creative pressure that came with shutting other people out, even if you weren't part of a perfect match. You could begin to enjoy a new sense of privacy. Watching TV with John. Being underwater with John. Being on the floor of a room in the Grand.

She'd told him at the end of his shift to walk straight up the stairs, casual. She waited for him on the landing. It was important that she control this small part of the process. Trimmed sunflowers in shapely vases sat on side tables. Little oil paintings looked sticky in their complicated frames.

As soon as she saw him she knew he was excited. Flushed face, sliding eyes. He looked older at work than he did at play. The white shirt and dark jacket never looked neat, exactly, but the attire suited him and he was clean and soft in the eyes, a lack of knives, a hint of stubble on his chin. The skirt she was wearing was faint and light against her legs.

They slipped into the room. John was wearing his sporty wristwatch with a fabric strap. She didn't like it. His skin carried that lovely fresh cucumber smell. He pressed her against the wall and got onto his knees. Edged her knickers down slowly, a little left and a little right, until they stayed taut around her calves, a thin thread of wetness in the cotton. He began to kiss her there. She didn't really know what he was doing. He didn't really know what he was doing.

She buckled a little in the moment where he found her clitoris with his tongue, but he lost his place soon enough, like a person reading a book on a beach, all elbows and breeze and no focus. She tried to picture the ocean between the curtains, to make herself come like she could when alone, but in the end she settled for a small fake shiver, a tremor of half-pretended pleasure, and he looked up at her with a smile that was almost shy, an attitude of glad relief. On the apricot rug he moved inside her. It lasted a couple of minutes longer than before. His shoulders felt huge in her hands. His movements were too fast but the room was bright and thrilling. Crisp linen, strange bed. Secrets. Slow down. She felt confident and composed as she stood naked by the window, fastening her hair and watching the sea. She sat back in an elegant chair — pure skin, he wanted her. She understood for a moment that the hotel was gorgeous. They took a bath together, John's foot between her legs. Tried to make love in the bath but actually that just didn't work. She would ask Sarah, if Sarah ever got back in touch, if there was a way of doing it right.

On the way out of the room there was a moment of horror. She looked up and saw Marina coming around the corner. Marina's eyes met hers and flitted to John and with a quick smile she kept on walking. This was bad, seriously bad, a pit of irate snakes.

In the shallow end of the pool John said, "Teach me your tricks, Freya Finch."

Freya found that when she tried to explain to him how to improve his backstroke — when she tried to break down her instinctive actions into sensible-sounding words — certain technical points that had always been confusing to her began very slowly to unravel. Her underwater breakout, for example, had always been too quick and too messy. She always clutched the side of the pool and threw herself back with vigour, but only briefly slipped under the surface. She tended to emerge into her first stroke after just a couple of seconds, the water agitated by her exit. This was fine when she'd first begun competing in swimming meets. The traditional school of thought was that the underwater portion of the race didn't matter much; every competitor started as badly as the next. But in her last few months of competing at County level Freya had seen a new breed of backstrokers coming through — guys her age like David "Blast-off" Berkoff, whom everyone at Brighton Swordfish tipped for gold in Seoul. Freya's swim team had been made to watch videotapes of Berkoff competing at the junior championship in Connecticut. A few coos and giggles. A boy you wanted to meet. In the taped race Berkoff had started with unbelievable speed, gliding forever underwater, a tightly streamlined yellow-capped torpedo of a boy, rapid little dolphin kicks propelling him on and on. Freya couldn't work out how he did it, could not conjure any version of his magic.

Once she came up with a description to give John, though, dividing Coach Dean's analysis into four or five simpler steps, in nontechnical language, she started to see how the theory might be put into practice. She started to see herself from different angles. Berkoff's blast-off lost a little of its mystery.

She held on to the edge at the deep end of the pool. Light from high windows made the water glitter. She coiled herself into a backstroke push-off position. The ceiling was panelled and some of the panels were missing.

As she flew backwards she shaped her body into a needle, one hand covering the other. The movement was familiar, the same as always, but now, as her body found its form under the surface, she made sure that the tiny bumps of her almost-biceps actually squeezed her ears. She whipped fast with her dolphin kicks, focused on her feet, kick-kick-kick-kick-kick-kick-kick, and they lasted longer than was normal. She shifted into a flutter-kick she'd never done before. One, two, three. Seemed to be under for ages. With her right arm still stretched in the needle position she flexed her left wrist a little, just a little, having to force herself out of the habit of keeping it straight, so it wrapped around the water and moved into the stroke, slow motion, piece by piece, yes. With her bodyline still long, her torso feeling steely, she found she could slip up through the skin of the water at a more slender angle than before — begging for air now, desperate for it — the liquid feeling quiet and thin. Out into the clamour. Gasping. She couldn't believe how few strokes it took to complete the length. The wall came too quickly. Her fingers bent back.

"Awesome stuff, Freya Finch."

She steadied her breathing and hauled herself out of the pool, pulled her goggles down around her neck and took her swimming cap off. She sat beside him, legs dangling in the water. Their feet were fluttering ghosts.

"Here," he said, smiling. She inclined her head towards him and he kissed her ear.

His ear-kisses were dumb. She loved them. Dumb. She put one arm around his shoulders. Put the flat of her other hand on his chest, the hardness of it, a few hairs at the breastbone that looked both old and new, foreign and familiar, squiggles of Arabic script. It was dumb. Even in here she could feel the heat building up behind his skin. She'd spent some time looking at his front, his back, bedding tangled around their intertwined legs, and had never managed to find a single pore. He didn't sweat when they kissed or touched each other. No part of him seemed to evaporate, no hints left behind, but in the moment you were with him the heat was yours. Clothes fell away, problems fell away. It couldn't last. He was Surfer John! Dumb.

Two girls walked past, their pale feet slurping on tiles. One of the girls glanced down at Freya. Her breasts were large. In a bad painting, perhaps even a painting by John, melons would be the suitable fruits. It was Sasha from the hotel.

"You!" Sasha said.

Freya responded in kind. She didn't like Sasha. She was one of those girls who only gave her energy to men. Instead of greeting John with a pronoun and an exclamation mark, Sasha touched his naked back and stooped to kiss his cheek.

"So you guys . . ." Sasha said uncertainly.

"Swimming," said Surfer John.

Sasha smiled at them like come wouldn't melt in her mouth. "Cool. This is Claire."

"Sure, I remember."

Freya said hello, niceties were exchanged. With her carefully shaped eyebrows, Claire had no choice but to look surprised.

"Yeah. Catherine loved that movie, by the way."

"Cool," John said.

"We should all go out together again."

John considered this. "Cool," he said.

"Bye then."

"Bye."

"Yeah."

When Sasha and Claire had trotted away, she and John sat in silence. She edged closer to him and touched a jewel of water on his back — one of the ones Sasha hadn't ruined. It started to break. It ran down his spine. He shifted, annoyed. He stood and squeezed the ends of his shorts. A stream of water hit the floor.

"Been hanging out with Sasha, then?"

"There was a group," John said. "Catherine. Pete."

She shook her head. So many names. What did it mean to live in a world where you lost track of all these names?

"You've got nothing to worry about there," John said.

"I'm not worried."

John shrugged. "There's no problem, then."

"So you haven't . . . I'm only asking out of interest."

"Listen," John said. "Nothing like that. But you know I don't want anything serious, right, Frey? I mean, you don't either. You're great. We talked about this."

He was doing that thing everyone in Brighton seemed to do: confusing a conversation they'd had with themselves with a conversation they'd had with her.

She shook her head again. He was dumb. The argument was dumb. Pears and doughnuts and surfboards. When the light of John's attention was settled on you, everything was warm. When it strobed elsewhere you felt incredibly cold.

Did he want to have dinner together tonight?

That would be great, but probably not, he was helping his cousin with something. She was mental, it was tricky. Which was a shame, because Freya had bought all the ingredients for shepherd's pie, his stated favourite, her mum's old recipe, and was thinking she'd cook it in Chef Harry's kitchen — ruffled potato peaks, Worcestershire sauce dashed into the meat, simple and warm and homely.

The next day preparations for Mrs. Thatcher's arrival went into overdrive. Hordes of special brandy glasses had arrived from Kent. Seven boxes of napkins from Scotland. Staff were given detailed briefing packs containing bios for key guests, starch for the collars of their shirts, and reminders on how to say Hello. The conference had been going on since Monday but everyone was still waiting for the important speeches to happen and the second wave of important people to turn up. One of her father's new catchphrases — "Got to cut down on unforced errors" — was getting a lot of airtime. Sometimes he elaborated on it with words about McEnroe, straight sets. A slipped shower head had concussed a guest on the second floor, Barbara had inflicted far-reaching injuries on a PR person, and a junior minister had been found asleep behind the bar at breakfast time, his pleated cummerbund draped over his eyes. Other than that, everything was fine. Since the cummerbund incident, the minister had been moving around the hotel gingerly, quietly, like a little girl who'd been told not to spoil her best dress.

There were only a dozen or so guests at the hotel who had no links to the Conservative Party. They'd made early bookings that needed to be honoured. Marina spoke to them all. Would it inconvenience them terribly if the bar was closed on Thursday night for a private event? Was there anything she could do to assure them that the increased security presence was no cause for concern? A whole room on the first floor was given over to specially ordered fax machines, two word processors, and something called a Laser Printer. Most of the male staff had visited the printer. They came back with tall tales about its innermost functions. A man who'd just moved into one of the new housing developments in Hove, where 200-year-old oaks had recently been cleared to make space for smooth driveways and neat unvarying gardens, came and gave the summer staff an "interactive workshop" on Improving Posture and Dressing to Impress. He was Austrian and his whole strategy seemed to be based around the idea that if you dragged people's insecurities into the headmaster's office and exposed them to ridicule, the insecurities would go away.

"So you think these tights are flattering

for you, yes?"

"Um," said Sally Woo.

Freya's father was desperately worried about all the CCTV they were installing. He said he hadn't expected so much noise. Men in overalls drilled holes. There were cameras on each of the landings, cameras at the ends of the corridors, cameras directed at the stairs, cameras high on the walls of the restaurant. She stood with him as he watched a new camera bracket being affixed. The installation was slow and methodical. Moose said his big regret was requesting that they avoid putting power cables along the skirting boards. They'd gone up into the ceilings instead. He was worried they were weakening the overall structure. "If lightning strikes, this place'll go to ground." There was high colour in his neck as he fretted and questioned. She had a sense that if she left him alone he might fall over again and this time he might not get up.

"Is this really necessary?" he said. "All this surveillance?"

His words made the men in overalls yawn. They continued their work in silence, smiling at each other whenever a female guest walked by, or a hip-swaying member of staff like Sasha. Her father popped another of his pills.

Climbing the stairs. Moving past scraps of paper. Reminders of her progress were taped to the walls: "you've just Reached step 15 of 45!"; "you've just Reached step 27!"; "step 33! The museum of lost content is NEAR!!"

The Captain's handwriting was a mess of red crayon. The oversized exclamation marks gave the staircase the vibe of a blood-drizzled crime scene. None of the dusty-stern professionalism of museums she'd visited on school trips. Sternness wasn't in the Captain's manifesto. His aim was "to make history personal." She liked the sound of this, but wasn't sure how the toy panda that always sat slumped in a dusty funk on step 36 fitted into his plan.

Two steps at a time, her lungs feeling huge. She had an idea that spending time with Surfer John was making her fitter and another idea, less spacious and admittable, that he was not an entirely healthy presence in her life. There'd been no contact from him today. He'd avoided her in the reception area.

There was a sign on the wall saying "ALL THE WORLD'S A STAGE." Someone had scrawled "ONE MELANOMA" at the end.

She reached a landing striped with light from a low window. She looked out at the sky. So small, so high, a kestrel. That or another of the hovering birds. She couldn't say for sure. On the sill were hairs and parts of dead flies. She turned and caught sight of herself in a tall dirty mirror. She saw in her face no information, no misinformation, only a person trying to be profound. On impulse she wrote "Ha" in the dusty glass. She stood back looking at her mirror image, the "Ha" above her head. Then she wrote "cliche" and stood back again. She couldn't remember if the accent was acute or grave. She missed French lessons, the basic escape of them. Her old red tennis shoes were decorated with Tipp-Ex, a move she now regretted. The lines had sunk and smudged, taking on the shape of a shaky mistake.

Ribbons dripped down from the door frame, each of them loaded with stitched-on bells — bells from cat collars, and dog collars, and two bigger ones that seemed to be from bicycles. She passed through them and found the Captain pouring water from a jam jar into a tiny kettle. It looked very much like one of the kettles they had in the rooms at the Grand. The Captain informed her that he wasn't due a tea break for another half an hour but that a man without a flexible schedule might as well be dead.

He invited her to lower her bottom onto the flat head of a stuffed crocodile. He'd overlaid the croc with various blankets. Taxidermy was one of the Captain's many interests but he'd admitted, on one of her previous visits, that dead crocodiles might be offputting to a certain kind of museum-goer, hence the blankets. He'd also expressed a distaste for people who killed deer and put the antlers on their walls. "Taxidermy's one thing, but I can never trust a man who mounts animals."

"So, has it been quiet, the last few days?"

"No no," the Captain said. "Lots of trade, lots of trade. Visitors. Susie was in here the other day, actually."

"My Susie?"

"Yep."

"That's funny."

"I humbly disagree," the Captain said.

"No, it's just . . . well, she never seemed that interested in this place."

"Oh, right," the Captain said, eyes falling. She saw that she'd upset him.

After scratching at the spidery veins on his cheeks the Captain shifted in his chair. As he did so the chair squeaked (the same squeak as always) and he jumped up in surprise (the same surprise as always), his eyes becoming rigid. He gave the chair a comprehensive assessment and sat down again with maximum slow-motion caution. He'd made a claim, back in June or July, that JFK had once owned this chair. It was a standard plastic chair with metal legs, a piece of furniture as unpresidential as any you could find, but there was something attractive in the idea that a clunky mediocre thing could have supported an extraordinary rear. You wanted to believe it. You thought, What's the harm?

She took in the product names and logos, the shine and tilt of crowded objects, the press of shapes and colours. A radio was on low and behind the churn of static there was solemn classical music playing. The area they were sitting in was the section of the museum that the Captain called Reception, the Curator's Office, the Membership Enquiries Room, and/or the Gallery of Modern Items Which Haven't Yet Been Lost. Behind him golden trees bloomed on silver wallpaper, and on corner shelves there were leaning piles of paper, large jars of gobstoppers, two small gnomes with chipped hats, and a wooden sign saying "Admire the Artist's Craft or Get the Hell Out." Actually the "C" of "Craft" had been scratched away; only a shadow of a curve remained.

To her left, a half-dozen tables of different heights and designs bore their different loads. Each heap represented a category of items the Captain was "considering." The principal question in any such assessment was apparently this: would X item one day be of interest to those studying "the way we live now"? There were silver moon boots, mittens on strings, and Cabbage Patch Kid dolls which, despite their unanimous chubbiness, were somehow suggestive of Susie. A mirror framed by a soft piping of Silly Putty. One Reebok Freestyle shoe with red laces. A see-through plastic box of cap guns. A see-through plastic box of spud guns. Two partially completed World Cup sticker albums (Argentina '78, Spain '82). An allegedly life-sized cardboard cut-out of the Jolly Green Giant. Finally he showed her a tub labelled "The Adventures of Slimer Hi-C Ecto Cooler" and a framed picture of Michael Jackson holding hands with E.T.

"Cost me nothing but time," he liked to say, surveying the clutter around him. But it was clear that all this had cost him a *lot* of time. Years, probably. Most of a lifetime spent collecting. He said what he loved was the euphoria of completion — getting a whole set of a particular stamp — but he also said that most of his projects resisted wholeness. A given category was rarely finite and there was always, also, the pull towards finding more impressive examples of what you already had. She thought of this place as basically a home for strays — items orphaned or dismissed. There was a lustre of love to it all. You needed to leave your cynicism at the door. Things otherwise neglected or forgotten. Give them some space and say they matter.

The Captain *did* kind of smell. But it was a comforting smell: that warm, dark, dusty-cupboard scent. He smelt of the attic where the Scrabble set lives, where the Christmas decorations are stored, where the spare tennis racket you'll probably never need lies on top of the inexplicable Subbuteo set. He smelt a little bit like the school did when you went back during holidays with a friend, maybe to check it was still there, maybe to use its fields for a run, and found that it was only half a school now, because a school was not fully itself without the human scuttle, the morning whispers, the clatter of locker doors, the laughter and bony bodies and lipstick swaps, the screech of rubber soles skidding around corners, the soupy clouds of sprayed deodorant, bra labels examined to confirm or refute claims as to sizing, tired arms draped over deeply scratched desks. Repetition. Lists. To go into school during the holidays was to be upset by its emptiness.

The Captain's head tilted and his jaw slackened. He seemed to be tuning in to some distant frequency. He coughed. "How's your father?"

"Oh, OK."

"Yes?"

She sighed. "Yeah."

"Good," the Captain said.

"He's relieved to be home. And to be at the hotel for a few hours each day."

"He should be careful," the Captain said. "A left-hander, is he?"

"How did you know?"

"They worry about everything," the Captain said. "Small matters. A cautious people. Comes from writing in exercise books in youth. The effort to avoid smudges. The need to cock the wrist. It's admirable, but . . ."

He began telling her about a chapter in a book called *The Public Image,* but at some point during his second sentence there was a staircase-creak and the bright sound of bells. She looked up and saw a thin arm parting ribbons in the doorway.

"Oh, hi." The arm belonged to a hairless man. He was one of those people who are all skin and joints: the lean, frantic body of a long-distance runner. There was a small purple bruise on the right side of his forehead.

"This is Freya," the Captain said. "Freya, this is Mike."

"Hello," Mike said. He seemed to struggle with the dusty light. Swatted at it, squinting, as if it might be persuaded to go and live elsewhere.

"Do you want tea, Mikey? I'm manufacturing some."

"I was just going to borrow that LP," Mike said.

"Ah yes, a new addition." The Captain foraged under the desk. "Here we are, here we go."

"Thanks," Mike said. "See you later, then." He disappeared step by step. Only the faint violin music on the radio remained.

"You lend stuff out? Like an LP library thing?"

"No no," the Captain said. "He's different. Lives downstairs, you see."

"On his own?"

The Captain cleared his throat. "With me."

"Oh, like flatmates."

"Almost exactly like that."

She thought it was good that the Captain

had a flatmate. She'd always imagined him alone. "So Mike's into Culture Club. How old would you say he is?"

"Even us oldies have preferences," the Captain said, and she thought she heard a note of reproach.

"Yeah, sure, I didn't mean —"

Preferences. The Captain seemed to be blushing. In the silence a vague idea became crisp and tight. Did the Captain have a lover? A lover who was a man? She'd been wrong on these matters before. She thought about Roy Walsh. She'd hoped for a while to see him at the pool. Like a stupid little girl she'd walked past the gym she'd recommended to him, peering in through the windows in case he was inside.

"You're very mysterious, Captain."

The Captain grinned a bigger grin than she'd ever seen from him before. He gestured at the room around him. "I have no biography, only this." He blinked.

The little kettle began to judder. They listened to it squeal. He made her a tea but left the bag in.

"How is everything else?" he said.

"Everything else is good."

The Captain put a finger in his ear. He wiggled it around. "Continue."

"Well, there's not much to say."

He nodded. The violin music on the radio gave way to the sound of a piano.

"I suppose one bit of news . . ."

"Yes?"

"I have a sort of boyfriend, I guess."

"Ah."

"Though not really." She waited. She wondered what she might hear herself say next. There was that old familiar dread of being misunderstood. "Labels," she said.

The Captain retrieved a sheet of sticky labels and held them up with a certain satisfaction. He began humming a tune. He broke off to enquire as to the length of the relationship. The figure was too pathetic to disclose so instead she said, "We're non-exclusive. I think so, anyway. And he's a little bit older. But they say that women are more mature anyway, don't they? So there's that."

The Captain leaned forward in his chair. "Dog years," he said.

"But we don't even really know each other. Not really properly, I guess. And he hasn't actually made contact today. So it's not a serious thing, for those reasons alone."

Which it wasn't, was it? The knowledge went through her in a quick chilly trickle. If it ended soon she wouldn't even have an excuse to be unhappy. She had a handle on maybe 1 per cent of John's secrets, and he in turn knew no more than 20 per cent of hers. Probably they were simply killing time with one another. There was probably only a certain amount of time to kill.

She thought of the TV her parents had bought in New York, off-white with rounded edges, and in the evenings the three of them — her, her dad, her mum — watching reruns of a show called *Rhoda.* The jokes about sex made Freya suicidal. Shut up, she'd think. Please God, shut up. Can't you see my parents are here?

The Captain fell into a very short power nap.

"Have you ever thought of leaving Brighton, Captain?"

"What?" He yawned. "Who's leaving? Me?"

"Brighton. You think you'll stay?"

"Pah! This place is a peach on a plate. Why would I leave?"

"It's the sea you like? The air?"

"No! Whole place. The Lanes. The little shops. All the colour and the culture. The range of resources for a man's rummaging. The *life,* if you're asking. Best place in the world, Brighton. People don't realise what they have, on the whole. All of us are frogs in warm water."

3

Moose was in his bed in his bedroom in his house. Since his return from hospital he'd been in love with the balding carpet. He'd felt an expanding admiration for the dust on the bedside table. The room belonged to him. The cosiness of real curtains and blankets. Plates and bowls, mugs that didn't match, the spider on the sill that refused to die. Choosing when to turn the lights off.

For Moose these were the days of soups in creative flavours: Freya's mushroom and sesame; Freya's split pea and celery; Freya's creamy artichoke hearts lightly fizzed with fried shallots. His daughter the cook. His daughter the marvel. The days of imagining Marina in a small white towel, on a distant beach, the sun, the sand, and reaching down, down under the blankets, and re-membering that his hydraulics had been rendered useless by the beta blockers. It was time to get back to full-time work.

During his first day at the hotel — an hour, no more — there had been champagne and cake, hugs from two dozen colleagues and friends, a kiss on the cheek from Marina. A rush of affection that moistened his eyes.

On the second day he'd worked for three whole hours. He spoke to a guest in a herringbone jacket. The guest told Moose that without cynicism and sarcasm the modern man was finished. The cross stitch in the weave. Brought to mind the bones of a fish. Moose, so often prepared to put diplomacy first, told the guest that he didn't agree. Cynicism and sarcasm were all very well, but only if underwritten by a proper depth of feeling. Irony might be the modern mode, but shouldn't someone sing the virtues of earnestness? This didn't mean turning away from the darker aspects of a life. It did not mean conspiring to make your days something falsely warm and neat. But it did involve looking closely at the dark stuff, paying attention to its variety of shades, its aliveness, the ridiculous and the terrible, the fart jokes and the tragedies. For to be alive, to be capable of laughter and surprise — this itself was a beautiful thing. All this he said to the guest and in response the guest said, "Churchgoer?"

Yesterday he'd done a five-hour shift. He'd seen a guest tipping George a ten at the door and intervened when the man reached the desk. "Let's get you an upgrade, sir." Head Office wouldn't approve, but Head Office hadn't just survived a heart attack. Also: it made good business sense. The softly spoken guy had the label of a luxury airline on his luggage. Probably came to Brighton a couple of times a year, a break before or after business meetings in London, or else he rarely came but had well-off friends who might. Upgrade him and send some wine to his suite. He'll tell people. They'll tell people. Men looking for a reliable home for their expense accounts: these were bread-and-butter customers. Certain limits on the kind of room his secretary can book for him without the company's finance guy expressing some alarm, but a generous allowance for meals, for drinks. And the cost to the hotel? Nothing. The suite was vacant until Thursday anyway. The late checkout associated with a suite jams up housekeeping a little, but only if he actually checks out late, and a businessman rarely does. Creaky cogs in Moose's brain were turning again. God, it was good to be back.

The first batch of conference-goers had been more or less well behaved. The occasional incident of major drunkenness had been tactfully dealt with by Marina. Most were there to applaud the minor speeches, the ones no one seemed to care about. Moose had watched some of the TV coverage. He saw how the cameras cut quickly from whatever weak joke had been delivered on the podium to the faces of the speaker's wife or sworn enemy, an attempt he supposed to add some human drama. Even the keenest among the Tories milling in the lobby at breakfast time, little plastic badges swinging around their necks, admitted it was the Big One that mattered. Mrs. Thatcher had briefly been in Brighton yesterday but, despite a last-minute flurry of phone calls from her Private Secretary's Assistant's Assistant, she had decided to stick with the initial plan: sleep in London, return Thursday night. The wait would only add to the eventual satisfaction. What was that line Viv liked to use about his diving? Happiness makes up in height for what it lacks in length. Robert Frost or another of her favourites. Early on she used to read him poems late at night and he understood so little except the rhythm, and that was lovely.

Thatcher snoring and dreaming in a bed he had checked. And he'd be there. Not in the bed. Not in the room. No no no. But in the building, heart beating. They'd talk at the big drinks function and then again maybe over breakfast. For the sake of his health he tried to rein in his excitement. Tried also not to guess at the number of weeks it would take him to get promoted post-visit.

When he told Chef Harry his daughter had been making him delicious soups, Harry told him she'd been going through the hotel's library of cookbooks, teaching herself new tricks, asking his advice when she couldn't work something out, test-running different dinners for two. Was all this for him, for his return? Her mother, when she could be bothered, had been a good cook too. He longed for a chocolate fudge sundae but it was completely out of the question.

He tried now to remind himself of that first year back in Brighton, him and a motherless teenage daughter returning to the secondary school she'd left behind. But all he could really remember was the incredible amount of little jobs to do, the lifts to and from school and swimming practice and netball and friends' houses at the weekend and the washing and cleaning, cleaning and washing. How, even when he started paying

Sandra to help out occasionally, other tasks filled his few spare hours and at work he was always exhausted. For the first time in years sleep ushered in no dreams and there was a comfort in that, wasn't there, in dreamlessness?

He'd decided he was going to buy his daughter a ticket to Spain. One of Marina's sisters had a spare room in an apparently safe bit of Madrid.

Cutting down on salt. The careful moderation of sugar. Never would another cheese croissant pass his lips. Not outside Bastille Day, anyway. Cigarettes only on very special occasions. When the promotion came. When Freya graduated. His fiftieth birthday. He had a timeline in his mind. It was full of light exercise and lots of salad. After a while he'd come off the beta blockers and his lower body would be back in business. He'd find the love of a good woman, or at the very least an average one, and settle down. He was no Patrick Swayze; he'd been aiming way too high. Marina. The idea of it! He hoped the lady in question would have feet no bigger than size seven. He hoped she'd make him laugh. In every other respect he was open to ideas.

His last few hours in the hospital were vague now. The decor of the ward had already shrunk from view. As soon as you were told you were to be discharged, the place could hold you no more. You drifted free of the whole world of scrubbed-clean suffering. Amazing how quickly you could take on the mindset of a visitor: this place isn't so bad; it holds a certain intrigue. When you know it only confines others, confinement doesn't seem so troubling. Add that to the lessons. Suffering is in your face or two hundred miles away, nothing in between.

His mother arrived at the Grand at the worst possible moment, thirty-six hours before Mrs. Thatcher. She had a gift for perfectly atrocious timing. He was in the midst of dealing with the Close Protection Unit, and also the plain-clothes Sussex police officers. Politicians were cluttering the reception area, politicians were swapping rooms, politicians were complaining about overbookings. They didn't understand that you *had* to overbook; had to assume one in ten wouldn't turn up. The hospitality industry was founded on this fraction, but some people went crazy, didn't care that you were going to cover their whole stay in the Metropole, didn't care for the implication that they perhaps could have called to confirm. Staff frowning. Staff flirting. The twitch of temporary security cameras, the yapping of small ineffectual dogs. Men with thinning hair and full smooth faces and that combustible mix of fatigue and wealth that made people step out of the way.

"It's me," she said, standing under the chandelier on her outstandingly abbreviated legs. That hunched posture. That forward tilt. Countering, he supposed, the constant impulse to sink back.

"Mum!" He kissed her. "So great to see you."

"Pipe down," she said. "I'm not one of your guests to impress."

"Mum." He sighed. "Not really a great time, really."

"You have five minutes."

"Well —"

"You do. Everyone does. Most jobs can wait a thousand years."

He took her into the restaurant, sat her down underneath a painting of a boat. He loved his old mother. Really he did. But he was busy, very busy, and she had a knack for distracting him from his goals. Her method was to tell him many sharp things he didn't want to hear about himself. It was death not so much by dagger as by a million unfurled paper clips. In her old age she was a great dispenser of tips and wisdom, around 5 per cent of it excellent. She seemed to favour a throw-it-all-at-the-wall-and-see-what-sticks approach. Probably the tactic ran in the family.

"Can I order you something?"

"I brought my own food."

"That's not allowed, actually, but —"

She unzipped her handbag. Gave him, with her usual flawless intuition, a freezer bag full of nuts. "Unsalted," she said, and removed a balled tissue from the sleeve of her cardigan. From a second freezer bag she began to feed herself splodges of dried apricot.

He asked her a couple of questions. She held up a finger to indicate that she was still eating. Robbed of conversation, he lifted the first nut to his lips. His saliva glands began gratefully welling, the tingling anticipation of a lovely savoury treat. The disappointment when the nut touched his tongue was huge. Without salt these things were pointless. To get through this exchange, what would he need? A better quality of snack, for sure. Also an enormous amount of alcohol combined with an enormous amount of caffeine. He waved at Shirley and ordered his first glass of wine since the infarction.

His mother's chin, badly receded these last few years, bobbed and creased as she chewed. One or two little hairs poked out from furrows in the flesh. He longed to lean forward and pluck them. When she was seated her long neck gave a false impression of stature.

"Heart," she said, taking a sip of water from a squat little bottle.

So then, she knew. Inevitable. The part of town she lived in was remote but rumours seemed to like the local soil.

"First thing to go when you run around all day."

"Is that so?"

"It's what I've read."

"The *Mail*?"

"That and the liver," she said. "Hits hotel workers in particular. What you need is to *think* less, and then do less. Simple. Get a couple of things right instead of this constant ridiculous —"

"Running around. Yes. I know."

"Accept your fate, Philip."

"Meaning?"

She chewed and inspected a further piece of soft fruit. "You'll die just the same as me."

"I'm pretty sure the running around hasn't been as bad for me, Mum, as the cigarettes and fatty food."

"Mr. Self-Aware," she said.

"I don't know why you always say that."

"Where's that Marina lady? I like her."

He coughed. It hurt.

Theatrically she sniffed. "How could you?" she said. "Not a word from my own son."

"I didn't want to worry you, Mum."

"How could my granddaughter not tell me? This is a double betrayal, make no mistake."

He sighed. "I told her not to. I didn't want to worry you."

"You always did make things up. If you scored two goals you'd say you'd scored three."

"That never happened."

"Terrible exaggerator."

"Untrue. That's you. How did you find out?"

"Freya."

"Well then," he said, feeling only a little let down. "It's not a double betrayal, is it, if she told you?" He thought for a moment. "How long have you known, then?"

"Eh?"

"How long have you known about my — the infarction?"

"Few days," she said.

"And you didn't think to visit me earlier?"
She was squinting.

He said, "How did Freya seem, when you saw her?"

"We had tea. Her visits are so quick. A boy in a car was waiting for her outside."

"A boy in a car?"

"I think so. Some kind of *sail* on top of the car. Like the car was a boat. She had a flushed look in her face."

"Who?"

"Your daughter."

"What do you mean?"

A sigh. "She was wearing a very short skirt, Philip."

"She's young, Mum. It's what they do."

"I know. I helped her take it up an extra inch."

"Oh."

She chewed on a dried apricot. "Yes, there's no avoiding it, she was wearing very sexual knickers."

"Mum, Jesus."

"There's a study in masculinity waiting to be written about you."

"What does that even mean?"

He drank half his glass of wine and felt his brain begin to soften. He settled on the not unpleasant idea that the boy waiting outside the house for Freya had been a taxi driver — Stan the Taxi Driver, probably — and chose to ignore the fact that Stan was seventy-something years old, a little beyond being called a "boy," and didn't drive a car that looked like a boat.

He *almost* enjoyed the first five minutes of any given exchange with his mother, the dry asides and minor duels. It was only by, say, the thirtieth minute in each conversation that he tended to dream of stabbing her with a cheese knife and selling her body to medical science.

Twenty-nine minutes had passed. He could feel a tingle in his fingertips. She told him to stop looking at his watch.

"You'd have been better off staying at the College," she said. She opened a piece of cling film, strips of dried mango within, another of her favoured snacks. He looked at all the bad luck in her eyes. It was there always between them, the fear it would pass on.

Chew chew.

Chew.

He'd finished his wine. It burned now in his chest. Watching her eat, listening to her eat — it killed all the hunger he had. The Listen to Your Mother Masticating Diet. Lose ten pounds in a month. He could hear policemen talking in the lobby. From the kitchen came the dim sound of Chef Harry shouting.

"I'm the happiest I've been," she said, unprompted.

"Good for you, Mum."

"It's true."

"I'm glad."

They talked for a while about a favourite café of hers that was closing down in the Lanes. Then Gillian, one of Moose's recent front-desk recruits, came up and said, "I'm sorry to interrupt."

Good, Moose thought. Gill sent from heaven. Little red-headed Gill who had ambitions, big dreams for herself. Show my mother how busy I am. Show her I actually add value. "What is it, Gill?"

"A party member . . . He wants a king bed, but there's only rooms with queens left, single or twin, unless we move someone."

"This is my mother."

"Oh, wow. Hi." Gill did a half-wave half-bow.

His mother smiled her shockingly sweet smile — the one she reserved for total strangers — and dispensed a perfect compliment about Gill's bracelet.

"Gill," Moose said, "is he on the list?"

"He's got a reservation, yeah."

"No, the Key VIP list."

"Oh, no. That's what I'm saying. He's not one of them."

He nodded and told her what she needed to do. Tell him you can get a king bed brought in for him. It's no trouble. We can get a removals company to bring one from a partner hotel. Tell him an alternative, though, is a room with two queens. Mention the room with two queens has more square footage and better bathtubs and there would be the second bed on which to spread out his clothes and conference papers — just a thought.

Gill said a wide-eyed "Fab" and ran off. Moose's mother scowled and shook her head. "Charlatan business," she said. "You'll be going to hell in a handbasket."

He watched her eating fruit and struggled with the idea that she might have once been young.

For most of her adult life his mother had seemed to prize plausibility and security above all else. "Don't get your hopes up." "Let me play devil's advocate." "What's not healthy is all your *ideas.*" Her credo seemed to be "Don't set yourself up for disappointment." In those days, she'd frowned at any mention of religion. She saw through plot twists in television series. People who took newspaper articles at face value were fools. Kidnapped children whose innocent faces filled the news would inevitably already be dead. She believed in an illusionless life of achievable objectives in which, if a person was lucky, they'd get 1 per cent of what they wanted. She liked to claim that obtaining the Maths teaching job at Varndean — which for some reason she insisted on calling the College, *the* College, as if there was only one — was an achievement Moose should never have tried to better.

These days she still held him to account for giving up on teaching and tutoring, for having made the wrong life and picked the wrong woman, but in most other respects she was different to the mother he'd grown up scared of. Her sharp dark hair had turned silver and her standard small-heeled shoes had been replaced with soft flat items she referred to as pumps. It seemed to him that the arrival of these pumps on her feet a few years ago had brought with it a corresponding shrinkage in bone mass and a new interest in going to St. Andrew's on Sundays.

God. Something had changed four or five years ago in her relationship with God, namely that He had started to exist for her. The conversion had at first appeared to be purely a practical matter. A means of installing herself more seriously into the local community. Meeting new people, telling them her stories, explaining that if you marry a red-faced English postman he'll die and leave you lonely and if you marry a Greek-restaurant manager he'll run off and leave you lonely. (A great hobby of hers was extracting universal rules from her own particular experiences.) Also, religion offered a harmless enough chance to get free tea and cake on Tuesdays. But somewhere along the line, belief had seeped into her. More than once in the last few months she'd expressed the idea that good people went to heaven and the bad ended up in hell. What he didn't know was how much of this was a tease, a show of false faith to rile him up. Underneath those thin cardigans a bony sense of humour lurked. He couldn't say with any accuracy where this humour ended and her earnestness began, and at times he thought that maybe, just maybe, there was something courageously gung-ho about faith, something wonderful that he himself should sample. Walking to the outer limits of knowledge and finding only a big wide wall, most people shrugged and traipsed back to safe ground. Only a few souls stuck around, climbed, threw themselves over the top. He didn't imagine they found much on the other side, but their hunger for perspective was humbling.

"How's the house?" he said.

"Perfect. Not that you'd know."

"I've been a little tied up with not dying."

"Join" — she swallowed — "the club."

"I'd rather not."

She began to look a little sheepish, was scratching at her ear. "Now. Speaking of the house . . . this month's payment, Philip."

"Ah," he said.

"There's more to life, but it all helps, you know." She extended her neck. "It gives me no pleasure to have been ruined by a Greek."

"I'll put the money into your account."

"I appreciate it. Does Vivienne know about your health?"

"No."

"Your wife doesn't know?"

"Ex."

"What are you saying? My ears."

"She's my *ex*-wife."

"And I'm your mother. Get used to it."

He felt the special heat of her censure. There was a certain look she could produce under pressure. It could tie a man to a rove of wild donkeys, drag him across several miles of mauled stone, and leave his bloodied body tangled on torn cacti, whining like the teenager he was when she was here.

"That Vivienne," she said. "She used to let you live in filth."

"Come on."

"Well, she did."

"I've been thinking a bit, Mum . . . Recently I've been thinking. I meant to ask" — here he paused for effect — "if you think about Dad much, these days."

She hesitated. "Do I think of your father? Well. I do. But only in the mornings." She chewed. "The evenings sometimes too. You do too, I suppose."

"Yeah, sometimes."

"I told you at the wedding," she said, and the moment was lost.

"I know, Mum. This is old ground."

"Old ground is the only ground there is," she said. "Your problem is you married an independent woman."

"What sort of woman should I have married?"

She seemed to give this careful consideration. "A dependent one."

"I wouldn't say *you* were dependent. When it came to Dad, I mean."

He knew his own compliment was false to the core, but nonetheless she nodded. "True," she said. "That's true. But your

413

father's terrible habit was —"

He closed his eyes. It worked. She stopped talking. When he opened them again she was rocking gently in her chair and he feared she was having some minor fit. But then he saw what she was doing. She was trying to get closer to him without making a big thing of it. The chair moved. She leaned forward and put her little rough hand on his. She left it there for a while.

"I've bought one of those new word processors," she said.

"Really? We're rolling more of them out here, but there's the potential for error. Wiped memory, and so on."

"Man from Curry's came to install it. Had a chin like a bum."

"Ha. What about your typewriter, then? You'll get rid of it?"

"Embracing technology," she said. "I want to do more newsletters."

"For what?" he asked, but she didn't seem to hear.

Going between the dozen vacant rooms. Smiling at every guest he passed. House-keeper after housekeeper kneeling in far corners, faces flushed, scrubbing. Vinegar on the mirrors. Hairdryer cords wound into neat coils. Vacuuming. Dusting. Steaming the curtains clean. All the things we call "cleaning," though there's a specific art to every task.

The bed-skirt check.

The pillow karate chop.

Knocking on the door to room 122, Thatcher's suite, using the heavy wooden block on the key ring.

There were two maids inside the suite. A houseman dragging dirty sheets from the bed. Moose muttered his thanks, pointed out that the windows should be opened to let in some fresh air, reminded them to get extra pillows (four extra anti-allergy; four extra duck feather), and made a mental note to ask Marina to arrange more fresh-cut flowers. He went into the bathroom, scent of fake lemon. He rearranged the Q-tips, the cotton balls, the two sealed nail files and the silver-handled lint roller. Everything was close to perfection, a 9 or a 9.5.

4

He walked across kerbstones painted red and white and blue. Overhead, flags were slapping in the wind. Curtains twitched in the windows of homes, glass soft with the last of the afternoon light, and men stared out from the drifting comfort of their cars after eight empty hours in the office. Dan wanted to know now what people saw when they saw him, what assumptions or judgements they made.

The morning news had predicted that Thatcher, in her Brighton speech, would present Labour as the enemy within. Supporting strikers. Letting the economy grind down. Traitors with no eye for the bigger picture. Kate Adie smouldering behind the camera, a woman whose burnished sophistication turned every word on her lips into prime-time truth, the BBC version of events. And if the device didn't work, what would it say about him? These last few nights his nerves had itched. His brain today felt overfull.

Sleeplessness. It seemed such a conventional response in the aftermath of an operation, and he wasn't even in the aftermath. The device hadn't yet entered the public phase of its life. Headlines, consequences. Normal rules didn't apply. The Larne–Stranraer ferry project had been long in the planning but quick in its own enactment. The pub attack on UDR officers had been over in less than an hour. The timer for the Hyde Park bombing was set short, simple engineering. Would it be found? Would it be damaged? Had he fucked it up? Had Patrick fucked it up? No contact from Dawson. Threat letters still coming. Last night he'd woken from thin, uneasy dreams featuring fishermen dragged into dark water, radios playing birdsong backwards, an animal hidden in his bedside cabinet tap-tap-tapping to get out. Sleeplessness led to fatigue. Fatigue to mistakes. A very simple equation. He'd increased his intake of spirits to smooth the edges off his thoughts, but the desired soft-warm haze rarely descended. The side effects, the headache, the dry mouth, the ruined concentration — all of this worked very well. It was just the drunkenness that wasn't happening.

As he walked past a stray dog peeing on a lamp post now he briefly imagined himself back into the Grand Hotel, looking out the window, thinking there was something bland about the English sea and sky most of the time, something huge and dramatic but disappointing, blank and grey and everyday. The prow of a ship unmoving, September's clouds falling into water, September's water rippling into clouds, grimy foam flickering on the tops of waves. The word "seaside," with its colourful sing-song, seemed to him to be a kind of false advertising. What he loved was grassland, shrubs. A sentimental preference for green. The dog limped away from the lamp post, looking only slightly ashamed.

The afternoon he sat on the bathroom floor with Patrick. The shine of the lino. Fluorescence riding the curves of the bath. With the timer device prepared you began to peel the wax paper from the slab of Semtex. You got lost in its specks and dents, its deep orange hue. Made him think of a particular cheese his uncle used to buy from Lowry's.

The wrapper had been halfway off when Patrick said, "No."

"No?"

"An alternative."

Went into the bedroom, came back with an open bag.

"Gelignite?"

Patrick nodded.

"Why?"

"Options. Play the percentages."

He said it was fresh from Enfield, County Meath. Twenty pounds. Top drawer. Mines and quarries. Mr. Nobel's invention. A refinement on dynamite, it was. Did you know that, Dan? A nice touch, no? We'll get the peace prize, with this. Or some fucker will, anyway. Some Labour Party grinner who gets in after Thatcher, sealing a suitable deal.

The memories were fine most of the time. You let them linger at the outer edges of your senses. What was unendurable were the doubts, the effort involved in not listening to them.

Some of the Union Jacks further up the road were wired to guttering or pipes. Others were more crudely secured, taped to window ledges or fencing. He passed a row of four or five homes that held other flags: the red-and-white Ulster banner, its central red hand steady under a crown. The banners had been up since July. Normally they would have been taken down by now. A sign from the Loyalists, clear and simple —

danger for Republicans passing through. Someone ought to climb up and burn them, burn all of them, including the flag he passed under now which bore, for some reason he wasn't able to fathom, a *left* hand, thumb open. If he ever moved away it would be his last act: he'd burn them. He glanced sideways at the house with the Land Rover. Behind the latticework of wire across the Rover's windscreen he could make out the sea-green of a bulletproof bib.

He should have taken the dogs on this walk. He tried to walk them twice a day but lately it was once.

The post office was boarded up. Finally, on his advice, they were replacing the window grille with proper bulletproof panes. The place had been done over twice in '83 and twice again this year, easy money because the owners were elderly. IRA Youth were involved. He knew this to be true. Dawson had never got back to him.

Faster, faster, past the police station with its pillared entrance and barred windows, a huge shadow-casting mass. The size of a concert hall, it was. A hundred mysterious performances going on inside. The library came into view and he slowed down to study new graffiti. The Loyalists were crude in their artistic efforts: jagged lines and shaky brushwork. No comparison with the detailed portraits of Republican legends, vast works on walls that flanked the Shankill Road. These murals were always at risk of redaction, black paint erasing Bobby Sands until a new portrait was formed, but with each revision the dead heroes had their appearance upgraded, a Chinese whisper of improving jawlines and eyes.

He remembered walking on Brighton Beach that first evening, the night they'd said he shouldn't leave his room. The walk had been uneventful but it had returned to him a sense of power in reserve, something bone-deep saved up for later. It had created, briefly, a double illusion of choice: the choice of the walk itself and the choice of whether ever to speak of it.

Before reaching the library, before finding a book that contained a lean chapter on knotweed, before punching wood-panelling in the dusty stacks for no good reason at all — before all of this he saw a man of Dawson's height and build in the street, wrapped in a mouse-coloured coat. He briefly believed it was him.

Japanese knotweed is a frequent coloniser of temperate riparian ecosystems, dirt tracks, roadsides and waste places.

He sat in the library. He was reluctant to

accept that his garden was a waste place. Maybe it was a temperate riparian ecosystem? He wasn't sure. The author, Jeremy P. Humphreys, didn't linger on definitions. How could someone write a book like this and come out of it alive?

As he flicked through pages in the library book he felt increasingly lost, a person lacking in traction. This was not a place that welcomed men like him. Would it go off? Did he want it to go off? His mother's haggard face. The blotchy wooden spatula that made everything taste of onion. The unfixed tap in the bathroom, the leak of unwanted thoughts. His mind seemed intent on dealing with every single thing except the text in front of him.

Everything in the library was brown. The curtains, the carpets, the desk, the library cards. The trousers of the old men who refused to speak in whispers. Everything except the librarian. He was grateful for her freckles, for her shiny apple face, for her green sweater and frizzy burnt-orange hair lifting just a little joy from the dog-eared drabness of the place. The ceiling was high but there was a lack of natural light. The largest window was behind her, the size of the road atlas he kept in the van, and the putty around the frame had cracked. Her nose was dotted with tiny pinhole pores. They made him think of sand and creatures burrowing. Day trips too. Trips to the Belfast Lough, his father and him, his mother back home cooking. The cold weight of Dad's binoculars on the bridge of the nose, the swirl of mudflats, the gleam of lagoons. The outer lough was rocky shore flecked with sandy bay. Long, wide, deep, calm; our gateway to the Irish Sea. The tides there were weak but noticeable. The moon pulls the water towards it.

He didn't talk to the librarian much. That, he would later think, was a shame. It might have been useful, maybe even instructive, to understand how she came to be here.

5

On the night before the big drinks event, Surfer John finally called.

"Freya Finch," he said in a squeaky voice. "This is Barry from school."

"Hi, Barry," she said.

Would she like to go for a swim tomorrow?

"No, Barry. The Prime Minister of the United Kingdom is arriving."

"The United Kingdom," Barry squeaked. "Does that include Worthing?"

She told him that it did.

"I love what she does with her hair!"

They met early again. She searched her purse for 10p coins. Even now the smell of chlorine made her nervous, a full-body anticipation of some oncoming competition.

When she arrived poolside in her swimming costume she found, as always, that John had already started his lengths. His muscular back. His swiftness and ease. She slipped into the pool and swam behind him for a while, struggling to judge distances, to keep close but not too close. After twelve lengths they paused at the deep end, breathing.

"Everything all right?" she said.

"Why wouldn't it be?"

"You just seem a bit off today."

Possibly this wasn't true. Possibly she was making it true by saying it.

"It's part of your over-thinking, Freya Finch."

He explained that they'd talked about this problem before. His eyes moved briefly to a pretty girl with short red hair. At some point in the last two weeks, without ever really acknowledging that she was doing it, she'd learned to follow John's stares, to look at the girls he looked at. She wanted the women he wanted, or rather to *be* the women he wanted, ideally while being herself.

"Not preoccupied, then?" she said.

He was looking only at droplets on the tiles. Smoothly he leaned in and kissed her. "You look nice today," he said.

She hated the tone in which he'd delivered these words. She let the silence shrink her discomfort down. Her fingers hurt from clinging to the edge and she said, "A holiday, maybe."

"What?"

"We could go."

"Come on. I wish. Where are we going to get the cash, Freya Finch? I owe my parents . . ." He shook his head, blinked, a confusion of calculations. *"Money,"* he said.

Various awkward observations passed between them. Eventually she said, "That old guy over there. His bald patch — it's the exact shape of Africa."

John smiled a fake smile. The eyes didn't light up at all. "That one over there," he said, pointing. "He's really tired."

She stared at him.

"What? Isn't that the game?"

The space between words was unswimmable. Her stomach was jumpy. Her guts were a string of Christmas lights fizzling out one by one, and the image wasn't even seasonal.

He turned away and carried on swimming.

In her previous life she'd thought the worst thing in the world was to sound needy. Let a note of desperation enter your voice when you're with a boy? Unthinkable. But now neediness seemed like a condition rather than a decision. Needy? Yes, I'm needy. Give me needy drugs. Relieve my neediness! She was in need and he was being a dick. Or she was being a dick. Both, probably, which was worse — the kind of equality you didn't want.

After more lengths she swam up to him and said, "If you don't want to see me again, that's fine." Hated the tremble her voice held. Hated that the words had gone wavy in her throat. Why had she even said it?

A pause. A pause! She wanted to die. To call someone's bluff and then discover they weren't bluffing — was there anything worse in the world? She was succumbing to a shameful sinking feeling, a sense that everything with a beginning had an ending.

"Look," John said, "I wasn't, probably, totally straight with you the other day."

"Forget it," she said. "I was being stupid. Let's swim."

"Frey."

"Don't call me Frey. You always call me Freya Finch. It's funny."

"It's about Sasha," he said. "The truth is I really like you, and stuff, but this thing with —"

"How about I show you a dive?"

"What? Look, Freya, the point —"

"The point is I'm going to try the ten-metre board. Have fun." She was out of the water and walking.

427

Self-consciousness came. It always did. One of the pleasures of being in the water was that you never thought about how you looked. The pool swallowed you up, insecurities and all. Your little-girl body took on a mature purity, your mind developed a sense of direction. The liquid connected you to everyone else. You knew exactly what you had to do. More speed. Less splash. Focus on the legs. Walking along the edge of the pool, the corrugated tiles that stopped you slipping, you felt none of this joy. You were close but you just couldn't reach it. There was a new heaviness in her legs. The water at her side, the elusive warmth of it, the impression of the whole safe thing.

She sensed her swimsuit was clinging to her bottom in embarrassing ways. She tucked a finger under the elastic rim. Sasha. *Sasha.* Think of the more important things. Like her father — he really was getting better, wasn't he? Like the doctors would look out for him. Like Anthony Haswell. Like Mr. Marshall. They knew about hearts. Good! Someone should know about hearts! "A lot of heart attacks are vicious but not malicious." This is what Dr. Haswell had said last week. Vicious but not malicious. Freya had tried to picture this combination of traits. All she'd managed to come up with was Abby Stephens from sixth form, cuttingly witty but fond of baking birthday flapjacks.

Fuck. He was fucking Sasha. It was so desperately predictable. It was the clichés that hurt the most. She'd always hated greeting cards with text printed inside, stock condolences or congratulations that preceded the event they addressed. Now whoever wrote those was writing her.

Anyone who cared to look up now as she climbed the metal ladder would see how her hips, in the tight black nylon suit, looked narrow as a fourteen-year-old girl's. Until recently this was a good thing, but these days you wanted to be Dara Torres or one of the even curvier swimmers. It was so hard to keep yourself pretty because prettiness was always changing, always shifting, which was what her mother had once said about truth — that a true thing in 1974 could be a false thing ten years later, and then true again when a new decade came. "Things change, Freya, I'm sorry." A way of saying "sorry" that drained away every drop of authenticity.

Probably John was comparing her goosebumps to the lovely constellation of water crystals on the nut-brown back of the girl in front. Three rungs higher, bum swaying smoothly, the girl's dark hair hung down the line of her spine and from behind she was so pretty, so perfect, that you wanted to reach up in one seamless motion and wring out her hair like a soaked rope just to touch her, be part of her, to connect with something pristine and confident and sustained so fully by itself. The ladder's bars were cold and her feet were squeaking on the steps and why was she heading up here anyway?

Diving like Moose taught her to do. But that wasn't from a ten-metre platform. And would he be OK? And had she ever even liked John, really? Wasn't she just distracting herself? That hurt all the more, though. The idea she'd only been playing at happiness, a stupid little-girl game.

She'd heard from someone who knew someone who knew someone that Sarah had found out about the thing she'd done ages ago with the trainee teacher on the golf course, which wasn't even a thing anyway because he couldn't keep it up, and it was ages ago now, back when she was a different person. Supposedly they were annoyed, Sarah and Co. were annoyed, annoyed at the fact she hadn't told them direct, or else they thought that she was easy, which was crazy because she'd only properly slept with two people ever and they'd slept with loads, and that's why they hadn't phoned, and thinking about all of this made her nauseous. Sarah and Tracy weren't nice people. The knowledge cut through her: they were not nice. And yet they were her friends, weren't they, so that was evidence that she wasn't nice either. What else could you draw from the facts? Why else did John not want her? Why, when it was finally all working well, did they look you in the eye and dismiss you? Why was she letting herself be dismissed? Why did she care?

Sometimes she felt she had no option but to destroy her father. A remark about his widening waistline or the stifling smallness of Brighton. She had no option but to nuke him straight off the map. There was something wrong with her and that was why she was being dumped for Sasha. Who wants to sleep with a stupid mean girl who doesn't even know how to please a man in bed? She was getting dumped by a guy she should have dumped before he dumped her.

Every muscle was tight. The pads of her hands were wrinkled and soft. Her swimming cap was tight. She would book a flight to Spain tomorrow. She'd heard of an agency who could get you cheap ones at short notice. She had £215 saved up. Screw Margaret Thatcher. Margaret Thatcher had nothing to do with real life. Margaret Thatcher was a person other people had made up. Her cap felt very tight. She owed Moose £9. She could calculate. John couldn't calculate. 215 minus 9 is 206. £206 was a fortune. Way too tight. She could go anywhere, surely, on £206?

She was at the top level of the diving tower. The high windows with their rounded tops made her think of churches. Through the transparent roof panels an open sky was breathing.

A hairy man hurled himself off the board in a cannonball that quickly became a cannonsplodge. She heard the fat smack of a fleshy entry. The air was thick with chlorine. The diving board stuck out and out.

She would be splashless. Serene. Toes lined up. Ten little piggies. A thought about the Conservatives who'd been in the hotel this week and of the word that so perfectly described their old-school outrage — Why hasn't my taxi arrived? Where are your other cognacs? — which was "aghast." When not amused, be aghast.

And what were hers? Her private rules?

Connect with nothing. Be bored or spiky. Mock or ignore. Take aim at easy targets. Keep a distance, keep a space. Be weak and weak. Go to bed with fuckwits. Be mean to customers. Was this her? Was it? She thought it might be. She was, as her mother had once succinctly said, "a perfect little shit."

The pretty tanned girl did an elegant dive. Now it was her turn. She thought of Samantha, a girl at school, and how Samantha had needed leather-and-metal ankle braces for a while, part of an *orthopaedic corrective programme,* and how around that time Sarah and Tracy were showing an interest in Freya, including her within their group, maybe impressed by her swimming, maybe noting her slightly improved looks, maybe appreciating her willingness to help with their homework — do it for them, basically. And Sarah and Tracy talked about Samantha's spasticity. They said that if Freya wanted to hang around with them they needed to know if she was really actual friends with Spaz Sam.

A chance to advance and be accepted. Never spoke to Samantha again.

It was the things you chose not to look at, the pieces unexamined, that survived as boiled-down sensations, stomach pains, squirming memories that made you ashamed in the night.

Balance and height. Toes together. Do not baulk.

Moose talked about the Tank. Respecting

the Tank and remembering there was nothing scary about the Tank. But the word Tank was not helpful. He might as well call it the Abyss or the Grave or the Nuclear Winter. Trying to impress John with a dive! Trying to avoid what he had to say. She turned away from the edge and walked back along the platform, squeezing past a man with huge hands. The man said "You OK?" and she climbed down the ladder, felt broad ground beneath her feet. John was standing by the lifeguard's chair, waiting, and although he wasn't watching the tanned girl climbing out of the pool, she felt sure that was where his eyes wanted to be.

After getting showered and dressed Freya went upstairs. She joined him at a table overlooking the pool. The space didn't deserve to be called a café. Everything about it was inconsistent with that uplifting continental word. The troll behind the counter was supervising half a dozen jaundiced cakes lying in an oblong plastic container, sick babies waiting to be rescued from this especially horrible ward, and thin brown coffee was dripping from the tap of a giant chrome cylinder beside the till.

"Basically," he said, "I really like you and everything, but I think we'd be better off as friends."

They could carry on as they were, he said, but he didn't want to do that in case he hurt her, because he could tell she was a person who had quite a bit of hurt in her already, like issues about her mum or whatever, emotional stuff, and now her dad being sick, even though he was getting better, and he didn't want to unbalance her further or anything because that would be shitty, wouldn't it?

6

Marty Clarke was speculating loudly as to what kind of sex life Thatcher might enjoy with Denis. It had started with Clinkie Hanson saying Arthur Scargill had her over a barrel — she was beaten now, she'd have to settle on the NUM's terms — and that had set off a string of dirty puns from Jim Clarke, Marty's brother, that climaxed in the inevitable one about Big Willie Whitelaw. Dan was leaning forward, weight on his elbows, eyes on the beer-soaked bar mat, trying to block all this out and hear what the radio had to say.

Mrs. Thatcher is expected, within the hour, to greet journalists outside —

In advance of tomorrow's crucial speech at the Conservative Party Conference, the Prime Minister has indic—

As always when Thatcher came up in conversation, anecdotes led back to Clinkie's year in the Blocks. Clinkie was a man who liked to stay groomed and he claimed now, for the hundredth time, that he'd bangled a little comb to keep his hair tidy inside. Like many of the guys who'd done time, he revelled in prison language. It marked him out as a martyred man. Nothing in the Blocks went by its real name. "Bangle" meant sticking something up your arse to prevent confiscation. A penis was a Fagin. Sinister and droopy-looking, a supposed receiver of stolen goods. If a guy was really good at utilising the spaces in his body — Bobby Sands's right-hand man being the obvious example — people called him the Suitcase, or the Holdall, or some other variation on luggage.

Sprinkling salt on a bowl of wet-looking chips Clinkie said, "They make sure to give you yer statutory requirements. You're entitled every month to one ounce of the salt and one of sugar. But if a screw was a real shit he'd give it you all at once, so he would. Pour it over your food, the salt and sugar and all, and when he went for his own dinner was when you'd start your secret Irish classes with the lads. You'd take a few bites of your shit-awful meal and come up with all the ways you could call the fella a cunt."

Marty yawned into his lager. "Major

bastard, the prison warden. Type a' guy who belongs behind bars."

Marty and Clinkie, after laughing awhile, slowly eased out of their performances. Their voices softened. They started talking about their kids. Clinkie was divorced. Marty was having marital problems. They sat there, comforting each other, drinking and talking. Smoking.

Down where the bar became the wall, Jim Murray worked his jaw from side to side. It was a nervous thing he'd been doing since June of 1979. "I'll quote you that you said that, Marty. Your kid's going to be just fine, you'll see."

A man Dan didn't know took a pretend toke on a pretend spliff and pretended to be happy about it. Billy Fitzgerald caught the man's eye and said, "Oh please." They disappeared out back and Clinkie chose that moment to start another story. Prison tales weren't what Dan wanted to hear. They brought thoughts about windowless rooms and all the various routes by which he might end up in one. Did he even want to be in the company of these men? Did he even belong? He wanted to belong. He liked most of these men. He took his drink and his much-mocked book on knotweed and sat at an unoccupied table by the fruit machine.

In six hours he'd find out if his timer device had been properly wired. In twenty-four he'd have full information about who was inside when it exploded. In forty-eight, a sense of whether he needed to go into hiding, of whether he was heading to the H-Blocks, of whether he'd spend a lifetime scrawling words on the wall with a finger dipped in shit, getting knocked about by guards. An idea of what new senselessness his actions might unleash.

Guys who got fatally knifed in the Blocks were described as going off air. The bar's radio was being retuned. It began to tell tales about the weather.

A tidy girl in a denim skirt walked in. Someone said, "Uh, the arse on that."

"Steady," the landlord said.

"Walks like —"

"Steady now."

The girl sat down and yawned. "Drink it in, lads, this is the closest you're getting." The men began to blush.

Dan looked towards the door and saw the scarred bald head of Mick Cunningham, your basic functional shit-eating grin and a body still stupidly bulky. He resolved to ask his advice. He needed the comfort of a dumb man's Don't Worry. Mick had been there from the beginning. Mick was all right.

"Remember that day," he said to Mick. "The trip home after the stuff in the field with the dogs. The beers. Do you remember? You had to swerve for that cyclist."

"Oh the fucker," Mick said. "Oh the fucky luck he had." Things like that could keep Mick furious for years.

He bought Mick another pint. It went down in twenty seconds. After shaking his glass to loosen a lingering swirl of stout Mick said, "If you told them everything in the debrief, Dan, I can't see why you'd be sweating. It's sounds stickin' out, far as I can see. Sounds sound all round." Gently he touched his injured ear. "What was the operation, anyway? I haven't heard much on the wires."

"Just a job. Nothing big."

"So you did a pedestrian number, it went off OK, and you told them the full works?" He grinned, gummy. "Celebration is more the sound of it, Dan. If I were you I'd find myself a friend and have myself a big little party. McCartland's busy, is all. Always a view on the next op, the next vol coming up. He's probably taking a lad to Parkhead. Celtic versus the Rangers, am I right? Times are changing. They cosy up to these kids."

"The recruits."

Mick nodded. "We've got Gerry as a

member, haven't we? People couldn't believe that. Now you've got to go for more diplomacy, I suppose. We need more people in the Department of Health, they say. In your bigger high street banks, the Post Office. The Brit Telecom. That's where it's at, isn't it? Clever kids in suits. Get them into your universities, into the licensing centre in Coleraine. Change minds bit by bit is the idea." He laughed.

"I suppose."

"I thought you were in favour of all that, Dan."

"I am."

"Well, why do you look like I just slipped one in your mammy? More and more I get it, Dan. I get there's something precious in the shite." He stopped and nodded to the landlord, said a hello to Marty too. "You've got to ask yourself, at some point, if we're just a bunch of fuckers addicted to failure, haven't you? Whether we've gotta be more imaginative than that. Whether we really want to wake tomorrow and find all our mates dead, or abroad."

"You make it sound worse than it is."

"Yeah? More imaginative than just pressing on with the same old patterns, I'm saying. Dead bodies here, dead bodies there, big fucken funerals and kids growing up

441

without parents, lads getting jail time when they turn eighteen. Know what I'm saying?"

"There's a balance, Mick."

"That's what I'm telling you. A balance."

"If we don't fight, the future gets smaller."

"Ha. Good one. It's pretty fucken small either way."

Dan tried to think of a response to this. "I need to talk to Dawson," he said.

"I know. I understand you." Mick scratched his head. "If the Brits wouldn't pull out in '72, when we took a chunk out of five hundred of their soldiers, why would the fuckers do it now? I ask myself that these days. That's all I'm saying."

"What's the point then?"

"Come again, Dan?"

"If it's not going anywhere, explain the point."

Mick shrugged. "You'd be hard-pressed to find a point in anything any fucker does. There's less and less of a role for what you and me do, Dan. Admit it. We're like the hard men of old. I mean — look at us." He grinned. "We're damaged people, aren't we, Dan? There's no place for us in the world we're trying to make."

Dan stared. It was the "us" that had once made the army attractive, and the "us" that in this moment really left him lost. "You know his wife, Mick?"

"Whose? McCartland's?"

"Yeah."

"Not intimately, if that's what you mean. It's been said before and I don't appreciate it."

"She's got one eye, has she? Was he lying when he said that to me?"

"No, wasn't lying on that one. She's a woman who deserves more."

With that, Mick turned away. Dan watched him feed coins into the fruit machine. The smell of sweat and stale ale was stifling, ashtrays overfull.

Somewhere clean: that's where he needed to be. Celebration. Distraction. Strangers. No talk of plots. And then it came to him: the hotel. A hotel he'd been to months ago, a night when Dawson had been keen to flash his cash.

Got to Cathedral Corner. Walked beyond the Sugarhouse Entry. Saw the Commercial Building. In a buried decade, thatched cottages had stood here. One of the cottages had been a draper's shop. An ancestor was supposed to have worked there. He passed the Ulster Bank headquarters. The building made him think of the Grand. High Victorian. One of those tall, intimidating facades that boys like to aim at with air rifles. From the apex, statues stared down in the dark. Sculptures depicting Commerce, Justice, Britannia. Masks and reliefs. Universals. In their little niches mythical figures lingered, their noses and chins worn away by the weather.

He walked towards St. Anne's, a church that was grey with old-world love, the air at once hazed and measured by cones of light from street lamps. He thought of the church in Brighton he'd passed on the last day of his stay, his route to the station, to freedom.

The hotel had taxis outside tonight. Eyes slid his way as he went through the doors. He was going to the bar, and no one would stop him going to the bar, and he wanted a drink at the bar. He was full of beer and dreams of nights when he'd probably felt a little less alone.

A man in a dark suit and tie approached. His face was full of gathers and tucks, the skin of his neck was pitted, the mouth was tight but twisted too. In his eyes were signs of a long adolescence spent bitterly battling acne. "What's your business?"

"Electrician," Dan said.

The man shook his head. "Catch yourself on, son. Your business here."

"Drink."

"Selling?"

"Drinking."

The man said "up." Dan lifted his arms like the little boy he was. The guy patted at Dan's armpits and ribs, his hands travelling down to the ankles. With a look of reluctance the man let him pass.

Sitting at the bar plucking nuts from a bowl he ordered a whiskey straight up. Not the Glenmorangie, he said.

The bar girl didn't think she had the Tullamore. Then she said, "Ah, I tell a lie."

No rubber beer mats here. Surfaces wiped and swept. Lights that hung down on metal strings along the bar, gold droplets waiting to drop. Everything induced your eyes to linger on wealth and its advantages. Dawson wasn't here.

Over there, at a table on her own, a woman in a soft blue dress. Not beautiful, but pretty. Smooth skin, television hair. She was sipping from a glass of yellow wine.

He finished the Tullamore in two quick swigs. An old conversation was coming back in him — gyms, swimming pools, Margaret Thatcher's schedule. Sick fathers. Couldn't let it grow.

He approached the woman in the blue dress before thought could murder impulse. Without the support of the stool he felt drunk. So much of life was lived in his own head these days. Shrubbery whipping low windows, a wind working up outside, and he put a hand on the chair opposite hers.

"Hi," she said. Soft, quiet.

"Hi," he said. "Hello. Can I —"

"Why not," she said, so he sat.

"I'm not disturbing your reading?"

"Nothing here. Gave up on it a while ago." She picked up the paper and read from the front page: " 'A drunk man set fire to a packet of peanuts and tried to make love to a lamp post, Belfast Magistrates' Court has heard.' "

He leaned forward, happy. "Sounds like a pretty good opener to me."

"You like a good lamp post, do you?"

"Not recently."

"But it's that kind of night, is it?"

"It might be," he said.

She smiled and her voice fell soft again. They talked about the whiskey. She said her name was Lena. Speech stalled after his drink was done and he had to wave twice to get another, plus one of whatever she's . . . Chardonnay, yeah. There was a clock on the wall with shapely hands and no numbers. Dimly he recognised midnight. He'd left his book about knotweed in the bar on the Falls. He could picture it between the wall and the fruit machine.

What part of town was she from?

Oh, around.

"Family here, have you?"

"Some."

A year, perhaps, since he'd slept with a woman. Everything these days seemed to flow into his work. Armies built up certain aspects of your character and folded others flat. It seemed to him that, of all the challenges his commitment to the Provos posed, it was the element of chance that really gnawed. The difference between life and death was as slight as walking home after the fourth drink instead of the fifth, rounding one corner instead of the next, forgetting to check under a car.

He sat back in his chair and resolved to get drunk. "Lena's not a common name round here, is it?"

"No," she said. "Are you disappointed?"

7

In the living room the fire was burning for the first time since February. Lying on the sofa she drew her legs into her chest. Her father was in his armchair, snoring. Between each slurping effort at breath was a long interval of silence, his lungs always late in knowing they needed air. These silences contained a moment of thinking he was fine, a moment of thinking he was probably fine, a moment of thinking he was going to die, a moment of realising he was fine, a moment of waiting to be afraid all over again — and then she'd think about her own breathing, and that sounded wrong too, like a word you turn over in your head too long.

A blanket pulled over his knees. An old-man nap before the big reception. The MPs. Mrs. T. Logs were glowing blue. There was the waggle of thinner flames up front. A sway of fatter flames behind. The wood was singing, crackling. Light touched the carpet, streamed across photo frames. She'd told John things, given him little parts of herself. He'd judged these things inessential.

"Make sure I'm awake by five, Frey." That's what her dad had said. Now it was 5:05.

She picked it up from the floor, the most recent postcard from her mother. She stared at the fireplace and blinked bright colours. A big flame puffed its chest and took in air. It rolled forward. A hissing sound loudened. The dots of colour bleached out behind her eyelids. Shouts from the slouchy boys next door. The *brrrrrr* of determined traffic. The scuffle and structure of a new school term, the criss-cross glances and one-liners, the depressing double periods, the arguments, the dipshit flared-up rumours, the constant pranks and inventive bitching — and it was possible to miss all this, all of it. On the windowsill her herbs were dropping leaves. Mint. Basil. Coriander.

Her mother's opener was "I hope this postcard finds you well," the closing line was "Hope your dad is enjoying his work," and in between these words the card contained only one sentence: "We're not up to much, but everything is fine." That was the sandwiching of it: *hope — fine — hope.* The word "everything" was crammed desperate against the edge, as grimly appealing as the *we.* Sometime during the last year her mother had lost a personal pronoun. Had the famous Bob been reinstated, or was this someone new? Did her dad read these postcards when they arrived on the doormat? She felt sure that he was meant to.

Sometimes when she was younger she'd wondered if she was adopted. Probably lots of kids did. She'd wondered in truth every time her parents were lame. You thought maybe they're not mine, maybe they don't belong to me; I'm from elsewhere, because I do seem a bit more special than them. Not a genius or anything, not even all that interesting, just more full of feelings, more three-dimensional. They are just parents, which is not the same as people, and I cannot see the world through their eyes.

She was a little shit, was she?

She'd knocked on her mother's door to demand that her school skirt be taken up, because no one wore it this long, because really was she trying to humiliate her or what? And she saw from all the smudged mascara that her mother had already been crying, and wow she cried often, wow she didn't stop; you'd think a normal human being would have dried up by now. "Give me some *privacy,*" Vivienne had said, or something like that, and from such small beginnings insults escalated. She hadn't realised parents wanted privacy. It did not seem reasonable that they should want it or get it, and she hadn't thought that her mother might have bigger things on her mind than the length of her daughter's skirt. "Self-absorbed." "Selfish." "You can be a perfect little shit, can't you?" "Like father like daughter, the world revolves around you!" So Freya wiped away her own tears, fresh-sprung, hot, and she nuked her. "At least I'm not a miserable worthless slutbag. At least I don't go around fucking ugly old men just because they have stackloads of money." Quite good. Nice rhythm. And after the tantrum there was silence, many hours of silence, and then her mother asked her how she had known, so she told her: I saw you kissing that man in that bar on New Year's Day. I saw you through the window. That guy Bob or Rob and the two of you drinking champagne. I was so ashamed. I wish most days you weren't my mother.

"To be cynical is a sin." That's what the priest said at church that one time she went, and she'd only gone because she thought God, on the off chance He existed, might see fit to make her mother visit her, actually care. She never meant to push her away forever. Always meant those words to be a nudge rather than a shove. A little nudge, a form of contact, intimacy inviting a response. And her father could have actually gone and got her mother if he wanted. He could have taken control at any number of moments. He could have done the grown-up thing. He could have actually tracked her down and shaken her and said listen, what are you doing, spend some time with your daughter and don't let the gap grow, or he could have shaken Freya and said the same. But he didn't like confrontation, did he?

Sarah lost her mum to cancer six years ago. People saw how bad that was and granted a special privilege of grief. But if your mum runs off with someone with a three-letter name — a name that happens to be the most stupid palindrome ever — she's a slut and your life's a *Carry On* film. People want to hear your gripes for a week at most, a quick summary of the dirtier details. After that, something changes in their voices and you realise you're being a burden. You've lost her but people don't treat it as a loss. On a scale stretching from everyday annoyance right up to Death, it lands closer to mislaid house keys than cancer. And time passes and Friday is Saturday, and Saturday is Sunday, and

Sunday night is the need to make your sandwich for school. And you just have to look at your tiny allotment of trouble, so small compared to that owned by others, and you have to say, "All right, no worries, I'll take it, it's mine." You have to acknowledge it's nowhere near a death even though she is gone, fully gone. And you remember the things she used to say to you when you were small and she thought you were asleep, the room pitch black and she would begin talking and talking, her breath against your hair and she would go on and on, softly chattering for minutes and minutes, and you loved it, you felt all the life in her running into you, the sugar rush of her feelings and thoughts. She existed to whisper into your ear.

At Columbia she'd watched the cheerleaders at the football games and thought how shiny they were, how gloriously unreal. Cheering and cheered. Leading and led. Sexy and giving off the air of having, all the time, sex. Throwing each other up into the air in huge flirtatious twirls and arcing back down with a reckless grace. The furrows of their skirts, the pleats and tucks. The silence between her father's snores. The gap between the whistle-breaths and the great inward slurps. Was he, did he, if. A daughter never responding to these lonely little post-cards.

"You can reach me on this number if you want." A line sometimes included and always ignored. Because how could a conversation like that happen? Like you'd say Hello, what did you have for breakfast today, Mum? How's the last half-decade been? The question on her mind more and more these last few weeks was how to know when she was choosing a thing as opposed to it being chosen for her.

The fire crackled and wheezed and her father's head moved forward. He rubbed his face as he looked at his watch and with great feeling he said, "Fuck." She pretended to be asleep.

8

He asked Lena what she thought the barman did in his spare time.

The reply came quickly: "Child killer, probably."

He blinked.

"Or," Lena added, "a collector of model aircraft. Tiny B-52s, let's say. Or maybe, if you really want to know, a Harrier Jump Jet. All laid out on his dining table, next to his sticky stamp collection."

"All stamps are sticky, I'd chance."

"His in particular," she said.

"Well. Jump Jets." He found he was looking at the blue frill of her bra strap. Felt his face gathering heat as he glanced away. After a pause she adjusted the shoulder of her dress and said her father had been with the armed forces. A vicar for a while in the British Army. The family had lived in north Devon.

"Man of the Church," Dan said, though

the word on his mind was Anglican.

"I think he probably would have preferred the RAF. The passion was planes but his eyes weren't good enough, see. He died last year. Don't ask if we were close."

"I won't."

"Everyone asks, that's all. It's the idea that it hurts more if you were close."

"Not true?"

She shrugged. "It hurts just the same either way. It hurts the same as it's worth." She looked to the wall and drank a good amount of wine. "By the way, I've strong views on nothing."

"Is your ma alive?"

"Oh," Lena said. "Always there with an answer. Though like a deaf woman it's rarely an answer to what you've asked."

He laughed. "I know the feeling."

"Originally from Poland. She was my father's cleaner, the vicar's cleaner."

"A scandal."

"Not a big one, though, by the standards of the Church."

"True," he said.

They drank and looked around.

"You know," he said. "I had that Latin waiter down as a tango dancer rather than a child killer."

"Did you?"

"I had him down as a tango dancer whose father had a stake in a — a hair gel factory. That's how he got the ticket to Ireland. His father cashed in some of those . . ."

"Dividends?"

"Know your finances, do you?"

"And you probably know your knitting," she said. "It's almost like we live in the twentieth century."

"I didn't mean —"

"Fuck off."

"Fuck you too, Lena."

She smiled and drank.

The conversations that went on around them were impossibly banal to his ears. A feature of most nice parts of town was that people spent a lot of time discussing the fact that the nice parts of town weren't as nice as they once were. The other drinkers gave off an air of negativity, snobbery, paid-down mortgages. While he couldn't say any of them looked exactly unkind, Lena was the only one who was alive to him.

Which aspect of her life to probe? They looked at each other. He imagined her past. It contained a year or two of trailing wildly through Europe, modelling for mail-order catalogues, being cornered by a prick in a well-lit Paris attic, sleeping on the streets of Rome and then building a new hard shell for herself here. It seemed a shame in a way to discover what was true.

"A gypsy king gets to be king by calling himself one."

"What?" she said.

"Sorry. Random thought for the night. Passed some travellers earlier. The gypsy king in a given group, he gets to be king by announcing it, I read."

"And then proving himself?"

"Maybe. But mainly it's a matter of confidence, is the point." His dick was hard against his inner thigh. "I used to swim," he said. "Do you swim at all?"

She shook her head and he tried not to let his disappointment show.

"You're a thoughtful one, aren't you?" she said.

"I can shut up any time you want. My friends are always telling me: Jack, why don't you shut the fuck up?"

"Are they?"

"No. Not really. My friends never say that."

"Because you're so fascinating?"

"Because my name's not Jack."

She laughed and touched her hair, took a slow slip of wine. Be bold, he thought. Do what's bold.

"I've money for a room," he said. "I'm

guessing you'll not be staying here otherwise. Would you join me for a drink, in a
good room? I doubt at these prices it's full."

A pause. "And why would I do that?"

"For a nice drink."

"I have a drink here. It happens to be
nice."

"How nice, though?"

"Any other reasons?"

"For what?"

"Why you'd want me in a room?"

"I'm outraged," he said. "I'm offended is
what I am."

"I'm lacking a boatload of the pre-sex
information, you know."

"There's pre-sex information? That's a
thing?"

"To be sure it is," she said. "Name, birthday, origin of that accent."

"My accent is pure Falls, as you'll know.
Once we're upstairs we can do our bit to
broker peace."

"Weakest line yet," she said. "I think I
even heard some English."

"Bollocks you did. It's you that has the
English."

"Maybe you don't notice it in yourself."

"Aye, bollocks."

"Saying 'aye' now, are we? Certain way

you say a thing. Your language lets you down."

"You should hand out a wee form when you first meet a guy," he said. "Client info."

She narrowed her eyes. He wasn't sure why he'd said it. A feeling he had in his gut.

"The thing is," she said, "I don't go in for racists."

"Oh?"

"Picking on my handsome Argentinian. The one who brought us our drinks. Nasty."

"I seem to recall you called him a child killer."

"Nothing nationality-specific in that, is there? Whereas all that stuff about greasy hair, stereotypes . . ."

They looked at each other for a long moment. She was quicker than he was. She was still smiling. He thought of it as a smile. At a neighbouring table a man was supporting his wife in conversation, murmuring affirmative words and corroborating facts. He wished he could swap his Tullamore for a vodka and water. He was sick of the bite the whiskey left in his nose. A platter of fruit travelled by and something about its molecular complexity, its sheer decorative excess, made his stomach do a flinch. He was drunk, for sure. Drunk.

"If you think I'm racist you've got it totally

wrong. You don't know me from Adam."

"Who's Adam?"

"Adam and Eve. Any bells?"

"Ding dong," she said.

"It's an expression, Lena."

"Oh" — she bit her delicious bottom lip — "I thought he might be a friend of Jack."

"Jack?"

"Jack who gets told by his friends to shut up."

"Oh . . . Jack."

He tried to smile but couldn't quite do it. Knew he was being teased but couldn't quite accept it. Felt a trace of the old embarrassment he'd experienced at school, knowing something he'd said wasn't right, or that he'd sniggered at the wrong bit of a naughty story. He looked at his face in mirrors these days and thought he could see the emotional muscle tone slowly going soft, replaced by little twists and twitches, and when he smiled the smile glowed with engineered cheer — the McCluskeys' flashing Santa. And now, sitting here looking at this beautiful woman — she was beautiful now; she'd been promoted from pretty to beautiful on account of being tricky to access — he was thinking of Dawson again and he could hear a dog barking and a new anger was rising up in him. He didn't know what to do with it.

"I couldn't be less racist," he said. "Not least with the Argies. The Falklands? You know about the Falklands? I'm hoping you don't subscribe to the standard propaganda."

"Boring," she said, tipping a last drop of wine through her lips.

His face felt stiff, warm. "No, it's not boring. They had no right to be there."

"*We,* you mean."

"The Brits. No right."

Her eyes shone as new wine arrived. A white cloth was draped over the waiter's sleeve. He filled Lena's glass and proceeded to pour an unrequested one for Dan.

"Everyone's a right to take back what's theirs," she said. "Do you disagree? Don't you, as a rule, like to take what you deserve?"

If there was a sexual connotation to this, an invitation to steer things back towards the personal, he didn't have the wherewithal to grab at it. "That's what the Argies did. They're the ones who took back what was theirs."

"In the night," Lena said. "Sneaking."

"You'd have preferred walking or charging."

"Seized the airfield and barracks, did they

not? Overnight with no notice, my brother says."

So then, a brother. He drank some wine and tried to act empty. "You mention advance notice, ultimatums. But why do you think Thatcher offered no ultimatum to Buenos Aires? Why do you think she gave orders to sink the *Belgrano,* no warning? Sailing west, it was, withdrawn from action."

"Presumably there aren't always warnings."

"With terrorists?"

"With war."

He mentioned the UN. She blinked. She didn't know. Her ignorance filled him with new fuel. "Discussions were going on in the United Nations in New York about — whatever — the leasing or whatever of the islands. Did you not read that, Lena? No? That's a huge thing, the main thing. There were discussions of the Argies having them back. So, what happens? Thatcher makes calls to get these discussions to collapse, I believe, many people believe. That's why the junta, as a last resort, revived their dormant old invasion plan. Because that's the context. Responsibility, you know? Here's more context: Thatcher's tough time at home, humiliated, mocked for being weak. Laughed at in the Commons, right?

463

So what does she do? The fair thing, the reasonable thing? Or the thing that will play well with the public, at the expense of lives? Fights aren't all about the fight, that's all I'm saying. They're always about something else. They're about — it's the past. Egos and . . . and weaknesses. About people silencing other accounts, pretending there's a single story."

He sat back. He felt in serious need of water. How long had he been talking? It felt like the longest speech of his life.

"Whatever you think of her," Lena said, "she took the islands back with decisive style."

"What, Lena? Please. Are you serious, Lena? The Tories? Style?" He leaned over to the next table, unoccupied now, and stole a fistful of nuts from a bowl.

"OK," she said. "Perhaps I'm not the authority."

"Neither am I. I'm not saying it's wrong, but. You should . . . you should *read* this." He tapped the newspaper. "Or a better one. Did you want some of these, the peanuts? I'm saying — all I'm saying is — you should be a bit . . . a bit *interested.*" He could hear the slur in his words, the excess volume.

"I've enough to worry about."

"Come on."

"It's the truth."

"For fuck's sake."

"What did you say?"

"You're a smart woman. You might be bored, but these are people's lives."

He was lecturing her on the value of human life. The irony did not escape him. His own words had struck him a dull blow to the skull. She looked away and played with her necklace. Gold bumblebee buzzing on a thin gold chain. Her cheeks had become flushed. The colouring doubled or trebled her beauty. But he'd lost her. He knew he had. He should have bottled his prattle.

She rubbed her forehead. The bar guy came to check everything was OK. Told them table service would be stopping soon.

"Listen," Dan said to him. "What part of Argentina are you from?"

"I'm from Uruguay," the waiter replied. "Originally I'm from Uruguay, but I've lived here for ten years."

The bare facts of the waiter's nationality left Dan lost for words. He crawled for something to say. He sneaked. "Hey," he announced. Why was he suddenly saying "hey?" "One more question. Maybe you could help me and Lena here. We have a terrorism query."

Why was he saying all this?

"We have a question for you about Maggie."

"Maggie?" the waiter said.

"Aye, that's right. Maggie."

The waiter puckered his lips. "Thatcher?"

"That's her. The one who's left Ireland to rot in the rain."

"Thank you," the waiter said. "But I am badly busy."

"Tell me, Badly Busy. Tell us. Is Maggie a terrorist?" He was sounding sneery. Angry. He hated himself when he sounded sneery. But if the waiter didn't listen properly, he'd take him by the throat. He'd squeeze the life right out of his smug little neck. "Like, you know, Jomo — Jomo Kenyatta. Or like, you'll know him, Menachem — his name is Menachem, something, Mena— I'm asking, what's the difference between a terrorist and a leader? Is it just about waiting for the times to change?"

The barman's hand moved to his throat and glided uninterruptedly down his tie. The supreme elegance of this gesture left Dan speechless.

Lena had decided to be amused. She watched the barman move around the room spreading his message that service was stopping. She swung her legs to the side of the table. "Had a few tonight, then?"

"It's complicated, is all I'm saying."

"Everything is."

"No, not everything. Most things are unbelievably fucking simple." Wake up. Join an army. Feel the frightening scale of the world.

She reached for her handbag and half strangled herself with the strap.

"Got to go," she said.

"What?"

"I have to go."

"I've offended."

"Ach, no. Nice to meet you. I've overrun a bit, that's all, and I'm a simple sort, so there you go."

She stood and held out her hand. It was as if this really had been all business, a promising transaction collapsed.

He looked at her. What to say? "OK. I enjoyed meeting you."

Her fingers slipped from his.

Everything in the bar looked peculiarly flat now. The Argentinian barman, the one who wasn't Argentinian, moved stiffly, like a practised drunk, past a line of two-dimensional bottles with strange chrome spouts. The ceiling and walls were drained of natural light and weather. Everything was bland and artificial, free of the unsettling effects of events. The darkened window glass offered only reflection now. Here he was, in a place of temporary safety, soon to know if his wiring had worked, and what the fuck was he doing?

He put down enough cash to cover the bill and a large tip. He rushed outside. She was in the street. He saw the dress first, then the hair. The hair was moving in the wind and she was trying to hail a taxi. The frailty of her wave made him think of his mother hugging him before he left for Brighton, scrabbling at his shoulders like a climber on a rock face, bound to nothing, bound to fall, knowing nothing, knowing something — but how much did she understand?

When he was close enough for Lena to hear him he said, "I've been up since quarter to four. Not sleeping. I'm sorry. Fatigue makes me more prick-like than usual. My name's Dan . . . Forgive that stuff."

She didn't turn around. She didn't flinch. Nothing seemed to surprise her. Maybe that's what real happiness was, he thought: the inability to feel surprised. But it could just as easily be a definition of misery.

The road was distinctly lit. Lamp posts were queuing up a hill. He could take it all in with a flicker of the eye: the closed-up shops; the railings; the metal bars guarding windows.

"I'll walk until I find a lift," she said.

"Let me walk with you, help you get a taxi."

"No. Yes. If you like."

They walked side by side. The pavement was peaceful. The only movement was the flutter of litter. A Lilt can rattled at the kerb.

The list of things they didn't discuss was long. Children, relationships, hopes, regrets, favourite foods, views on sex, friends alive, friends dead, break-ups, disease, famine, love, all the different kinds of leave-taking that make up a life. They exchanged maybe a hundred words, but the silences between felt special. He tried to hold her shoulder but she rolled it away. Cold and pebbled, her skin; he'd expected it to be warm. He looked at the shine of her eyes and sensed there was nothing he could do.

Maybe I should just ask, he thought. Would I be able to kiss you? Would that be OK? He wasn't sure how it would sound. Like a fourteen-year-old's zitty plea, prob-ably.

They were perfectly still, facing each other. He looked down at his watch, regis-tered the time. A bus stop. She decided to take a bus. A bus came and she moved towards its hissing doors.

He gave her a half-smile as they parted. That he could manage even that was a credit to his ability to pretend. This was nothing. It didn't matter. In a few hours it would be a well-lit morning and he'd read the newspaper, see the accounts of the bombing, and accept that this moment on this street with this stranger was never a part of the story. She doesn't like you. Move on.

On the walk back he laughed at himself. The idea that a cold brute, a prizefighter, needed the warmth of a good woman. It was the saccharine stuff that Hollywood sold and he wasn't a prizefighter, was he? He was an electrician and what he needed was sleep.

He'd get into bed is what he'd do. He'd get home and sleep soundly. He wouldn't wake to the letter box tonight. If they wanted to put something through the letter box, let them. He wouldn't wake in the night and think how noisy the bed sheets were, a crashing sea all around him. He wouldn't wake like he had these last three weeks with the dippy idea of the ocean in his mind, mouth dry with dread, hand grappling for a glass of water. He simply would not wake.

9

Moose felt daft with adrenalin. One hundred per cent alive for the first time in weeks. Finally it was happening: light laughter; gaps in chatter. Silence was smoothed by classical music. The old gramophone had been procured with events like this in mind. He was circulating through the bar area with a silver tray balanced on the splayed pads of his fingers. The more competent of the summer girls were doing the same, weaving tactfully through gaps in the partygoers. Twenty elegantly dressed men and women. Thirty. Forty. The space was filling up nicely. Tories, lords. The accident-prone staff he'd tidied away backstage: restocking chiller cabinets, fuelling security staff with coffee.

Freya's allocated task in advance of the Prime Minister's arrival was to keep champagne topped up. She was being rheumy-eyed and unhelpful. Already she'd dropped two flutes. The first mistake sent champagne splashing up Sasha's legs. He needed her to be on top of her game. After sweeping up fragments from the second glass he asked her what exactly was wrong.

"What do you think?" she said.

"I'm supposed to know?"

"No."

"I'm not?"

"No."

"Is it because I rushed you, getting ready?"

"No."

"Are you trying to annoy me by over-relying on the word 'no?' "

She lifted an eyebrow at this.

"What exactly, or just vaguely, is wrong?"

"Nothing," she said.

Since then he'd been intermittently trying to get his daughter to talk, but her only concession to reciprocity had been to take a bowl of nuts from his hand — nuts that had, after a dozen tiny sampling sessions, left telltale hints of glitter on his fingers. She gave him, in lieu, a side plate of carrot sticks. Each stick radiated outward from a central ramekin of taramasalata. He resented her for being a blot on his happiness, and hated himself for thinking of his own daughter as a blot. He relocated her to the reception desk. She stood behind it, shoulder to shoulder with Surfer John, silent. What came to mind was a Christmas where he and Viv had sent her upstairs to think about why torturing Grandpa was bad.

"Caroline," he called.

"Yes, Mr. Finch?"

"Be great if you could help Elena top up the champagne."

"Sure, no problem."

If they were all like Caroline his job would be easy-peasy.

Did the salmon blinis need a little squeeze of something? Would it not have been better to serve them with precise little slices of lemon? He was sure he'd requested lemons. He wondered whether the volume on the gramophone was pitched just a little too high.

He moved between groups, hoping key individuals noticed his name badge. He was being hands-on, a boss who wasn't afraid to get involved. He was serving up miniature fish cakes with a self-deprecating air, a years-since-I've-done-this smile, but was nervously aware that the point of such self-deprecation was that other people should notice and appreciate it, thereby balancing the ledgers of modesty and praise in his favour. The ministers each had in their information packs a handwritten note signed by Moose. Printed at the bottom was his full name and title, but you could never be sure, could you, what people read and what they skipped. This was his show and he had to have faith.

Some of the men and women were raucous already and others were whispering in corners, exchanging hushed thoughts about the PM, placing stress on unremarkable syllables. "I just think un*less* the Lady can pull something exceptional out of the bag, something out of the ordinary, then what we might be looking at tomorrow is, you know, don't you think, if we're *to*tally honest . . ." Fifty of them now? Sixty?

Marina was with a PR woman. Both of them were holding hefty Filofaxes. A call Maggie would need to make to Scargill. This evening, from this hotel, a call that could change the course of history. He loved overhearing little titbits like this. In hospital he'd felt the press of cancelled life all around him. Tonight put him back in the world.

A lady with a sequinned neckscarf was contemplating a selection of soft cheeses.

"Pursuit of income equality!" someone said.

Over there, by the painting of Harold Wilson, a Welshman was telling Jorge that politics was a matter of give and take — "we give the English our coal, and the English take our water" — and Jorge was giving him the kind of smile that succinctly expresses complete and utter incomprehension.

John Redwood was seated next to one of two dozen flower arrangements purchased at stupendous expense. Redwood touched his chin and nodded as a young guy in a polka-dot bow tie talked to him about a "small idea I have." On Redwood's face was a frown of amused concern.

"The Lady's view," Redwood said eventually, and Moose missed a few words as someone thanked him for a canapé, ". . . do *not* need that, those things, to help them find work. A great myth!" When Redwood was happy he looked like Spock from *Star Trek*. In other moods he was Liza Minnelli.

Conversations mixing with other conversations.

"Secondary issue."

"Well, that I'd agree on."

"Probable cause."

"More or less exactly it."

"Two hundred thousand, though, is not enough for contempt of court."

"Pass the . . . ?"

"I just can't get excited about Durham."

"Would you . . . ?"

There was the clinking of fragile glass. Earrings as elegant as the chandeliers overhead. Pockets of choking cigar smoke through which Moose held his breath. He tried not to cough because coughs, when they came, still detonated pain: overlapping, pouncing jolts of it. There were a lot of polished skill-sets around. A lot of firm handshakes and air-kisses. Smiles too big to be fake, too bright to be true — which made them what? Full lips. Empty eyes. He tried to ignore the momentary sense that it was all a vicious pantomime.

At the end of the bar five important men had been in conversation for perhaps an hour. Geoffrey Howe, the Secretary of State for Foreign and Commonwealth Affairs, was among them. He seemed to be talking about the differences between humans and animals. He broke off to throw a fishcake down his throat.

Dinner jackets identical but for the width of the lapels. White shirts with studs instead of buttons. One or two maroon cummerbunds and shoes of uniform shine.

Some further food disappeared from Moose's platter, some napkins from his hand, and one of the group told Mr. Howe that the distinction between humans and beasts was our ability to be coolly rational.

"No no," another said. "Our deep capacity to — well, to *feel,* yes?"

"No," Howe said, "you're right."

A young aide Moose had earlier seen sweating in the restaurant now dropped a canapé on the floor. "I am so s-s-sorry," he said.

Moose walked over to John and Freya. Freya was still opting for silence. Fine, be that way. He clutched John's shoulder, a ball of muscle.

"When the Key VIP arrives, John, alert me immediately."

"The Key VIP?"

"MT."

"MT?"

"Jesus, John, is there anything going on in there?" He tapped John's forehead with his finger. He did so much harder than he'd meant to. "The Prime Minister."

John yawned and said sure no problem.

Babble at the edge of a dream. Breastbone pain. He'd have to keep slow and calm, look after his heart. Tiredness was already coming for him, trying to steal away the night's opportunities.

Sir Anthony Berry was talking to an aide. Moose quietly interjected and asked if everything was all right with the room. Berry had been due to stay at the Metropole, but after a last-minute cancellation Marina had squeezed him in.

"Oh, absolutely," said Berry. He was the ideal guest, polite to a fault, hair carefully combed. "Happy a space became available. Thanks for all your help."

A simple thank-you: it could mean so much. The smallest acts of appreciation were magnified tenfold tonight.

Staff who were awaiting the allocation of further tasks had been told to stand with their hands behind their backs, but he saw from his new vantage point behind the bar that one or two still had their fists sunk into their pockets. The slumped ones tended to cluster together. The Poor Posture Club. When managing a large staff you had to keep an eye on all the factions; you couldn't let the peripheral groups get disgruntled. Some of the waiters' shirt collars looked wrinkled, and this was irritating. He'd supplied everyone with a little spray gun of starch, bought at his own expense from the Blue Door Launderette.

Plain-clothes Special Branch men stood motionless at the edges of the room. They had brisk, assertive eyes and when they spoke Moose thought only of right angles.

So tall and solid-looking you felt a hundred gut-punches wouldn't move them. Another eight or nine of them had, he'd noticed, been dispatched to the car-park area. Others were posted on the first-, second- and third-floor landings. It seemed an embarrassingly comprehensive security effort given the only halfway-visible threat was the presence, outside the front entrance, of six or seven student types in itchy-looking clothing. Was one of them Susie, Freya's friend? Was that why Freya was in a murderous mood? Beyond the window these skinny probable-vegans rocked on the balls of their feet and chanted, "Stop the rot, stop the rot," without ever quite clarifying what the rot was, or how to stop it. He wondered what it would be like to be one of them, a person who devoted their days to the pursuit of major change. It occurred to him that his own life had been devoted to the opposite activity: the attempt to mould capriciousness into something respectably firm. He ate a blini.

A couple of top-tier journalists had arrived, a BBC guy and someone with a column in the *Telegraph,* and in their faces Moose found the closest mirror for his own tensely contained excitement. They ducked in and out of various groups, leaned onto tiptoes every time the revolving door whirred. Tomorrow's dinner in the Empress Suite would be journalist-free. He needed to check with the External Events Manager that all was running to plan. He couldn't see her. He sought out Marina instead. Marina usually had the answers.

She was bending to retrieve a napkin someone had dropped behind one of the gooseneck high-backed chairs. The napkins were conference blue, ordered especially from a supplier who'd seemed to understand Moose's obsession with shades and textures in a way his own staff never had. As Marina got to her feet he moved to stand beside her and she said, "It's not so beautiful when it's full, is it?" There was something a little mournful in her voice. They watched the twitch and throb of the party, women throwing their heads back in laughter, pearls strung around their elegant necks.

"The bar?" he said.

She shrugged. "The hotel."

"Not you as well."

She frowned.

"Freya," he said. "The people that I — that I care about, they're depressed. Accommodating people is what we do, Mari."

"Were you always such a functional man, Moose?"

Functional. The word conjured up the big joyless filing cabinet in his office. "There's nothing wrong with something fulfilling its purpose, if that's what you mean."

Her eyes went bright. She seemed about to laugh. Something malicious he hadn't seen before? "What is your purpose, do you think?" she said.

"My purpose?"

"I am curious."

"Well, today it's about keeping Thatcher happy, isn't it?"

"And Freya?"

"What about her?"

"She seems miserable, you said. I agree."

"I don't know what it's about. If you know, I'd appreciate knowing."

Marina twirled the napkin she'd retrieved from the floor. Several dots of red wine were sunk into the stitching. If this were Viv, she would be holding it further from her body. Viv would have it pinched between forefinger and thumb, at arm's length.

"If you know something," he repeated.

"No. I don't know what she's feeling."

Behind her, through the window glass, a greenish night took shape. "Maybe she's got a boyfriend," he said. "She's been out a lot. Maybe it's boyfriend trouble. There was a

481

kid called Tom who used to hang around a lot."

"Have you asked her?"

He shook his head. "If you had a daughter you'd know that questions like that never get answered. They stare at you in a way that suggests you're a nutcase from outer space, Mari, and that the kindest thing would be to laser you into the ground. *Pow. Bzzzzzz.*"

He expected another smile, a warmer one, but her lips didn't move. Had he been insensitive? Perhaps her own childlessness was a source of pain? Her easy warmth with Engelbert suggested she'd make a good mother. It wasn't necessarily too late.

"Engel OK?" he said.

"Yes. In your office."

"Good."

"I hope you don't mind?"

"Of course not."

"Emma is babysitting. He'll sleep soon, I hope."

"Set up camp in the side room?"

Marina nodded. "She's trying to tire him out. Last time I looked, they were making a castle from tinfoil. My sister would kill me if she knew he wasn't sleeping."

"Have they found my rolls of tape? For the — the construction?"

Now the smile came. "Tell me, why do you need all this tape?"

"I buy in bulk," he said. "Saves the hotel money."

"What about friends?" Marina said. "Who is she friends with at the moment?"

"Emma?"

"Freya."

Someone downed a glass of champagne and said, "Ahhhhh." A few jackets were being positioned on the backs of chairs. One woman had a bow tie draped around her neck. Mrs. Thatcher was definitely late.

"Well," Moose said, "there's that Tracy girl. The one with the, how do I put this . . . with the fashion sense? And of course Susie Thingy, who I think is currently outside protesting against our Prime Minister, which is interesting. Have you noticed that there seems to be a fair amount of chatter about the PM's speech tomorrow? About how if it doesn't go well she might be, you know . . ."

"I thought they don't see each other so much these days. Freya and Susie."

"Yes, yes. Did I know that?"

"An argument one or two weeks ago."

"How do you hear this stuff?"

She shrugged. "People tell me things."

"That's what I've always thought about

myself, that people tell me things."

"Maybe you don't listen to what they are telling."

"That seems a bit harsh."

"Also silence," Marina said.

"Sorry?"

"If you create a silence, people speak."

Silence fell. Moose made a point of not speaking.

Marina said, "She's swimming again, no?"

"Yes, yes. She's definitely doing that. We went together, actually."

"That was weeks ago."

"It went well, though."

"You had a heart attack, Moose."

"Well . . . true."

"I was talking of recently."

"Right."

"Who does she swim with these days?"

"Who with? One of her old swimming-team friends, I think. She's a grown-up, Mari."

"Such as?"

"As?"

"Which friends?"

He sunk his fist into a flap pocket of his jacket. He'd cleared out all of the coins. Usually coin-play gave him comfort, the quick answer of cool metal in his hand.

"Mari, is this an interrogation, or what?

I'm supposed to be able to name them? Are you suggesting" — someone shoved past him, rude, thoughtless — "that I'm, what, a bad father in some way? Because I'm trying to make the best of a tricky situation, you know. Her mother I get nothing from. I get sweet FA from her mother. I know I'm only a mediocre dad." He capitulated to a pathetically painful cough. "I'm trying my best."

"Where are the sausage rolls?" someone shouted. Another pocket of laughter erupted. For a split second Moose felt an incandescent urge to turn a gun on everyone in the room.

"I'm not so familiar with the divorce benefits here," Marina said.

"What?"

"The sweet FA. I don't know what this involves."

Was she being funny?

"I've spent years pursuing dead ends, Mari. What I need is —"

"A photograph in the paper with Margaret, and some glowing endorsement. I know, and I do not think you are a mediocre dad."

Photograph. The word was triggering a memory. "Your exhibition, Mari. The picture of the pig and the islands. Tell me I haven't missed it."

"Not yet. Don't worry."

"God. Good. I want to know the date. And this is not ego, Mari. This is me trying to get a career going. Why? So Freya can go through university without having to stack shelves. So she can get an education and have a good life. Corny but true."

"Does she actually want to go to a university, though? Is that *her* idea of a good life?"

"She'll go eventually. She's smarter than all of us put together."

"So smart she will do what is expected of her, as women must."

"Look, Mari, I don't expect you to understand. If I'd had certain opportunities that Freya has. If I had had the encouragement that —"

"I am hearing a lot of *I* here," Marina said, and in saying it sounded so terrifyingly like his mother that Moose wondered, briefly, whether he could ever again bear to fantasise about rolling around with her on a sunny square of grass in . . . Somerset? Dorset? Which got better weather? OK: he could, he could.

He was feeling a little dizzy now, light-headed, regretful about that last glass of Coke. The doctors hadn't said anything about Coke. They'd just advised him to avoid cigarettes and "sugary and fatty foodstuffs." How much sugar could there be in a modern glass of Coke? Just a dash, these days, surely.

"Mari," he said, "I admit it's partly personal. I feel . . . I just feel . . . I feel like if I could do one perfect thing, you know, I'd be happy."

In response Marina began to say something about daughters, but at that moment Moose saw, on the far side of the room, the familiar red jacket of the Captain. He seemed, oh God, to be talking to the Secretary of State for Education and Science. How had he slipped past security?

"I'm going to have to deal with this, Mari. Sorry. He's cornered Sir Keith."

A gap opened up between Patrick Jenkin and Kenneth Baker. Baker was heading for great things, people said; he'd need to catch a moment with him later. He took the gap, closed in on the red jacket. The injection of pace left him breathless.

"Your Excellency," he said to Sir Keith, which was definitely the wrong form of address.

Keith Joseph stared at him, a face full of tortured intensity. His features thinned into a wince and he wiped the wince with a conference-blue napkin.

The Captain whispered something to Sir

Keith and Sir Keith said, "We'll come back to that, we will. Have the two of you met?"

"Of course," Moose said. "Of course." He slung a friendly arm around the Captain's shoulders, surprised by the way his fingers seemed able to press between the bones. He said, "Sir Keith, not wishing to interrupt, but would you like me — well — I could introduce you to Mr. Jenkin or Mr. Baker over there, perhaps?" He tried out something between a wink and a blink, still clutching the Captain's fragile shoulders. Steering them, in fact, in the direction of the bar. A man like the Captain could probably be bribed into silence with a drink or two. An outright ejection from the hotel would risk making a scene. Nice guy — Moose meant him no harm — but he was out of place here. This was a private function.

Sir Keith's gaze fell on Moose's name badge. "I can assure you, Mr. Finch, that I don't need to be introduced to either of the two gentlemen you mentioned."

"Ah, of course, not introduced — not *introduced* as such — I just meant —" He did a quick sideways nod in the direction of the Captain. Saving you! Saving you! He's fun but a little bit crazy!

"I would say, in fact," Sir Keith went on,

488

"that I probably speak to those gentlemen as often as I do to my own wife. Moreover, the — the Captain? Yes. Well, the Captain and I were in the middle, as it happens, of a conversation about environmental issues."

"Right," Moose said. "As if the environment's a priority!" He swallowed and studied Sir Keith's increasingly grave expression. He was fucking this up. He really was. "In times like these, I mean." Stop talking, stop talking. "You know, the rich–poor divide and . . ." This was bad. This was digging yourself a hole. A Moose in a volcano with a shovel, rumblings from below. Natural disaster with extra lava. He waited for Sir Keith to speak.

"The environment," Sir Keith said, "is among the most important of concerns. What you may consider to be background scenery is of course — Hello, James, how do you do? — the very thing keeping us alive."

"Makes me think," the Captain said, "of those lines from Auden."

"Yes?" Sir Keith said. "I'm not familiar."

The Captain recited a line of poetry, something to do with faces in public places.

"Ah," Sir Keith said. "I must make a note!" He looked bafflingly happy, his eyes soft and moist.

"I always prefer," the Captain said, "to be outdoors, don't you? The environment. The elements. The sea. Whereas events such as these — a fandangling job at curation, don't get me wrong — but public men such as yourself cooped up in small rooms, the faces in private places . . ."

"Oh, absolutely," Sir Keith said. "Refreshingly honest. I take no offence. In fact" — he leaned in, chuckling (chuckling!) — "I couldn't agree more, truth be told."

Moose looked on, astonished, as the conversation continued to blossom. The Captain brushed crumbs from his jacket. His hair looked extra white and his cheeks teemed with uncommon colour.

"Though I would like," the Captain said, "to speak to you about another matter at some point too. One concerning education and health. I believe you have links to the pharmaceutical industry? I'd like to discuss what we can do to address a growing problem, a global problem I've already written to Mr. Peter Tatchell about. It concerns prejudices and — sincerely — preventing many deaths. But perhaps I'm taking up too much of your fine-sung time."

"Not at all," Sir Keith said. "You have my ear."

Fine-sung time? What did it even mean?

Moose shook his head and walked away. You misread people and misread people and misread people again.

Marina was still standing by the curtains, bare arms crossed, back straight, hair and heels reflecting lamplight. "The Captain still seems to be here," she said.

"Yes. That's true. Holding it together pretty well."

Sasha walked by, yawning. A minister touched Karen's wrist and asked her about cake, or possibly his coat.

Marina said, "Freya has been going there a lot, no? The Captain's museum."

"The what? Oh. That." Paparazzi were beginning to throng outside, a mass of denim jackets and camera bags, which meant —

"She went there twice this week, I think."

"Why?"

Marina shrugged. "Because she finds him interesting, no? Or is a little bit alone."

There was a burst of activity in the lobby. Voices. Flashbulbs. Marina saying, "Keep *calm,* Moose. Don't rush. Your health."

"Calm" was on your marks. "Rush" was equivalent to a gun going off. He barely heard the word "health." He lurched through bodies, elbows out, using the silver tray as a shield. Maggie was here, Maggie was here, and she was what this party was missing.

Some of the photographers had spilled into the hotel. They were saying "Prime Minister, do you have any comment on . . . ?," "Prime Minister, what do you say to the . . . ?," "Prime Minister, do you plan to . . . ?" Someone trod on his foot. A police officer was shouting. So many arms and legs. He wedged himself against a painting of Napoleon, chest aching, foot hurting, the blur of black-tie all around. John was a head's height above the rest, close to the door. He looked confused, hopeless. He was saying "Excuse me, hello." Freya might have knocked them all into shape but Freya — where was Freya?

A man with a walkie-talkie appeared on the stairs. Who was he? Where from? With a few authoritative words this man managed to restore some semblance of order, but there were still too many people shifting for Moose to get a glimpse of Mrs. Thatcher. The plan to line staff up along the stairs no longer seemed actionable. John wasn't ac-tioning it. And Plan B was . . . Why didn't he have a Plan B? Had he learned nothing? Light from chandeliers fell in shards, il-luminating shoulder-dandruff.

He slipped through a few of the more half-hearted spectators. Here the crowd tightened around him. Ducking down he saw between tights and trousers a pair of shoes that could be hers. Brown shoes, scuffed, like his mother sometimes wore — they were not very prime ministerial. The roundness of the ankles surprised him.

A thin zigzag of space opened up. This was his moment. He raised his eyes, savouring every second on the way to her face. He saw the hem of a tweed skirt, he saw the wrinkled bend of a waistband, and it was at this point — the point at which he was straightening his back and beginning to stand tall — that a Special Branch guy barged him into the shadows.

10

Four-something in the morning, the moon's soft display of emotion, the night bright against closed windows. Dan was nearing the end of his long walk home. Knotweed on his mind, the lost library book, unspoiled face of the receptionist girl, a woman's hand slipping from his. He was going to have to pay a pro a lot of money. Glyphosate sprayed over the garden. A non-selective herbicide. Kills everything and poisons the soil. Find Dawson and give him a dose? Keep it all for himself? He could imagine the tearful hangover tomorrow. He could imagine the day after that, waking up to no headache, the small pure joy of health restored. He could imagine hearing the Saracens slipping into low gears and men raiding his home, everything falling apart. He could picture the book on knotweed in a puddle of ale, a crowd of dipsos around it, the land of old smoke and the city of myths. There was no real life. Not here, not anymore. Everything pretend. He was drunk.

He gifted a burp to the chill night air. He was booze-snug, insulated, full-bodied, cloudy. He thought he could hear a hysterical mosquito whining at the loss of summer. He tried to clap it dead. Girl in the blue dress had boarded her bus. Could feel the cold only on his lips, on the tip of his nose. His ears ached. They ached with nothing. In his assessment he'd need to be sick very soon. Could feel his weight shifting wildly as he walked. Waterbed head, a motherfucking dream. He loved Ireland, he loved Belfast. He loved it with nothing.

No cheers or shrieks to be heard in these streets. No raids of houses as far as he could see. It had gone off and the news hadn't filtered through. It hadn't gone off and there was no news. It had been found and defused, a press release shaped, clear roles assigned and the past flattened down: heroes, villains, survivors; everyone assigned their proper role and thinking in threes. He tried to find comfort in the fact that whatever had happened or not happened had by now happened or not happened. People wanted love, they thought it made them whole, but caring about other people was exactly what cracked you open. He cared and didn't care.

He felt cracked open now. He didn't feel it until he thought it. It was the thought that shaped his fate. He was cracked.

As he got close to home a change of atmosphere occurred. His mind registered this in stages. First the scent of burning leaves. He breathed it in and hoped it would steady him. He liked the spice of kindling things. Then above a twitching street lamp a dark mass of shifting air. There were flecks of glitter within. Ash?

For a moment he wondered dumbly who would have a bonfire at this hour. Gradually the fog on his thoughts burned off and an upsurge in sensory detail came: siren noises getting louder; people moving in the street. He realised he'd been aware all along of an orange glow clinging to the bend in the road. The fire was nearer than he'd imagined.

He moved off the pavement, onto the stuttering white line. In the houses either side of him windows and porch lights flickered to life. Front doors were swinging open, more people waking up. They staggered and rubbed their eyes. He felt he was picking his way through an intricate dream.

The chemical tang thickened and he spat. The orange glow was thinning into specific tongues of fire. Only a hook of moon above.

Ash falling softly on rooftops. Clouds like steel wool expanded in the sky. He was running — a burnout, a burnout.

It might be number 12. It might be 42. Feet hitting concrete. Legs absorbing shock. Nothing in his mind was properly fused. The ground was harder than it had been before. He sprinted until the road was straight.

Again the truth revealed itself in increments: the property on fire was number 17; number 17 was where he lived; he lived with his mother and his mother would be home.

He stopped dead in the street. The night arranged around him was all motion now. He was seeing the neighbourhood as if for the first time. The small crowded houses, the patchwork gardens. The air of dilapidation and minimum love. His eyes winced in their sockets. A tropical warmth souped him. It was a warmth that told you this couldn't be Ireland, and then you saw the embattled bystanders, the rich plumes of smoke rising up from burning property, and you heard the skid of a tyre, and the shouting of commandments, and the quiet prayers recited at the edges of the flames — all the things that told you it was.

The right side of his house was melting away. The flames were leaning, extending.

Enjoying themselves. Ten or twenty men were at work hurling water out of buckets. The roof. The fencing. As liquid sped from the buckets the men swivelled and grunted, ran to refill, sweating into their sleeves. The stooped figure of Ancient Jones was among the helpers, half killing himself with each bucket-thrust.

Empty of strength Dan watched the collective effort: good Catholics and good Protestants trying to save his home. Among these mixed civilians he felt a crushing need to sleep. "He's snattered," someone said. People pointed. "Is that . . . ?"

The men urged their women to stay clear, but some of the women threw water nonetheless. Two or three he knew from the club, the ones with that special moxie, that defiant spark, the extraordinary refusal to relent that you find in people punished too long: the blacks, the Jews, kids sleeping in the street. What he felt in this moment was close to joy. Call it acceptance, acquiescence. It came even before he saw his mother sitting on the kerb unharmed. This thought: I've got what I deserve. It came even before he saw that his house wasn't the only one burning. Twenty doors down there were a few slight flames from the home of the next Catholic family.

I've got what I deserve. There is an order to events after all. The bomb has gone off. Revenge has begun. This is lads from Loyalist groups clutching their lists. This is the proper reciprocation of damage and it gets quicker every year. There were tears in his eyes. Ash in the air. Love in his heart. The anger had gone. He blinked and wiped his face. He looked for rumours of light in the sky. What a time to get sentimental, he thought, and cursed his wasted years.

He watched the dark loop on the roof. A ten-foot TV aerial he'd helped to install aged fourteen, melting. First thing he ever did that worked. He saw it and thought of his CB radio. He used that radio to talk half the night with people across the Province. Catholic, Protestant. One of the girls on CB had a handle, a call sign, which had caught his attention straight out: "Perfect Shankill Kiss." They spoke for a few nights. They met in person outside a pharmacy in town. It was where all the CB freaks leaned against lamp posts. If he had anything worth swapping, she said, she'd swap it for a kiss. There were bins on the pavement back then. He took from the top of one of these bins an almost-clean copy of *Rushlight* magazine. Gave it to her. Wad of Wrigley's on the corner of the cover. They kissed. She complained he kissed too wetly. There were happy months in which they went to the pool. Ridiculous to cling to a romance like that. When his CB radio broke, he took it apart under his uncle's supervision. They put it back together and it worked. He used it less and less. The fixing was more fun than the listening. Perfect Shankill Kiss began kissing someone else.

His mother on the kerb was flanked by other women. They were smoking. He could not believe they were smoking. Through the soft haze of cigarette smoke mixed with the smoke of burnt belongings he saw up the skirt of one of these old women, glimpsing the beige mysteries of her underwear.

11

He had to pick himself up. No one helped him. Maybe there were too many people for any one person to feel responsible. Maybe they just didn't see?

It was all too hectic. A wedding reception times five. He begged Marina to get a grip on things, to use her feminine wiles, and she gave him a look that said he'd phrased that very badly. He went to the toilet to breathe deeply and be alone. The simple smells of soap and bleach. The dreamy tinkle of urine in the bowl. Took an aspirin. It left a bitter taste in his mouth. Imagined conversations drip-dripped through his thoughts.

Really, Margaret? Me?

You.

Me? The major national speech on leniency? Me?

I need a man I can trust, Moose. I think you're the man to deliver the speech.

Not the Secretary of State for Education?

No.

Not the . . . not the prisons guy?

No, I'm asking you — you — to be the man to deliver it.

Even though I'm arguably lacking pizzazz?

Nonsense, you genius. The way you made those beer ice cubes, that time, so you could keep your beer cool without diluting the beer?

You saw that?

I see everything.

He woke with a jolt, a sense of being watched. Trousers around his ankles. His heart hurt.

By the time he'd buckled up and straightened his tie and acknowledged to himself that sleeping on the toilet constituted a new low, the crowd in the bar area was of a manageable size. Good: he'd have proper time with the Prime Minister.

He leaned onto tiptoes and looked around. Was that . . . ? No, not her. Maybe behind . . . ? No, no. The crackle of a throat being cleared. A man with a cane saying, "I took a bus once." Whatever story followed could never live up to the audacity of that opening line.

A tall, needle-faced young man was standing in front of him — the man who had helped call for order on the stairs when the

Prime Minister was working her way through the lobby. Moose had seen him a few times these last few days without knowing exactly who he was. He had a pointed chin that preceded him into confrontations with people you suspected he hated.

"Hi," Moose said. "I don't think we've —"

"Edward Peterson," the man said. "Logistics."

"Right. The Prime Minister's team."

Peterson's smile was pure hygiene, the expression of a guy about to floss. The teeth were big. The mouth couldn't quite hold them. It was a miracle the lips didn't bleed. There was saliva pooling on his gums and shining on his bottom lip and when he closed his mouth to swallow there was a faint, squeaky sucking sound, like a cloth being used to polish cutlery.

"How can I help then, Mr. Peterson?"

"The Lady," he announced, "is now upstairs."

"Oh. Already?"

"Amendments to her speech. End-of-day phone calls. It's a busy time. Will there be coffee?"

"Of course."

"Dark roast, or . . ."

"Well, there's a selection."

"French?"

"I'll show you some options, Mr. Peterson."

Edward Peterson looked a little crushed by this. One more decision to make.

"Who showed her up to the room, Mr. Peterson?"

"Your colleague," Peterson said, pointing.

John strolled towards them. "Yo," he said.

"Yo?" Moose said.

"It's a greeting," John explained.

Moose couldn't let the disappointment swallow him. He tried to smile. He sighed. Tomorrow, he thought. I'll speak to her tomorrow. "You, John? You showered her upstairs?"

"That I definitely didn't do."

"Showed, I mean. *Showed.*" His tongue was still asleep. "Is the PM OK up there, in the room?"

"Yeah. Seemed happy."

"You showed her up there with who? With Freya?"

John shifted his weight from foot to foot. "I think Freya had something else on, maybe. I took her up with the boss, along with her secretary person. Cynthia?"

Edward Peterson nodded. The sharp drama of his chin. It swung down like a pygmy pickaxe, or something very similar that made sense. Moose once again rubbed his eyes to bring reality back.

"All good fun," John said.

"Good fun?"

"Yeah, she's actually" — John hesitated, flicked a glance at Peterson — "she's actually really chilled, Mr. Finch. I talked to her about wetsuits."

"Wetsuits."

John opened his mouth. Moose held up a hand to indicate that he had no interest in hearing about wetsuits, dry suits, any kind of suit. "And the boss is . . ." he said. "Our GM is here right now, John? That's what you're saying?"

"Yeah. With this Baker bloke."

"Baker? There's a baker here?"

"Surname," John said, grinning. "Yeah, he's the one who's taking over, right?"

Moose shook his head.

"The GM position," John said simply. "Richard Baker."

Silence.

"Yeah," John said, a new uncertainty in his voice. "You've met him before, right? Or he's met you, anyway. He came in the other day too. He's the one taking over as overall manager here, is what he said. Came in with Mr. Price from Head Office. They announce it before Christmas, right?" After delivering these lines, John began to look increasingly unsettled by the silence around him. "Your new boss!" he added cheerfully, then frowned again when this latest effort failed. "You knew the GM was stepping down, right?"

"Now," Peterson said, "about the dinner tomorrow night. I have to tell you that it'll be the Lady's birthday — did you know? — so there is a change of plan, alas, and she will not in all likelihood be attending."

"Not . . ." Moose swallowed to steady his voice. Baker? Price? "Not attending, did you say?"

"There's actually something else planned now, at the Metropole. There's a preference for the dining room there."

Behind Edward Peterson, champagne was being poured. It surged right up to the rim of each flute, full of cocksure fizz, only to subside back down into a single meagre gulpful.

Someone was holding his hand, he realised. Freya was next to him now and holding his hand. Warm. He wasn't feeling well.

"The dinner?" Freya said to Peterson. "You're saying she can't make the big birthday dinner in her honour?"

Peterson made a clicking noise with his tongue, sucked in some more saliva. "If by *she* you mean the Lady, then yes. Who's in charge here, actually?"

"You're saying the Prime Minister can't make it," Freya said.

"I've said it now at length, yes. People here seem to have a talent for repetition."

"Just like that. Can't come."

"Excuse me?" Peterson said. He looked around as if to ask if this latest outrage was being recorded. The answer was yes. A security camera had its boxy gaze fixed upon them.

"Do you know how much work goes into these things?" Freya said.

"I beg your pardon?"

"This has been planned for weeks," Freya said. "People's work. All this food, basically. This changes a lot of things, so it would have been good — polite — to have known sooner."

"Sadly," Peterson said, "there are pressing national and international issues. Things going on beyond your plans." He touched the tip of his chin.

"You're not even sorry."

"Extraordinary," Edward Peterson said, laughing. "Perhaps I should be speaking to the new manager."

"The who?"

"Mr. Baker. The new —"

"You could have told us in a different way," Freya said.

"I don't think I know who you are." He blinked. "Now, Mr. *Finch,* second issue. We could do with that human with the tattoos from Kalle Infotec back here, to set up three further fax machines in the temporary office, and my own recommendation would be, let's see, that we start by —"

On and on Edward Peterson went. Moose, if not quite having an out-of-body experience, was definitely having an out-of-joint one. The GM job had gone to someone else. Could it be true? He knew it was. It was over.

There was a fold-out table he'd positioned against the wall several hours ago. A dozen laminated name badges remained. They were arranged in three rows and the spaces between the rows were exactly right.

"Mr. Peterson," he said, squeezing his daughter's hand, "we'll sort everything out. You needn't worry."

"Good," Peterson said. "I'm glad we've reached an understanding. I look forward to seeing the coffees you have to offer."

Before turning away from this exchange, Moose took a final look at Edward Peterson. There was something about his sly expression. Something about his reiterated request for caffeination. Something about the damp, satisfied pout that cost its owner so little effort. Something about Peterson's pleased brown eyes moving from him to Freya, from Freya back to him, as if deciding which of them he was most inclined to deride. There was something about all of this that caused a guy rope in Moose's professionalism to begin to creak and twist, and murderous thoughts to begin to blossom.

He thought of the Captain talking to Sir Keith, and he thought of his daughter having to put up with this young man's rudeness. He thought of the hopeless promotion he'd put so much energy into, and of the possibility that his promised advancement had been nothing but a dangled incentive, a way to keep things ticking over while the current GM eased into a notice period. He thought about these things and the cancelled dinner tomorrow and about whether he'd been pushed out because of his health, or had simply never ever stood a chance at becoming GM, and felt he needed to say something, to convert some of his thinking into words, not just for himself but for his view of the world — a view which had no room, he realised now, for careless people like Edward Peterson. After a dozen long seconds in which a variety of semi-clever insults were considered and dismissed he said, "Mr. Peterson?"

"Yes?"

"Second thoughts, go fuck yourself."

He came close to following this up with a punch but was worried he might hurt his hand.

12

Freya was in the ladies' loo, crying and applying make-up, staring into the mirror. The door opened. Marina.

"What are you doing, darling?"

"I'm crying and applying make-up," she said.

Marina stood in the doorway, absorbing this remark. Then she blinked and said, "It is best to divide this into a two-stage process. Otherwise you look like a melted panda."

Freya sighed. The slab of grey stone in which the basins sat had a theatrical shine tonight. She put the eyeliner down. Earlier in the week someone with over-plucked eyebrows had complained that the lavatory lighting was insufficient for the proper plucking of eyebrows. Bulbs of greater wattage had been installed above the mirrors. Every natural pattern in the stonework showed, skylines and trees and thin and thick clouds.

"We can talk," Marina said.

"I'm fine. It's nothing."

"The quality of nothing has not such need to hide itself."

With a pink tissue Freya blew her nose.

"I've been seeing a Shakespearean," Marina said. "It's finished now. His toenails scratched me in bed. He's very successful at everything, but there were the toenails — scratch scratch scratch scratch scratch. It's very boring, also, to be around someone so pleased with themselves." She glanced at herself in the mirror. "Your love life, Freya. Is that what's making you so sad and messy?" She placed her handbag by a basin. She took a hairbrush out. "Shall I?" she said.

There was an awkward moment — it seemed a strange offer — but Freya didn't have the energy refusal might require. There was a single chair against the wall. The toilet attendant they used for events had already left for the night. "Here," Marina said. She turned the chair to face the mirror. Freya sat down and Marina moved behind her.

"I know you saw me," Freya said. "Coming out of the room the other day."

Marina began to run the brush through Freya's hair in long and even strokes. She separated sections. She eased the brush through knots. The brush made a scuffing electrical sound that came straight out of childhood.

"I'm such a cliché."

Marina looked up.

"A big fat cliché. He's with Sasha now."

Marina laughed. "John?"

"I think so, maybe."

"If anything, darling, I think you are . . . Yes, under-clichéd. It is Sasha who is the cliché. It is John."

Freya stared at her own reflection, and at the face of Marina floating above it, and for a moment thought she could smell the too-strong perfume of Wendy Hoyt, hairdresser ordinaire.

"You could do with being a bit more whingeing," Marina said. She rested the palm of her hand on Freya's head. "I mean, you look a bit pathetic now, yes. But generally, a bit more emotional — it would be good. You are more like what a man should be, but isn't."

Freya opened her mouth and closed it.

"It's OK to be sad sometimes, Freya. You almost lost your father, yes? You already lost your mother. Your friends have gone to colleges. You thought you would be all alone."

Something about the simplicity of this summary caught Freya off guard. A barefooted lady in a silky dress came in, humming a tune, heels dangling from her left hand. Freya said, "Use the ones in the restaurant."

The humming stopped. The door closed. Easy.

"That's the spirit," Marina said. She put the brush down, rested her hands on Freya's shoulders. "It gets you thinking, no?"

"What does?"

"Your father being ill. It makes you think about your mother."

"A bit."

"It makes you think about what it would be like if you never saw her again, and it stayed like this. If news came tomorrow that she was dead, that it was *her* who'd had a heart attack. Or that she'd actually been dead for weeks and you'd missed the funeral. Months, maybe. Longer."

It seemed to Freya that Marina was getting into the swing of this a little too easily.

"You are a lovely girl, Freya. You don't have to feel, every time you do or think something that isn't lovely, that these feelings are your fault."

"I don't. I don't think they're my fault."

"Well," Marina said, "that's good."

"You." Why not say it? "Everyone's in love with you, Marina. My dad, everyone. I wish

I could be more like you."

"When I take off this make-up," Marina said, "it is not pretty. My face is like an animated raisin, Freya. Sunshine — I wish someone had warned me. You're going to work in documentaries one day."

"Me?"

"You're going to work for David Attenbrow. You're going to go to amazing places, Africa. You're going to get mud in your socks and they will underpay you but you'll be happy, and you'll meet a cameraman who is a bit short, maybe, but makes you laugh."

Another guest came in. Freya was thinking that most cameramen would surely be tall. The guest used the toilet and handed Marina a fifty-pence piece. She walked out without washing her hands.

"I guess," Freya said. "Whatever happens, even if he gets sick again, I guess I'll manage."

"Pah," Marina said. She got up and rinsed the fifty-pence piece under the tap, then put it in the pocket of her skirt. "Manage. Who wants to manage? Fuck that." She looked in the mirror again. "I lost someone I loved once, you know? My husband. I joke about him. I make things up. I make it like we weren't in love, and it's funny. People prefer

things that are funny, yes? But he was —
it's not something to discuss. But he was a
person I loved. And when you come out of
the initial feelings about it, the feeling
depressed, it's not like you're improved. You
just feel different, yes? And the thoughts
can come back at any time. Maybe you just
have to settle for saying something like this.
Something like, 'My mother does imperfect
things, and so does my father, and so do I.'
If you want an alternative to feeling all
chewed, you can choose to think that. A
choice. I mean, I know it is still a bit . . .
what would you say?"

"Lame?"

Marina's lips threatened a smile. "Lame.
But maybe it is still worth thinking. It's not
that all parents are worth the worrying.
Some definitely are not. Some are lame. It's
much more simple and selfish than that. If
you get in touch with your mother again
and give her another chance, one of two
things will happen. You will develop some
kind of relationship, or you won't. Either
way, you will have done what *you* can do. It
is always better to clear the air, even if the
air often stinks."

"Is that an Argentinian saying?"

"No," Marina said.

The lights above the mirror did not flicker.

"You're quite good at this, Marina."

"I have spent money on cheap wisdom. But the best thing I heard? It was free. It was about one of those parties that everyone gets invited to, where the night comes and you don't want to go, and you want to make an excuse and stay at home with a movie. You know the ones. It would be inconvenient to go for an hour — that's all, inconvenient. You are tired or something. Hungover. Maybe you have a cold. But for the person whose party it is, it would mean a lot if you went. And my friend said to me that for most of us, for decent people, the choice each day isn't between doing something good and doing something bad. It's between doing something good and doing nothing. So, this is my advice, if you ever want it: always go to the party."

There was silence for a while. Marina kissed the top of Freya's head. "OK?" she said.

"OK."

Always go to the party. Maybe there were worse rules to live by. It didn't seem to cover every eventuality, but maybe in time it would.

Marina said, "Let me know if you feel like going to the pool sometime. I'm actually an excellent swimmer."

"Yeah?"

"I am good at most things," she admitted.

"My dad told an important guy to go fuck himself. One of the Prime Minister's staff."

Marina tilted her head and said, "I am lending his decision my support." Then she left without a further word.

Freya went outside. She'd delayed the inevitable for too long.

"Hey, Sooz."

Susie nodded.

"Has the protest — has it been good?"

"Well," Susie said, "it's ongoing, obviously, so." She was wearing a baggy red jumper and feeding bubble gum into her mouth. She looked determined as she chewed, a muscle flickering in her jaw, and there was a hint of practised disappointment in her eyes. A few other protesters stood nearby, each armed with a banner. No one Freya recognised from the day outside Amadeo's café. Moon-faces on narrow necks, some of the necks wrapped in scarves, a cold October wind coming in from the sea.

"It's tough to make people care," Susie said. "Not you, I'm not having a go. Just people who expressed an interest, you know? Everyone expresses an interest in making their voice heard, and then, in the end, they're too busy watching TV, or doing

their nails, or having massive sex or whatever."

"Bouncing ping-pong balls into their
beer," Freya said.

"Yeah, I watched some of that."

"You did?"

"If you press your face up against the glass
you can see most of the inside. Sebastian
got his bag confiscated by one of the security
guys."

"Oh."

Susie shivered. "Yeah. He was waiting by
the cook's entrance just before ten, like we
planned with you" — she blinked — "but
apparently this security guy came out and
took his bag and said . . ."

"Yeah?"

" 'Bugger off.' "

Unlikely as it seemed, Susie was smiling.

"So . . ."

"So apparently he wants to be a lawyer,"
Susie said. "Sebastian, I mean. His dad
wants him to work for his firm, this place in
London called Hangers, so he can't risk doing any more stuff for a while, in case he
gets a criminal record, he said." She took a
pack of Hubba from her pocket. "Want
some?"

They chewed and looked at their shoes.
Seven policemen with skin of varying rud-

diness were standing by the hotel entrance, drinking steaming coffee, one from the cap of a shiny flask and the others from cardboard cups.

"I've been trying to hang out," Susie said. "I've been trying to see you. Just to ask how your dad is, or whatever. I heard and stuff."

"Yeah."

"Didn't you get my messages? The ones saying let's just hang out?"

"I've been really busy. Distracted."

"Your dad," Susie said.

"That and other stuff, yeah."

"Is he OK?"

"He's fine, I reckon. Thanks for asking."

It was cola-flavoured Hubba. She'd never had a cola-flavoured Hubba before. She hadn't known it was a flavour they did.

Being together in the dark. It reminded her of sleepovers, camping. The way your eyes scanned around in the dim, waiting for some creepy shadow to be cast, ears attuned to outdoor sounds, some real and some imagined. Looking at Susie now she felt something. Not a rush of love, but a definite trickle. The start maybe of a reasonable flow. Nothing but bubbles emerged from their lips. It was all in sync and quiet. With a couple of side glances they decided which policeman was the best-looking of the group. With a smile they located the worst. Freya wanted to say I'm sorry I've ignored your messages, and I'm sorry I told the security guard about Sebastian, but hoped it was enough to think it, feel it.

She drew Susie in for a hug, a bony body pressed against hers. Funny how good a simple hug could be. Susie's hair smelt of herbal stuff.

"My dad found out he's not going to be the next general manager."

"What? Oh."

"Yeah."

Susie's eyes were shining. "He wanted that, didn't he?"

"Really bad, yeah."

"Brutal," she said.

"Yeah."

"My mum says it's a week of bad news. Did you hear about Wendy?"

"Hairdresser Wendy?"

"Yeah. She's really ill."

Freya laughed. "Always."

"No, seriously. They scanned her head and found this growth. She's going to need a load of treatment. An operation."

"Wendy Hoyt?"

"Yeah. A tumour. Apparently she's been having headaches for ages. They didn't spot it. My mum knows her husband."

"That's terrible. That's really . . . it's awful."

"Yeah, I know."

Could it really be true? Wendy?

For a few minutes they talked about how awful it was and then, with frowns and headshakes, conceded that they'd run out of ways to talk about it. They'd buy flowers tomorrow, take them to the salon, ask the staff if there was anything they could do.

"Are you still seeing that guy, Frey-Hey? I heard that you might be seeing a guy. Stephanie's cousin, the spotty one . . . he lifeguards at the pool."

"I'm . . . yeah, not seeing him anymore."

"Bothered?" Susie said.

"Nah."

"He was a bit gross, I expect, was he?"

She chewed. "No, he wasn't gross. He was Surfer John."

"Nooooooo."

"Yeeeeeeess."

"What were his nipples like?"

"His *nipples*?"

Susie shrugged. "I always imagined they'd be cool. You didn't sleep with him, did you?"

"Of course not."

"Good."

Susie raised her banner. The banner bore the slogan "Only Machines Should Be

522

Made of Iron." It was a very low-cost banner. The handle part seemed to have been constructed from several dozen ice-lolly sticks wound together, possibly the Mini Milk ones. It was such a hopeless effort that you couldn't help but feel proud of Susie, the makeshift commitment she showed.

"It's a play on a lyric from one of the Red Wedge bands."

"Clever," Freya said.

"Yeah. There were more of us last night, a *lot* more. Mainly Irish Freedom Movement guys. We were up there, the coast. Protesting at this meeting by these right-wing people called, like, the Monday Club. They threw coins at us. I kissed this guy, actually. He was married, which was cool. All this stuff is quite good for meeting guys. Not a Monday Club member, obviously. A fellow protester. But he was the guy who was in charge of letting off our stink bomb, and he dropped it and it went off early, when we were still in the hall. Whole room hummed of rotten eggs."

"Turn-off."

"Yeah."

"And his poor wife."

"Huh?"

"So you're not going to throw a stink bomb in there, while Thatcher's in bed?

You're not going to get someone else to do Sebastian's job?"

"Nah," Susie said. "I told them I had a friend who worked at the hotel, and that it would be horrible for the people working there, so."

"Did you?"

"Well, that's what I hinted at, yeah. They take my views on stuff pretty seriously."

Raised voices, a laugh. Two of the policemen were arguing about how long it would take to walk from here to Upper Beeding. One of them had a proper beer belly, his shirt buttons undergoing some major strain, and he was saying it would take at least two and a half hours. The slimmer one seemed to be saying only two. Possibly they were both right: a belly like that could easily cost you thirty minutes. It felt at times like people in Brighton, and maybe in the UK as a whole, were only interested in distances — how far one place was from another, and how long it might take to close the gap given selected variables. Weather. Quality of roads. The narrowness of lanes and the quota of slow-moving tractors. She listened to the sea, the lovely lucid wash of it, coming in, going out, coming in, going out.

Susie said, "Is your dad still no closer to getting dirty with Marina?"

"Actually —"

"No way."

"Well, I've just got a feeling, that's all. Who knows. The hospital stuff seems to have made them closer, and apparently she's just split up with someone. A guy who sounds suspiciously like Mr. Barry from English."

"Barry Balloon Eater?"

"Yeah."

"Brutal. I don't know how Bazza does it. But you'd feel all right about it, would you? If your dad and her got together?"

"I actually really like her."

"You do? You never seemed to."

"No, she's good. She sort of always says what she thinks."

"So do I," Susie said. "I mean, that's what people say about me, anyway."

"Yeah."

"Did you see her? Mrs. T?"

"No. You?"

"Few seconds," Susie said. "Threw an egg."

"As in stink bomb?"

"As in free range."

"Three points?"

"Got the bodyguard."

"Ah, two points."

"One max."

"No splat?"

"Hard-boiled."

"Ah."

"I wasn't sure how long to keep them in for," Susie said. She nodded at a couple of the other protesters, packing up to leave. "We could have one of our beach walks, Frey-Hey?"

"Now? It's pretty dark."

"Only if you want to. It was just an idea."

Freya twisted on the ball of one foot, a soldier type of thing. An idea. "OK then. Yessir. Let's go."

She began a slow march in the direction of the sea, wishing she had her warm jacket to hand. It was the kind of stupid walk Moose used to do to amuse her when she was small, ill, afraid, totally snot-soaked or bogged down in fever. He did it while her mother fetched a cool damp facecloth.

She paused to give Susie time to slip her rucksack on. Stared into the dark. Brown leaves patterned the pavement. They must have blown a long way. There were no trees along this part of the King's Road. There was the smell of turning earth and —

For some reason she was in the road, on her stomach, in the road. Hands gritty, stinging. On her belly on the ground.

There was noise all around her. Not quite

a thunderous rumble, not quite a shattering crack. It was a single deep sound with an unbotched quality, the force of a command, and it stretched out and out, thinning into a vicious whine, and Susie, incredibly — ha— Susie was lying on the other side of the road, against the iron railings.

Freya's arms all glittery. Glitter for some reason in the tiny downy hairs. Muck in her mouth that she now spat out. The air was fogging up and she heard people moaning. Dust was pattering down all around her.

13

Moose was in his office when the ceiling came down. As he fell to the floor he saw himself in a car on a road, wheels rolling as he drove down the middle lane to nowhere, vehicles roaring to the left and the right — a race, a dream. Then his sticky eyes were opening and he saw that the room had become a cloud, a malarial thickness to the air. There were places where the wall had crumbled away and he'd been looking for a letter, had he? Correspondence containing a promise of promotion. His leg was trapped under a concrete block.

He coughed and thick black sludge found his hand. Pain sprung in his chest; he fought for breath. His office door was hanging off its hinges. Slants of electric light came through the old spoiled wall. His leg. His face. He heard someone shouting "Please!" and realised it was him.

He touched his cheek. A string of something sticky came away. It clung to his fingers and he didn't understand. Plaster dust was coming down in fuzzed aimless flurries, everything eerily quiet. His leg was trapped. Fractured hatstand, dulled bricks. Broken painting in its frame. Couldn't move his leg. He was wheezing. The world was pressing at his chest. Bits of lamp and bits of table all around. Outbreaks of shredded furniture. The atmosphere was larded up with incredible dust and nothing here was whole. He was taking air in quick breaths, *ah, ah, ah.* He coughed. Vomited. Light crept from the doorway. He was a moth inside a lantern for a moment. The heaps of debris all around were so rich in different textures of grey-and-black crud that they achieved a kind of abstraction. Evil taste in his mouth. *Ah, ah, ah.* He took it all in, this small wrecked room, the astonishing evidence of his situation.

Slapping Susie. Susie saying "Gurghh" and opening her eyes. There was blood on her chin and her mouth was fully huge. Her left foot was twisted around the wrong way, Freya saw. Susie looked and screamed. Mrs. Cooke was over there in a blood-spattered dress, begging the night air for water. She was holding her fox drape in one hand.

The Grand Hotel. The brickwork wedding cake her father had encouraged her to admire so many thousand times. She was thinking of the cliché that you can't believe your eyes. The night sky had eaten into the roofline. The wound in the building went three floors deep. Smoke gushed up out of the dark space where rooms were supposed to live. The railings of balconies arced down, trailing off into nothing. Rubble tumbled in from left and right. She didn't know what had gone wrong with the rules of the world. She stood there with all she'd learned. It amounted to nothing.

A man staggered out of the hotel's entrance, covered in dust and moving onto all fours, scrabbling over rubble, an expression of wary amusement on his face, unsure if he was being teased. He stood and looked back at the building. He shook his head as if the Grand had badly let him down. Twisty bits of balcony at Freya's feet. Pieces of brick and blown-out glass. Susie seemed to survey the damage too, then remembered her foot was fractured. She started to scream again.

Freya lay down with her friend and took her in her arms, spoons, didn't know what else to do. "Be all right, Sooz. It'll be all right." Everything so quiet. What do you do with a foot that's the wrong way round? A dozen people staggering out in ripped dresses and suits, indecent and ashamed, their hair all turned to grey, and why were none of them screaming?

"Hello?" Susie said. "Hello?" She was shaking.

Freya held her. "Best wait here for help."

Another man coming out of the entrance. He had a beer glass in his hand. The liquid was grey, the same grey powder that coated his shoulders and shoes, like a cape on his shoulders and toecaps on his shoes, and he took a sip which turned into a spit and vomit shot out of his mouth. A woman ran out in her underwear shouting "Bomb" — good, someone should be shouting, *good* — and then an old man, naked except for one sock, one shoe, emerged from behind a pile of bricks in a way that couldn't be real. His skin was pink and slack down one side of his body. You could tell he didn't yet know he was hurt. The not-knowing gave him a kind of power. She closed her eyes and held Susie tighter.

Rumbling building. Soft chatter. Susie was mewing and rocking back and forth. A cloud of grey puffed out from the hotel's entrance and silently swallowed the moon. Freya watched the cloud move towards her and Susie. It did so with a dreamlike lack of speed. It was dust, not smoke, just dust from a thousand different surfaces and spaces. It was expelled all at once, disgusting dust. It seemed for a moment like it might pick them up, this dust cloud, and drop them somewhere clean and sane.

She was facing the water, coughing and spitting, and the cloud was scribbling out to sea. Some thoughts had settled into place and the first was My dad is in there, oh God. He's in there, isn't he? He is.

The ceiling groaned and the walls coughed up rubble. Moose winced and covered his head with his hands, saying "Please." Hot chips of plaster came down through the soup at different speeds. Heavy brickwork followed. Pipes and tiles clattering. Chunks of stone burst lazily around him, sending up more dust, making cruel music, and something sharp and hot found his ear and caused more wetness to flower there. He screamed "No!" as a dull force shoved him in the throat and "No" again as more music consumed him.

The room gloomed and the air was out of him again. He was a whimpering dog now, nothing more. There was a cry from somewhere high as he panted. It faded into the endless whistle in his ears. His leg was pulsing. His eyeball too. He thought of all the gloop inside him, the way it seemed so desperate to get out, and he felt himself going limp — back into darkness, a dog.

He woke to the foul smell of sewage. Through the thick stink of grey he watched the wound on his leg. It shivered. Why? Why had this happened here? Who? His body was convulsing less now. His wheezing was slowing, his airways adjusting.

Paper did a dance. With his weight on his elbow he took a fistful of these whirring papers — they were warm, they were his, they were kind — and now he was stuffing paper into the wound in his leg, paper into flesh and flesh becoming paper. The wound seemed to gurgle less. It had been a good idea.

Break it down. Break this down into steps.

The mottled concrete block that trapped his leg had a promising crack across it. He couldn't shift a big block, but he could maybe shift two smaller ones. He needed to work the crack and make it material. Please God, I know I have ignored You for years. Let my daughter keep her life. Anyone else I will let You have. It is evil but I will let You have them.

She was outside, was she? He was 90 per

cent sure she was outside. As percentages went it was nowhere near enough.

It burned to blink. Through stinging eyes he looked again at all this mess. There would be dozens of other wounded people in this building, people dying or dead or trapped on different floors, alone. Humans, creatures, suffering. It doubled his pain to know this. He started weeping. Could not help it. A gift of life gone. The weeping eased his eyes. A breeze came now and this was lovely, no sulphur scent at all.

Come on, you fool. Come on.

He twisted his body to the left. Paused. Tried to use his elbow as a kind of jack — winch himself backwards, free his leg. Didn't work.

Freya was outside, definitely. Would be outside in the air, the clean dark air, his daughter in the fine night air outside. Please let her be outside. She was outside. He coughed. Maybe with Marina, in the air outside. He'd seen Freya going out. If she was all right outside then everything else would be all right. All right. Ah, ah, ah.

Vision blurring again, he lifted his good arm. Felt for the crack in the concrete block. Dug his fingers in. Paused for breath. Got his fingers in there, squeezing. Try to burrow. It didn't work.

The darkness was now more red-brown than grey and something black swept down, a bird or bat he thought, but it clattered in front of him and he saw what it was: a fucking security camera, a ghost from the future.

This time he gave himself ten seconds before stretching his right arm up. His plan was to get a grip on the other concrete block. The one behind him, planet-sized, causing him no bother at all. And none of this was the old hotel's fault — he would not let anyone attribute blame — and he backed his palm into the block and clutched its upper edge, an awkward angle for his hand. Everything required calculation: every breath, every movement. Well: he could calculate. Calculation was one of his things. He counted to five, panting, waiting for the next wave of pain, and another explosion of rubble came down, the building's most vicious sneeze yet. When he recovered and got to five he gave himself an extra two. He tried to grip the smooth surface, haul himself back with his fingertips, unwedge his leg. He cried out, "Give me a chance." His chin was wet. He was grateful that his leg was numb. Lost his grip and the back of his head hit concrete. A howl. It didn't work. He sensed now that his life was over, that death was the one constant thing, the destination he'd been heading to these last few weeks or years. He moaned and thrashed at this naked unfairness, pulled at his clothes in despair.

Then he thought, No. Just: no. He began to go wild on the concrete block. Began to go out-your-brain mental. He was all clawing, all thumping, all eyeball-surprise. He had an idea of unseen people urging him on. People saying, Come on, Moose, come on. Moose, come on. People thinking, Moose, Moose, I never liked you much, Moose, you've got a stupid name and a slow history and you're a bit of a wet blanket, Moose; you're a bit strange and soft-spined and irrelevant to what we're interested in, Moose, but come on now, let's get it together.

When he tired of his own frantic attack he saw that the crack in the block had opened up. Two sides of stone had relaxed into a roof around his knee. There was a change in the pressure in his leg. An astonishing happiness filled his heart.

He began twisting himself, breathing, oh, oh, oh. He saw his lower leg, the first sign of it, pale and swollen in his shredded trousers, an appalling sight but where was the pain now? Hello, pain, where are you? It had nothing left to attack him with. He howled as he hauled himself back, saw the pale pressed flesh shuffling out from under the concrete. Welcome back, lower leg! A blood rush now. A sense of what survival might mean. Pulling, twisting. Biting his lip. Imagining Father Christmas going ho, ho, ho. The *pop* of his leather loafer coming off. His foot was attached to his leg. Thank you for this gift, thank you.

He turned himself over. Considered the triangle of light on the other side of the room. Began planning a route through the debris. He was counting out seconds as crocodiles. He was allowing himself three crocodiles with his eyes still scrunched. One crocodile, two crocodiles, three. Who cared if he'd never done anything newsworthy? Day to day he had a daughter. Day to day he had shelter. His daughter would be outside and she would be one hundred per cent fine. He paused to warn the heavens that he would tolerate nothing less. He was in tears again as he crawled.

There were firemen now. Sirens. Red lights, blue lights, a confusion of noise. Police shouting "Back from the building! Back!" Women in tattered dresses, men open-mouthed in the night. Chattering teeth and an ambulance.

She tugged at a fireman's sleeve, needy. "My dad."

"Breathe!"

"I'm already breathing! My dad's in there."

"OK, OK." The fireman removed his hard hat. The fireman was in fact a firewoman. Her blonde hair was all balled up at the back and her eyebrows were drawn on with a pencil. Give me information, the firewoman said. His name, what he looks like, the area of the hotel he'd be in.

"Finch," she said. "Philip. Moose."

The firewoman shook her head. One lick of hair came loose. She made some notes on a folded piece of yellow paper and said we're doing what we can, I'm sorry. If you think he was on the ground floor that's good. She said this and then she put her enormous yellow hat back on, gave a policeman the piece of paper, pointed at Freya and whispered some words. Gone.

A tanned man wearing a baggy jumper and sports shorts was crouching over Susie. He had Twiglet legs. All he said about himself were the words "off duty" and then "I don't sleep so well." He was touching Susie's ankle like he could heal it by the power of thought alone and basically the stage was set for a miracle. In a minute he'd fix everything else. "This will be . . ." he said. "I'm sorry, this will be . . ." and Susie whimpered right up until the point where he stuffed a hanky in her mouth. Her eyes went wide with fear. Freya failed to intervene. He took Susie's foot firm in both hands and twisted it viciously, an awful cracking sound. Susie's muffled scream; her bared teeth biting down on the hanky; her swelling eyes as it happened. He pulled the hanky out of her mouth, strings of spit bending onto his hand. Susie fought for breath. Bit her lip. It bled. Her body was convulsing. He told her, "Better now, better. You don't want to leave these things too long." The foot was facing the right way. Calmly he waved to a paramedic. "I need a hand here, when you have a moment."

Freya found a woman who looked official. The woman was just shaking her head and muttering, shaking and muttering and waving her papers like papers could help, but as she looked up something jumped in her eyes and she threw her arms around Freya. Freya had never been hugged this way before, with so much warmth and so much need. She felt in fact that up until now she had only ever been held by the edges of who she was. She also felt trapped. She kissed the woman on the nose, fully no idea why, and the woman let go and Freya was free. Ran for it. Tripped over rubble. There were sorry flickers of orange in the air. She tried again to get into the hotel.

"Get *back*!"

Another long shining line of fire engines leaning into the bends of the road. A barbecue smell and wafts of something toxic. Rubble coming down in groups of two and three, ice cubes from a tray. The sight of a man in flip-flops, vomiting. A vigilant old woman, silver hair shooting forward from the crown, poking at a camera lens with her rubber-tipped stick. Dust and a dozen people coughing. A fireman saying, "Get back. Get back."

An old man approached her. "Might you perhaps help me find my wife?"

"I —"

"Please? We've been married thirty years."

A woman said, "God. Skipper! Did you see my dog? Skipper!"

"I'm sorry," the old man said.

"Are you sure? Skipper! He's a dachshund. Skipper!"

"Sorry," Freya said.

"Skipper! Skip!"

"I'm very sorry," the man said. "I'm looking for my wife. We've been married thirty years."

"Skip!" the woman called. "Skipper! Skip!"

Surfer John found her. He was covered head to foot in filth. She told him she was completely done with hugs. He said, "You're in shock." She said, "Irrespective." She said, "You've got to help me find my dad." He stood there looking dumb and kind, not quite a lemon but a definite citrus.

Groups were forming. A minister and his wife were pacing the pavement, the wife wearing a necklace of unaffected pearls. A bathrobe, a pair of slippers. She was saying, "I will not be flapped." Someone else said, "The Lady is secure, the Lady is secure." A tiny cheer rose up into the neutral night sky. Two dozen people in nightclothes. Firemen shouting "back back back." Felt like every emergency vehicle in the United Kingdom was here now. Ladders extending up from fire engines. Men in huge clothing climbing onto balconies, vanishing into the building. Who would do this? Where was her dad?

John Redwood from the thingy unit, the Policy Unit, bottom right corner of Moose's "Briefing Bios" document; John Redwood pacing around saying, "After all that, I've left the bloody speech in there!" Another guy saying, "We need to cut the Kinnock stuff. Where's Ronnie um? We need to yes recast in case of —" People seemed to fall into two camps, the panicked and the merely inconvenienced. Another dinosaur rumble from the building. "Back, back, get *back.*"

A fireman came out carrying a box of teacups, set it down on the ground and ran back in. A paramedic said, "Water from the hose. Eyebaths." People staggering blind, rubbing at their eyes, she saw them now, saw them quietly forming a queue. She was so grateful for this minor demonstration of order. She wiped the tears from her eyes.

Sir Keith Joseph was wearing silk pyjamas and a fine patterned dressing gown. He looked miraculously clean sitting there on a red box of government papers. He was humming and rocking very slightly from side to side.

"Have you seen Daniel, is he staying here?"

"Have you seen Amy, was she staying here?"

"There's coffee and wine in the Metropole, bar opened, Blitz spirit."

"Metropole evacuated, another bomb."

"Get her back to Downing Street."

"There's no other bomb."

"She won't go."

"Fuck's sake."

"Skipper!"

"Police stations."

"She's safe."

"Have you seen my wife?"

"Second device."

"Hospital."

"What to do?"

"We've been married thirty years."

No one wanted to help her find her dad. Surfer John talked to the policemen. They wanted names of staff, a floor plan.

A cat ran across the road in several smooth leaps, ears pinned back, body lengthening and lowering as it crept under a car — Barbara. Her tail disappearing, only the yellow eyes aglow.

Glass shattered.

"Get back!"

Voices and torches, dust, luminous jackets, yellow tape, bathrobes, dust, police, cameras, lights, dust. A helicopter had begun to hover in the sky.

Dan's mother had been taken in by Mrs. Whelan: cocoa and a bath. When he walked into the living room he found her sitting on the sofa. Books on the shelves had been arranged according to their colours, yellows blending into greens, the Whelans' OCD thing. Outside, smoke still poured from his home.

He stood in front of her. "Ma," he said. She complained and leaned to the left. The TV was in the corner, murmuring in black and white. She said she was trying to watch it.

He sat beside her and turned the volume up. Minutes and minutes of pointless shite before the newscaster said Mrs. Thatcher had survived. The news emptied Dan's head. He felt only relief. He would fall into history's footnotes, become one of its unseen failures. The newscaster's next revelation: Alistair McAlpine was talking to Marks & Spencer about opening early, to sell clean clothes to those "affected." Cut to Thatcher saying the conference would go ahead as planned, no delay to the speeches. Cut to a picture of Marks & Spencer. Marks & Spencer! A great British success story was piecing itself together. A nausea began to swell in his stomach. Cut to the Grand Hotel still standing, a chunk torn out. Cut to a doctor standing outside the Royal Sussex hospital, curly grey hair. He said the number of dead could not yet be ascertained, the rescue operation continues, so do the efforts to treat the wounded. The word "wounded" crawled inside Dan. The word "dead" did nothing. He turned the sound down, looked around the room. Through the window the sky was such a smooth black that it seemed a thing he ought to be able to feel, a blackboard or a piece of slate.

He tried to put his arm around his mother. She moved away. Did not even lift her chin from her hands. "Come here," he said. "Come here."

His mother shook her head. Three or four women who'd been in the kitchen came into the living room now. One said, with undisguised excitement in her voice, "She's lost everything, Dan. Give her time."

He stood and said no. "Half the building's being saved."

"What?" his mother said.

"Ma, there's no fresh fire out there now, only smoke. We can rebuild."

"Come on, Dan."

"We can. Some of the belongings, Dad's things, they'll be salvageable. And Jones's home is mostly OK. Don't mistake me, these people will pay."

She shook her head and pinched the skin of her forearm. "These people," she said.

"We could have lost more, I'm saying."

She laughed again. "Who are you talking

about, Dan? Who is it you're calling 'these people?' These people are the only people here."

He began to explain. She shook her head, did not want to learn. His skin still tingled from all the ash that had fallen upon him. His clothes stank of smoke.

"Some things," he said. "Some of it we'll get cleaned up and will be fine. We'll hold on to some of it, we will. Things aren't as bad as you think, Ma."

Slack skin, liver spots, eyes greyer than before. She seemed to have aged ten years in the last two hours. The other women in the room were whispering. She said, "Things aren't as bad as you think, Dan? True. Things are worse than you think. Being general, they're much, much worse."

"No."

"Catch yourself on, Dan. You no longer look like my son."

He tried not to linger on this.

"Insurance," one of the women said, as if insurance covered families like his in neighbourhoods like this.

Kind Mrs. Whelan arrived bearing a teapot and an assortment of mugs. She settled her tray on the table, touched it twice.

His mother spoke again. "I didn't know

what was happening, Catty." A nickname unused for years. "A brick came through the bedroom. I was watching the little TV in the bedroom about the bomb and the brick — a brick, you know? I mean I was expecting something but. The brick came through like this. I looked out the back. A brick like they knew. The garden was having a fire. I took a couple of the half-good cookbooks and went out like this for the door."

"It's OK," he said.

"Why weren't you here, Dan?"

"I was with friends."

"Friends. You're never this late."

"This time I was."

"Where are my cookbooks? The cookbooks are out there. I couldn't find the golf club. You expect me to believe."

"What?"

"That the timing."

"What?"

"A coincidence," she said. She was beginning to weep, to shake.

"Stop it," he said. He told the women to leave the room. They did not leave. "Ma, it's OK."

"The *news,*" she said, vicious. "Look at it. I had a phone call! Hour before the brick. They said that. And. And Provos boys, those

547

boys with the scarves, they'd been hanging around an hour before and I heard that —"

"What do you mean? What did you hear?"

She was crying.

"Stop it," he said. "Don't cry on me. You're not making sense."

"The news," she said. "The news."

She was weeping and it made him desperate. It crushed all the air inside him. Again he had his hands on his knees. Again he was looking away and trying to breathe. Fidgeting for space, for air, always, endless.

"Or the Loyalists. Loyalists. They've burned houses elsewhere, Dan. Retaliations already begun. Streets back from here, houses burning. They're always so quick when there's a mainland attack, it's like they've a list, a list."

"Calm down, Ma. Stay calm."

"Thatcher survived, Dan."

"You think I didn't catch that?"

"It's made her a martyr, Dan."

"No."

"Yes."

"It's nothing to do with us."

"Nothing she'll do from now on will matter. She'll be the woman who was bombed and didn't blink."

"Why would we care? It's not relevant to us. Why would you even tell —" He glanced at the women in their semicircle. Their eyes moved towards the TV.

"They're saying she won't even put back her speech!"

"Stop."

"Not even a delay, Dan! And people have died."

"Whoever's done this to us is going to pay. I'm going to make them know — they'll know what they've done."

"Oh, they know! They already know. All the wounded people on the telly, Dan, and they've done nothing wrong, have they? They're like your da, Catty."

"I'm talking about here."

"There, here. It's all the same, Dan. They're pulling them out half alive."

She was whimpering; he was whispering.

"Stop it please," he said. "You're embarrassing us, Ma."

Clear snot was running down into her mouth and she was shaking on the sofa, allowing the event to destroy her. Embarrassment was the word and he didn't know why. How was he not yet beyond embarrassment?

She said, "I should never have let that Dawson McCartland into my garden."

"Quiet now. Be quiet."

"There might not even be a minister dead,

they said. Not one! But there's dead bodies already on the news — women who weren't ministers who were staying there, women and wives, and now Belfast's burning, look."

"Stop, Ma. Control yourself. We got the letters."

"The letters!"

"What happened on the mainland — it means fuck all to us. This is just weird timing — this is . . ."

He thought again of what she had said about Provos boys hanging around the house. He thought, No, they wouldn't do this. Use me and get rid of me? Dawson? No.

"My whole life is over," she said. "Over. My whole life up in flames because of you and your kind and your father dying for nothing. What would he say now, Daniel? What would he say, Daniel, if he saw you —"

No. Couldn't hear this. Wouldn't. He wheeled around, deliciously free of thought, deeply impressed by his own disgust, and with the back of his hand he hit her face. Saliva streaked from the corner of her mouth. His knuckles stung. He stood there for a moment, amazed by himself, as the women touched their hair and looked away.

■ ■ ■ ■

Dawson came the next day with money and a plan. He said Dan would need to spend some time abroad. He said that the army looked after its own. He had pictures of the Loyalists who had set fire to the house. "Time to start a new life, Dan," he said. He said he had been on leave.

"Compassionate?"

"Annual."

"Fuck, Dawson —"

"We all need a break," Dawson said.

Dawson talked about Thatcher, her lack of empathy, her inability to imagine herself into other people's shoes: the miners, the Catholics, those with another view. He talked about the distance she'd created within herself, the distance necessary to do her job.

Dawson did not talk about the victims in the Grand. He did not talk about the dogs that had died in the fire, the charred bodies in Dan's garage. He did not talk about all the hate he surely felt.

Dawson said he had tickets for the Celtic Rangers game and would gladly give them up.

Moose grabbed at his belt. There was a new exhilaration at the margins of his pain, an old edgy in-the-gym feeling. Whipped the belt right out of the loops, a gesture learned from nowhere. A bit of Harrison Ford juju that wasn't really him. He got the belt around his bad leg and tightened it, let it be.

In his head now he was one hundred per cent Harrison. The Beatles were playing "Hard Day's Night." The triangle of electric light was where he was headed. It was the only sharp thing in the swarm of the room. He heard water trickling in an unseen space.

What are you going to do? Best you can, best you think you can, which is everything. He performed an unlikely sit-up. Pain lived between his ribs. The motion bought him momentum for the next few desperate gestures. Licking his split lip, breathing fast and crawling slow, pausing at intervals to say "No."

He saw his own progress as fragment-to-fragment. Get to the broken chair leg. Breathe. Get to the Sellotape hoop. Breathe. Get through the thick fog to the flattened tinfoil castle, dragging the bad leg behind him. He could feel the crinkle of vulnerable foil under his hand. There was fire in his veins, smoke in his flesh. "Ah," he said. "Ah, ah, ah."

He couldn't do this. Couldn't keep moving. His lungs were full of dust. But he was moving, was he? He was doing this. Trying. Every inch coughing up blackness was a sort-of-almost progress. He felt oddly invested in himself. If he had a flag he'd stick it in the middle of Engelbert's tinfoil castle. He had no flag. Never mind. Move on. Beyond the castle was a steaming mountain made of wood. The crook of a pipe there. A cistern. And beyond —

Here was the thought that kept forming: Marina had said Engelbert was asleep in the side room. Where was that side room now?

He looked behind him. The potted yucca was there but the doorway wasn't. All was rubble and dust. Somewhere in his mind he heard the word hero. The idea was irresistible. This agony might have a shape. He wanted to disprove life's lesson tonight: that it made no sense at all.

There were voices behind him. Footsteps. Coughing. A muddle of well-meaning human sounds. Cones of light. Torchlight. Warm torchlight on his skin for a faint electric instant and then gone. The torch-light did not illuminate anything. It simply showed you the extent of the darkness all around. He made a shouting sound, noise not language, and brickwork came down and spat dust in his face. Might as well go to the yucca, the disappeared doorway. There was a chance he would find a little boy beyond. He coughed and spat. He groaned and shrieked. He squeezed his leg to hurt the pain.

He crawled towards the plant. Avoid the mountain of rubble to the left. Go right. Oh, oh, oh. Take the road more taken. "No." The path less troubled. "No." Back over the tinfoil castle, saying only the word "no." Find the next bit of rubble. Get it in your sights. To get through this! To get through this. "I'm sorry," he said, but he was not sure what for.

He swallowed blood. He crawled into the area where the side door should have been. He got onto his good left knee. He wrapped his arm around concrete. He hauled, fell back. He spat and put weight on his left knee again. He hauled at more stone, think-ing of Engelbert beyond, and the fourth or fifth time he did this he rose up to half-height and spat and saw, through burning eyes, an opening and a — a boy, standing beyond, very still.

The boy's skin and clothes were dark with dirt. His eyelids snapped up like blinds. Those live-wire white eyes. A pink mouth began to blink.

"Engel?"

The boy began to climb. Over the rubble he came, moving towards Moose on hands and knees, real or not real, something in between. The area in which he moved was no longer a room. It was a space owned by improvised alcoves, heaps of stone and twisted metal. Racy little tears sped down Engel's cheeks. They left clean paths behind. Time slowed and progress was slow. There was torchlight behind Engel's head. There was a fireman emerging through a further half-gone wall.

"Engel," he said. "Not to me. Back there."

The boy did not obey. He had his goal and with the blind stupidity of youth he was climbing like a little motherfucker. Climbed, he climbed, over the mountain he climbed. And then he stopped, maybe confused by all the light now shining near him. Maybe understanding.

"Torch," Moose said. "Behind you, torch." His voice was a rough whisper now, too small and thick to be his own; he knew that he was losing himself.

The fireman behind Engel was drifting towards them. Debris crunched under his boots. Engel waited. There were jabby shadows overhead. Another fog breathing out its ghosts. We are unseen, he thought. The fireman doesn't know we're here.

His fingers did not want to clutch at stone. His grip was relaxing, opening to the world. He had to force himself to claw one final time. He grabbed a piece of stone and threw it. He did not see where it landed. He heard only the noise and the absence of noise. The fireman turned. Torchlight flooded Engel. No one said a word.

Moose watched the fireman lifting Engel. Felt such a pure rush of happiness, sugar on an exhausted tongue. The fireman would now be discovering how warm the boy was. Amazing the warmth a child's body gives off. Heat monsters, the lot of them, a lifetime of potential packed in. He imagined Freya so small again and he was holding her, kissing her forehead.

He opened his mouth to shout to the fireman — the formality of saying I am here, me too, help me out? — but all he had left was a croak. He was croaking like he had as a boy in bed, woken in the night by a bump in the dark, fear taking his voice and hiding it. He threw another stone and nothing happened.

Engelbert was carried away over the fireman's shoulder, arms hanging down like he'd been caught mid-dive. But he'd look up at him soon, wouldn't he? And then the fireman would turn and see that he, Moose, was lying here: a battered Deputy General Manager. But the fireman continued to walk away with Engelbert, everything quiet and slow.

Survivors fanned out around the wounded hotel. Some were in the cordoned-off section of the King's Road. Others were further back against the railings. Freya was sitting in a huddle of strangers, waiting, legs crossed like school assembly. Her sense of time was slipping. She'd been out here in the dark for weeks. She was as close to the Grand's entrance as allowed. Some of those rescued were lifted out on firemen's shoulders. Others were carried on stretchers. One was a minister with a long sad face, limp and alien in his bedclothes. Was her father still inside? Had he been carried out? Had she missed him? Was he lost? Was it over? Everybody cared but no one knew.

The uniforms and walkie-talkies, the police tape making spaces smaller. It screamed as it came off the roll. And how do these things end? Where basically do they stop? The shadows cast by events like this. For all she knew they could ripple on forever.

She sat and tried to make her thoughts cohere. The adrenalin had gone and she was sick with slow despair. There was a DO NOT DISTURB sign on the ground. She wanted the power of the night to die down into the mundane. She wanted the extraordinary to go back to being ordinary, please. She vomited. People moved. Please do not disturb.

The first trickle of dawn was a breaking egg yolk in the sky. She blinked and it resembled something else. The light came slow and wide across rooftops, warming long sections of crumbled stone, and she felt her youth being packed away, a piece of paper folded over and over, half-thoughts and quarter-thoughts, gone.

She told herself stay positive. She told herself Brighton was built on the wreckage of itself. It said so in "The Brighton Fact Pack," kept behind the desk for curious customers. You burn Brighton down and it rises from the flames like that fire bird, arched neck, pinkish feathers — from the flames. Brighton was burnt down by the

French in fifteen hundred and something. Survived. It was hit by the great storm of 1703. Survived. Windmills thrown. Houses flattened. Boats sunk. Survived. Survived Hitler. Survived each twist of history. Booming in the twentieth century. Thriving. Surviving. You thought it was finished but you were wrong. Brightonians were survivors. Many of them were lame and old and hampered by terrible dress sense, but they were survivors. The English were survivors. The Irish. The Scottish. The Welsh. Think of Lowri "The Look" Morgan. Make a sheep-shagging joke in class and she'd nuke you. She didn't need words. A mascara-thick glance was all it took. The glance said you were lucky to be alive.

And he would come, wouldn't he, out of the dreaming hotel? Her hands were dirty. She wiped her eyes. She wanted her dad back now.

Tomorrow there would be water creeping onto Brighton Beach. He could relax now, stop struggling. He could let the hotel take his weight.

In his wrecked office Moose saw lime greens and yellows. Time slowed and an image came from colour. He rolled onto his back and looked at the peeled-away ceiling and he saw it, an image of himself. He was on a three-metre springboard, thunking his weight down to get going. The air was clear and bright. The board did what it was asked to do. It flicked him high, his body suspended in nothing, revolving with perfect grace.

He waited to see himself fall into the water. Here the image flickered out. He tried to reimagine it, but the dive would not take hold. He blinked. He was not in the air. He was in the rubble of this hotel on the surface of the earth. Earth was the proper place for grace. This was the last thing he knew. His humanity was tangled up with the humanity of those trapped in other rooms. They were more real than him. He existed for them. He had never been so afraid. All the people he couldn't be, all the stories he couldn't hear, this is what life was. He held on to the last few weeks as he stretched out and died. Held on to the daily battles with his daughter, to the factless beauty of a broadloom rug, to the private moments history so rarely records but which make up the minutes in the hours. "Please," he said, but it did not help. Someone had considered this fair.

On the day Roy Walsh checked out of the

Grand she had stood by the desk to say goodbye. She had thought she would get to know him. The distance hadn't closed. Whatever held people together had gone or was missing all along. He waved at her. He said "take care." The revolving door ushered quarters of salty air into the lobby. The glass wings of the door kept moving long after he had left. She felt the slightest sadness. An absence more vivid than a presence. She sat behind the desk and finished her book. There was never true silence here. Sometimes she was grateful for that. Silence and peace were not the same thing. She heard fragments of conversations from the street, laughter and shouting, voices crossing borders, seagulls bickering on the shoreline, the outside coming in. In the dark bar area a stranger stood up and bumped into a table, then a chair.

AUTHOR'S NOTE

Five people lost their lives in the bombing of the Grand Hotel. Many more suffered serious injuries. Several survivors were permanently disabled by the blast.

In June of 1986, Patrick Magee was found guilty of planting an explosive device in room 629, and of murdering the five people who died as a result of his actions. He received eight life sentences. In 1999, he was released from prison under the terms of the Good Friday Agreement.

Evidence was presented during Patrick Magee's trial that a second bomber may have assisted him in the room during his stay. This evidence included room-service records and the eye-witness testimony of a member of the hotel's staff. Speculation about a second bomber has also been fuelled by suggestions made by Magee and his counsel that fingerprints found on the hotel registration card — evidence used to identify him as "Roy Walsh," the man who checked in — could not in fact have been his. Several IRA members have faced convictions in relation to elements of the Grand Hotel plot, but the second bomber in room 629, if there was one, appears never to have been found.

This book is a work of fiction. The three principal characters — Dan, Freya and Moose — are inventions. Many of the incidents in the book are entirely imagined too. There are large gaps in what is known about the bombing of the Grand Hotel and I have tried, over the last few years, to imagine myself into those gaps. For those seeking reliable guides to the situation in Northern Ireland, past and present, there are many good non-fiction books available. One of the most extraordinary is *Lost Lives,* a work by David McKittrick, Seamus Kelters, Brian Feeney, Chris Thornton and David McVea. It aims to record every death suffered during more than thirty years of conflict.

In 2009, Jo Berry, whose father was among those killed in the explosion at the Grand Hotel, founded an organisation named Building Bridges for Peace. In fulfilment of the organisation's mission she now works side by side with Patrick Magee to promote peaceful conflict resolution throughout the world. www.buildingbridgesforpeace.org

ACKNOWLEDGEMENTS

Thanks go to:

Diana Miller, Jason Arthur, Oliver Munday, Iris Weinstein, Erinn McGrath, Katie Burns, Kathleen Fridella, Betsy Sallee, Jordan Rodman, and everyone who worked on this novel at Knopf and William Heinemann;

Clare Alexander and the team at Aitken Alexander Associates;

Gillian Stern, Dwyer Murphy, Anjali Joseph and Dan Sheehan;

The Society of Authors and the K. Blundell Trust;

Brigid Hughes, Rob Spillman and Michael Archer;

Amy and the family.

In the last few years, excerpts from earlier drafts of *High Dive* have appeared in *A Public Space, Tin House* and *Narrative*. Work feeding into the novel has also been published by *Guernica* and *Granta.* Without the support of these literary journals, and of all the people listed above, I wouldn't have finished the book.

ABOUT THE AUTHOR

Jonathan Lee is a British writer whose recent short stories have appeared in *Tin House, Granta,* and *Narrative,* among other magazines. He is the author of two novels published in the UK: *Who Is Mr. Satoshi?,* nominated for the Desmond Elliott Prize, and *Joy,* shortlisted for the Encore Award for Best Second Novel. *High Dive* is his first novel to be published in the US. He lives in Brooklyn, where he is an editor at the literary journal *A Public Space* and a contributing editor for *Guernica.*